BERWICK

Also by LJ Ross

THE DCI RYAN MYSTERIES:

1. *Holy Island*
2. *Sycamore Gap*
3. *Heavenfield*
4. *Angel*
5. *High Force*
6. *Cragside*
7. *Dark Skies*
8. *Seven Bridges*
9. *The Hermitage*
10. *Longstone*
11. *The Infirmary (Prequel)*
12. *The Moor*
13. *Penshaw*
14. *Borderlands*
15. *Ryan's Christmas*
16. *The Shrine*
17. *Cuthbert's Way*
18. *The Rock*
19. *Bamburgh*
20. *Lady's Well*
21. *Death Rocks*
22. *Poison Garden*
23. *Belsay*
24. *Berwick*

THE ALEXANDER GREGORY THRILLERS:

1. *Impostor*
2. *Hysteria*
3. *Bedlam*
4. *Mania*
5. *Panic*
6. *Amnesia*

THE SUMMER SUSPENSE MYSTERIES:

1. *The Cove*
2. *The Creek*
3. *The Bay*
4. *The Haven*

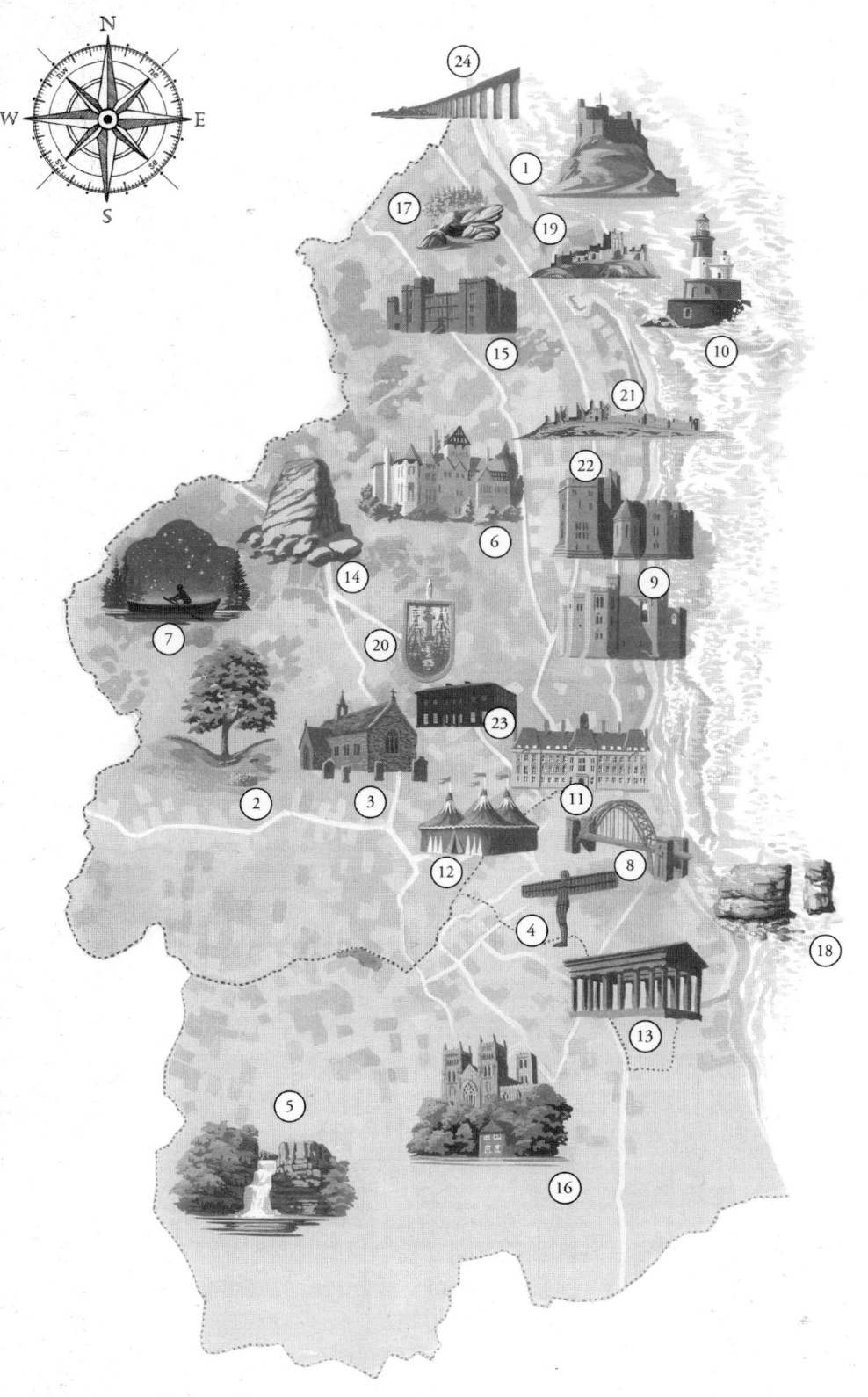

BERWICK

A DCI RYAN MYSTERY

LJ ROSS

CENTURY

UK | USA | Canada | Ireland | Australia
India | New Zealand | South Africa

Century is part of the Penguin Random House group of companies whose addresses can be found at global.penguinrandomhouse.com

Penguin Random House UK,
One Embassy Gardens, 8 Viaduct Gardens, London SW11 7BW

penguin.co.uk

First published 2026
001

Copyright © LJ Ross, 2026

The moral right of the author has been asserted

Penguin Random House values and supports copyright. Copyright fuels creativity, encourages diverse voices, promotes freedom of expression and supports a vibrant culture. Thank you for purchasing an authorised edition of this book and for respecting intellectual property laws by not reproducing, scanning or distributing any part of it by any means without permission. You are supporting authors and enabling Penguin Random House to continue to publish books for everyone. No part of this book may be used or reproduced in any manner for the purpose of training artificial intelligence technologies or systems. In accordance with Article 4(3) of the DSM Directive 2019/790, Penguin Random House expressly reserves this work from the text and data mining exception.

Cover artwork and map by Andrew Davidson
Cover layout by Riverside Publishing Solutions Limited

Set in 11.5/16pt Minion Pro
Typeset by Riverside Publishing Solutions Limited

Printed and bound in Great Britain by Clays Ltd, Elcograf S.p.A.

The authorised representative in the EEA is Penguin Random House Ireland,
Morrison Chambers, 32 Nassau Street, Dublin D02 YH68

A CIP catalogue record for this book is available from the British Library

ISBN: 978-1-529-97894-0 (hardback)
ISBN: 978-1-529-97895-7 (trade paperback)

Penguin Random House is committed to a sustainable future for our business, our readers and our planet. This book is made from Forest Stewardship Council® certified paper.

"Where there is no imagination, there is no horror."

—Sir Arthur Conan-Doyle

CHAPTER 1

Newcastle-upon-Tyne

Christmas Eve

Of all the things Linette Winterbottom hoped for when she awakened on that crisp, wintry morning, dying a violent death certainly hadn't been one of them. Indeed, the prospect hadn't featured at any point during her fifty-one years, though she'd always known in some far-off, abstract sort of way that death comes to us all, eventually. Still, she might have hoped to die peacefully in her sleep, rather than drowning in her own blood.

C'est la vie.

Or rather, *c'est la mort*.

Until the moment her lifeblood seeped from her body onto the threadbare rug in her living room, Lin's day had been going rather well. That is, if she discounted a shaky start in the form of her elderly neighbour, Gertie, with whom she shared a love-hate relationship as well as a thin partition wall separating their respective flats. The old battle-axe presented herself at Lin's front door shortly after seven o'clock to say that she'd purchased Lin's latest book, *Island Mystery*, very much against her better judgment. She proceeded to hand down her verdict on the story in the manner of a crusty, care-worn judge presiding at the Old Bailey, and Lin barely had time to scrub the sleep from her eyes before the cantankerous old coot rounded things off by telling her that it was a bloody good thing she'd managed to pull something decent out of the bag, for a change.

With neighbours like hers, Lin thought, *who needed terrorists?*

She'd forced her mouth into the semblance of a smile, skin stretching tightly over her teeth until the muscles in her jaw ached with the effort. She stood there in faded Christmas pyjamas while Gertie rolled on, all the while imagining ways in which the woman might suffocate on the folds of her wrinkled neck, or trip over her orthopaedic shoes and take an unfortunate tumble down the stairs. The thought alone was enough to elicit a genuine smile, and Lin had waved her neighbour off with a cheerful promise never to write another 'bad' book again.

After that, things had improved somewhat with a rare visit to the hairdresser, who'd spruced up Lin's mop of grey frizz as best she could—though, as the nineteen-year-old natural brunette had been at *pains* to point out, she couldn't work miracles.

Gertie might have had a point, Lin thought, *when she'd complained about the 'youth of today' having no respect for their elders and betters.*

Once she'd recovered from the pique, there followed an early lunch at an upmarket restaurant in town with another impossibly young woman named Saffron, who introduced herself as the public relations assistant assigned by Lin's publishers to 'manage' her, now that one of her books was actually selling enough to warrant such investment. Consequently, she was subjected to all manner of exceedingly helpful suggestions about how to *connect* with readers, how to write *engaging* newsletters and, best of all, how to grow her following on a new social media platform they called *'Tip-Top'* or *'Tik-Tok'* or some such nonsense. Lin had nodded, smiled, and polished off a healthy plate of eggs benedict, lamenting the Good Old Days when all she had to do was write stories and cultivate some sort of mystique.

As she'd mulled over the artful, exciting ways in which she might create a new persona for herself, Lin slopped a dollop of eggy sauce down her smart navy blouse—one of the few she owned. With no time to make a change, the remainder of brunch was spent mopping up the damage, including hovering beneath a drying machine in the Ladies' toilet, all the while trying not to notice the pained, pitying expression on the face of the young woman beside her, who was no doubt wondering how she'd ended up drawing the short straw babysitting a woman without basic hand-eye coordination.

Being a consummate professional, Saffron said nothing of the mishap, and they made their way to a nearby bookshop where Lin was due to give a talk and sign books for readers. For the first time in years, a healthy crowd had gathered to get their mitts on a copy of *Island Mystery,* the latest thriller from the woman they knew as Lin Oldman— 'Winterbottom' being too humdrum a surname to inspire 'thrills and chills', and 'Linette' being too *female* a forename to inspire widespread purchasing from male readers of a certain generation, or so her literary agent had told her when she'd begun her career, thirty years before. Mind you, the back-stabbing Judas had dropped her from his books as soon as her sales had begun to dwindle and she'd developed what publishing teams liked to call 'bad track'. Lin had argued...no, she'd *begged* them to give her another chance to hit those bestseller charts, but all to no avail. Since then, she'd bounced from one publisher to the next, desperate to stay in print at any cost, until accepting peanuts in exchange for a mediocre story had become the norm.

It kept the wolf from the door.

Until, it didn't.

That's when she'd started running courses, passing on her wisdom to wannabe writers who fancied a chance at the Big Time. But none of them had her talent, Lin was sure of that. She'd always known she was special.

Hadn't everybody said so?

She remembered being a young twenty-something, taking a first-class train to London and a fancy private transfer to her new publisher's gleaming office, the proverbial red carpet having been rolled out for her arrival. Men and women in bold colours and smart suits waxed lyrical about how she'd be the next Barbara Taylor Bradford, with her name in lights. They told her she was gifted, and, for her sins, Lin believed them. Decades had passed since those heady days and she'd scraped a living here and there, putting on a show for the occasional few who turned out for a library talk or to learn about 'the craft of writing'. Throughout those long, lean years, the only thing that sustained her was the sure and certain knowledge that she was above the rest.

She had to believe it.

Then, one day, Fate stepped in to lend a hand.

It gifted her a manuscript. Unpublished, unpolished, but *good*, so very good. It didn't matter that it wasn't hers. Lin had taken it, claiming it as a pirate did to buried treasure, clutching it in her sweaty palms without regret or remorse.

After all, why should its true author succeed, where she had failed?

It wasn't *fair*.

That young woman had already won the lottery of life, as far as she was concerned. Anna Taylor-Ryan had looks, brains, a happy marriage and—it pained Lin to admit—a certain way with words. *Naturally*, she assured herself, the original manuscript would *never* have made it past any reputable agent's desk, so roughshod was the prose…but, with her own additions here and there, her own *elevated* style, she'd been able to make a silk purse from a sow's ear. That purse would take her all the way to the bank and back to the top of the charts, where she belonged. In fact, the more she thought about it, the more Lin realised that she was *meant* to find that manuscript. By the time she'd tinkered with it here and there, the story was more hers than anybody else's, anyway.

Linette thought this as she smiled and signed copies of the book, admiring the gilt-edged hardbacks with a *purr* of appreciation.

Yes, she thought. *She was back where she belonged, and nobody was going to take this moment from her.*

They'd have to kill her, first.

While Lin spoke expansively about her latest novel to a group of enthralled fans, Doctor Anna Taylor-Ryan battled the early afternoon crowd milling around the Christmas markets in the centre of Newcastle. The scent of caramelised nuts and mulled wine filled the air, spilling from large, steaming cauldrons inside quaint, chalet-style stalls. People walked arm in arm, bundled up against the wind that swept up from the river and through the old Georgian and Victorian streets of Grainger Town, its stone facades decorated with strings of twinkling white lights. Anna paused to rub her shoulder, which ached beneath the smart red coat she wore. The skin was still sore and bandaged, and could've used some anti-inflammatories, but she was reluctant to take pain medication—not in her condition. Unconsciously, a protective hand strayed to her stomach, still flat beneath the layers of clothing she wore.

Would Emma have a little sister to look forward to, or a brother?

Smiling at the prospect, she made her way towards Fenwick's, the stately old department store at the head of the street. Thinking of the family she and Ryan were building together, her thoughts inevitably strayed back to a time when she'd felt entirely alone in the world, and the only person she'd been able to rely upon was herself. Her father hadn't exactly been a model parent, not least in his treatment of her mother, before she died. Andy Taylor had been a handsome man with an ugly temperament; one given to taking the quickest, easiest route, no matter whom he trampled on the way. He was handy with his fists, which was a polite way of saying that he could be an angry, violent man, and the few times he'd shown a kind word or deed had not been enough to outweigh that fundamental flaw. To top it off, in the years following his death, Anna learned that her father had also been one of the leaders of a secretive cult known as 'The Circle', whose exploits included murder and corruption, all in the name of self-advancement. Its members claimed to act on behalf of a shadowy 'Master' and practised a dogma that was nothing more than a stolen mix of Paganism and Satanism, cobbled together to lend their murderous tribe a patina of legitimacy. It was no wonder she'd spent years avoiding long-term relationships, and had never considered herself 'maternal'. She hadn't wanted to risk loving someone, only to be hurt all over again when they let her down.

That was before she met Ryan.

Maxwell Finley-Ryan, she amended, with another smile at the idea of him ever being known as 'Max'. Perhaps when he was younger, but certainly not as the man she'd come to know and love. To all who mattered, he was simply 'Ryan', a person of his own making.

Theirs hadn't been a tentative, slow-burn relationship. Oh, no. It had been an instant supernova in which two minds and hearts sought out their perfect match and came together in explosive style. Against every realistic probability, they'd found their own particular needle in an enormous haystack containing billions of others and life had never been the same again. In an unnervingly short amount of time, Anna found she *could* imagine holding a baby in her arms, because she knew that the man who would be its father was one worth having. As the child of a lesser specimen, she wouldn't have settled for less.

With these thoughts circling her mind, Anna found that she'd walked as far as Waterstones, the largest of several bookshops in the city. Later, with the benefit of hindsight, she'd think that it would have been better to stay away and avoid seeing the evidence of her work having been plagiarised so flagrantly, but she hadn't known Lin Oldman was giving a talk at that very moment. Nor had she expected to see an enormous display of the book she'd named *The Island,* gracing the front window of the shop, with a new name that proclaimed it as somebody else's story. *Island Mystery* was a bestseller already, and its reviews had been spectacular. Tears blurred her eyes as she looked at the rows of books, with their beautiful, gilt-edged jackets and iconic silhouette of her childhood home. Beside them was a framed photograph of the author, but, instead of looking at an image of herself in moody black and white, Anna stared into the smug-faced expression of a middle-aged woman who thought she had triumphed.

Anger coursed through her veins, the anger of a woman whose heart had poured onto the pages of that book and whose story was uniquely hers to tell. Like so many times in her life, another person had stolen something sacred and precious, this time a piece of her identity.

Anna dashed away a tear, and fumbled in her bag for a pack of tissues.

The lawyer she and Ryan had spoken to had been kind, but realistic. It was possible to fight the publisher, he'd said, and to sue them for all they were worth, but it would be a long, expensive and emotionally draining battle. With a new baby on the way, a three-year-old ready to take on the world, and a loving partner who'd support her no matter what she decided, Anna knew it would be a selfish act to demand her day in court.

It wasn't worth the heartache.

Not at any cost.

BERWICK

Anna was about to turn away when the doors opened beside her, letting out a wash of applause from the audience seated within. She edged forward to look through the glass, scanning the backs of their heads until she came to a face she recognised.

Lin Oldman.

Only then did she notice the sign on the door advertising, 'AN AUDIENCE WITH LIN OLDMAN—BOOK AND MINCE PIE INCLUDED!'

Before her mind had an opportunity to dissuade her, she stepped inside.

"I think we have time for some questions from the audience."

The bookseller in charge of running Lin's event turned to face the crowd and waited for hands to raise before selecting whoever was quickest off the mark.

"The gentleman in the second row, in the tweed jacket—"

"Thanks," he said, and a roving microphone was thrust in front of him. "I—ah—well, I have to say, I loved reading *Island Mystery*. I hope you won't mind me telling you, it felt like you were back to your best—"

Lin kept her smile in place, while the bookseller cast her a wary glance. Over the years, she'd come to know the author seated on the small podium beside her, and her ego was practically the stuff of legend.

"Thank you," Oldman said. "How kind of you to say so."

"I wanted to ask a question about that cult you were writing about…you know, the 'Syndicate'," he continued. "Was that based on anything real, or was it all from your imagination?"

Lin swallowed, finding her throat as dry as the Sahara. "*Well*," she said, and reached for the water jug to buy herself some time.

"You know all fiction tends to have a basis in reality, but, in this case, it came from the depths of my imagination."

"Really? I thought it might have been something to do with that 'Circle' case up on Holy Island, a few years back—"

Persistent bugger, Lin thought. "Well, naturally, writers do take inspiration from real life—"

"Seemed pretty close to the mark, if you ask me," he interrupted. "Did you have to do much in the way of research?"

"I—" Lin began to say, while a bead of sweat ran down the length of her spine.

"Yes, I'd be very interested to know how you came up with that story."

A new voice carried across the room, clear as a bell and laden with meaning. Heads swivelled and Lin scanned the crowd until her eyes locked with the hard, unforgiving stare of the woman whose work she had stolen.

Anna Taylor-Ryan.

Lin's heart thudded against her chest, and a layer of sweat beaded her skin. Then, she reminded herself that *she* was the name in the room; it was *she* the readers had come to see, not some *nobody* who'd never make it past the starting blocks.

She tilted her chin, managing to affect an air of regal condescension. "Inspiration can strike anywhere—"

"At a creative writing session, perhaps?"

The bookseller looked between them, picking up on a tension that was palpable. "Well, I think that's about all we have time for," she began to say.

"You haven't answered my question," Anna snapped, and took a step forward. "I asked whether you found your inspiration at a creative writing session. In fact, I wonder whether that inspiration was laid out for you, neatly, in a manuscript somebody else had written."

BERWICK

Lin turned an ugly shade of puce. "If you're suggesting what I *think* you're suggesting, I would advise you to retract that statement immediately, unless you want to receive a writ for slander—"

"You stole my story!" Anna burst out, and nobody was more surprised than she. "You took my manuscript, made a few token changes, and sent it to your publisher with your own name on the front. You should be ashamed!"

There was a stunned silence, while the audience waited to see what would happen next.

Lin composed herself and then stood up, very slowly. "That is a very *serious*, not to mention entirely *spurious* allegation," she said, in the manner of one explaining something to a slow child. "I don't know who you are," she lied. "But, in the course of my long career, I've met individuals like you before. People who convince themselves they've come up with something original, when they haven't. You have my sympathies, because I'm sure it's disappointing to find out your idea wasn't original after all, but, *really*, there's no excuse for barging in here like this, especially at Christmastime."

There were a few twitters around the room, a couple of tuts and headshakes. Seeing them, Anna's eyes burned with unshed tears, anger vying with humiliation.

"You're—you're *lying*," she said, tremulously. "I can prove it!"

"I think we've all heard quite enough," the bookseller said, and made a desperate signal to another bookseller to move along the dark-haired woman with a murderous expression in her eye. "I think it's time for you to leave."

"I'm going," Anna said, but turned to lance Oldman with one final Parthian shot. "You've written your last chapter in this business. You'll never write another word, I'll make sure of it."

Something in her tone caused the smile to slip from Lin's face.

Was that a threat?

Anna turned and stalked back out into the gathering darkness, feeling a welcome rush of cool air against her overheated skin.

There was an awkward silence in the wake of her departure.

"There's always one, isn't there?" Lin joked, eliciting a few laughs. "Now, who's ready for a mince pie?"

But later, as she penned her last signature for the day, she thought of the look on Anna's face as she'd turned to leave.

...written your last chapter...

...you'll never write another word...

If looks could kill, she'd be dead already.

CHAPTER 2

Later that day

Thrusting all thoughts of publishing disputes to the back of her mind, Anna squared her shoulders and prepared to face down another foe, one far more stubborn and intractable than the last.

Her daughter.

All Emma had to do was eat some of the broccoli on her plate. A single floret of the green stuff would do, but she was having none of it. Anna had tried asking politely, then she'd tried disguising the offending vegetable in some pasta sauce, only to have it weeded out again. She'd tried distraction, then humour and cajolery, all to no avail, but at least she had one last trick up her sleeve—one known to every parent in the land as a last resort to inveigle even the toughest of toddlers.

Bribery.

"If you eat some of your broccoli, Emma, you can have sticky toffee pudding for dessert. How about that?"

"I don't *like* broccoli!" Emma declared, crossing her little arms over her chest in a move so adorably mutinous, her mother was forced to hide a smile.

"You liked it last week," Anna reminded her. "In fact, you told me the broccoli looked like little trees on your plate, and eating them made you feel like a giant."

"Well, *now*, I don't like it," Emma said, neatly circumventing any references to a time in the recent past when her tastes might have been less discerning. "And I don't *want* to be a giant, anymore. I want to be a detective, like Daddy."

There came a soft chuckle from across the room, where Ryan's mother was seated in a cosy spot beside the fire.

"Emma reminds me so much of her father, when he was that age," she said, with fondness. "Fiercely independent and stubborn as a mule. I think it comes from my side of the family," she added, as a self-deprecating nod to her own wilful nature.

Eve Ryan set down the newspaper she'd been scanning, took off her reading glasses and propped them atop her head before moving to join her daughter-in-law and granddaughter at the kitchen table. Rascal, the golden Labrador who was now more of a gangly teenager than a puppy, raised his head from where it had been resting against her slippers and loped after her.

"He loves you," Anna said, and reached out a hand to ruffle the dog's ears.

"We keep each other company," Eve admitted, before fixing her granddaughter with a beady eye. "Now, young lady, what's this I hear about you not eating your vegetables? How do you expect to be able to grow big and strong?"

The doorbell rang, and Anna excused herself to go and see who it could be. Ryan wasn't a man in the habit of forgetting his keys and, besides, he wasn't due home for hours yet. She supposed it was probably a delivery courier, or perhaps one of their new neighbours coming over to introduce themselves.

It turned out to be neither.

"Mrs Taylor-Ryan?"

BERWICK

Anna looked between the stern faces of two plain-clothed detectives. She didn't recognise either of them from Ryan's cohort of colleagues at the Northumbria Police Constabulary, but she'd have pegged them as fuzz from a mile away; there was a look in their eyes that was unique to those in their profession, which she'd come to recognise after living with one of their number for the past ten years.

"That's right," she said slowly. "Are you looking for Ryan? He isn't home yet—"

"We're not here to see your husband, ma'am. We're from Durham CID," the older of the two replied, and reached for her identification. "It's you we'd like to speak to, if we may."

Anna's brow furrowed as she read the names 'Detective Sergeant Lauren Bell' and 'Detective Constable Kieron Vale' on their warrant cards.

"You're a long way from home," she remarked. "Has something happened at the university?"

Anna continued to teach History to undergraduates and doctoral candidates at Durham University a few days per week, and it was her only remaining connection to the area. She'd once lived in a little stone cottage on the banks of the river, but that was a long time ago.

They didn't answer her question.

"Do you mind if we come in?"

"Um..." Anna couldn't think of any decent excuse to leave them standing outside in the cold, so she gestured them inside. "Yes, of course. Would you like a cup of tea?"

They declined politely, and she led them through to the living room.

"What's all this about?" she asked, and a creeping feeling of dread began to spread over her skin, prickling the fine hairs on the back of her neck. She folded her arms across her chest, unconsciously adopting a defensive stance.

To her surprise, DS Bell recited the standard police caution.

"Do you understand?"

"I—I don't—I mean, yes, I understand," Anna stammered. "I'm sorry, I'm a bit confused. Why are you here? Have I done something wrong?"

"We'd like to ask you some questions regarding your relationship with the writer known as Lin Oldman."

Anna's stomach performed a slow somersault. "Look," she said, taking the bull by the horns. "If this is about what happened earlier today—"

"That depends," the sergeant replied, mildly. "What happened earlier today?"

"Well, you know, at the bookshop," Anna said, with a touch of embarrassment. "I suppose I *was* a bit rude, interrupting her talk like that, but I don't think there was any need for her to complain to the police…"

She broke off, unnerved at the sight of the younger detective taking notes.

"You admit there was an altercation at Waterstones bookshop in Newcastle upon Tyne, earlier today?" DS Bell queried.

"I'd hardly call it an altercation," Anna demurred. "I interrupted Lin Oldman's talk to ask about the provenance of her most recent novel, knowing full well she couldn't answer because she stole the story from me."

They seemed not to hear the last part of her statement, and proceeded along their dogged line of enquiry.

"Did you threaten Ms Oldman, verbally, in front of a large audience?" Bell persisted.

Threaten? Anna thought.

"I would never—" she began, and then remembered her furious parting words, something along the lines of *Island Mystery* being the last words Oldman would ever write.

She closed her eyes briefly, then opened them again.

"I was angry with Ms Oldman because she plagiarised my book," she explained, as calmly as she could. "Seeing the woman waxing lyrical about the inspiration for her novel was a bit rich for my blood, so I called her out about it, that's all."

"Did you seek out Ms Oldman, in order to threaten her?"

"Of course not!"

"Mummy?"

They all turned at the sound of a small voice entering the room.

"*Emma*," her mother said, and hurried over to draw her close. "Where's your grandma?"

"I'm here," Eve said, entering the room belatedly with a tea towel in hand. Her older, wiser eyes took in the situation immediately, as well as the worry marring Anna's expression. "What can I do?"

Before Anna could formulate a response, DS Bell interjected.

"I presume you're the little girl's grandmother?"

Eve nodded, and slid protective arms around both of her girls.

"I am," she said, in the same clipped, well-rounded tones she'd gifted her son. "Is there a problem?"

"It would be helpful if you would agree to look after her, at least until her father returns home," Bell said.

"What?" Anna said, and took an instinctive step forward. "*Why*?"

"I'm not leaving my mummy!" Emma said, and clamped her arms around Anna's leg in the manner of one who would Not Be Moved.

The sergeant fixed Anna with an impassive stare, which conveyed a clear message: they could do this the easy way, or the hard way, and the choice was hers.

"Come on, sweetheart," she said, and crouched down to look into her daughter's face. "Everything's going to be okay, these are just some of Daddy's friends from the police station. They need me to go along with them and answer some questions."

She hoped that was all.

Anna pressed a kiss to Emma's cheek and exchanged a glance with Eve, who nodded and leaned in to bestow a brief, hard hug.

"I'll call Ryan," she whispered.

"Thank you," Anna said, and held onto Ryan's mother for a few more seconds before drawing away. "Tell him there's nothing to worry about; my conscience is clear."

Eve nodded, and cupped a warm hand around Anna's cheek. "Chin up, sweetheart," she said softly. "You've faced worse demons."

The demons in their present nightmare had the decency to wait until Eve had removed her granddaughter from the living room, well out of earshot, before striking their next blow.

"Anna Taylor-Ryan, I am arresting you on suspicion of the murder of Linette Winterbottom, also known as Lin Oldman," Bell said. "You do not have to say anything—"

Anna heard the words as if from a great distance, while black spots began to dance in front of her eyes.

Murder?

"Wait a minute—"

"—but anything you do say may be taken down and used in evidence against you—"

"—wait—you said Lin Oldman was—*murdered*?"

Anna looked between the two officers, eyes pleading with them to listen.

"I didn't kill anyone," she said. "I swear it."

"Let's talk about it down at the station."

They instructed her to retrieve a coat, which Anna did, walking dazedly from the living room to the porch where their coats hung in cheerful disarray. She saw her daughter's pink duffel coat, decorated in a pattern of gawdy white unicorns, next to her husband's woollen overcoat that he tended to wear off-duty. It carried a lingering scent of his aftershave, *Cairo* by Penhaligon's, and she reached for it instead of her own, wrapping the generous material around her as a kind of comfort blanket for herself and the baby she carried.

"I'm ready," she said softly.

When they stepped outside, there was no glimmer of stars to soothe her spirit, nor the gentle lap of waves against the shoreline where they liked to walk the dog each morning. Instead, the sea was a turbulent roar, crashing against the dunes with all the ferocity of an angry god, while the clouds loomed darkly overhead, foreshadowing all that was to come.

CHAPTER 3

Detective Sergeant Frank Phillips cast a nervous glance at the speedometer on his friend's car, which continued to edge upwards at an alarming rate, and comforted himself with the knowledge that he was unlikely to live long enough to see England win the World Cup, even if he *did* manage to survive the hair-raising journey from Newcastle to Durham. All the same, he'd rather keep what little hair he had left firmly on his head.

He looked across at the forbidding profile of the man seated in the driver's seat and drew in a fortifying breath.

"Now, just try to stay calm, lad—"

"I *am* calm," came the snarled reply.

"Aye, you seem as cool as a cucumber," Phillips muttered. "Look, I know how you feel—"

"Has your wife been arrested for murder, Frank?"

"Not yet, but she's threatened it often enough."

In other circumstances, Detective Chief Inspector Maxwell Finley-Ryan might've laughed at that, but he didn't have the heart.

"I can't understand it," he said. "Durham CID wouldn't tell me anything over the phone."

"They can't," Frank reminded him. "They have to treat you as a family member, not a fellow officer."

Ryan gave him a withering look.

BERWICK

"I'm not sayin' it's what *I* would do," Frank assured him swiftly. "But you know their team took a lot of flak after all that business at the cathedral a couple of years ago. They've got to be seen to be goin' by the book."

He paused to roll his burly shoulders, which ached after an early morning boxing session down at Buddle's Gym.

"It'll all turn out to be a storm in a teacup, you wait and see," he continued. "Everybody knows your lovely lass wouldn't hurt a fly."

Frank hadn't forgotten *that lovely lass* was also adept at handling a rifle, when the occasion called for it, but he pushed the thought from his mind and concentrated on being a good friend to the man who might have been his senior in the police hierarchy but was, in all other things, a surrogate son, favourite nephew and loyal partner, all rolled into one.

"This wouldn't be the first time one of us got banged up, now would it?" he carried on, with forced cheer. "In fact, it wasn't so long ago *you* were the poor bugger behind bars, as I recall. I've had a few raps on the knuckles in my time, and the less said about wor Jack's shenanigans, the better. It's a rite of passage, that's what it is."

Ryan thought back to the time he was wrongfully accused of murdering Mark Bowers, one of The Circle's former cult leaders. "That was different," he said quietly. "And besides, there's something else to think of—"

He broke off, and his hands flexed on the steering wheel as they flew along the slip road that would take them into the centre of Durham.

"Something else?" Frank prompted, once his stomach righted itself.

"Anna's carrying our baby," Ryan said softly. "I swear, if they've hurt her, in *any* way—"

The muscle in his jaw clenched, and his eyes burned like chips of silver ice, worry outweighing the joy of second-time fatherhood for the moment.

"A baby? That's *wonderful* news, lad!" Frank said warmly, and put a hand on his friend's shoulder. "As for Anna...well, she comes from hardy stock. She might look delicate but she's strong, that one. She'll pull through."

"I know she's strong," Ryan murmured. "But this situation would be stressful for anyone, never mind a pregnant woman in her first trimester. The shock of the arrest could harm the baby, as well as her. What if she miscarries because of this? It's happened before."

It had? Frank thought, and grieved for his friends' loss.

Many years ago, when he and his first, late wife thought of having a family together, Laura had suffered several miscarriages. They'd given up trying after a while, and then, by the time they'd begun to consider other ways of becoming parents...well, the cancer had robbed them of any future they might have had. He'd never imagined he'd be fortunate enough to love again, let alone have the privilege of fatherhood, but it was funny the way the world turned. Denise and Samantha were all he needed in the world, and he thanked his lucky stars for them every day.

None of which was any help to his friend, at that particular moment.

"Now, don't start thinkin' like that," he declared, and patted Ryan's shoulder again. "As far as we know, Anna and the baby are doin' fine. They're a decent bunch, down in Durham, and they know she's your wife. More importantly, she's *my* friend, and they'll not muck about if they know what's good for them."

Ryan couldn't help but smile. "Thanks, Frank," he said, quietly. "My head's reeling...I know she was angry with Oldman for stealing her work—we both were—but I can't imagine Anna would ever act on it. It isn't in her nature."

"Aye, I know, lad. Let's get there in one piece, and see what's what."

With studied nonchalance, he nodded towards the car ahead of them, whose rear end approached with alarming speed.

Ryan tapped the brake pedal.

"You should've let me drive," Frank said.

Now, Ryan *did* laugh.

"Thanks," he said. "I needed that."

Frank administered a none-too-gentle punch to his friend's bicep, and was pleased to hear a satisfying *yelp* in response.

"Still got it," he said with a wicked chuckle, and then folded his hands over his paunch. "Not far now, lad."

Ryan rubbed the circulation back into his upper arm. "I don't know what to say to her, Frank."

"Hm?"

"Anna," Ryan muttered. "I don't know what to say to her, when I see her."

Frank turned to him with warm brown eyes, filled with understanding. "You'll find the words," he said. "Never fear."

But he was afraid, Ryan thought. *In fact, he was terrified.*

What if—

What if it was true?

What if his wife was a killer?

It went against everything he stood for, everything he fought to avenge each day in the office he held. He'd lost a sister to a murderous madman and seen other families in the throes of grief and loss, too numerous to count. Only in very rare circumstances could he find it in his heart to forgive or, at least, to try to understand the destruction people inflicted upon their fellow man. Sometimes, it was a case of revenge, other times it was insanity, duress, coercion, provocation or diminished responsibility, but at the end of every avenue was a body lying on a slab at the mortuary. He saw their ghostly faces in his memory and made no distinction between 'good' and 'bad' victims. However they behaved in life, there could be no justification for somebody ending it prematurely without following the proper wheels of justice.

What happened when those wheels failed, in an overloaded system under threat of corruption and bias?

Ryan's mind whispered the words, and he knew they were true. Any overstretched organisation could be vulnerable to errors or oversights, no matter how well-intentioned. It was an unfortunate fact of life, but it made no allowance for the people who fell between its cracks.

He only hoped Anna wouldn't turn out to be one of them.

CHAPTER 4

Durham Police Station was in keeping with the greatest traditions of modern government architecture. That is to say, it was an uninspiring edifice which not even the addition of a few limp Christmas decorations could do much to relieve. Ryan could only imagine it had been erected as punishment, not only to the community who were required to look at it, but to the police personnel who were required to work within it. He thought this as they made the short journey from his car—parked flagrantly across double yellow lines—to the main entrance.

"Ready?" Phillips asked, watching his friend keenly.

Ryan nodded, and continued to stride across the asphalt like an avenging angel, long legs eating up the ground. His face was set into uncompromising lines and Phillips took a moment to send up a prayer for whichever unsuspecting desk sergeant was about to get it in the neck.

As it happened, the desk sergeant was a woman by the name of Wendy Dickens, and she was far from unsuspecting. She'd served more than twenty-five years on the Force and, while not immune to Ryan's physical charms—which were *considerable*—she had enough good sense not to succumb to them.

"DCI Ryan and DS Phillips," she said, primly. "Long time, no see!

Is your business here today personal or professional?"

Ryan raised a single eyebrow, and she had the grace to blush.

"*Personal*," he enunciated. "You have my wife in custody for murder, as I'm sure you're well aware."

"Well," Wendy said, and folded her fingers on top of the counter. "DS Bell is still interviewing your wife, so I'm afraid you'll have to wait. There's a seating area for family and friends over there—"

"I'm not about to sit there like a lemming while—" Ryan began, through gritted teeth.

"How's Alan doin' these days?" Phillips cut across him, and put a steadying hand on his friend's rigid back. "Heard he came through the chemo like a trooper."

Wendy knew Frank Phillips of old; in fact, she seemed to recall a couple of dances and a few midnight fumbles way back in the early eighties, before she'd met Alan and he'd met Laura. They might not have been right for one another, but she knew Frank to be an honest, decent man with a twinkle in his eye which never dimmed. He might have been trying to butter her up, but that did nothing to lessen her pleasure at having him remember her husband, who'd recently survived the greatest battle of his life.

"He's on the mend, Frank," she said, warmly. "Thanks for thinkin' of him."

"Aye, well, mind you tell him there'll be no duckin' out of next year's Great North Run, just because he nearly died o' cancer. It's no excuse for bein' lazy, y'nah."

Wendy's lips twitched. "Go on with you," she chuckled, and took not one bit of offence, knowing as she did that Frank had nursed his own late wife through the ravages of the same disease and not been as lucky in the outcome. "You're welcome to tell him yourself, if you want to call in, sometime."

"I will," Phillips promised.

Conscious that Ryan was vibrating with suppressed rage, he moved on to the matter in hand.

"Howay then, isn't there anythin' you can chuck our way about his missus?"

Ryan continued to hold his tongue, never more grateful that Frank was doing all the talking, since he was in no mind to be civil.

"Frank, you know I'd like to help you out, but—"

Phillips leaned on the counter, and, just for a moment, Wendy was reminded of the man she'd met thirty years before. He might've been a trifle slimmer, then, with a bit more hair on top, but he still had those lovely, button brown eyes and a smile that could light up a room.

"You know we'd do the same for you," he crooned.

She fiddled with her pen and cast a furtive glance around the lobby to see if her boss happened to be within earshot. Then, she leaned forward, keeping her voice low.

"All right, I can tell you this much," she said, conspiratorially. "That author—whatshername? Lin Oldman. She was found dead in her flat, just down the road from here. Her neighbour found her, apparently. She heard unusual noises and a loud thud, so she went around to complain and ask Lin to keep it down. When there was no answer, the neighbour started to worry and called the police."

Ryan gathered up the scraps of information like a starving man.

"What does it have to do with Anna?" he wanted to know. "Why have they arrested her?"

They needed sufficient grounds, he thought. *What could they possibly have that was so incriminating?*

But Wendy shook her head.

"You know I can't go into all that," she told them, leaning back again to signal the conversation was over. "I'll let the SIO know you're here—"

"Who's runnin' the case?" Phillips asked.

"DS Bell," Wendy told him. "Now, if you'll just take a seat, I'm sure it won't be too long."

"I'm not going anywhere until you tell me whether Anna's rights have been observed," Ryan said, in a tone that brooked no refusal. "She's pregnant, and I have concerns about the impact this will have on the baby. Has she seen our solicitor, yet?"

"Miss Fairchild signed in twenty minutes ago," Wendy said, flicking through the log book. "However, her services were refused. As for the rest, so long as Mrs Ryan told the team about her pregnancy, I'm sure she would've been looked after."

Refused? Ryan thought, wildly. *Why would Anna refuse to see a solicitor?*

Wendy watched the play of emotions on his face, and felt for him. "We're only doin' our jobs, you know," she said, softly.

He swallowed a sudden constriction in his throat, and gave a jerky nod of thanks. "I know. Thank you."

"Ryan?"

Both men spun around at the sound of approaching footsteps, which belonged to Detective Sergeant Bell.

"Lauren," Ryan said. "What the hell's going on, here?"

She didn't bother with any pleasantries, understanding correctly that he was in no mood for small talk. Despite the circumstances, she knew Ryan to be one of the best in their business, and respected him for it. As one of the incorruptible officers in her own command unit, she had him to thank, in part, for bringing about a widespread cleanup in their division, washing it free of some of the less desirable elements so that she and others like her could spend their time solving crimes and seeking justice, rather than battling obstacles and closed doors. In happier times, they'd laughed at conferences and worked together on cross-command investigations, so it gave her no pleasure to see him standing on the other side of the fence, cap in hand.

"Let's walk and talk," she said, and didn't wait for a response but turned and made for a security door, beyond which lay the interview suite. "Your wife's in one of the rooms down here, taking a comfort break. She looked pale when she arrived at the station, so I offered her some refreshment and some personal time before her interview began."

Ryan knew her to be a fair-minded woman but, somehow, the evidence of it did nothing to allay his fears.

"She's expecting our baby," he said quietly.

Bell paused to look at him, and then turned back to the keypad, unwilling to show any sympathy, however much she might have felt it.

"That explains it," she said. "Mrs Ryan *did* mention she was feeling nauseous, so we've done our best to make her as comfortable as possible…but, as you know, we have to ask our questions and have them answered."

She pushed through the door and led them down a long corridor painted a dismal shade of grey, to match their present mood.

"Has she seen a solicitor?" Ryan asked, playing dumb for Wendy's sake.

"A solicitor attended, but was turned away," Bell threw back over her shoulder. "Your wife says she's innocent of any crime, and has no need of a solicitor."

It was a common reaction, Ryan knew. Those who believed themselves innocent, or wished to *appear* innocent, often refused the help of a solicitor. Perhaps it was an act of defiance, or further evidence of their plea, he couldn't be sure. However, morals were expensive commodities, and it was far better to have someone fighting your corner when the occasion called for it.

"Why wasn't I contacted immediately?" he asked, as their footsteps clattered across the linoleum floor.

Lauren stopped, and gave him a cool stare. "We *did* try and contact your office," she told him. "The mobile number you have listed on the staff database is out of date, you know."

Ryan opened his mouth, then shut it again. He'd meant to update his profile after being issued a new smartphone, but there always seemed to be something more important to do.

"I'll see it's updated," he muttered. "I was closing the investigation up at Belsay Hall, or I'd have been here, sooner. What possible grounds do you have for arresting Anna?"

Lauren sighed inwardly. The decision to arrest Anna Taylor-Ryan had been hers to make, and she'd known it would ruffle a few feathers, but since Anna was the only person with any semblance of a motive to kill Lin Oldman, she'd been left with no choice but to play it safe and bring the woman in. It was on the tip of her tongue to refuse to share any further information with Ryan, given that he was not his wife's legal counsel nor a member of the investigating team, but there was a code between the men and women who avenged the dead. It may have been unwritten and unspoken, but it was as tangible as the nose on her face.

You helped one another, whenever you could.

Lauren shrugged. "The victim, known as Lin Oldman, was found dead in her home only a few hours after your wife was filmed making a public death threat towards her."

Ryan and Phillips looked at each other, then back at her, their faces twin masks of comical surprise.

"A *death* threat?" Frank squeaked. "I don't believe it—"

"See for yourself," Lauren said, and brought up a social media app on her phone. A moment later, they were treated to wobbly footage of Anna, dressed in her red winter coat, standing in the centre of a seated crowd pointing an accusatory finger at the speaker, who was none other than Lin Oldman.

You'll never write another word…

Ryan winced at his wife's voice, which rang out clearly in the video footage and was followed by an audible gasp amongst the bookish audience. The video ended with a monologue from its creator, a woman calling herself 'CatLadyReader1958', who gave a blow-by-blow analysis of the drama, much like a pundit on *Match of the Day*.

"The video was posted almost immediately after Oldman's talk ended, and went viral in a few hours," Lauren said, slipping the phone back inside her breast pocket. "It'll be a feeding frenzy, once the news of her death breaks."

Ryan's brows drew together in a hard line. "I won't have my wife's name dragged through the dirt," he warned her. "You have absolutely no evidence, other than the fact she lost her temper with the woman who'd stolen her story—"

"Allegedly," Lauren put in.

"*Definitely*," he corrected her. "We have the original on file, and planned to sue."

"Some might say that gives your wife even more of a motive to kill."

"Howay, man!" Frank said, with feeling. "There's a big difference between *tellin'* someone they're for it, and actually *doin'* it, otherwise I'd have killed *this* one's sorry arse a hundred times over, by now."

He crooked a thumb in the direction of Ryan's chest, in case there was any doubt.

"Besides, as far as I can see, she never actually threatened to *kill* the woman, did she?"

"It was implied," Lauren shot back.

"I want that story taken down," Ryan barked. "It has the potential to be taken wildly out of context."

"We don't have any grounds to demand that the platform remove it," Lauren replied, and was sorry to disappoint him. "You're a senior police officer, Ryan. You know we can't show favouritism to our own, and, in any case, the content of that video doesn't defame your wife."

Ryan stuck his hands in his pockets, unable to argue with the truth of that. "When did Oldman die?" he said, in a sudden change of direction. "Has the pathologist given any indication of postmortem interval?"

Lauren pressed her lips together, drew in a deep breath through her nostrils, and then let it out again. Here was another thing she hadn't intended to share, but, since he'd had no opportunity to confer with his wife, she supposed there could be little harm in Ryan knowing.

"Pinter says Oldman had been dead less than two hours by the time first attending officers forced entry and found her body," she said. "We know her neighbour called the police after hearing a suspicious noise shortly after five o'clock, so it seems reasonable to assume time of death was sometime around then."

"CCTV?" Frank prodded. "Any witnesses?"

But Lauren wasn't about to tell them everything they knew, such as the fact the single working CCTV camera around the back of Oldman's apartment block had been broken, nor the fact they didn't have a single witness who could verify the identity of anyone entering or leaving the property around that time.

"I'm about to interview your wife again," she said. "As a courtesy, I'll allow you to observe from the viewing room—"

"Please," Ryan said, and put a hand on her arm, compelling her to listen. "*Please*, Lauren. She might need me, just to be there beside her."

DS Bell began to shake her head, then a memory of how vulnerable she'd felt during her first trimester with her son flashed back into her mind. Some might say it made no difference whether a suspect was pregnant, but a smarter detective knew that, to get the most from an interviewee, you needed them to feel as relaxed as possible. People tended to talk more freely.

"You can sit in the interview," she decided. "So long as you don't say a *word*—not *one* word, Ryan. Do you understand me?"

He held out a hand, the gesture taking her by surprise.

She shook it.

"Agreed," he said. "Thank you."

CHAPTER 5

It was like seeing an exotic flower growing in the middle of a concrete pavement.

The thought sprang into Ryan's mind as soon as he saw his wife sitting in the interview room, her elegant hands folded neatly in her lap, head bent in quiet, unspoken defeat.

Anna.

His heart ached for her; every atom yearning to take her into his arms and shield her from the world. She looked up as he entered the room behind DS Bell and DC Vale, and he watched her expression shift from listlessness to elation, then something akin to shame, unshed tears lending her eyes a luminosity that only made her more beautiful.

"*Ryan,*" she said, and began to rise from her chair.

He crossed the room and caught her up against him, feeling her body tremble, her arms clinging tightly to the back of his shirt.

"I didn't do it," she whispered against his chest. "I promise you, I didn't do it—"

Ryan drew back, only so that he could hold her face in his hands. "I know," he told her. "You don't need to tell me."

She let out a long breath, and could have cried at that simple admission of trust.

"Let's get down to it," DS Bell said. "The sooner we begin, the sooner this will be over."

They nodded, and, once they'd seated themselves, Ryan reached across to take his wife's cold hand between both of his own. Lauren read out the formalities for the benefit of the tape recording, then looked at the woman seated across from her with assessing eyes.

"To pick up where we left off, I believe you were about to tell us where you went after leaving the bookshop?"

"Are you sure you don't want a solicitor?"

Lauren shot Ryan a frustrated glare, but supposed she couldn't blame him.

"DCI Ryan, your presence here has been permitted under the strict condition you wouldn't seek to impede our investigation, and only because your wife has waived any legal representation," she reminded him. "You are not present as a member of the investigating team—"

"I understand that," he said, but offered no apology. "All the same, it's always been my custom to check at the beginning of every interview under caution that an interviewee understands they've waived their right, and are entitled to change their mind. Or are things done differently in Durham?"

Lauren's teeth ground together, but she gave a curt nod.

"I didn't catch that," Ryan said.

"*Yes*, we have the same procedures in Durham," she hissed, and sucked in another deep breath before continuing. "Mrs Taylor-Ryan—"

"My wife is an academic doctor," Ryan interrupted again, with maddening politeness. "Therefore, the appropriate title should be used, don't you think?"

Anna squeezed his hand. "It doesn't matter to me," she whispered.

But Ryan shook his head. "It matters to me that you're afforded the respect you deserve," he said.

Lauren had seen Ryan play hard-ball with people before and had privately admired him for it, but that was before she'd found herself on the receiving end.

"*Doctor* Taylor-Ryan, we understand you've waived your right to have a solicitor present during this interview. Do you understand that waiver, and do you wish to amend it now?"

Anna could feel her husband's watchful eyes on her, but shook her head. "I understand," she said. "I don't need a solicitor present."

Lauren might not have agreed with her reasoning, but applauded the sentiment. "All right, let's continue. You were telling us about your disagreement with the late Linette Winterbottom, known as Lin Oldman, at the Waterstones bookshop in Newcastle earlier this afternoon?"

"I don't know what to call it," Anna said, and rubbed a tired hand across her eyes. "I suppose it was a disagreement, of sorts. She claimed to have written the book—*Island Mystery*—from her own imagination, and I disagreed with the veracity of that claim."

"Must've made you angry, seeing her there like that," DC Vale chimed in.

Is that a question? Ryan wanted to say, but kept his counsel, for now.

"I think it would make any sane person angry," Anna said, with a calmness she scarcely felt. "To be the victim of theft is never nice, is it?"

"To be the victim of murder is worse, wouldn't you say?" Vale shot back, and Ryan felt his hackles rise—even in the certain knowledge it was a ploy he'd used countless times before.

"Of course," Anna replied. "I wouldn't suggest otherwise."

"Ms Oldman denied your accusation, didn't she?"

Anna nodded and then, remembering the tape, murmured a simple 'yes' in reply.

"That must have made you even angrier," Vale said. "Especially when she made you look a fool in front of all those people."

Anna felt Ryan's hand tense, and replied quickly before he had time to rip the poor man's head off. "I won't deny that I was angry," she said. "But the anger made me upset and tearful, not murderous. As for making me look like a fool…well, I've had worse things happen. It's not nice, but I'm a grown woman. I can handle my own impulses, DC Vale."

"Somebody couldn't," Lauren said, leaning forward to drive the point home. "Somebody lost their temper with Ms Oldman so badly, they spattered her brains across the rug in her living room—"

On cue, her constable spread out a number of crime scene photographs in a fan on the table, each depicting the battered, lifeless body of what had once been a well-known writer of mysteries.

Anna glanced at them, then away again.

"There's no need—" Ryan began, but Anna squeezed his fingers to silence him.

"If you're hoping to shock me, then you have," she said quietly. "I might have been more shocked, ten years ago, when I hadn't seen half of the things I've seen as the wife of a murder detective. But, still, I feel the same human response any normal person would, which is revulsion and pity for the person she once was."

They listened, watching her face for any tell-tale signs of guilt.

"I might not have admired Lin Oldman as a person, but that doesn't mean I'd ever wish this upon her—or anyone, for that matter."

Convincing, Lauren thought.

And yet…

"Where did you go after leaving the bookshop?"

Anna lifted a shoulder. "I—let's see. It must have been around three o'clock. I'd planned to wander around Fenwick's, but, after what happened, I abandoned that idea. I needed to sit down for a little while to steady myself, so I went to the café at the Laing Art Gallery."

Lauren looked across at DC Vale, who shrugged.

"It isn't far from the bookshop," Ryan explained. "About a five minute walk."

They nodded, and made a note.

"How long did you stay at the café?"

"Oh, not long," Anna said, trying to cast her mind back to that same afternoon, which felt like a lifetime ago. "Fifteen minutes, maybe? It was busy in there, and I had a headache. Besides, I was conscious of the time, and I needed to think about getting home. Ryan's mother, Eve, was watching our daughter and I didn't want to be away too long."

"Where did you go after leaving the café?" Lauren asked.

"I made my way back to the multi-storey car park on Dean Street, but I stopped at one of the stalls to buy some fudge on the way down. The Christmas markets are still going, as you know."

They nodded, and took down the name of the stall.

"What did you do after you bought some fudge?" Lauren asked.

"I went back to my car and started driving home, at around four o'clock," Anna said, and offered the make, model and registration plate, inviting them to check the parking app for details of when she clocked in and out. "Traffic was pretty heavy, so it took around an hour to get back to Bamburgh. I just made it in time to start giving Emma her dinner."

"You didn't make any stops along the way?"

They needed to be sure, for everyone's sake.

"*No*, I didn't," Anna said. "I certainly couldn't have made an hour's detour to Durham, murdered Lin Oldman, cleaned myself up, and still have made it home by five o'clock. That's if I knew where the woman lived, which I don't."

There was the *slightest* note of facetiousness to her tone, because it was getting late, and she'd had quite a day.

Lauren exchanged a glance with her colleague, who nodded his unspoken agreement. They could check Anna's version of events with the fudge stall, CCTV at the Laing Art Gallery, and with the city's parking administration, if need be. It remained true that Anna Taylor-Ryan had a strong motive to kill; whether she had the mettle for it remained uncertain.

However, she was right about one thing.

There was no way she could have made it all the way to Durham and back again, in time to be arrested at her home in Bamburgh by six.

"Would you be willing to provide a DNA sample—so that we can eliminate you completely from the investigation?" Lauren asked.

Ryan opened his mouth to protest, then thought better of it. Anything that would exclude Anna, once and for all, could only be a good thing.

"I have no objection," she said. "I've never been inside Lin Oldman's house, and I've never touched her. You won't find any part of me at the crime scene."

"Well, then," Lauren said. "You've nothing to worry about, have you?"

CHAPTER 6

It was late by the time Frank Phillips arrived home.

When he did, he turned off the car's engine and allowed himself a rare moment to admire the view. The timber and glass house they'd bought, at a significant discount, from Ryan and Anna was more than he could ever have dreamed of. He had never been a man moved by material things; he was less concerned by inanimate objects than people who lived and breathed. But then, he'd never expected to be in possession of both. His childhood had been what some would call 'humble', but, for all they might have lacked, Frank could credit his family for having taught him the value of hard work, not to mention resilience. It was easier to weather the punches life threw at you, from time to time, when you had nothing to lose. The boy he'd once been, scrapping with the other lads in the narrow, terraced streets on the banks of the Tyne, had allowed himself to imagine a steady job, a steady home, and perhaps a couple of children, someday. Nothing too fancy, just a little less hardship than his own parents had borne.

How blessed he'd been, Frank thought, as he sat in the quiet car looking at the strings of twinkling Christmas lights hanging from the branches of the trees and over the porch. A giant, inflatable snowman wobbled on the pathway, welcoming visitors with its maniacal white face and bulbous arms. A bargain from a bric-a-brac fayre a few years ago, he seemed to remember, and still going strong.

More's the pity, Ryan might have said.

Chuckling at the thought, Frank heaved his tired bones from the car and, with a small shiver at the shock of cold air, crossed the driveway towards the house. Lanterns hung from a covered veranda, like beacons guiding his way through the night, and he followed them.

Inside, the house was aglow.

Christmas ornaments vied with poinsettias for space on the hallway table, while cheerful garlands wound through the spindles on the staircase. From the living room, he could just make out the closing scenes of *Home Alone…no*, he amended swiftly. *Home Alone 2: Lost in New York.* He popped his head around the door to find his daughter, Samantha, lying on the rug with her head propped in her hands, giggling away while Harry and Marv met their match in a young Kevin McCallister.

"I bet that one hurt," he said, as a paint can smacked the bandits squarely in the face.

She looked around at the sound of his voice, and her face broke into a smile.

"Dad!" she said, and scrambled to her feet to give him a tight hug. "You're back late!"

Blinking away unexpected tears, Frank pressed a kiss to the top of her head, and met with some form of hair glitter that promptly stuck to his chin.

"Aye," he said, swiping it away. "Sorry, petal. I was—er—held up with somethin' down at the station. What the heck's this?"

Sam looked up and giggled all over again. "You've got it all over your chin," she said, tugging at the sleeve of her top to wipe away the pink hair glitter.

"Thanks," he said, and gave her cheek an affectionate pat. "Is your mam in the kitchen?"

"Think so!" Sam said, returning to her film. "She was listening to that old music again—"

"Er, I think you mean, that *classic* music," he corrected her, with a wink. "I'll not have Bing Crosby's name taken in vain."

"Isn't he dead?"

"That's beside the point," Frank said, with a throaty chuckle. "Off to bed after this one, mind."

She nodded, and he stayed a moment longer, thinking how tall she was becoming, and how lovely. She was another blessing, he realised; perhaps the very best of all.

Humming *White Christmas* beneath his breath, he wandered into the kitchen to find his wife listening to Nat King Cole on the radio while she thumbed through a case file at the kitchen table. Hearing him enter, she looked up and smiled warmly.

"There you are," she said.

My, but Denise MacKenzie is one hell of a woman, he thought. It wasn't just the striking red hair, nor the bold green eyes that spoke loudly of her Irish heritage. It wasn't her intelligence, nor the wit she frequently employed to manage a man like himself. It all helped, but none of it could match the simple essence of who she was: a fighter, a friend and a fearless leader who'd chosen him, of all people.

Him!

Frank Phillips.

Without a word, he walked over to where she was seated and took her face between his hands.

"You're a sight for sore eyes," he told her, and then planted a deep, loving kiss on her upturned mouth.

"What was that for?" she asked.

"Does there have to be a reason for a man to love his wife?" Frank countered. "You're sittin' here, as pretty as a picture, and I was thinkin' how lucky I am to have you and Sam to come home to. That's all."

Denise smiled, and took his Christmas tie in her hand to tug him back down again.

"Well, in that case, kiss me properly."

He barely had time to wonder what his own kiss had been, if not a proper one, before he was shown the difference.

"I still can't believe it," Denise said, once they'd ushered their teenage daughter to bed and reclaimed the living room for themselves. "How are they holding up?"

Frank let out a gusty sigh, watching but not really seeing Jimmy Stewart talk to a giant rabbit on the television.

"*Y'nah*, Ryan was puttin' on a brave face, but he was narf shaken up," he said, taking a sip of whisky. "As for Anna, the poor lass looked dead on her feet, by the end—and that can't be good for her."

"No," Denise murmured. "Especially not…"

She broke off, unsure whether Anna had given her permission to share her good news about the baby. As it happened, that horse had already bolted.

"You *never* knew before I did!" Frank exclaimed, and outrage made his accent all the more pronounced.

"Well, now, don't get your knickers in a twist about it," Denise said, watching him fold his arms across his chest, on the brink of what she liked to call a 'man sulk'.

"Calls me his 'best friend'—"

"I hesitate to remind you, but we've only just closed one murder investigation, we have several others on the go because crime doesn't stop at Christmas, and Anna's only just been released after being arrested for murder. It's possible Ryan might have had other things occupying his mind."

Frank pursed his lips, and grunted. "Well, when you put it like that, I s'pose you're right. But, *still*, this is a clear breach of the Man Code."

"Oh?" Denise said, amused by the whole thing. "What else does the Code say?"

"Well, let's see," he said, and started ticking things off his fingers. "For starters, no funny business allowed with any female member of your best mate's family, especially their sister. That's a cardinal rule of the Man Code."

"What about male members of the family, or non-binary?" Denise wondered aloud.

"Don't start gettin' into semantics," Frank said. "*Any* close family member is a definite 'Hands Off'."

"Or else?"

"Or else," he repeated, ominously.

"What about distant cousins?"

Frank gave this serious thought.

"If they've never met before, then it's allowed," he declared. "It's a different business if a bloke's cousin lives three doors down."

"Mm hm," Denise said, nodding thoughtfully. "And, what if the cousin or family member is willing? Don't they get a say in their own destiny?"

"Destiny, my arse," Frank said, with feeling. "No good ever came of a bloke shaggin' or shackin' up with his best mate's daughter, sister, cousin, mother, aunt, or *great*-aunt, for that matter. If owt was to happen, the friendship would be ruined for good."

Denise found she couldn't really argue with that.

"What else is in the Man Code?"

"If a bloke's got trouble in his nether regions—"

"Nether regions?"

"Aye," Frank repeated, and looked pointedly at his crotch

area. "His *nether* regions, whether it has to do with pestilence or performance, his mate's not to go blabbin' it to all the world. If asked directly, it's always a case of 'back trouble'."

"Back trouble," Denise repeated, and her smile grew wider. "Didn't you have back trouble a few times, last year?"

He lifted his chin.

"That was *entirely* different," he said, with dignity. "I'd had a long week, and I was on that damned blasted cabbage diet at the time. Anyone would be off his game in circumstances like that and, besides, this body's like a finely tuned machine. It needs *meat* to run at full speed."

He flexed a bicep, to make her laugh.

"Is that your way of saying you'd like a ham and pease pudding stottie?"

"You read my mind."

A few minutes later, as Frank chomped his way through honey-glazed ham with all the trimmings of the season, conversation turned back to their mutual friends.

"Hopefully, they'll be able to exclude Anna's DNA quickly, and that'll be the end of it," Denise said, with a wide, jaw-cracking yawn. "I feel for her, being put through all that, but I suppose we might have done the same."

Frank licked his lips, and scowled. "They're scrapin' the barrel, if they think Anna could've had a hand in that woman's murder," he said. "She's a gentle soul."

"She is," Denise mused. "But she's tough, when she needs to be. I think anyone is capable of murder in the right circumstances."

"So you've told me," Frank said, and she laughed again. "But the circumstances weren't exactly optimal, were they? Anna would've had to leg it back to her car after leaving the bookshop, battled her way through city centre traffic to get down to Durham before Oldman came home, killed her as soon as she arrived, and then hot-footed it back to Bamburgh in time for tea. That's miles and miles of drivin', for one thing, and too many 'ifs', 'buts', and 'maybes' to count. She couldn't have known where Oldman lived, or when she'd be home, for a start."

Denise nodded. "Too many variables," she agreed.

"It's like I said from the start," he said, polishing off the last bite. "They were just followin' up all the leads, dottin' all the 'i's, and crossin' all the 't's. That video made things look worse than they are but, now they've met Anna and spoken to her, they'll not give her another thought."

"I'm sure you're right," Denise said, and tried to ignore the small, niggling doubt boring its way through the lining of her stomach. "But the question remains: who wanted Lin Oldman dead?"

"Probably some other poor bugger she stole from," Frank said. "It'll all come out in the wash. Howay, bonny lass, let's curl up for a snuggle on this sofa and watch the rest of the film. It's a wonderful life, isn't it?"

Denise smiled, and rested her head on his broad chest, feeling the steady beat of his heart beneath her cheek.

"It is," she agreed.

CHAPTER 7

Detective Constable Melanie Yates stared at the empty living room in the little house she owned with her ex-boyfriend and fellow detective constable, Jack Lowerson. It was a cosy space but, without him and the cat, it felt much too big.

And lonely, she added silently. *Very lonely*.

She sank onto the edge of the sofa, unable to prevent a reel of memories flooding back, of times when they'd sat on that very cushion together, talking over cases, watching films and…well, everything in between. Honesty compelled her to admit that those happy times had mostly been before her kidnapping, and the long months afterwards when she'd tried to heal her traumatised mind. In that time, she hadn't thought very much of Jack; not *really*, not in the way she should have done. She was grateful to him, as a patient might be to their carer, but she hadn't appreciated the depth of selflessness he'd shown her, especially during the worst times when she'd been very difficult to live with. He'd held her hand during therapy, supported her afterwards, been there for her when she'd suffered paranoia and crippling night terrors. He'd even swallowed his own hurt when she'd told him she needed to get away—far away—from the memories, to try to piece herself back together again. He'd thought only of her wellbeing and set aside his own rejection, which, she admitted, she'd dished out time and time again.

In the privacy of her own company, Melanie realised the love she'd felt for Jack had never been as great as he deserved, nor as great as the love he'd felt for her. She hadn't realised it, of course, until after the fact; hindsight being a marvellous thing. The simple truth was, if she'd loved Jack half as much as he'd loved her, then she wouldn't have wanted to leave him to travel the world alone. She'd have wanted him by her side, even as a quiet force while she healed herself. If he was the other half of her soul, he would never have been a burden or an impediment to her healing process. The truth hit her forcefully, and she grieved the loss of what had never been, shedding some tears as an old Hitchcock played quietly on the television.

There were degrees of love, she thought. A person may feel they couldn't love their partner any more than they did, that they had reached the pinnacle of romance, but then, when compared to another relationship theirs is left to feel hollow and immature. Though it was painful for her to admit, Melanie knew she was more than half to blame for their failure; she'd dragged her heels after the prize had been won. Jack deserved better, and she truly hoped he'd find that in his new relationship with Charlie. She seemed to be a genuine person with a good heart, not to mention a little boy who was cute as a button.

Jack had always wanted kids.

Knowing they'd made the right decision did little to salve the hurt, but, above all else, she hoped she would always be his friend, and a friend would want him to be happy.

And she did.

Almost immediately after the thought entered and left her mind, there came a knock at the door. Mel looked down at her ragged Christmas pyjamas, thought of the wild hair she'd bundled into a pony tail and rolled her eyes at the world.

She traipsed to the door and threw it open, to find Charlie Reed standing on the doorstep.

"What are you doing here?"

Mel couldn't prevent the outburst, having used up every scrap of Christmas cheer in her discussion with Jack, earlier in the evening.

"I know I'm probably the last person you want to see tonight," Charlie said, quietly. "But...do you mind if I come in, just for a moment?"

Mel was rarely lost for words but, for a moment, she could only shrug.

"I'm sorry, I'm not—"

"Please, don't apologise," Charlie said, and put a gentle hand on her arm, taking them both by surprise. "It's very nice of you to let me in, at a time like this."

Mel didn't pretend to misunderstand. "It wasn't your fault," she said, because it was true.

She turned and led the way towards the kitchen, where there was a half-drunk bottle of wine in need of finishing.

"Thank you," Charlie said, taking the glass Mel held out to her. She didn't bother to mention she'd never been a fan of red wine, because it was an olive branch and she'd be a fool to refuse it.

"Did—did Jack forget something?" Mel asked, after a healthy gulp. "He said he was taking a bag, to give me a bit of space, but did he forget his toothbrush?"

"No, no, it's nothing like that," Charlie said, and set the glass down on the countertop. "I wanted to come and see you tonight because, firstly, I want to be your friend, Mel. I admire you very much as a detective, having read over so many of your reports while you were away in Thailand. I heard nothing but praise from everyone. I don't believe any man should come between two women who could be the greatest of friends."

Mel smiled at that. "How do you propose we...overcome the situation?" she asked. "We all work together, which is a bit awkward day to day, don't you think?"

Charlie swallowed. "The fact is, it should be last one in, first one out," she said. "I'm the newest member of the team, so I should be the one to find a transfer. It isn't right that you should feel awkward amongst your friends."

"But didn't you say we should be friends, too?"

"Yes, I hope so, but I'm not foolish enough to expect that sort of thing to happen overnight. I've caused enough heartache—"

"You didn't cause any of this," Mel assured her, and took another gulp of wine before grasping the nettle. "The fact is, I threw away my relationship with Jack the moment I left for Thailand. I even *told* him not to wait for me, and to find someone else. I barely replied to any of his e-mails...as far as he was concerned, I'd disappeared and forgotten him for good. It was arrogant of me to expect him to sit around, twiddling his thumbs, on the off-chance I'd come back, one day."

Charlie picked up her wine glass, finding herself in need of the Dutch courage, after all. "And you did," she said. "You came back for him."

"No," Mel confessed, in a pained voice. "No, Charlie, I didn't come back for him. I came back for myself. I thought I'd slip back into my old life, including my relationship with Jack, because it was comfortable and safe and...I suppose, I felt a bit jealous when I saw how he looked at you."

It was an act of generosity for one woman to admit that to another, and Charlie accepted it with good grace.

"It must have been confusing and upsetting," she said. "I'm sorry."

Mel swallowed. "Anyway, I've grown up a lot over the past couple of years," she said. "Almost being killed and overcoming a breakdown tends to do that to a person."

Charlie opened her mouth to agree, then closed it again. Perhaps they'd talk of her own sorry tale another time, over a different bottle of wine. "I think you're very strong," she said. "I know Jack admires that in you, too."

Mel looked at her, then back at her glass. "I credit him with helping to mend me, when I was broken," she said, and looked up and into Charlie's kind eyes once more, this time with a flash of warning. "He's a good man, Charlie, believe me. He's made a few mistakes, as we all have, but he has a good heart. The best, really, and he's trying to be better all the time. I was foolish not to appreciate and love what I had with Jack, and I've paid the price, but I won't make that mistake again. I hope, if another good person comes along, I'll recognise it, next time."

Charlie's lip wobbled, and she resisted the urge to throw her arms around the other woman in solidarity alone.

"They'll be lucky to have you," she said, in a choked voice. "I believe there's somebody for everyone out there, Mel. Just because you didn't find the right fit this time doesn't mean someone isn't out there just waiting for you to find them."

Charlie paused to add something even more important.

"I won't pretend companionship isn't nice," she said. "I know what it is to feel lonely and alone, abandoned and rejected, but I don't think you're any of those things. I meant what I said—if you feel the slightest bit uncomfortable sharing an office with me, I want you to tell me straight away. Friendship is more important than almost anything else."

Tears filled Mel's eyes because, sometimes, somewhere, she was sure Jack had said similar words which, without knowing it, Charlie had echoed.

In the very back of her mind, a door closed quietly.

"I think you're right," she said, after a moment. "There is somebody for everyone, and I believe Jack met his 'somebody' the day he met you."

She held up a hand to stave off any words Charlie might have spoken.

"I'm happy for him—for *both* of you—because I know love isn't easy to find. Thank you for your offer to transfer, it's kind of you, but I think we're both grown up enough to muddle along together. What d'you reckon?"

Charlie returned the smile, and nodded. "I'd like that."

"I appreciate the courage it must have taken to come and see me, especially on your own," Mel added. "I'm no dragon, but it can't have been easy."

"Jack wanted to come too, but I told him this was something we needed to do," Charlie said. "Besides, if I can deal with murder suspects and the fallout from Phillips' bowel movements, I can have a civilised chat with a lovely woman I hope to call a friend, one day."

Mel nodded. "For the record, I think you're strong, too, Charlie. Single parenting must be hard, especially in our business, and I know your mum's multiple sclerosis is getting worse. You deserve happiness as much as anyone, and more than most."

"Thank you," Charlie said, swallowing a hard ball of unshed tears. "I'm so pleased we talked."

"Me too," Mel agreed, and then added brightly, "See you at work on 27th?"

Mel walked her to the door, where Charlie paused to venture one last olive branch.

"Are you doing anything tomorrow?"

It was Christmas Day.

"I—God, I haven't even thought about it. My parents are abroad, at the moment, so I suppose I'll just have a quiet one, here."

Charlie cleared her throat. "I understand if it's too soon, but you'd be very welcome to come and eat with us—around two? My mother will be there, and a couple of other friends, so it won't just be Jack and me. I can't promise you won't be roped into doing some jigsaw puzzles with Ben, but there'll be turkey and roast potatoes to make up for it."

It was a genuine offer, Mel realised, and she marvelled at the kindness. It was on the tip of her tongue to refuse it, but she decided to be brave and start as they meant to go on.

"Thanks, Charlie. That sounds great."

Charlie beamed at her, and then gave her a swift, hard hug.

"Happy Christmas—and thank you."

When she'd locked and bolted the front door again, Mel walked back into the living room with its half-hearted Christmas decorations and looked around, pensively. There must have been a Christmas miracle, because she no longer felt tearful and the empty room didn't feel half as lonely as it had before.

Feeling lighter, she flopped down onto the sofa and flicked through the channels until she found what she was looking for.

Elf.

Melancholy melted away in the face of Will Ferrell dressed as one of Santa's little helpers, and, as the credits rolled sometime later, she fell into a contented sleep.

CHAPTER 8

27th December

Three days later

Ryan awoke to the sound of gulls seeking breakfast along the shoreline, their calls carrying on the wind across the dunes and through the cracks in the old sash windows. The sky was still dark while the village awakened and he knew that, if he could've spared the time to wait for it, the sunrise would be spectacular.

The sunsets were even better.

Anna opened her eyes and looked across to see Ryan silhouetted in the twilight. He was unselfconscious, his long, naked body resting lightly against the window frame, and she could only be glad the house wasn't overlooked by any elderly neighbours suffering from high blood pressure.

"What time is it?"

"Six-thirty," he said, and moved to sit beside her. "Go back to sleep, if you can."

"I'm awake now," she said. "It won't be long before Emma will be up, anyway."

He brushed his lips against hers, and tucked a long strand of dark hair behind her ear.

"How are you feeling?"

"Still tired, embarrassed, ashamed—"

"You've nothing to be embarrassed about, and nothing to feel ashamed for," he said, pulling her into his arms. "You didn't break any laws. You called out a dishonest woman, who happened to be murdered later the same day. That's bad luck, but it's behind you, now. We had a lovely Christmas, and, whenever you're ready, we can instruct the solicitors to sue Oldman's publishers and have that book removed from sale."

Anna felt the warmth of his bare skin against her cheek, heard the steady beat of his heart, and was surrounded by love. "Thank you for being my champion."

Ryan smiled. "You don't need to thank me for that," he whispered. "I love you. It's part of the deal."

She rubbed her face against his skin, unwilling to let him go, just yet. "Are you back in the office today?"

He sighed, and drew back so he could look at her. "Yes," he said. "We caught a case while we were wrapping things up at Belsay Hall. Body parts, dragged from the river, which we still haven't managed to identify."

She pulled a face.

"Sorry," he muttered. "I should have remembered that kind of talk isn't good for the morning sickness."

"It's okay, pregnancy nausea isn't confined to mornings. It can happen at any time of the day," she said, wryly. "Although, it doesn't seem as bad, this time around."

"Famous last words." He chuckled. "Will you be all right? I can take another day off—"

"I'll be fine," she said. "Don't worry about me. Your mother's still here, and I have Emma to distract me."

Ryan ran gentle fingers over her arm.

"The DNA check should come back soon," he said. "It's been Christmas and Boxing Day, so there won't have been any technicians working in the lab, but Lauren will have put a rush on it, if she has any sense—which she does. They'll get to it as soon as they're back at work today. It's just a formality, in any case."

"But an important one," Anna said, and felt another flutter of unease in the pit of her stomach. "I'll be glad to see the back of all this."

"Me too," he said, and kissed her again. "Stay here, while I bring you up a cup of tea and something to eat."

"You don't need to go to any trouble," she protested. "I can—"

"I know you can," he said. "But I want to."

Anna leaned back against the pillows, turned on the bedside lamp and watched her husband tug on some pyjama bottoms, presumably so his mother wouldn't be scandalised by the sight of her grown son wandering around the house naked.

He turned and flashed her a devastating smile. "Did you turn on that lamp to get a better view?"

She wriggled her eyebrows. "What if I did?"

"Pervert," he said.

"Guilty as charged."

"Howay, man, Frank! Gan' canny!"

Phillips held up both hands and danced away from his sparring partner in the boxing ring at Buddles, the decrepit old gym that had been an institution for more years than he'd been alive—which was plenty to be getting along with, as his knees reminded him daily.

"I *was* takin' it easy!" he bellowed back, and did a little fancy footwork to gee up the small crowd of onlookers.

In answer, the other man muttered a good-natured insult and

lunged forward to administer a solid right hook, which Frank dodged easily.

"I'd better be gettin' on," he said, after they'd exhausted themselves a few minutes later. "The place has probably been fallin' apart while I've been gone."

The two old friends exchanged a sweaty, one-armed hug, bumped boxing gloves and started back towards the dilapidated storage area that doubled as a changing room.

"You got much on at the moment?" Harry asked, after they'd covered the usual chat about their respective holidays and turkey dinners. "Heard about that business up at Dunstanburgh, a while back. Wouldn't'a thought an old bird could've run an operation like that."

"Takes all sorts," Frank replied, cheerfully. "And, you know what they say—"

"It's always the quiet ones? Aye, that's true enough," Harry said, and scrubbed his face with a towel. "We've seen plenty o' them through these doors, over the past forty years, eh?"

Frank nodded, and sat on the bench to begin tugging on a pair of socks featuring a pattern of holly leaves.

"Anyone been givin' you trouble, lately?" he asked, casually.

Harry cast a surreptitious glance around the room, and decided it was neither the time nor the place. "Let's have a pint sometime, eh?"

Frank looked up into his old schoolfriend's face and nodded. "If there's owt worryin' you—"

"Give over," Harry said, all smiles again. "I'm gettin' too old for all this, that's the trouble."

Talk turned to other things but, as he set away for Police Headquarters, Phillips found himself wondering if he should have been more forceful in pushing for the truth. Something had been worrying his old pal, who wasn't easily worried as a rule. On the other hand, managing informants was a delicate business, especially when you'd played football with them as a nipper.

He decided to stop in for that pint, after work, and get to the bottom of it.

Jack Lowerson stood in line at the Pie Van outside Police Headquarters and reflected that its name was something of a misnomer nowadays, since the little mobile eatery had expanded its offering to all manner of goods beyond pastry and meat. He deliberated for a moment, then decided to play it safe.

"Just the usual coffees," he told the proprietor. "Four—"

"Aye, I know, four white americanos and two black," the man said, cheerfully. "You sure you don't want a few turkey stotties to keep your strength up? I've got some o' those veggie sausages you like, n'all."

Jack didn't know whether to be flattered by the fact he'd bought in vegetarian sausages for a single patron amongst the hundreds working at Police HQ, unless there was another covert vegetarian hiding amongst the ranks.

"No thanks," he said. "I'm trying to be good, after stuffing my face with Quality Street over the past few weeks. I'm sure there's another veggie who'll snap them up, though?"

"Nope," the man said, definitively. "You're the only one, as far as I can tell. There's a few folk tryin' to be gluten free, but they all fall off the wagon when they get a whiff of freshly baked bread. Just like you, when you sniff the fried bacon after a session down at the pub, eh?"

Jack wished he could say he'd never had a weak moment in which he'd forgotten that he didn't eat meat, especially after a heavy night on the town, but he couldn't make any such claim. *In vino veritas*, so the saying went, and it was never truer than for a part-time vegetarian nursing a hangover.

Ten minutes later, he entered the open-plan offices of the Criminal Investigation Department laden with everything from coffee to croissants, turkey and stuffing stotties for the carnivores amongst them, and a single floury bap overstuffed with vegetarian sausage and some sort of green mayonnaise which he was already regretting.

"Need a hand?" Denise laughed, spotting him from her desk across the room. "Here, give some of those cups to me, before you go flying. *Jesus*, Mary and Joseph, are you planning to feed the five thousand?"

Her lyrical Irish accent was even more pronounced than usual, and he guessed correctly that she must have recently been speaking to her family, back in Ireland.

"Are you and Frank heading over to the Emerald Isle with Samantha?"

She nodded. "We decided to stay at home for Christmas, but we're hoping to get across to Kerry for a few days in the New Year. It'll depend on what's happening here, though, won't it?"

"Oh, I'm sure Ryan won't mind—"

"What won't I mind?" said the man himself, entering the room with his usual dynamism, slinging his coat over the back of a chair. "Because if you're thinking about roping us into doing another half-naked charity calendar, you can think again. Fool me once, Mac, but you'll not fool me a second time."

"I second that," Jack said, remembering when the pair of them had stood in nothing but novelty Christmas boxers, him holding a kitten with miniature reindeer antlers atop its head, while Ryan posed like James Bond with an unloaded gun in his hand, looking as if he'd been born to it.

As for Frank—

The less said about 'Naughty Santa', the better.

Mercifully, Denise interrupted his train of thought, which was probably for the best. "I was just telling Jack, we were hoping to get over to see my parents for the New Year."

"Of course, you should," Ryan said. "We can cover anything that comes in, if need be. Besides, there isn't too much on at the moment aside from the body parts case, is there?"

The other two shook their heads.

"Mel and I secured the scene," Jack said. "We've got a bit more information, now we have the pathology report—"

"Let's have a briefing once the others come in," Ryan said. "Where are they, anyway?"

"Frank should be here any minute," Denise said. "He had an early session down at Buddles to try to burn off some of the turkey calories. As for the girls, *well*, I wouldn't be surprised if Mel decided to take the day off."

Jack looked as though he wished the ground would swallow him alive.

"Isn't she well?" Ryan asked. When no immediate reply was forthcoming, he looked between them and raised an eyebrow. "What are you not telling me?"

"It's a personal thing, boss," Jack said. "The fact is, Mel and I decided we weren't right for each other. We both knew it, after she came home from Thailand, but we made things final on Christmas Eve."

"Sorry to hear it," Ryan said, searching the younger man's face. "Although, I have to say, you don't seem too cut up about it."

"That's probably because I've fallen for someone else," Jack said, and shifted his feet. "Charlie and me…well, we've grown pretty close over the past few months, and I s'pose it forced me to be honest about my feelings."

Ryan barely suppressed a sigh. "I'd like to know when this place became a singles bar," he grumbled. "Must be something in the water around here—"

"*You* started it," Denise pointed out. "Anna was a police consultant when you met on Holy Island, as well as being a witness—"

"All right, all right," Ryan said, holding his hands up. "That may be true, but that doesn't give His Nibs here the right to go rampaging through CID like Casanova's Ghost."

"Chance would be a fine thing," Jack put in, to make them laugh.

"As your friend, I'm delighted for you, because Charlie's a lovely woman and I hope you'll be happy together," Ryan said. Then, after a short pause he added, "As your *boss*, I could knock your heads together, because this'll be bloody awkward around the office with all three of you, won't it?"

"Maybe not," Denise murmured, and pointed discreetly towards the door. They turned to find Charlie and Mel walking side by side, each holding a fresh mug of tea and chatting about something or other, looking as thick as thieves.

"How the hell have you managed to pull *that* off?" Ryan demanded of Jack, in an undertone. "Are my eyes deceiving me, or do they look… *friendly*?"

"We're all grown-ups, you know," Jack said, loftily. "There's no reason they shouldn't be friends."

"Pull the other one," Denise snorted. "Tell us what dark magic you used."

"It was Charlie's idea," Jack admitted. "She went over to talk to Mel and clear the air, and the next thing I knew, we were all having Christmas dinner together, Charlie's mum and half of the waifs and strays of Newcastle, included."

"That was very good of her," Ryan said. "Nobody's at fault in your breakup, so she didn't have to play peacemaker, but she did it anyway to make things easier for everyone."

It demonstrated good leadership skills, he thought, and made a mental note.

"You're an exceptionally lucky man, Jack," he declared. "Now, stop mooning around and get to work."

As Jack wandered off to distribute food to the masses, Denise put a staying hand on Ryan's arm.

"I wanted to ask how Anna is doing? Can I help with anything?"

Ryan shook his head. "As soon as the DNA check comes back, we'll all rest a bit easier. The whole debacle cast a shadow over Christmas Day," he admitted. "We tried our best not to think about it, but we're only human after all, and Anna's feeling especially sensitive at the moment."

Denise nodded. "It's one thing to watch us arrest people, but it's another to be the one in handcuffs," she murmured. "And then, of course, with the baby on the way…"

"At least they spared her the handcuffs," he said, and ran an agitated hand through his hair before letting it fall away again. "I wish to God she'd *never* gone to that creative writing session, last year. If she hadn't, that awful woman would never have stolen her manuscript and published it as her own, and Anna would never have had anything to do with her."

Or be a suspect in her murder, he added silently.

"Anna couldn't possibly have known any of this would happen," Denise said. "Is she doing okay, aside from the waiting taking its toll?"

"She'll be anxious until the results come through, but I keep telling her there's nothing to worry about," Ryan said. "Anna's never been to the woman's house, so there's no way her DNA could possibly find its way there."

MacKenzie nodded. "Come on, let's discuss a different murder, to take your mind off things."

Ryan grinned. "Careful, you'll turn my head with that kind of talk."

CHAPTER 9

"You broke my heart, Jack."

Phillips delivered this statement in the style of Al Pacino as *The Godfather*, and cupped the younger detective's face in his hands.

"What're you on about?" Lowerson was bemused, having never seen that classic film. "And why are you talking in that dodgy accent?"

Phillips scratched his chin with the edge of his knuckles. "Respect, kid, it's all about *respect*—"

"It's all about a *sandwich*," Ryan said drily, as their team settled around a long table in one of the conference rooms. "I thought you'd sworn off stotties for the New Year, anyway?"

"That's a scurrilous lie," Phillips burst out, reverting back to his native Geordie. "Here I was, thinkin' we were all pals, but the minute my back is turned, you gannets stuff your faces and don't leave so much as a *crumb* for muggins, here—"

He thought it wise not to mention that he'd stopped in at the Greggs drive-thru for a cheeky sausage roll, on the way into the office.

"The early bird catches the worm," Denise reminded him.

"*Et tu*, Brutus?" Frank whispered, and his wife merely smiled and blew him a kiss. "I'll remember this, next time one of you lot is starvin' to death and beggin' for a bite of me ham and pease puddin' stottie."

"You're more likely to see a pig fly than find me begging you for a bite of mushed lentils," Ryan assured him. "But the warning is duly noted. Now, if you don't mind shelving any plans for revenge, at least for the next hour, we'll get down to the business of murder, shall we?"

Phillips folded his arms across his chest and huffed.

"Good," Ryan said. "Now that all the excitement of Christmas is behind us, we can turn our minds to the owner of the various body parts that were dragged out of the water at North Shields fish quay, the other day. Jack? Mel? You've been handling that one, so what do we know about our mystery body, so far?"

Ryan leaned back in his chair and picked up a blue biro, which he proceeded to twirl around his fingers while he waited to see how the two of them would handle their working relationship from now on.

"Um—"

"Shall I—"

They spoke in unison, then fell into an awkward silence.

Not terribly encouraging, Ryan thought, and rolled his eyes inwardly. "Mel? Why don't you start us off," he suggested.

"Okay, sure," she said, and made a show of checking her notes. "Things were delayed a bit over Christmas, but the team over at the new lab managed to find a DNA match to someone already on the database—"

"New lab?" Ryan queried.

"Aye, it's the one to do with the university," Frank told him, unhelpfully.

"Newcastle University," Denise answered, before the question left Ryan's lips. "There's been a load of investment in forensics, mostly through the university so they can train up new staff or provide internships for students studying at the Faculty. Tom was telling us about it, before Christmas, because they've asked him to be a visiting lecturer."

She referred to their most senior Scenes of Crimes Officer, Tom

Faulkner, who'd worked as a consultant for Northumbria CID for so long, he was considered a part of it.

"Investment is always a good thing, in our line of work," Ryan said, and there were murmurs of agreement. "I'm not so keen on the prospect of losing our best forensics expert to a gaggle of spotty teenagers."

"Ah, now, be fair, lad," Frank said, with a twinkle in his eye. "They're not *all* spotty."

Ryan snorted.

"Don't get me started on the body odour," he said, darkly. "Their noses are so de-sensitized, the scent of a rotting cadaver probably doesn't register."

"Probably ideal, in the circumstances," Charlie was bound to say.

"Speaking of cadavers," Mel steered them none-too-gently back to the point. "Whatever was dragged from the river doesn't make up a full body, but the parts that've washed up so far belong to Terence Pearson."

Frank spared a moment for the sausage roll sitting heavily in his stomach, and wondered if it would stay there much longer.

"Why does that name ring a bell?" Ryan wondered aloud.

"Could be Terry Pearson," Denise said. "Son of Terence 'The Terrier' Pearson Senior? He dropped off the radar a few months ago, when his wife reported him missing."

"It's one and the same," Jack confirmed, and pulled out the Missing Persons report filed six months prior. "He has quite a sheet, as you can imagine. Assaults, arrests for armed robbery, all the way through to fraud and trafficking charges. Nothing stuck, either because witnesses changed their stories or suddenly dropped off the face of the Earth. Then, back in August, Terry's wife, Keri-Jayne, reported him missing when he didn't come home after more than forty-eight hours."

"She took her time," Denise remarked.

"Apparently, he had a habit of going AWOL for days on end, then turning up again as if it was completely normal," Jack explained. "I suppose he was away taking care of his father's business, whatever that entailed."

"In her statement, Keri-Jayne also suggests he might have been having an affair, so he could have been with this other woman," Mel said, as he scan-read the file. "She didn't have a name or address, it was only suspicion on her part, and, without any mobile phone data, the investigating team didn't find any information to corroborate that."

Ryan nodded. "Tell me more about Pearson Junior," he said, rocking back in his chair.

"Well, if he were still alive, he'd be forty in February," Mel began. "He and Keri-Jayne have a teenage daughter, Mia, who's seventeen. The wife went to school with him, and got to know the family well before she married into it. They were childhood sweethearts, if you can imagine it."

"Awww," Ryan said, with a touch of sarcasm. "It's nice to think that, when he'd finished maiming, killing or stealing, Terry would stop off and pick up a bunch of flowers on the way home."

Frank chuckled.

"Let's face it, gangland murder is the obvious answer here," Ryan declared, pushing back his chair to pace around the room a bit while he considered the facts. "My concern is that Pearson vanished months ago, but we're only just finding him now, in pieces. Why didn't he turn up sooner, if somebody wanted to send a message? It defeats the object, if the body isn't discovered."

There were nods around the room.

"Pinter's only just getting to the body, now," Mel reminded him. "He was tied up with other cases, but he says he should be able to give us some preliminary thoughts in a week, or so."

"Oh, I think we can do a bit better than that," Ryan said, in the tone of a man who intended to pay the good doctor a personal visit, at the earliest opportunity. "It's amazing what a couple of theatre tickets and a bottle of whisky can do to speed things up, down at the mortuary."

There were more nods around the room, and a few knowing smiles.

"What do we know about Terry's last movements?" Ryan asked, after taking a swig of coffee that was, by now, stone cold. "Who was the last person to see him alive?"

"His wife and daughter," Jack replied. "Keri-Jayne and Mia were both at home on 6th August, getting ready to go to the hairdressers and school respectively. He had a cup of tea, ate a slice of toast, and said he'd see them later."

"Doesn't that imply that he'd be home later that evening?"

"Apparently not," Jack said, shaking his head. "It was something he often said before heading off, but it could have meant anything, or so his family say."

"No indication of threat or particular mood?" Ryan asked.

"Not according to their statements," Jack replied, tapping the paperwork in front of him. "That being said, the family don't have the best relationship with us, so it's more than likely they gave monosyllabic answers or chose not to share anything beyond the basic facts."

"Assuming those basic facts are true," Denise pointed out. "What about his workmates? His father? Did they question Terence Senior about his son's whereabouts?"

Mel nodded, fishing out the next statement from the pile.

"Terence gave a very basic statement," she said. "The upshot is, he claims Terry never came into work, and the last time he saw him was the night before, on the fifth, at their usual drinking hole."

"Which is?"

"The Magpie," Mel said, and pulled an expressive face to indicate that it was not a 'family friendly' establishment—unless you belonged to the Pearson family.

"Maybe we should pay Terry Senior another visit," Ryan said.

"Unfortunately, he died of pneumonia after protracted liver failure six weeks ago," Jack said, having already looked into the man's whereabouts. "He'd been on the list for a transplant for a while, but the winter finished him off."

"Check out the circumstances, to be sure," Ryan told them. "We need to know if Terry's death was an isolated incident, or whether his father was another victim of the same killer."

Jack nodded, and made a note to follow up.

"Jack? Mel? You carry on digging into the background, find out all you can about the Pearsons. Speak to the National Crime Agency, if you need to, and colleagues in narcotics and vice, because there'll be plenty of crossover. This needs to be a multi-agency, multi-command approach, so set up a meeting with everyone as soon as you can."

"Will do, boss."

"Denise? Charlie? Look into cold cases associated with the Pearsons and flag any you think could have led to a retribution killing," Ryan said. "Go back and ask questions."

They nodded, and started to gather up their things.

"Frank? You're with me."

"Always," came the ready reply. Then, as an afterthought, "Where we gannin'?"

"To meet the grieving widow."

"Right y'are."

CHAPTER 10

As it happened Keri-Jayne Pearson was not at home, and so Ryan and Phillips swapped one Pearson widow for another, and took themselves off to talk to Terry Pearson's mother instead. They didn't know what to expect from a home belonging to the matriarch of a well-known crime family. In their time, they'd seen everything from former council houses knocked through, to weird, Brutalist mansions with plastic lion heads, and *actual* mansions built of stone and marble. In the case of Keri-Jayne and Terry, they'd opted for a large but unprepossessing new-build property in the village of Dinnington, on the western outskirts of the city. Where a crime boss chose to lay his proverbial hat depended not only on taste and predilection for expensive things, but on their appetite for work-life balance: some preferred to commute from the suburbs for a hard day's criminal activity, whereas others preferred to remain in the thick of it, where they could keep a finger firmly on the money.

In the case of Terence Pearson Sr and his wife, Patricia, it seemed they'd opted for a middle ground. Theirs was a modern, faux-Tudor mansion on the outskirts of the city, which must have been impressive when it was first erected, back in the late eighties. Now, its rendering had faded from ivory to dirty beige, while the tarmacked driveway sprouted weeds between its ageing cracks. Rot had long since taken a chokehold on the wooden Tudor façade, and chintzy curtains reigned supreme at the faux-mullioned windows. A Bentley saloon was parked on the driveway, but it was as old as the house and peppered with rust around the fenders. In all, it spoke of faded grandeur; shadows of an empire that had once been great, much like the broken remains of the Emperor Hadrian's wall, a few miles yonder.

"The Pearsons used to be a big name, back in the day," Frank remarked, peering through the windshield as they pulled up to the kerb outside. "You sure this is the right address?"

"It is," Ryan assured him, noting the twitching curtains.

"I thought there'd be a bit more…" Frank turned his finger, searching for the word.

"Bling?" Ryan offered.

"Aye! Well, there's usually a few sculptures on the electric gates…a couple o' souped-up SUVs on the drive, a dog barkin' your ears off, that sort o' thing."

"Maybe crime doesn't pay as much as it used to," Ryan said. "There's bound to be a dog, somewhere around here—"

As if on cue, they heard an incessant bark coming from the direction of the house.

"Knew it," Ryan muttered. "What's the bet it's a pit bull?"

"Nah, it's probably a Staffy cross," Frank countered, as they slammed out of the car and began making their way up the drive towards the front door. "Rottweilers are out of fashion."

"They don't seem to have much in the way of security, otherwise," Ryan said, having taken a comprehensive scan of the vicinity and finding it wide open to intruders.

"Old Terrier Pearson used to have a rep as long as your arm," Frank said. "I remember him, from way back when I started as a bobbie. He was always a proper little gobshite, even then, but havin' a rep like that can keep you safe at night."

"What about when that rep's gone?" Ryan mused. "The lack of

security could also be down to the fact the Pearsons are no longer a force to be reckoned with."

"Their empire's well and truly shot to pieces now," Frank agreed, keeping his voice down as they approached the front door, where the sound of barking grew louder. "With both Terries gone, there won't be anybody left to carry the baton."

"Did Terry Jr have any siblings?"

Phillips shook his head, thinking back to the information they had on file. "No brothers, but, now I think of it, there *was* a sister. Maybe she's the one to watch out for, nowadays?"

"Let's see if you're right," Ryan said, and raised a finger to ring the doorbell, which featured an ornamental brass frame and a plate that read, 'RING FOR CHAMPAGNE'.

They waited, and the door opened as they were about to ring again. Rather than finding seventy-two-year-old Patricia Pearson on the threshold, they were greeted by a young woman who, they couldn't help but notice, was very striking. Long, blonde hair trailed in waves over one shoulder, while a pair of luminescent blue eyes looked between them from a perfectly symmetrical face. She wore a hoodie featuring a series of prancing reindeer over plain black leggings, while her feet were encased in slippers fashioned to look like elf boots, which only added to the overall image of a beautiful *ingenue*. In her arms, she held a miniature poodle, who gave out one last *yap* for good measure.

Not exactly a guard dog, Ryan thought.

"Hello," she said, sweetly. "Can I help you?"

"I'm Detective Chief Inspector Ryan and this is Detective Sergeant Frank Phillips, from Northumbria CID," Ryan said, and held out his warrant card for her to inspect. "We'd like to speak with Mrs Pearson, if she's in?"

Mia Pearson leaned her body against the doorframe and ruffled the dog's ears.

"My grandmother is getting old," she said, with a note of apology. "She's in the early stages of dementia, which means she often gets confused and upset. It's been especially bad, since Grandpa died."

Grandpa, Ryan thought, struggling to think of a former crime boss as something so…

So…

Cuddly.

Pushing that discomfiting thought aside, he fixed the young woman with a hard stare.

"I take it you're Mia—Terry's daughter?"

She smiled slowly, and in such a way that spoke of experience beyond her years.

"You know my name," she said.

"It's in the file," Frank snapped. "Howay, pet. It's gettin' nippy out here, so let's not bandy words about. Is your gran at home? We've got a few more questions to ask about your grandpa's death."

"Why? He died of natural causes."

They might have questioned the extent to which long-term alcohol abuse could be considered 'natural', but it wasn't worth the argument. In any case, the girl had already connected the dots.

"It's because you found my dad," she said, in a flat voice. "You found his body, so you're wondering if Grandpa was murdered as well."

They said nothing, partly because they were taken aback at how candidly she spoke of death.

"A woman from your department came around to tell us he'd been found," Mia carried on, with a shrug. "We all thought he was dead, anyway."

Before they could pass comment, another woman's voice carried on the air.

"Mia? Who's at the door? If it's those bloody Jehovah's Witnesses again, tell them to bugger off!"

Pat Pearson emerged from the living room, and came up short when she clapped eyes on the two men in the doorway.

"Oh," she said, heavily. "It's *you*."

Pat's beehive up-do had seen a little help from the local hairdresser to maintain its platinum blonde shade, but the rest of her was all-natural and bore the evidence of a lifetime spent looking the other way. Her mouth was pinched, smoker's lines having dug deep into the folds of her skin so that a web of wrinkles spread in a fan around her mouth, to match the ones either side of her eyes, which had once been as boldly blue as her granddaughter's. Her voice was deep and gravelled, the product of more than fifty years inhaling nicotine.

"Finally coming to speak to me about Terry, are you?" she began, folding her arms across a generous bosom. "Keri-Jayne told me your lot had been around to see her. Nobody thought about *me*, did they? I'm only his mother!"

She was growing more agitated, and began to gesticulate with the cane she'd been using as a walking support.

"I'm sorry you weren't told in person," Ryan said, taking the opportunity to step past Mia and into the house. "I'll speak to my staff about it."

Though Frank might have been a dab hand at dealing with prickly witnesses, he was forced to admit that, when it came to persuading prickly *female* witnesses to be cooperative, his friend had the edge. Thanks to a combination of film-star good looks and a fancy Southern accent, most women between the ages of eight and eighty ended up melting over Ryan, like ice lollies over a bonfire.

"Well," Patricia said, patting her hair a bit. "I suppose it couldn't be helped."

Frank marvelled as Ryan proceeded to sympathise with her loss, while steering her towards the living room as though there wasn't a chasm of difference between their two worlds.

"Hang on—" Mia began to say.

"It's too late now," Frank advised her, in fatherly tones. "It's like looking directly at the sun. Your gran's been dazzled."

"Put the kettle on, love," Pat called out.

Mia rolled her eyes, but stalked towards the kitchen while Ryan and Phillips followed Patricia into the living room, where she gestured for them to take a seat.

"You know, if my boys were here, you wouldn't've made it up the driveway," she said, coyly.

Ryan settled himself on a sofa fashioned to look like something from Louis XIV's court at Versailles, upholstered in a silky pattern of gold and pink fleur-de-lis, which matched the deep pile pink carpet covering the floor. His eye passed over a framed picture of Patricia and her late husband taken ten or fifteen years ago, when both man and wife had been enjoying the fruits of their labours on a working holiday to the Costa del Sol. Tanned, dressed to the nines in designer gear and sporting sunglasses that were too large for their faces, Pat and Terry Senior posed beside a marina full of yachts.

"Little Terry took that picture," Patricia said, and they couldn't be sure whether her voice was husky thanks to an outpouring of maternal grief, or the erosion of her voice box. "I remember that day."

"Why don't you tell us about your boys?" Ryan suggested, and thanked Mia for the cup of tea he had no intention of drinking, when she re-entered the room.

"Terence was always a bit of a charmer," she said, and patted the seat next to her to indicate Mia should sit beside her. "Your grandpa was always a bit of a one, wasn't he?"

BERWICK

Mia opened her mouth as if to speak, but the question was rhetorical.

"I remember the first time we met—*properly*, I mean," Pat reminisced. "Terence and me, we knew each other as kids, but I never gave him the time of day. He was—"

She almost said, *poor, uneducated, dirty, a scrapper in every sense of the word.*

"He was just a lad, back then," she said. "My ma and his would chat around the doors, and he'd come over for a bit of dinner, now and then, and to see our Matty."

"Matty?" Ryan queried, while Frank took notes.

"My brother," Pat said. "He moved to Australia, years ago."

She delivered the information curtly, which suggested she hadn't been impressed by her brother's decision.

"It wasn't until my eighteenth birthday, down at The Bottom Club," Pat continued. "I remember, Terry walked in wearing a dark suit and this natty little tie…I thought he scrubbed up well, for a lad from Walker."

"Did he ask you for a dance, Gran?" Mia said.

Patricia remembered her late husband asking her for a lot more than that, but she wasn't about to say as much.

"He was a proper gentleman, he was," she said, looking down at her tea to hide her lying eyes. "We were inseparable, after that."

There had been something intoxicating about a young Terence Pearson, especially when he was earning a bit of money from the Garrisons, who'd been the ruling family back in those days. She knew what kind of pies their fingers were in; they all did. The question was whether you were content to stay a worker drone, or rise to the top, like Terry had always planned to do. She'd seen it in his eyes, all those years ago: ambition, focus and, yes, the violence had been there, too. He'd never once raised a hand to her, not in all the years they were together, but the same couldn't be said of many others who'd crossed him. Terry could be mercurial, but she'd known him since he was a boy and knew how to handle him, how to cajole him out of one of the black moods, and theirs had been a happy enough life—especially, so long as he kept the dirty side to his business away from her front door.

She'd heard rumours about other women, over the years, but chose to ignore them.

Terry wouldn't do that.

Not to *her*.

Not to the kids.

"Mrs Pearson?"

Pat came to attention again, and fixed her gaze on the handsome detective, ignoring his stockier counterpart entirely.

"What's that, love?"

Ryan forced himself to smile. *Softly, softly,* he reminded himself.

"I was explaining why we'd come to see you today," he said. "Are you happy for your granddaughter to be in the room? We may need to discuss some sensitive details?"

"I've already told you, my grandmother is unwell, and often becomes confused," Mia said, and her eyes were like chips of blue ice, daring them to argue.

"Oh, she *does* look after me!"

Patricia looked at the young woman perched beside her, and patted her cheek with a calloused hand. "My Mia is all I have, now," she said, before emitting a hacking cough which led both men to wrinkle their noses. "I'm old, now, but you should have seen me, in my heyday. I'd have climbed you like a monkey tree—"

Ryan swallowed hard, trying very hard not to imagine it, while Phillips stifled a laugh behind his mug of tea.

"Ah, well, if you're happy to proceed, we need to ask you both some questions regarding Mia's father, and your son, Terry," Ryan said, in a 'no-nonsense' tone.

Pat sighed, wheezily, and hiked up her bra strap. The action drew the attention of everyone in the room, including her granddaughter, for no other reason than curiosity that the laws of Physics and gravity could withstand so flimsy an article, in the face of such tremendous pressure.

"I've already given a statement to your lot," she said, snapping them all back to attention along with the elastic. "I can't tell you anything else."

"Me too," Mia put in. "Dad was at home for breakfast on 6th August and he seemed totally fine…or, at least, just the same as usual."

She gave a half smile in acknowledgement of the fact they were aware of her late father's profession, and a cheerful demeanour hadn't been a necessary skill to have.

"He left, saying something about 'seeing us later', and that was that."

A brief silence ensued, which Ryan was happy to prolong. In some cases, silence could loosen tongues, most people feeling compelled to fill it with chatter, but it seemed Pat and Mia Pearson were immune to that particular tactic.

"Was Terry involved in any, ah, *business disputes*, at the time of his death?" he asked. "Anything to give you cause for concern?"

Pat gave another wheezing laugh. "Look, love, Terry was always into something or other," she said. "When you're an entrepreneur, you can expect the odd unhappy customer, can't you?"

Entrepreneur? Grandpa? Romantic? Ryan's mind boggled at the choice of words.

"Anybody unhappy enough to kill him?" Frank asked. "Any threats?"

"It's like Gran says," Mia replied, and gone was the sweet, innocent tone she'd first employed. "Besides, Dad never told any of us about the ins and outs of his business. We wouldn't have a clue whether anyone took a dislike to him, so much as to—to—"

She broke off, suddenly overcome by emotion.

"Aw, now, *there, there*, my pet," her grandmother crooned, and tugged the unwitting girl's head against her breast before casting them both a disappointed glare. "*Now* look what you've done, with all your questions. We're grieving, for pity's sake! We don't know anything about anything. You'd be better off speaking to Angela—"

Both men came to attention.

"Who's Angela?" Ryan asked, not having seen the name anywhere in the paperwork, and Pat looked at him as though he were a halfwit.

"My daughter, of course." She tutted. "Terry's older sister. The two of them were close, or used to be. Maybe she knows something we don't."

They took down the details of Angela Pearson, who was living in Amble, a quiet fishing town further up the coast.

"One more thing—" Ryan began.

"We've told you all we can," Mia interrupted him, having apparently made a miraculous recovery. "There isn't anything else to say, so, next time, come round when you've found Dad's killer, or we might start to feel a bit harassed. Know what I mean?"

With that, ever so sweetly, she showed them the door.

CHAPTER 11

Back in the relative safety of Ryan's car, Phillips looked across at his friend. "*Well*," he said.

"Indeed," came the heavy reply. "Do you want to start the debrief? I'm still reeling after getting a slap on the arse from Grandma Pat."

"Aye, she was a bit handsy," Phillips agreed, although it had been funny to watch. "Fancy, blaming it on early-onset Alzheimer's, n'all…"

"She's got a nerve," Ryan said. "That, and a strong forearm."

Phillips let out a laugh. "You could always make a formal complaint, but I'm not sure the CPS would take forward a prosecution…"

"Oh, put a sock in it," Ryan grumbled. "You're only jealous nobody's slapping your arse these days."

"Actually, y'nah, Denise has always loved gettin' a good handful—"

"Oh, *God*!" Ryan cried, and covered his face with his hands. "I don't want to know about what your wife does with the end of a spatula, Frank. I don't need any more nightmares."

"Actually, it's usually the back of her slipper—"

"FRANK!"

Phillips chuckled to himself. "Alreet, let's get back to business," he said. "For starters, that lass in there is only a few years older than my Samantha and, if that's the kind of smart-arsery I've got to look forward to, y'can keep it!"

"And I thought you'd talk about how contrived her tears seemed to be, and how little she seemed to care about her father's death."

"Aye, well, I mean that's obvious, isn't it? Anybody could see that. It's her *attitude* that worries me—"

"Spoken like a true father."

"You'll be worryin' about all this, soon enough," Frank said, ominously. "Once the hormones kick in, you've had it. I hope wor Samantha doesn't start all that flirty nonsense with men old enough to be her da. I'll hit the roof!"

Ryan started the car's engine, assuming correctly that this was just the beginning of a tirade.

"I *mean*, all those 'come hither' looks she was givin' you, back there. All the eyelash flutters—"

"That was her grandma," Ryan corrected him.

"They were as bad as each other!" Phillips roared. "One's practically a bairn, and the other's gettin' o'er Penshaw Hill!"

He waggled a finger towards Ryan, who was navigating the car through a network of streets that would take them along the coastal route towards Amble.

"I don't mind tellin' you, lad, there've been times when I've wondered what it would be like to pull the lasses in like you do. Moths to the flame, and all that. These days, I'm not so sure my blood pressure could handle it."

Phillips paused, and reconsidered the matter.

"Actually, I probably *could* handle it," he admitted, and gave a bawdy laugh. "But, all jokes aside, that Mia was a wily one, don't you think? Especially for her age."

"I agree, but then, consider her upbringing."

Phillips made a rumbling sound. "And her gran? She seems all reet in the heed, if y'ask me—"

"My thoughts exactly," Ryan said, steering carefully around a group of kids gathered in the street, half-heartedly puffing on vapes and scuffing their heels against the tarmac. "Should we have a word and move this lot along?"

"Ah, they're not doin' any harm," Frank said, having made an educated assessment. "They're in a gang, but not the kind we should worry about."

Ryan nodded, and turned back to the road ahead. "Pat and Mia are adamant they don't know anything about Terry's death," he said. "I wonder if they'd have more to say if we put them in separate rooms, down at the Interview Suite?"

Phillips scratched his cheek. "Aye, they may well do," he agreed. "Seemed to me, Little Miss Eyelashes was doin' her best to get us out o' there, before her gran could really tell us anythin' at all."

"She's clever," Ryan said. "Let's not forget her threat to us, at the end."

"About police harassment? That was designed to put the wind up us," Frank said. "Unluckily for her—"

"You're already windy?"

"Har bloody har," Phillips replied.

There was a momentary lull, before Phillips spoke again.

"It gets to me sometimes," he mused.

"What does? The baked beans?"

"*No*, you daft bugger. The fact we're doing all this runnin' around for some no-good, who probably never regretted a thing he ever did in his life. Doesn't feel right, does it?"

Ryan looked across at his friend, then back at the road. "You know how this works," he said softly. "We treat them all the same, in death, no matter what they did in life. Every action has a reaction. Every murder we avenge leads us closer to keeping the general public safe. If we start making judgments about who deserves what, playing judge and jury, it's a slippery slope."

Phillips knew it, and yet… "Even if we find out who killed Terry Pearson, and maybe his da, too, we won't find justice like a pot at the end of the rainbow. They'll wriggle off the hook, somehow, if they're part of a rival gang. They always do."

"Not *always*," Ryan averred, and there was a gleam in his eye. "This could be the end of a long thread in need of unravelling, Frank. You know how you love sniffing out new criminals."

Phillips made an appreciative sound. "Aye, there's nothin' better than uncoverin' a fresh nest," he said. "Been a few years since we had a good gangster, come to think of it—"

"Good?" Ryan cut in. "I rather thought being a gangster precluded the possibility."

"You know what I mean," Phillips said, waving away semantics. "One of the *proper* baddies, who really gave us a run for our money. Y'nah, Jimmy the Manc, or—"

"Bobby Singh?"

"Aye, he was a piece o' work," Phillips nodded. "Not forgettin'—"

He broke off, unsure whether to say the name aloud and rake over old wounds.

"It's okay," Ryan said quietly. "You can say his name. In fact, I'll say it…*Keir Edwards*. The Hacker."

Phillips cleared his throat. "Aye, he was the worst of a bad lot."

He clicked his fingers, as if discovering a new theorem. "We should go *undercover* again!"

Ryan was dumbfounded. "When were you *ever* undercover?"

"Plenty o' times," Frank said, breezily. "I was probably so deep undercover, you didn't even know I was there. *That's* how undercover I was."

Ryan rolled his eyes. "You forget, I've seen your attempt at going undercover, that time we had to scope out a strip club. I've never seen anybody look less comfortable, and that includes the time you asked me to hold your hand during a prostate exam."

Phillips sniffed. "You know fine well, we were *arm wrestlin'* while the doctor was doin'...whatever he was doin' down there. It was a perfectly manly distraction, that's all it was!"

"Mm hm. Tell it to the judge, Frank."

Phillips pursed his lips. "Come to think of it, I'm due another check-up—"

"No."

"What? I haven't even asked you anythin'—"

"*Absolutely not.*"

"But—"

"It's Jack's turn to arm wrestle with you at the doctor's," Ryan told him, as they joined the coastal route northbound. "Same goes if you're having your balls checked. I've seen a lot of things, Frank, but I'm not ready to see that."

Phillips laughed richly. "Aye, fair enough. I should ask Denise, but..." He shrugged. "It's a man thing, isn't it?"

"I'm sure she's seen it all before."

"Aye, she has. In *fact—*"

"Oh, God, I've done it again," Ryan muttered, and pressed the pedal to the metal as they motored towards Amble, hoping the car's velocity would drown out the sound of his sergeant's voice.

CHAPTER 12

Amble was a small coastal town thirty-odd miles north of Newcastle, situated in a part of Northumberland Ryan's team knew very well. It had been a few years since the ferryman had been found dead at the nearby hermitage of Warkworth Castle, only a stone's throw from Amble on the other side of the Coquet River, but only a matter of months since they'd investigated the weird and wonderfully toxic plants of Alnwick's Poison Garden, a few miles upriver. It was almost impossible not to stumble upon a castle or fortification older than the United States, which was why it held such fascination for those who visited from the New World. Conversely, for those born and bred in the area, it would be easy for familiarity to breed contempt, so that towering battlements weathered by time and toil became par for the course.

Even if his wife hadn't been a noted local historian, Ryan would still have found the old stones impressive to behold. He imagined who had lived there before—not the Earls, Barons, Lords or whatever they might have been, but their servants, guards and the serfs who worked the land to sustain those enormous estates. He wanted to know *their* stories, to wonder about the songs they sang and tales they told around an open fire as they sheltered from the unforgiving weather and supped on bowls of hearty broth.

"Fancy some clam chowder, before we go and see Angela Pearson?"

Ryan looked over at his sergeant and wondered whether the man had a sixth sense, after all. "I was just thinking about broth, and then you suggested chowder."

Phillips was never one to snub an opportunity, especially for a late lunch. "It's because we're so *attuned*, that's what it is," he said, pressing the advantage. "When you've been mates as long as we have, and worked together longer still, you can't help but know what the other one's really thinkin'—"

"I'm not really hu—"

"Even before they know it, themselves," Phillips added smoothly.

Ryan checked the time on the dashboard and bowed to the inevitable. "Fine," he muttered. "Half an hour, tops."

"I can work with that," Phillips said, and almost licked his chops.

"Where should we go?"

"Sky's the limit," Frank exclaimed. "Seafood's the best, obviously. There's still a workin' harbour, so you get plenty of fresh fish hereabouts. There's a load of nice places that've opened up, these past few years—"

"Pick one, before I change my mind."

"It's like askin' me to pick a favourite child," he mumbled. "There's Jasper's…The Old Boathouse…The Amble Inn…The Fish Shack—"

"Frank, it would be quicker to rent a boat and catch our own fish, at this rate."

"Okay! Alreet, let's try Fishy on a Dishy," Phillips decided. "We'll have to come back tomorrow and try a different one, to make up for snubbin' the others—"

"Don't push your luck," Ryan warned, steered the car towards the marina. "Incidentally, that's an excellent choice, and not only because of the food. It's owned by Angela Pearson and her husband, according to Pat."

"See? There's that sixth sense, again," Frank exclaimed.

Or pot luck, Ryan thought, but didn't have the heart to say.

"Go on, what am I thinkin' now?"

Ryan turned into the public car park, switched off the engine and swivelled to face his sergeant with an expression that would have told the most *simple* simpleton that he was in no mood for mind games.

"How about you go first," he said. "What am I thinking now, Frank?"

Phillips clocked the drawn eyebrows, the slight twitching of the jawline muscles and general air of a man close to the edge.

"That you need a holiday, before you throttle me with my own tie?"

"You're right," Ryan said, and gave him a clap on the back. "You *can* read my mind, after all."

The wind was bracing when they stepped out of the car.

"Brr!" Ryan shivered, turning up the collar on his winter coat. "You'd think I'd be used to the weather up here, by now."

"You southern pansies are all the same!" Phillips called out, over the howling sound of the wind and waves slapping against the harbour walls.

Frank clenched his jaw, to stop his teeth chattering while he hurled insults about being sensitive to cold weather. "Could be time to start thinkin' about layerin' up," he tagged on.

"I'm already wearing layers," Ryan replied, keeping his head down against the wind rolling in from the sea.

"Not *clothes*, you pillock! I'm talkin' about cultivatin' a Winter Hibernation Layer! Athletic bodies are all well and good, when you're young. But, as you get older, you need a bit more paddin'."

Ryan chuckled.

"You take my advice and start neckin' a few pies," Phillips continued. "Spend a bit less time runnin' around and a bit more time with your feet up on the sofa, and you'll soon see a difference. You never know, it might help with your other affliction, n'all."

"I'm terrified to ask," Ryan said. "But which affliction would that be?"

"There's plenty I could mention, but I was thinkin' of your bein' like catnip to females," Frank replied. "If you put a bit more beef on your bones, you might find you get a few less slaps on the arse, although I can't promise there won't still be a market for it."

"It's not like you to be politically incorrect," Ryan said, deadpan. "You don't have to be a certain shape to be assaulted by impertinent grandmothers, you know. Perviness comes in all shapes and sizes."

"Don't I *know* it!" Phillips said, and tugged open the door to the restaurant, where both men let out a contented sigh as they were greeted by warm surroundings and the tantalising scent of good cooking. "What I may lack in height, muscle and hair, I make up for with a sparklin' personality and hips like John Travolta. It's a devastating combination."

"Well, it's not your modesty, that's for sure," Ryan drawled.

Before Phillips could formulate a pithy response, they were approached by a smiling woman of around forty. Her greying auburn hair had been swept up into an artful Bohemian scarf atop her head, which featured a pattern of lobsters which drew the eye and a certain amount of envy from the good sergeant. Naturally, if he'd known they'd be making a trip along the coast, Phillips might have looked out one of his embroidered ties featuring shells, boats or little dancing seagulls, but he was sadly unprepared.

"Table for two?" she asked.

"Yes, please," Ryan replied, and they followed her to a table beside the window.

"Are you visiting?" she asked politely.

"Aye, that's right," Phillips replied, reaching for one of the menus. "What's the special for today?"

She smiled, and reeled off an impressive selection of fish and lobster.

"Is the restaurant associated with the 'Fishy on a Dishy' Catering Company?" Ryan asked, after they'd placed their orders.

"Yes," she replied, slipping her notepad back into the pocket of the trendy canvas overall she wore, instead of an old-fashioned pinny. "It's part of the same company, and we do the catering from the kitchens here. Did you want to place an order for an event? I can give you one of our package menus, if you like?"

"Actually, we were hoping to speak with the owner, Angela Pearson, or her husband, Kevin Riley. Are they in, today?"

Angela's eyes became shuttered. "Are you one of Terry's men?"

Ryan didn't know how to feel about being mistaken for a gangland thug, but decided to worry about it later. "No, were from Northumbria CID," he said, and drew out his warrant card as discreetly as he could, having a care for her place of business and their fellow patrons, who might be locals with tongues that could wag. "We need to talk to you about your brother, Ms Pearson."

"I go by Riley," she corrected them, because it was important to her. "I've been Angela Riley for a long time."

"Sorry," Ryan said. "Our records aren't up to date."

She swept her eyes around the room, which continued to thrum with contented chatter and the occasional clatter of crockery or glassware.

"I have a break coming up in about twenty minutes," she said.

"Can we talk then, please? It will attract less attention than if I walk out now."

"No bother," Frank said, amiably. "We've got our lunch comin', anyhow."

"My cottage is just around the corner," she said, and rattled off an address they already knew. "I'll meet you there."

Angela started to turn away, but Ryan was struck by something she'd said earlier.

"Mrs Riley? Why did you ask if Terry had sent us, when you know he *couldn't* have done?"

"I'm sorry, I didn't mean to give offence," she said, misunderstanding him. "It's just that, you know, you're both men in long coats, with watchful eyes. I suppose you reminded me of his lot."

She still wasn't catching on, which begged the question—

"Mrs Riley, has anybody been in touch to inform you of the news?"

She frowned. "What news? I'm afraid I'm more or less estranged from my family, Detective Ryan, so I wouldn't have heard about any family news, if that's what you mean. Why? Has something happened?"

Ryan and Phillips exchanged a glance.

"Would you rather wait until your break to talk about this?"

Angela shook her head and slid onto one of the free chairs beside them, no longer concerned by appearances. "Please, tell me what it is I don't know."

Ryan schooled his features into professional compassion. "In that case, I'm very sorry to inform you that your brother, Terry, was found dead recently. We believe he was murdered, after being reported missing back in August."

"*August?*" she whispered, and put a hand over her mouth.

"You didn't know he was missing?"

She shook her head. "No, I—as I say, I don't really keep in touch with my family. Perhaps they thought he'd gone abroad, or that he'd turn up, sooner or later, so they didn't think it was worth mentioning."

Ryan thought of the news coverage about Terry's disappearance, but it was true that his murder hadn't been reported yet. It was plausible that she wouldn't have heard about his death, especially if nobody in the family circle had informed her. To the wider world, Terry Pearson was still a collection of anonymous body parts, dredged from the Tyne.

Unfortunately for Angela, there was more.

"Your father, Terence, has also passed away," Ryan said, gently.

"I did hear about that," she admitted, and swiped a tear from her eye. "Kev and me, we thought about goin' to the funeral, but..." She trailed off, sadly. "I know it must sound heartless, but I've built a new life, and I don't want to be sucked back into the old one," she said, after a few seconds ticked by. "He wasn't the easiest father to grow up with, and we had very little in common, really. He could never understand why I married Kev, and moved out here."

Before they could ask any further questions, a waitress arrived bearing a tray of steaming food.

"I'll leave you to eat," Angela said, rising to her feet again.

They watched her walk briskly towards one of the side doors, behind which they assumed there was a store room or bathroom.

"It's amazing, isn't it?" Frank remarked, dabbing the edge of his lips.

"The soup?"

"No, human nature," he said. "That woman probably has a hundred good reasons to choose not to keep in touch with the family she was born into—God only knows what she'd seen or heard. But, when we told her that her brother had gone, she looked as though she was on the verge of tears."

"As you say, it's human nature to feel compassion," Ryan said. "She may remember Terry as a little boy, before he began murdering people and dealing drugs to kids. He was her brother before he was a mob boss, after all."

"Aye, people change."

Unaccountably, Ryan thought of Jack and Mel, then of himself and Anna. They'd gone through various stages of chrysalis in their lives, especially during the past ten formative years. However, in some things, their values remained the same.

So thinking, he reached for his phone to check for any messages from Durham CID, but was irritated to find none.

"Everythin' alreet, lad?"

Phillips' eyes were keen over the rim of his spoon.

"Anna's DNA results," Ryan said. "I was expecting them to come through today, but they haven't. Probably just the usual administrative delays, holding things up."

Phillips kept his eyes trained on his soup. "Aye, that'll be it."

CHAPTER 13

Back at Police Headquarters, Jack Lowerson scrolled through the replies he'd received from colleagues in Vice and Narcotics, then leaned back in his chair and folded his arms.

"There aren't as many flags as I thought there'd be," he said. "It's the same story when I try searching the database for connected investigations. Terry Pearson or his dad haven't flagged in any major investigations for eight or nine years, at least."

Melanie popped her head around the edge of her computer monitor.

"I'm finding the same in my searches," she said. "The Pearsons and any known associates were involved, somehow, in most major crime investigations locally back in the seventies, eighties and into the early nineties—"

"Allegedly," Denise's disembodied voice chimed in, from somewhere across the room. "We couldn't pin the wily old git for any of it, more's the pity."

"*Allegedly*," Mel corrected. "But that was more than thirty years ago."

"Narcotics tell me they haven't considered Terry Pearson as anything more than a small time operative, riding on his father's name most of the time. Apparently, he didn't have the same kind of gravitas as his old man, either."

"It's the same story with the Cold Cases I've been looking at," Charlie said, swinging on her desk chair. "There's quite a few mentions of Terence and some close calls for him on cases back in the late eighties, especially. As for anything more recent, it's as though he went into retirement."

"He did," Denise replied, and found herself dreading the prospect. She supposed there were some who looked forward to long days mooching around watching *Midsomer Murders*, punctuated by the occasional Viking River Cruise or a weekend trip to the golf course, but she couldn't imagine it herself.

Not yet, anyway.

"Denise?"

"Hm?"

"You looked as though you were about to say something," Charlie prompted.

"Actually, I was thinking about Scandinavian cruises and daytime telly," MacKenzie quipped. "But that's not important. I was going to say, old Terry Pearson handed over the reins to his son and heir around the mid two-thousands, as far as we can tell. That corresponds with his name appearing less and less frequently in our case documents. What about Terry Junior? Was there a spike for his name, instead?"

"A few pops for assault, but none of the victims chose to proceed," Jack replied. "He was interviewed under caution a bunch of times for drugs trafficking, but nothing was ever traced back to him, directly. There was always a fall guy to take the rap; that's how these organisations operate."

"You can see a pattern of decline, if you really look for it," Mel chimed in. "I'll put together a timeline of major arrests or court appearances and see if any other names keep coming up alongside Terry's."

"Good idea," Denise said. "Remember, we're looking for potential killers motivated by revenge, or somebody who intended to send a message to others. Terry offended someone, so we need to look closely at rival gang members in the area."

"I was wondering about that," Charlie said, and all eyes turned to her. "I was thinking about what Ryan said before, about the delay in finding the body. What if Terry wasn't dismembered in order to send a message, but the exact opposite?"

"You think they wanted to hide his identity?" Jack said, and Charlie nodded.

"Why else remove his fingertips and his teeth? Why weigh down the body in a bag, to keep it underwater for as long as possible?"

"We don't know for certain that the fingertips were deliberately removed," Denise cautioned. "The limbs were underwater for some time, and there was barely anything left of the extremities. We should wait until the pathologist sends over his report before jumping to any conclusions."

"I agree," Charlie said. "But, as a working hypothesis, if somebody didn't want to send a message about Terry and, in fact, hoped he wouldn't be found for a good long while, we have to look for a slightly different motive."

"Such as?"

"Fear," Charlie said. "Accidents happen, even in Terry's world, don't they? What if someone didn't mean to kill him, and panicked? They could have dismembered, anonymised and hidden the body as best they could in order to avoid repercussions from the criminal underworld."

The others ruminated on the prospect.

"Cutting up a body isn't a walk in the park," Jack pronounced, with the authority of one who had never so much as cut up a chicken breast. "You'd need a fair bit of strength."

"Not necessarily," Denise said. "Butchery is about skill as much as strength."

This time, all eyes turned to her.

"I'm not speaking from personal experience," she said, holding her hands up. "But I often gave my old da a hand carving up venison or pheasant. It's a messy business, but, if you know where to slice, it isn't as laborious as you'd think. Just look at Pinter; he's as skinny as a rake, but he's cut up more human beings than you've had hot dinners, Jack."

The very thought was enough to turn his stomach.

"I wonder why anyone would *choose* to do it," Charlie thought aloud. "How old d'you reckon Jeff Pinter was, when he decided that handling and dissecting cadavers was his calling in life?"

"I can't imagine Jeff as a young man," Mel replied, and screwed up her face in concentration. "Nope, as far as I'm concerned, he's always been balding and middle-aged, with bony fingers. I refuse to believe he once had hair."

They all laughed, but it wasn't an unkind sound; theirs was a team that took turns in ribbing one another, so Jeff's inclusion in that ritual was a sign of acceptance in their little tribe.

Had he been there, it would have thrilled him.

"I have some pictures from old office parties," Denise said. "I'll have to fish them out of the archive and let you have a look at how we all were, back in the dark days before Ryan appeared on the scene."

Jack was enthralled, as he always was by any talk of his mentor.

"That's something I find hard to imagine," he said. "Northumbria CID, without Ryan? I can't picture it."

"Things were run by Gregson and his underlings, back then," Denise explained, and there was a note of resentment in her voice to reflect the crimes their former superintendent had committed, and the shame he'd brought to their profession. "Me, Frank and a few others were probably outcasts without knowing it, since we were some of the only ones *not* on the take, or part of Gregson's 'circle'. It'd been going on for years without us knowing the half of it; there were just a lot of unexplained deaths, lost paperwork, bogus confessions…all of that, but the whole thing was managed with military precision. There were unexplained deaths, but never *so* many as to attract too much attention. Lost paperwork, but always a believable excuse. So-called confessions from credible witnesses who turned out not to be credible, at all. When I think back, the scale of the operation was remarkable. It took years to unravel."

"Do you think everything has unravelled now?" Charlie asked.

Denise felt a chill, as though someone had traced a finger along her spine. She knew the younger members of her team awaited a cheerful response; something about having cleaned up shop, once and for all, justice having prevailed.

But this was real life.

"Progress takes time, and it isn't linear," she said, truthfully. "We've made huge inroads, but there'll always be bad apples in every barrel. It just takes time to find them, sometimes."

"Speaking of bad apples, another e-mail's just pinged through from the Drugs Squad," Melanie said, and Denise was grateful for the distraction from memories best consigned to the past. "They've sent over some details about the new kids on the block; a crime family based out of London, with extensive links to Russia and Eastern Europe. They're setting up outposts in the Midlands and here in our manor. Wait, I'll bring up their file."

Mel hummed beneath her breath and then let out a long whistle.

"Well, this may not be strictly professional but, as I'm newly single"—she paused to wink at Jack and Charlie, to let them know there were no hard feelings—"I'll go out on a limb and say this might be one of the best looking baddies I've seen outside of the movies. It's a pity he's probably some sort of psychopath."

Deciding to roll with the banter, Jack rose from his chair and walked around to look at her monitor.

"Okay," he said, and gestured the others over. "I'll sacrifice my manhood and agree…this dude looks like one of the Hemsworth brothers."

"Which one?" Charlie asked.

"Does it matter?" he replied.

"Yes," all three women replied.

"Bloody hell," Jack muttered. "Okay…the one who played *Thor*. Whichever that one is."

There were murmurs of appreciation, even from Janet, the Super's highly conservative new personal assistant, who happened to be passing in the corridor outside.

"Stand aside, children," Denise said, and they parted like the Red Sea. "I'll be the judge of—oh, *Sweet Baby Jesus*. Now, that just isn't fair, is it? Would you look at those cheekbones…"

"Well, now I *have* to come and look." Charlie laughed.

"I'm not sure I want you to," Jack said, dubiously. "You might have second thoughts about law enforcement and decide to become a gangster's moll, once you catch a glimpse of this bloke."

Charlie laughed again, and the smile was still on her face as she rounded the bank of desks and came to join the small crowd around Melanie's computer monitor.

"Well?" Jack prompted, when no remark was forthcoming. "Should I worry?"

The others chuckled, and Charlie told herself to speak, to smile, to say *something*.

Anything.

"He's—he's certainly easy on the eye," she said, tremulously. "But, as Melanie says, he's a psychopath."

"*Allegedly*," Denise said.

"What's his name?" Jack wondered.

"Alexei Rachmaninov," Mel replied, skim-reading the short biography they had on file. "Aged thirty-six, eldest son of Dmitry Rachmaninov, now deceased. One brother, one sister, both here in the UK, both suspected lieutenants within the organisation. Drugs and people trafficking, mostly, but also some more sophisticated tech scam operations, identity theft, hacking, extortion…there's quite a list."

"Rachmaninov…where've I heard that name before?" Jack muttered.

"He was a classical composer," Charlie said softly. "Known for his piano concertos."

Jack was impressed, so failed to notice the sickly grey pallor to her skin or the slight tremble to her hands, which she kept balled tightly by her sides.

Alexei, she thought, and felt sick.

Charlie remembered the day he'd introduced himself as 'Alexander' and held open the door for her at the Outpatients Unit in Yorkshire three years ago, where her mother was due to be seen by a neurologist. Alexander told her he was there to visit his father, who was gravely ill and was unlikely to live much longer. Her foolish, trusting heart had gone out to the handsome, chivalrous stranger and, when he'd asked her to have coffee, it had reminded her of a scene in one of those Richard Curtis movies. You know, where a harried young woman bumps into the man who will turn out to be the love of her life, but she has no idea at the time. Reeling from the shock of her mother's recent diagnosis, and feeling the impending weight of responsibility it would bring, Charlie had grasped the chance for company.

In the coffees, dinners, walks and, eventually, evenings that followed, Alexander made Charlie feel as though she was the only woman in the world. He told her she was special, smart, and beautiful.

He behaved as though he valued her mind and spirit, not merely their casing. He shared his memories of childhood, some of which might have been true, and, just like all the other women he deceived, she fell for the act—hook, line and sinker.

Charlie couldn't have known she'd been targeted and chosen carefully, months before, nor that his men had watched her movements, noting her schedule, workplace, home address and the fact she had a very small circle of trusted friends and family. She was vulnerable to a certain kind of predator, and this one wanted a body on the inside who could be manipulated and manoeuvred. His opinion of women was so low and his experience so vast, Alexander—or, *Alexei*—never once doubted his ability to control a young, attractive woman with romantic ideals. He knew all about her likes and dislikes long before they met, and set about exploiting that knowledge to maximum effect. In the end, Charlie was convinced they were in love and that she'd found her soulmate in life. She felt so *lucky*. He told her he worked away quite a bit, since he was a senior salesperson for some kind of artificial intelligence research company, and made it sound as though they were doing the work that would eventually cure all known diseases.

Lies, she thought. *All lies.*

It was only when two officers from Ghost Squad cornered her in the womenswear department of Marks and Spencer that the truth came crashing down. Alexander Rachmaninov didn't exist, but Alexei Rachmaninov did, and he was a highly dangerous man. He'd been grooming her, to use her as a mole within the police, and they hoped she hadn't been foolish enough to share any sensitive information from Major Crimes.

No, she'd assured them, as her heart shattered. There had been no information sharing, or improper breaches of protocols. She turned over all the devices she owned, and invited their digital forensics personnel to check them for anything untoward. It was a demeaning process, and she wondered if the men and women tasked with filtering through her messages had a few laughs at her expense, no-doubt wondering how anyone could be so naive.

Once they were satisfied she hadn't turned over access to police files, or any other sensitive data, they invited her to become an undercover informant, instead. How would she like to maintain the relationship and pretend she knew nothing, allowing things to pan out as Alexei intended? Instead of feeding him useful information, a sting operation could be set up and executed far more easily with her help.

Charlie had declined.

They might have caught her in time to prevent any sensitive information sharing, but they'd arrived much too late to prevent something far more important—

She was pregnant.

Only a couple of weeks, but the test was positive.

She remembered standing there in the department store, clutching a pair of maternity leggings close to her breast, fearful the vacant-eyed man from Ghost Squad would look down and spot the tags.

"Charlie?"

Abruptly, she returned to the present. "Sorry, I was miles away. What did you say?"

"I was saying, we should set up a meeting with Drugs Squad to see if they can tell us anything that could point to a connection with Terry Pearson," Mel repeated.

Charlie rubbed an absent hand over her stomach. "Good idea," she said. "I'll be back in a sec."

She walked from the room as steadily as she could and then, as soon as she reached the empty corridor outside, broke into a run.

CHAPTER 14

Angela and Kevin Riley lived in a quaint fisherman's cottage overlooking the sea, its battered stone walls painted a hardwearing, masonry white. Despite the season, it was a well-tended home, with a garden that was small but perfectly formed. An old bell hung outside the front door, and Ryan gave it a tug.

"They've probably had a chance to talk things over while we were finishin' lunch," Phillips said, beneath his breath, which was clouding on the cold air.

"They've also had *months* to confer, if they needed to," Ryan reminded him, considering Terry had been missing since August. "I don't think the time it took you to inhale that soup would have made too much difference."

Presently, the door opened, forestalling any further conversation.

"Hello again," Angela said. "Come in, out of the cold."

They stepped inside a cosy hallway painted in a shade of blush pink that gave the effect of being somewhere far warmer. A log fire crackled in the living room beyond, which was as small as the rest of the house but furnished in more earthy tones to create a feeling of instant welcome.

"You have a lovely home," Ryan remarked, to put her at ease.

"Thanks," Angela said, looking around at the nest they'd created. "It used to be very run-down, but we've renovated it, over the years. I'll just go and get Kevin, he must be upstairs. Would you like anything? A drink?"

"That's kind, but we're both fine, thank you."

Phillips sighed inwardly and waved farewell to the prospect of tea and a custard cream to round off his lunch.

"Have a seat, and I'll be back in a minute."

Frank didn't need to be asked twice but, while he settled himself on the sofa, Ryan took the opportunity to wander around the room.

"You're like a tiger, prowlin' around the place," Phillips hissed. "You're makin' me dizzy—"

"DCI Ryan?"

Angela re-entered the room with a man of around fifty in tow, who ticked every stereotypical box for being a middle-manager within local government, an electrical engineer, or perhaps the regional supervisor for a telecommunications team. They supposed it was wrong to make value judgments based upon appearance; but, it was their job to read people, and this man wore the expression of someone institutionalised by office hierarchy. He wore beige from head to toe, which matched his beige skin, mid-brown eyes, mousy brown hair, and features that were entirely bland and forgettable.

He would have made an excellent spy.

"Mr Riley? I'm DCI Ryan, this is Detective Sergeant Phillips."

Kevin's weary, watery brown eyes ran over the hand Ryan extended, before taking it into his own limp-wristed grip. Phillips, who had hoisted himself off the sofa as a matter of courtesy, was treated to a similarly flaccid shake which he could have lived without.

"Angie says you're here to talk about Terry?" Kevin said, and perched himself on the edge of the sofa. "The last we heard, he was still missing, but we reckoned it was more likely he'd buggered off to Ireland."

There were tax breaks to be found in Ireland, they knew, and plenty more besides for an enterprising soul.

"We're investigating his *murder*," Ryan said. "Before we get to that, I wonder if you'd tell us a bit about yourselves?"

He didn't wait for them to acquiesce, but simply ploughed on.

"Mrs Riley, we understand you own the restaurant and catering business, is that correct?"

Angela nodded. "Yes, I set it up when we first moved here," she said. "I went to catering school when I was eighteen, then worked in one of my father's restaurants in Newcastle for a few years, so I learned the ropes of running a hospitality business. I think he wanted me to manage that side to his empire, but…"

She broke off, and looked down at her hands while she considered how best to speak ill of the dead.

"Let's just say, his business ethos didn't align with mine," she said. "I met Kev when he came in for his work's Christmas party, one year, and we hit it off."

Looking between them, it was difficult to imagine the mild-mannered man sitting before them as a young, vibrant lothario flirting with a younger Angela, but it must have happened, somehow.

"And what line of work are you in, Mr Riley?"

"I'm a structural engineer," he replied, and recounted having spent his early years working for one of the larger firms in the North East before deciding to open his own freelance business when he and Angela moved to Amble, all of which they would be able to verify later.

"Do you work alongside Angela at the restaurant, too?"

To this, Angela laughed. "Kev wouldn't know his way around a kitchen," she said, and rubbed his arm in a gesture they found mildly condescending. "Would you, love?"

"No," he replied, robotically.

"Jonah helps out, sometimes, on the weekends," Angela told them. "He seems to have inherited my cooking genes."

"Who's Jonah?"

"Oh, sorry, that's our son," she said, and pointed towards a framed picture sitting on one of the side tables, depicting a sullen teenager, tall and lanky like his father with the same shade of mid-brown hair.

"Is he here, too?"

"No, he's at a friend's house," Angela replied, with a touch of defensiveness. "He doesn't know anything about his uncle, or who he was, so there's nothing he could tell you."

Ryan left it alone for now. "You told us you hadn't seen your brother, Terry, in quite some time," he said. "Can you remember exactly when that was?"

Angela looked at Kevin, then back at Ryan. "It must have been several years ago," she said. "I can't remember the exact date, but Jonah was about ten or eleven. Terry and Kerry-Jayne came into the restaurant with Mia, who's a couple of years older than Jonah. It was all very awkward. We just don't have anything in common, anymore."

Frank caught Ryan's eye, and the latter nodded imperceptibly.

"The thing is, when we spoke to your mother, she seemed to think Terry might've visited you more recently," he said. "Are you sure you haven't seen him, lately?"

"I'm sure," Angela replied, without pause. "I don't know why my mother would say that, because I haven't seen him in years."

Ryan turned to Kevin. "And you, Mr Riley? Have you seen Terry, lately?"

"I think he'd have told me, don't you?" Angela interjected.

Ryan said nothing, because he'd lost count of the times one spouse lied by omission to another, or simply fabricated an entirely different truth.

"Mr Riley?" he prompted, but Kevin shook his head.

"It's like Angela says," he replied. "Neither of us had seen him for years. It's definitely true, then?"

"Is what true?" Ryan asked.

"That he's dead?"

"It's definitely true," Phillips said, with feeling. He'd seen the pictures of what was left of the man. "Why? Do you have some reason to doubt that?"

"No, no," Kevin replied, seeming to shake himself. "It's just…it's hard to believe he's really gone. He was such a big character, or liked to think he was."

Ryan spoke with them for a while longer while Frank took notes, circling back around to questions he'd asked before, to be sure their answers didn't change. It was a delicate dance he'd done too many times to recall, but the effort reaped nothing of immediate interest. As far as the Rileys were concerned, Terry was no longer a part of their lives and they wouldn't have the first clue who might have wanted to kill him, except to lament his chosen lifestyle. They were sorry he was dead, but equally unsurprised because the risks came with the territory.

"If we have any further questions or updates, we'll be in touch," Ryan said, and fished out a business card he kept for moments such as these. "In the meantime, if you remember anything else, give me a call or speak to one of my team."

Phillips waited until they were back inside the relative privacy of Ryan's car before passing comment and, when he did, it was exactly as Ryan had predicted.

"Did you get a feel o' that man's *handshake*?" Frank said, disgustedly. "It was like shakin' a dead fish."

Ryan opened his mouth to respond, but found he didn't know what to say.

"Makes you wonder why people bother at all," Phillips grumbled, and began rifling through the central console in search of hand wipes or sanitizer. "Leaves you feelin' dirty, that's what it does."

Ryan had to laugh, because it was true. "Aside from his inferior handshake, what did you make of the pair of them?"

"Unusual match," Phillips said, and scrubbed his hands together. "Mind you, I can't say much about that. Anyone lookin' at me and Denise would have to wonder what she ever saw in me."

It was said without any irony whatsoever, and Ryan smiled to himself. Anyone who knew Frank Phillips or Denise MacKenzie would also know they were perfectly matched and, as for what the red-haired Irish beauty saw in her shorter, slightly more rotund husband, they could take their pick between kindness, loyalty and good humour, just for starters.

But Ryan wasn't about to tell his friend any of that.

"We've *all* wondered that," he said, because it was expected. "Still, I know what you mean. Opposites can attract, but maybe that pair have more in common than we realise. Angela wanted a quiet life, a different life to the one she'd known before. Perhaps Kevin offered her that opportunity."

Phillips made a non-committal sound. "It's always the quiet ones to watch," he said. "If y'ask me, there was somethin' shifty about Kevin Riley. Could have been his lazy eye, I s'pose."

Ryan reversed out of the narrow parking space with the ease of one born with superior spatial awareness, and steered them in the direction of home.

"He didn't seem at all surprised that his brother-in-law was dead."

"Aye, but that's not unreasonable," Phillips said. "We all know what Terry did for a livin'."

"Yes, but it was more than that," Ryan said, and braked to allow an elderly lady to cross the road. There wasn't much choice in the matter, considering she'd stepped into the road without warning. "Do you think she's okay?"

Phillips considered the woman's demeanour, and then nodded. "Aye, she's cantankerous, not demented."

Ryan was impressed. "You can tell that, from here?"

"She gave us the finger, so that was a bit of a giveaway."

Ryan laughed, and decided there was plenty to look forward to in his dotage.

"Anyhow, you were sayin' about Kevin?" Frank prompted.

"Yes, I was going to say, I thought he seemed relieved to hear that Terry was dead. He wasn't surprised, he was *relieved*. That's why he wanted to double check it was true."

"That was a bit of a funny thing to ask," Phillips agreed. "It's not like we make a habit of payin' house calls on the off-chance folk might be dead."

"It's possible he's relieved on his wife's behalf," Ryan offered. "If Terry was the reigning boss, there was always a chance he'd try to re-enter their lives, or pop up unexpectedly at the restaurant, as he did before. Now he's gone, that possibility doesn't need to hang over their heads anymore."

"Well," Frank said. "We know one thing for certain."

"What's that?"

"One o' them is lyin'."

"Oh, that." Ryan nodded. "Yes, on the one hand, we've got Patricia Pearson claiming Terry visited his sister recently. On the other, we've got the sister and her husband telling us they hadn't seen Terry in years. It's a mystery, all right."

"We love a good mystery," Frank said, with a glint in his eye.

"That we do," Ryan agreed. "Let the games begin."

CHAPTER 15

"Has anyone seen Charlie?"

It had been more than half an hour since she'd left the office, and there'd been no sign of her, so Jack was beginning to feel concerned that she was unwell.

"Denise? Would you mind popping your head into the ladies' to see if she's okay?"

MacKenzie checked the time on the large, industrial wall clock above their heads, and nodded. "I have to head off to collect Samantha from her friend's house in a minute, so I'll check on my way out."

Denise chucked her phone and keys into the tan leather bag she tended to use for work and glanced across to Charlie's desk area.

Her jacket was gone.

"Are you sure she didn't have an appointment, somewhere?" she said. "Her jacket's gone, so it looks as though she's gone out."

"No, I'm sure she said she'd be back in a minute," Jack murmured, turning to Mel for confirmation. When the latter nodded her agreement, he rose to his feet. "She was still wearing her jacket, I think. It's a brown suede blazer."

Denise moved around the desk and put a reassuring hand on his arm. "I'll go and look now."

She made her way along the corridor briskly, smiling as she passed colleagues that she knew, and almost collided with the superintendent as she pushed through the swing door into the ladies' room.

"Oh! Sorry, ma'am."

Detective Chief Superintendent Sandra Morrison continued to shake the excess water from her freshly washed hands.

"Easy, tiger," she said, with a smile. "Running late for something?"

"I'm heading home in a minute, but I'm looking for Charlie Reed. Is she in there?"

Morrison looked back over her shoulder. "I don't think so," she said.

Both women stepped inside the facilities, which boasted a long, rectangular space with a bank of sinks along one wall and a number of cheap stalls along the other, all of which were unoccupied.

"Nope, nobody here," Morrison declared. "Is it urgent?"

Denise sighed. "I don't know, really. It's a bit odd… She left the office about half an hour ago, saying she'd be back in a minute, and we haven't seen her since. It's not like Charlie to disappear without saying 'goodbye'." She fished out her mobile. "Let me try giving her a call."

Morrison had places to be, but was intrigued enough to linger.

Denise selected Charlie's number, but the call was immediately redirected to voicemail. She tried again and was met with the same response.

"Strange," she murmured.

"Maybe something happened with her son, so she had to nip off?" Morrison suggested, and Denise grabbed at the possibility.

"Yes, that could be it! I don't have her mother's phone number, but Jack will. I'll ask him to call her and ask if she's heard anything."

Before she could dash off, Morrison caught her arm. "One last thing, while I have you," she said, keeping her voice low despite the fact they were the only two in the room. "Do you know if Anna's DNA results have come back yet? I don't like to pester Ryan about it, but it would be good to draw a line under everything, wouldn't it?"

MacKenzie couldn't agree more. "I know they were expecting something today, but I haven't heard from either of them and it's getting a bit late in the day, now."

Morrison felt a pang of unease. "Okay," she said, as cheerfully as she could. "You know where I am, if you need me."

"Jack's calling me, Charlie. What should I do?"

Charlie's mother held out her mobile phone, so her daughter could see the name illuminated on the screen.

"Don't answer it," came the curt reply.

"He's called several times now, which means he must be trying your mobile, too," her mother replied. "You'll have to speak to him, either on the phone or when he comes home this evening. At this rate, I wouldn't be surprised if he came home early; he'll be getting worried."

Charlie closed her eyes briefly, her nerves ragged. "What should I say to him, Mum?" she whispered, and when her eyes opened again they were bright with tears, which were an indulgence she refused to allow. "Should I just come out with it? I can see the horror on his face, now, when he finds out Ben is the son of a gangland criminal and I'll be—I'll be—"

Her voice hitched and fell as she fought to suppress the raw emotion clawing its way through her skin.

"He'll still love you," her mother replied, softly.

But Charlie couldn't, or wouldn't, hear it. The unexpected and unwelcome reminder of Ben's true father had ripped open a wound that was only just beginning to heal; Alexei's handsome face a visceral reminder of the fool she'd once been, and the pain she'd once weathered. Any dreams she'd had of a normal family had been destroyed the day she'd found out who he truly was, and she'd done the only thing she could, which was to *run*. She'd lied, and told him she was moving to Australia, and not to follow her. She'd taken her mother's maiden name, Reed, and headed further north to the wilds of Northumberland, taking the first job she could find in the constabulary closest to her mother, whom she'd needed, desperately.

She'd given birth to Ben without his father to hold her hand, but her mother had held it, instead. Of course, she'd considered all the options available to her; nobody would have blamed her for terminating the pregnancy, given the circumstances, but she had already fallen in love with the burgeoning life inside her womb, and would not be parted from it.

She knew she had to protect it, at all costs.

Now, that cluster of cells was a bright-eyed, blond-haired bundle of joy she'd named Benjamin, and he would be two years old in a matter of weeks. He had no idea about the dangers that could befall him, nor the anger his true father may feel, if he should ever learn of his existence and of her deception. Their fragile bubble could burst at any moment, and, for a while, she'd forgotten that. In the safety of Jack's arms, cocooned by the warmth and friendship of a new team, she'd forgotten the danger that lurked beyond the county lines of Northumberland.

She'd been a fool to imagine she could relax, or be content.

A fool, again.

The phone began to ring again and, this time, she took it from her mother's hand and stabbed a button to quell the incessant sound.

"You have to tell him, Charlie."

"I can't. I need to start packing our things and looking for a new job, somewhere far away," she replied. "It's the only way to keep Ben safe."

"Are you sure his father will try to—?"

"I'm sure," Charlie muttered. "If he finds out about Ben, Alexei will try to take him. He isn't the forgiving kind."

In the background, they heard the jingle of a well-known children's cartoon playing on the television, followed by the sound of her little boy singing along at the top of his lungs. Her heart shattered at the thought of how close he'd come to finding a real father, one that deserved to have him. They might have been a family, she, Ben and Jack, with her mother as a live-in grandma with an infinite supply of cuddles for all of them. It had been a wonderful dream come true, but that's all it was.

A dream.

Just then, they heard the sound of a key turning in the lock outside. Charlie knew it would be Jack, coming home to see what the hell was going on, as her mother had said. He'd be worried and confused, shocked and hurt when she told him she would be leaving, but anything was better than being dead.

Just as she knew Alexei could never forgive her deception, nor would he forgive another man for standing in his place as Ben's father.

He'd kill Jack first, and then come for her.

"Charlie? Charlie!"

Jack's footsteps sounded along the corridor of her nice little maisonette flat in Gosforth, which she'd been so proud of, only that very morning. When he appeared in the doorway, she thought she'd been ready to face him, to say what needed to be said, but a single look at his face was enough to test her resolve.

"I'll leave you to it," her mother said, and leaned up to bestow a brief kiss on Jack's cheek before making her way into the living room to be with her grandson.

Bemused, Jack turned to Charlie, one sweeping glance taking in the open suitcase lying on the bed and the clothes piled high beside it.

"What's going on here?"

Mindful of young ears, he stepped into the bedroom they'd shared for all of four days, and shut the door behind him.

"Charlie?"

Feeling her knees weaken, she sat on the edge of the bed and focused on a point somewhere just above his head.

"I'm sorry I left the office abruptly," she said, in the same calm, unemotional voice he'd heard her use with victims' families, or difficult witnesses. "I panicked, and needed to be with Ben."

Jack shook his head, totally at sea. "Why? Has something happened?"

She could feel her heart hammering against the wall of her chest, like a caged bird. "I—it's more a case of what happened three years ago," she stammered.

He moved to sit beside her, and she didn't stop him. After all, he may no longer want to be anywhere near her, soon enough, and she'd be leaving at the first reasonable opportunity, anyway. She would need to soak up these last intimate moments together, committing his scent to memory, along with the sound of his voice and the feel of his hand holding hers.

"Tell me what happened three years ago."

"I met a man—by chance, or so I thought," she began, in a small voice she hardly recognised as her own. "I'd lost my dad, and my mum had only recently been diagnosed with MS. She'd come to live with me, temporarily, in Yorkshire, which is where I was based at the time."

Jack said nothing, only listened.

"Anyway, one afternoon, I'd taken Mum for a meeting with her consultant neurologist at the hospital," she said. "She'd left some notes in the car, so I ran to get them. On my way back inside the hospital, I ran into Alexander. He bumped into me, or I bumped into him…

it doesn't matter. He was charming and kind and handsome, Jack. All the things a woman would want."

It was only the truth, he thought, but it hurt all the same.

"You're talking about Ben's father?"

She nodded. "We weren't together long," she said. "Only a few months and he lived in London, so it was more of a long-distance relationship, if you can even call it that."

"I don't care about whether you were married—" he began, trying his best to understand what the problem could possibly be.

"It isn't that," she said. "Just—let me finish, Jack. Let me get this out, if I can."

He squeezed her hand. "Sorry," he murmured. "Go on."

"Almost everything he told me was a lie," she said, in a brittle tone she couldn't quite hide. "His profession, his family, his reason for being at the hospital, *everything*. Even the name he gave me was only half-true."

"What do you mean?"

She looked at his hand holding hers, and then up into his kind brown eyes.

"His name wasn't Alexander, it was Alexei. Alexei Rachmaninov."

CHAPTER 16

Jack stared at Charlie for several seconds, while his brain computed the information she had given him.

Alexei Rachmaninov was Ben's father?

"How—?"

"I know what you must be thinking," she said, pushing to her feet so she could pace around the room and no longer have to see the disappointment lurking behind his eyes. "You're wondering how I could choose to have a child with a man like that, aren't you?"

Jack frowned. "No, I—"

"You're wondering how I could tolerate it, knowing me as you do and the principles I stand for, aren't you? How could I set those principles aside and sleep with a man like that—"

She heard the rising note of hysteria in her voice, and Jack heard it too. He came to his feet, and crossed the room to take her shoulders in a gentle hold.

"Charlie, you're putting words into my mouth," he said. "He lied to you from the outset, and never even told you his real name. I'm not wondering how you could be with someone like that, because you believed you were with a man who never really existed. I'm not questioning your principles, because you cared for someone who deceived you and turned out to be the worst kind of person.

I don't need to ask any questions because the answers are obvious, but I'll listen to whatever you want to tell me. I only have one thing to say, which is that I love you, Charlie. I love Ben, too."

It was everything she could have wished for, and she longed to throw her arms around him, bury her face against his neck and allow him to hold her and believe that everything would work out for the best. Unfortunately, she'd learned that life wasn't like the pretty romance stories in books or on television, where the bad guy got his comeuppance, and the good guy got the girl.

If only.

"It isn't as simple as loving someone," she said, and hardened her heart to say what needed to be said. "Alexei Rachmaninov is a brutal, ruthless man who was bred to believe that men are superior to women, and nothing is more important than bloodline. No matter what he thinks of me—he probably thinks I'm nothing more than a failed mark he planned to use for information—he *will* want Ben, if he finds out about his existence, and he'll want to punish me. He'll hurt anybody who gets in the way of that, including you, Jack. I can't allow that to happen."

"You don't know for sure," he argued, and tried to reach for her again, but she stepped away from his grasp. She needed to, in order to remain strong.

"I read his files," she said, and turned to stare unseeingly out of the bay window overlooking their small back garden. "Ghost Squad found me and told me everything, one afternoon while I was picking up maternity clothes. They invited me to read it for myself, so I could be sure they weren't fabricating or embellishing any information about the man I thought I loved."

Charlie turned away from the window, her eyes haunted by the memory of that day.

"What I read made me sick," she said. "I'd given my body to a man who'd been accused of sexually assaulting young women, killing and seriously injuring men of all ages, and was suspected of all sorts of other crimes. He'd never been convicted, because people were terrified of the repercussions if they gave evidence. But it was there in the paperwork, for any fool to see what he was."

Jack ached to hold her, to comfort her and tell her everything would be fine, but she didn't want or need platitudes. She needed *strength* and *security*, and to know she no longer had to face the storm alone.

He began to formulate a plan.

"I'll speak to Ryan first thing tomorrow and tender my resignation, or put in for a transfer to another constabulary," she said, in the momentary silence. "So long as he was still in London or Europe, I felt reasonably safe, but now that his organisation has grown and extended operations in the North East, I need to get Ben and my mother as far away from here as possible. It's the only sensible thing to do."

Jack took her shoulders and turned her around to face him.

"The most sensible thing to do is to empower ourselves with a better understanding of his operations," he said. "We should find out everything we can about his organisation, then track his movements and learn his routines, if any," he said. "We play him at his own game, so we know where he is at all times. As for personal security, tell me about your online presence—could you be found, easily?"

She shook her head. "I don't think so. I've kept Ben and me off any social media platforms, including opting him out of any nursery photographs," she said. "Everything to do with our address and phone number is ex-directory. I use my mother's maiden name, rather than my father's which is the one listed on my birth certificate and on my official record."

"What's your father's name?" Jack asked.

"What?"

"I'm curious." He shrugged.

"Clough," she said. "I'm registered as Charlotte Jean Clough."

"Does 'Jean' have a special significance?"

She knew what he was doing, of course: he was trying to de-escalate her stress levels with idle talk, so she'd calm down and listen to whatever he wanted to tell her.

"Jean was my maternal grandmother," she said, obligingly. "She died shortly before I was born, so it seemed fitting to name me after her."

Jack reached up to brush the hair from her eyes, and curved a hand around her cheek.

"You don't have to be afraid," he said. "You're not alone, Charlie."

She wanted to believe him, so badly.

But—

"You don't know Alexei as I do," she said. "He's entirely without remorse. He doesn't experience human emotion as we do, Jack; he mimics it, to get whatever he wants out of people. I had to lie to him and say I was moving abroad to take a job opportunity, and you'd think the months we'd spent together were meaningless. No woman walks away from him, usually, but as soon as he thought I was of no further use to him, I might as well have been invisible. It would have been upsetting, except it played exactly into my hands at the time. He's so used to getting his own way with women, I assumed he'd be angry."

"Especially when he looks the way he does," Jack muttered. "Probably thinks he's God's gift."

"Beauty is only skin deep," she said, and, this time, she curved a hand around his cheek. "The way you've been with me, with my mother and my son…Jack, you're the most beautiful man in the world to me."

"Frank always told me I had a good face for radio."

"Well, he'd know."

They smiled together, until hers faded.

"I can't compromise on safety," she said again. "Please understand."

"I do, Charlie. But you don't have to run anymore. It's no life for you, or for Ben. I'd only trail after you like a lonesome puppy, anyway."

Their cat raised her furry black head from where it had been lounging against some of Charlie's clothing and gave a short *miaow* in disgust.

"All right," he amended. "A lonesome kitten. Is that better?"

The cat gave him a baleful look, then resumed her previous position snoring amongst the folds of Charlie's woollen jumpers. The latter lifted the cat gently and transferred her into the largely disused cat bed sitting in the corner of the room, then turned back to Jack in resignation.

"I know you want to help, Jack, and wave some sort of magic wand, but you can't."

"We don't *need* magic," he said, firmly. "We need to do what we do best, which is enforce the law and protect the public. There's another reason you can't carry on running, Charlie."

She waited.

"If you're right about everything this man is, there isn't anywhere you can run to," he continued, with brutal honesty. "If Alexei Rachmaninov finds out about Ben, and gets it into his head to take him from you, he'll make it his mission to find you *wherever* you go. You'd be forever looking over your shoulder, waiting for the day he turned up on your doorstep. The only difference is, you'd be alone, without the support of the people who care for you."

"Can't you see? It's *because* I care that I don't want to put any of you in danger!" she cried out. "I have enough to worry about keeping Ben safe, let alone my mother, and you, and—and—"

"You don't have to be a martyr, Charlie."

His words had the desired effect of taking her breath away.

"You think I'm trying to be a *martyr*?"

"Aren't you?" he countered. "What else would you call slinking off into the shadows, like the scared girl you used to be, rather than the bold, bright, capable woman you are now?"

She was so outraged, she missed the compliment.

"How dare you suggest that I'm some sort of coward? Do you have *any* idea how difficult it's been, these past three years?"

"Prove me wrong, then, Charlie. Stay and face this, and face him. We'll do it together. Me, you, and the whole bloody army at CID, if we have to."

She saw the love shining in his eyes, heard the conviction in his voice, and felt herself weaken.

"What if something happens to Ben? I'd never forgive myself."

I'd never forgive you, either.

"You know I'm right about Rachmaninov," Jack said. "He won't stop at the border of Scotland, Cumbria or County Durham. It doesn't matter where you go, he'd use whatever network he has, whichever contacts on his payroll, to find you. The risk is just as high elsewhere, if not higher."

She turned away, needing to think clearly, because, in that moment, she loved him so much it was a physical ache in her chest.

"I'll give it until the end of January," she whispered. "If I still feel that things are too risky here, I'll leave."

"If we can't neutralise this threat by then, I won't ask you to."

He held open his arms, and she walked into them, feeling the warm, comforting thud of his heartbeat through the wall of his chest. He raised a hand to caress her hair, and she felt the brush of his lips against her temple.

"We'll beat this together," he murmured.

From her position on the other side of the door, Charlie's mother clasped a hand to her mouth, relieved beyond words. She'd liked Jack Lowerson from the moment he stepped into their lives, but had often wondered if he had the guts to father a young boy who was not his own.

She needn't have worried.

It was obvious Jack loved her precious little family, and that he'd do his best to protect them. Charlie had spent too long in survival mode, doing all she could just to get through the day, and she deserved to have a partner in life who could share some of the load. Her greatest wish was to see Charlotte smile again, as she'd once smiled. She wanted to see her daughter laugh and be playful, as though life was only just beginning. Having heard all she needed to, she turned and made her way back to the living room, where Ben was building towers with his colourful Duplo blocks. She watched him for a moment, and wondered if he knew how greatly he was loved.

"Grandma?"

"Yes, cutie-pie?"

"I need a wee-wee."

She chuckled to herself, because, while some talked of murderous gang leaders, her grandson's greatest worry in life was whether he'd make it to the potty in time.

It was a great leveller.

"C'mon, then, tiger! Race you to the toilet!"

CHAPTER 17

Shortly after five, Ryan steered his car into the historic, seaside village of Bamburgh, where he, Anna and Emma now lived in a "new" old house, which they were renovating with all the speed of an Ice Age glacier. The village still bustled with locals and tourists making the most of their final days of festive holiday before returning to their normal lives, and the shock of a long, cold January. For now, they bundled themselves up in thick layers to brave the long, sandy beach at the foot of the castle, which stood atop its mighty perch on a crag of volcanic rock, a fitting watchtower and indomitable fortress for some of the first Kings of England.

Ryan eyed the tourists like a true local, eager for the day when the picture-perfect village would be theirs to enjoy once more, without having to share it with a constant stream of social media influencers who seemed largely oblivious to the needs or rights of others, so long as it meant they could capture a bit of content to monetise. The thought reminded him of Anna's recent experience as the subject of one such salacious content creator, who'd filmed her outburst for the clickbait of others and without any thought for the impact that might have.

The world was full of amateur journalists, he knew, and the instantaneous nature of their so-called reporting could be dangerous;

there was something to be said for taking a pause before clicking 'upload', it afforded one a greater chance to fact-check, for a start.

As if the Universe had read his mind, Ryan's phone began to ring, and a brief glance at the caller ID told him it was the one he'd been waiting for all day. He pulled his car into a space on the village green, uncaring of the sign which clearly read, 'NO PARKING AT ANY TIME', flipped on his hazard lights, and answered the call.

"Ryan? It's Lauren Bell."

"Hi, Lauren. Do you have any news for me?"

Straight to the point, as always, she thought. No chit-chat about their respective Christmases, or whether Santa had been good to them, and that was fine with her.

"Yes, I do," she replied, and prepared to deliver the news none of them had expected. "The results came in around twenty minutes ago, and they're not quite what we were expecting. Ryan, I'm going to need you to bring Anna back into the station, as soon as possible."

Ryan stared out of the windshield and watched one of his neighbours crossing the street, a small bag of groceries dangling from one hand. Spotting him, they raised a hand in greeting, which he ignored.

"Why?" he asked, and, unconsciously, his grip tightened against the edge of his seat.

"We found various DNA samples at the crime scene, including one that was a full match to the DNA sample your wife provided," she said. "Another sample we recovered was a partial match to your wife's DNA."

He tried to make sense of it all, mind racing to find possible explanations for how Anna's DNA could have found its way into Lin Oldman's flat without her ever having been there.

It didn't look good.

"What do you mean, 'partial' sample? How is that possible?"

"I think it's best if we discuss everything face to face," she said.

"Are you going to bring Anna in this evening, or would you rather wait until tomorrow morning? I know it's quite a drive from where you are."

"I—no, let's get this over with," he said, in a flat voice. "We'll be there as soon as we can."

He was about to ring off, when she added, "Ryan? I'm sorry about this. I really am."

On another day, he'd have thanked her, just as he'd have waved back to his neighbour. Instead, he found himself struggling to muster the energy to drive home and face the woman he loved, who carried their second child, and who happened to be the prime suspect in a murder investigation.

Ryan sat there for several minutes and then started the car again.

Time to face the music.

Rascal was the first to greet Ryan, as he let himself through the front door of the elegant, if a little dilapidated, Georgian house they called 'home'. He allowed himself a momentary respite, hunkering down to the dog's level so he could administer a scratch behind the ears, followed by a thorough belly rub.

"Oh, to be a dog," he murmured, as the animal rolled around, wagging its tail in cheerful abandon.

"Daddy!"

Emma's footsteps echoed around the hall as she raced towards him, as fast as her little legs would carry her. Ryan came to his feet and braced for impact, only slightly winded when she bounded into him with the force of a baby elephant. He lifted her high up into the air, strong arms holding her with ease, and she laughed delightedly, as she always did.

"I missed you," she said, and wrapped her small arms around his neck.

"I missed you too," he replied, and gave her an extra squeeze. "Where's Mummy and Grandma?"

"Grandma's reading a book upstairs, and Mummy's helping me make dinner," Emma declared, proudly. Only then did Ryan notice the suspect stains on the front of her dungarees, and something that looked suspiciously like flour.

He looked down at his navy coat, and saw that he was right. "Let me guess what you've made," he said, pretending to think about it. "Dinosaur soup?"

She giggled, and shook her head. "*No*, Daddy! Dinosaurs are egg-stink!"

"Extinct," he corrected her. "Hm, perhaps some dragon casserole?"

She giggled again. "Dragons aren't real, Daddy!"

"My mistake," he said, grinning. "How about…a cake?"

She bobbed her head up and down. "Yep! It's a Victoria sponge cake, with jam inside," she told him. "Why do they call it 'Victoria'? Why not Emma?"

Clearly piqued that nobody had thought to christen a cake with her name, Ryan set her back on her feet.

"It was named for a very old queen, called Victoria."

"How old is she?"

"Er, well…she's not alive, anymore."

"You mean she's DEAD?" Emma almost shouted, and Ryan hushed her, so as not to wake up the aforementioned dead in the cemetery down the road.

"There's no need to shout about it," he said. "But, yes, she died a long time ago."

Emma tugged on his hand, solemnly. "The butterfly in the garden died."

It had been at least six months since Emma had found the fallen butterfly on their patio, at their former house, but the loss had clearly been a memorable one.

"That was very sad, but—"

"And, my friend Theo? His bunny rabbit died."

"Well, I'm sure—"

"There was a dead squirrel in the road, by the hedge, when we were driving in our car. Do you remember, Daddy?"

Ryan was starting to sweat. You'd think he'd be accustomed to talk of death, but it was unnerving coming from the mouth of a small child.

"Yes, I remember. You know, the important thing is not to dwell on it."

"What does 'dwell' mean?"

He almost slapped a palm to his own face. "I'll tell you, after we've had a slice of cake. How does that sound?"

"Okay!"

She skipped ahead, calling out to her mother, something along the lines of dead queens liking cake. By the time Ryan caught up with her, there was a slice waiting for him on the table, and Emma was already tucking into hers. Anna was fiddling with the radio, trying to find her favourite channel, *Absolute 90s*, and turned with a ready smile on her face.

"Hello! You're home early, today," she said, and abandoned the radio to cross the room and bestow a welcome kiss. There must have been something in his demeanour that gave him away for, when she drew back, she frowned. "Anything the matter?"

Ryan's eyes flicked towards Emma, who was munching her way through sponge and icing while turning the pages of a picture book.

"I had a call from Durham CID," he said. "The results of the DNA test have come in."

Anna read his expression with the ease of long experience, and found the answer to her unspoken question there, in the deep, stormy grey-blue depths of his eyes.

The results were not good.

She stepped back, and her chest rose and fell in one shaky motion. "I don't understand how that's possible," she whispered, careful not to allow any of her inner turmoil to spill over and upset the little girl sitting a few feet away. "It's *not* possible."

She shook her head, not knowing what else to say.

Ryan moved over to the kettle, to give himself something to do. "I have to ask," he said, once the water had set to boil. "Are you absolutely sure you've never been inside Lin Oldman's flat, under any circumstances?"

Anna tried not to feel hurt by the question, nor the fact he'd even asked it. Ryan was a logical man, who responded to situations such as these by taking things in stride. He needed to be sure she hadn't forgotten anything, nor overlooked anything that could be relevant, before progressing to the next step, whatever that may be.

"I'm sure," she said. "I would have told you before, if I'd ever been inside her apartment."

Ryan nodded, and began pouring water over a couple of tea bags in Christmas-themed mugs. "DS Bell wants me to take you back to the police station for further questioning," he said. "She offered tomorrow morning, but I thought you'd want to get it over with, if you're up to it?"

Anna rubbed her hands over her arms, which felt very cold despite the warmth of the kitchen.

"If your mother is happy to look after Emma, then I'll go tonight," she said, and started to move towards the door, intending to go in search of Eve Ryan. At the last moment, she paused and turned back to look at him. "I've said it before, but I'll say it again: I have nothing to hide."

Ryan abandoned the tea, and covered the distance between them.

"I believe you," he said, cradling her face in his hands. "There's always an explanation, even if it isn't obvious. We'll find it, together."

Anna felt an invisible weight lift from her shoulders.

"Mummy?"

They turned to see their daughter brushing crumbs from the table onto the floor, where the dog waited to hoover them up.

"Yes?"

"Grandad Charles used to say that if something looks like a duck and quacks like a duck, then it's a duck."

"What made you remember that, darling?"

"Daddy said there's always an expla-nay-shun, even if it's not always ob-vee-us," she enunciated. "That made me think of the ducks."

Ryan smiled, remembering his late father. "Your grandad was right; sometimes, the most obvious answer is the right one."

"I wish I knew what the most obvious answer is to my current problem," Anna confessed, in an undertone.

"We're not armed with all the facts," Ryan said, and curved an arm around her shoulders so he could pull her against him for a hug. "Try not to worry, we'll get to the bottom of this. Trust me."

"So long as *you* trust *me*, that's all that matters."

Ryan tipped her chin up so she could look into his eyes and see that he was telling the absolute truth, when he said, "Anna, I'd trust you with my life."

CHAPTER 18

While Ryan and Anna made the return journey to Durham, with a little help from Bon Jovi and Bryan Adams to ease the passage, Denise MacKenzie and Frank Phillips collapsed side by side on their living room sofa.

"*Eeh*, lad alive!" Frank declared, to the world at large. "That's a turn-up for the books."

"Which part? The bit where we found out Charlie had a secret child with a ruthless gang leader, or the part where one of our best friends' DNA was found at a murder scene?"

"They're hot topics, but I was actually thinkin' of Samantha tellin' us about her friend's parents gettin' divorced. They always seem so lovey-dovey whenever I've seen them."

Denise was baffled. "Of all things, *that's* what sticks out to you, from the news of the day?"

"Aye, well, I wouldn't be surprised if there was some hanky-panky goin' on outside the marital bed, if y'nah what I mean—"

"Frank, I'd have to be a raging moron not to understand what you mean."

"Let's not forget, they've got a *giant* pampas grass sittin' on their front lawn."

"What does horticulture have to do with it?"

"*Howay*, you can't tell me you don't know what a pampas grass means?"

"I've a horrible feeling you're going to tell me."

"Back in the seventies and eighties, it was the universal sign that the house was open to swingers," he said. "It was like a bat signal for all the locals who fancied a bit o' rumpy-pumpy in the cul-de-sac."

"It sounds like something from a Benny Hill sketch," she muttered, before something struck her. "*Hang* on a minute! How the heck do you know all about pampas grasses and cul-de-sac swingers. You used to live in a cul-de-sac!"

"So did you," he reminded her, and wriggled his eyebrows for effect. "However, I'll have you know I've never accepted any of the many offers I've had to throw my keys in the bowl. I'm a one-gal-guy, as Bing Crosby once said."

"He did?"

"In *High Society*," he reminded her.

"Oh, right. Anyway, never mind Bing Crosby! Stop trying to deflect," she accused him.

"It's common knowledge." He shrugged, and avoided her gaze lest she ask any more probing questions, particularly about the hot and sticky summer of 1989...

Luckily for him, her sense of self-preservation far outweighed idle curiosity.

"*Well*," Denise drawled. "Now that we've covered the gossip section of this evening's discussion, perhaps we could move on to more pertinent matters? Namely, how the hell are we going to keep Alexei Rachmaninov from finding out about Charlie and Ben? As for Anna..." She exhaled a long breath. "It just doesn't make any sense. Just looking at the logistics alone, I can't see how Anna could have gone all the way to Oldman's flat, killed her, and then made it home to Bamburgh before five. It's not humanly possible, unless she's learned to fly."

Unless they made a mistake in estimating the time of death, she neglected to add.

"She's in a fix," Frank agreed, and scratched the stubble on his chin. "Listen, pet, you don't think she might've—?"

MacKenzie shot him a warning look. "Of *course* I don't think Anna's involved; she's the most honest person I know."

Frank twiddled his thumbs. "Alreet, let's think laterally. D'you think anyone might've planted her DNA, to get her into trouble?"

"Anna's DNA?" Denise queried, and then shook her head again. "I can't imagine who'd want to do that to her. She doesn't have any enemies."

"That we know of," Frank corrected her.

As his words hung on the air, the living room door burst open and the pair of them jumped in shock.

"We've run out of Coco Pops," Samantha announced, as though it was a national emergency.

"Are you tryin' to scare the last bit of hair off my head?" Frank cried out. "As for cereal, we'll add it to the shopping list, but nobody's runnin' down to Tesco tonight, if that's what you're thinkin'. What d'you think you're on—your granny's yacht?"

Sam jutted out her hip and folded her arms.

"But there's *nothing* else to eat," she complained, and her parents stared at her in equal parts shock and outrage.

"Are you kidding? There's a fridge full of leftovers, a cupboard full of Christmas snacks and treats, and about ten bowls of fruit dotted around the house, so you'll not starve to death," Denise said, her voice dripping with sarcasm. "Now, hop to it, and come back when you're in less of a sulk."

Sam huffed, and slunk out of the room.

"I think we forgot to mention one other calamity that's befallen us," Frank said, darkly.

Denise turned to him, aghast.

"We've got a teenager." He nodded, confirming her worst fears. "Worst of all, it looks like the hormones are ragin'."

"Oh, Frank, bless your heart," Denise said, and patted his hand as she might have done a slow child. "The hormones haven't even *started* to rage, yet."

The terror on his face was priceless.

Returning to the police station in Durham felt like an outtake from the movie *Groundhog Day*, even down to the duty sergeant at the main entrance, Wendy Dickens, who appeared not to have moved from her perch behind the front desk in several days.

"Hello again," she said, her cheerful voice belying the concern she felt at seeing the couple back in her manor, both looking anxious and drawn. "Have you got an appointment?"

"Yes, could you let DS Bell know we've arrived?"

"Are you expecting counsel to join you?"

Ryan's jaw clenched, because that had been a sticking point between him and his wife yet again. He still believed legal representation was worth having, regardless of the fact she was innocent, whereas Anna flatly refused.

"No," he snapped. "It'll just be us."

Wendy invited them to take a seat on one of the wipe-clean chairs while they waited but their rear ends had barely touched the green pleather before they spotted DC Vale hurrying through the turnstiles to usher them towards the interview suite. While he was grateful not to have been kept waiting, Ryan wondered whether the urgency denoted something other than good timekeeping.

"Thanks for coming in," DS Bell said, when they entered the interview room. "Do you need anything for your comfort, Dr Taylor-Ryan?"

Anna took one of the metal seats arranged around a table nailed to the floor.

"Just some water, please."

When they were settled, Lauren started the recording, read out the date, time and names of those present, issued the standard caution and prepared to face Ryan's wrath, once again.

"Doctor Taylor-Ryan, is it correct that you've waived your right to have legal representation?"

"Yes, that's correct."

"And you don't want to change your mind?"

"No, I don't."

Anna could feel Ryan seething in the chair beside her, but his hand continued to hold hers, warm and steady.

"Very well, then. We're here today to discuss the results of a DNA comparison that was made by our forensics team, in which we compared the DNA sample you provided to us after your arrest, with a number of blood and other trace samples found at the victim's home. Before we discuss those results, is there anything you want to tell us, or any amendment you wish to make to your previous statement?"

"No," Anna said, very clearly.

Bell cleared her throat. "In that case, if you could turn over the paper in front of you...yes, that's it. This is a copy of the results received from those analyses. You'll see some data given there and, highlighted, are two relevant columns. Can you see that?"

"Yes."

Ryan's eyes scanned the document, drinking in the facts and figures.

"Listed beside case sample number LW834, which is described as low copy number DNA sampled from paperwork found inside the victim's desk, is a match to your DNA profile. As you'll see, the results indicate the likelihood of that trace sample belonging to anyone else as being somewhere in the region of one in three billion. Can you see that?"

"Yes," Anna said, and took a sip of water to ease her dry throat. "I can see it."

Lauren steepled her fingers together and eyed the beautiful, doe-eyed woman sitting across the table. In a career spanning more than thirty years, she'd come across every kind of suspect. Some looked the part, shifty and malnourished, or enormously bloated on steroids, as though they'd stepped straight off the pages of a crime novel, but others didn't. Some presented as gentle, or far too beautiful ever to have committed a heinous, bloody crime. But she knew that was psychological bias. She'd come to learn that everybody, without exception, was capable of violence in the right circumstances and how they happened to look, speak or dress made very little difference, except when faced with a jury who might feel more disposed to be lenient towards killers they found attractive.

"Can you offer any explanation as to how your DNA might have come to be on that paperwork?"

Ryan opened his mouth, but Anna was faster.

"You haven't told me what the paperwork was," she said. "While I'm sure that I have never entered the victim's home, I can't possibly comment on how my DNA could have found its way inside without knowing what that paperwork was. I need some context."

Fair enough, Lauren thought, and turned over the next page.

"If you turn over to the next document, you'll see it's a printed image taken from the scene, depicting a close-up photograph of the paperwork in question. The area where the sample was found is indicated by a small yellow marker, although there were several samples taken from the same sheaf of papers, all corresponding to your profile. Can you see that?"

"Yes."

"The paperwork appears to be a printed manuscript, entitled *The Island*."

Anna held the image up close so she could be sure, before setting it down again. "That's the manuscript I lost," she told them. "It has to be."

"Which manuscript would that be?"

She'd already related the story of how she believed Oldman had stolen and plagiarised her work, but they wanted to hear it again, presumably to see if her account changed.

"*The Island* is the original manuscript I wrote," Anna told them, for what felt like the tenth time. "I printed off a copy to take to a creative writing class, a while ago, which was being run by Lin Oldman. The idea was to garner constructive feedback before taking the plunge and self-publishing, or sending it off to an agent. Unfortunately, I left the document behind and, when I went back to retrieve it, the pages were gone. I assumed it had been tidied away by the cleaning team at the venue, or pilfered by somebody simply to read out of interest. I didn't think of it again, until I came to self-publish the book and found that Oldman had beaten me to it. Her version, *Island Mystery*, was much too close to my original to have been coincidence, and it was obvious she'd taken it and passed the story off to her new publishers as being her own work. Ryan and I sought legal advice, but we were told it would be a long, expensive and stressful process. I was still thinking about our options when I saw Oldman marketing the book at Waterstones in Newcastle, on the day she died."

DS Bell tapped a finger to the image on the page.

"We found this manuscript hidden behind a panel in Oldman's

desk," she said. "It's circumstantial, but it does tend to corroborate your account that it was stolen, and therefore needed to be hidden away."

Anna let out a long, slow breath. "So, you believe me?"

"At this stage, I'm willing to accept your account of how LCN DNA came to be on the manuscript, since we were unable to find any other full matches to your DNA profile anywhere in the victim's home, which would be highly unlikely if you'd bludgeoned her and attempted to make a speedy getaway."

Anna looked across at Ryan, relief shining from her eyes, but he knew there was another unanswered question that had the potential to cause far greater heartache.

"On the phone, you said there was another partial match," he said.

DS Bell nodded, and pulled out another image taken from the scene of the crime, this time depicting the bloodied remains of the author formerly known as Winterbottom. She considered showing it to Anna, but pity stayed her hand, and she kept its contents hidden, for now.

"Yes, that's correct," she said. "A number of skin fragments were found at the scene, as well as various fibres and other samples. In cases such as these, where the victim is found in a high traffic area of the home, we tend to find a lot of alien DNA samples which muddies the waters because many of them turn out to be legitimate members of the family or the victim's circle of friends."

Lauren paused, took a swig of tea, and then continued.

"In this case, we found a number of skin samples that registered as a partial DNA match to yours," she said. "Do you have any idea how that might have happened?"

Anna was an intelligent woman, but stress could fog even the finest mind, and hers was already struggling with the cumulative weight of the past few days.

"I—I don't know much about DNA," she admitted. "But, from what I've gleaned in the past, in order to have a partial match with another person, the two samples need to belong to family members. Is that right?"

Bell nodded, and Ryan continued to hold her hand between both of his own, waiting for her to come to the same unbelievable conclusion he had, earlier in the evening.

"That isn't possible, though," Anna said. "All of my immediate family are dead. Could the partial belong to a distant member of the family, perhaps some cousin I've never even heard of?"

Bell shook her head.

"The match denotes a close familial connection," she said. "Usually, a parent or a child."

"One of our children is three years old, and the other one hasn't been born yet," Anna said. "I presume you'd agree that rules them out. As for parents, as I say, they're both dead. The only other family I had was a sister, Megan, but she was murdered on Holy Island ten years ago."

"Yes, I remember," Lauren said. "I'm sorry for your loss; nobody deserves to die that way."

Anna took another drink of water, and made a conscious effort to push the memory to the recesses of her mind.

"The fact is, I don't see how this result could possibly be a close familial match to mine, because my family are all dead," Anna said, battling frustration. "I can only imagine there's been some sort of mistake."

At this, DC Kieron Vale spoke up for the first time. "We thought the same thing, ourselves, so we asked the lab to double check their findings," he said. "That's why it took a bit longer to come back to you with the results."

Anna looked between them, and then at Ryan, whose face remained carefully neutral.

"I don't understand," she said, shaking her head. "Do I have another brother, or a sister I know nothing about?"

Ryan turned to the other detectives in the room. "There's more you're not telling us," he said, and his tone held a warning. "You must know the sex of the person the sample belongs to, for instance."

Anna's hand began to tremble, and Ryan held her fingers gently between his own.

"Yes," DS Bell admitted. "We do. The sample contained an XY chromosome, which tells us it belongs to a male. The broader similarities between that sample and yours, Dr Taylor-Ryan, tells us it belongs to a male member of your immediate family. Do you have any brothers?"

Anna could hear the blood rushing in her ears, and her chest felt tight.

"No," she said, very softly.

"I'm sorry?"

"*No*," she repeated. "There was only my father. He didn't have any brothers, so I don't have any uncles, either."

There was a short, tense silence, in which they heard the faint ticking of a clock and the distant sound of traffic in the streets beyond.

"It couldn't have been him," Anna repeated, to herself as well as the others in the room. "He's dead and buried. He fell from Lindisfarne Castle onto the rocks and was killed, years ago."

"Unless he didn't die," Ryan said, and Anna turned to stare at him, open-mouthed. "Anna, what if your father's still alive?"

Suddenly light-headed, Anna pushed to her feet. "I'm sorry, I—I need to get some air—"

Memories raced through her mind of a man who was a chameleon;

at once playful and kind, chasing her and her sister along the sand when they were small, as well as hard and quick to anger, with hands that could inflict bruises and cuts. She remembered her mother crying softly through the bedroom wall, and smelling alcohol on her father's breath.

She remembered her father crying, when word got around about her mother's death.

He killed her, they whispered. *Andy Taylor killed his wife.*

Those poor little girls.

"Anna? *Anna!*"

Ryan moved like lightning to catch her as she fell, her mind no longer willing to remember the fear and shame she'd lived with as a child, nor the day she'd learned her father had gone, too. For all that he was, he was all they'd known, and all she and Megan had left, except each other.

For ten years, Anna thought she was the last of her family to survive.

She'd been living a lie.

Flashing images of her father at different stages in her childhood flooded her mind until she could stand no more, and she succumbed to a peaceful oblivion, held safely in the arms of the man who loved her.

CHAPTER 19

Anna slept for much of the journey home, while Ryan drove the ninety-minute distance from Durham back to Bamburgh. His hands were confident on the wheel, despite the smattering of snow that had begun to fall through the darkening night, and his eyes never wavered from the road ahead, except occasionally to glance at his sleeping wife and the child she carried.

Much had changed in the ten years since he'd first met Anna on Holy Island, where he'd sought sanctuary from the oppressive grief and relentless media coverage of his sister's killer. At first, the tiny island of Lindisfarne had delivered the peace it promised to all pilgrims who went in search of shelter there. The tide rolled in twice daily and cut the islanders off from the mainland, so theirs was a hallowed world, where religion and faith mingled with tradition, but even those like Ryan, who followed no particular dogma nor believed in any god, found a spiritual peace. For him, the island was a perfect combination of sea and sky, of space and intimacy, and of the knowledge that history was alive in the broken ruins of a priory that traced its lineage back to the Dark Ages and beyond.

For all its beauty and mysticism, there was a danger in staying too long in that hidden world. Ryan remembered a growing feeling of restlessness that came from knowing that, however much the island

and its people had welcomed him, he did not belong there. He was not one of them. Yet, despite knowing it, he remembered feeling at an impasse; stuck, inert, and unable to leave. A purgatory of sorts.

Until the murder.

When a local girl's body was found in the priory ruins, he'd come alive again. It was a sad confession, Ryan supposed, but a true one: he was born to do the work he did, which very few people had the stomach for. He could face the darkest minds, and the darkest deeds humanity could inflict, and muddle through lies and deception to wheedle out the truth, however buried it may be. With every victim he avenged, he drew a little closer to his own redemption. He didn't need any psychologist to tell him what he already knew about himself, which is that he tried to save people with a relentless energy in order to atone for being unable to save one woman who'd mattered so much.

His sister, Natalie.

Her death had been the breaking of him, and the re-making of him. Without it, he would never have gone to the island, and would never have rebuilt himself as a productive member of society. He would never have met his wife—the young Doctor Anna Taylor, as she'd been, back then. Hired as a local consultant on pagan and other early Anglo-Saxon religious practices, Anna had the additional benefit of having been born on the island, and knew its people and landscape as only an islander could.

He remembered wanting her on sight, that very first time he'd seen her standing in her father's old pub, beside her sister. She'd irritated, needled, aroused, amused and antagonised him, in all the best ways. It had been a constant education, and a humbling experience. When her sister was murdered, he and Anna found they had something else in common, both having lost their only sibling, but it wasn't something to toast over dinner.

Ryan remembered everything as if it happened yesterday.

He thought of Anna's father, Andrew Taylor, and the role he'd played within a cult known as 'The Circle'. Somewhere between freemasonry and Satanism, its ethos was a muddle of beliefs, cobbled together to provide a veneer of legitimacy. Dogma was crucial to any faith-based organisation, and The Circle was no different. For those who needed ritual in order to be loyal, its leaders provided that in spades. For those who needed a bit of dinner theatre, a few masks and cloaks, a bit of chanting...well, they'd provided some of that, too. But, make no mistake, the enterprise was all about money and power, as so many things were. God or Satan had nothing to do with it.

Andy Taylor died years before Ryan's arrival on the island, a supposed suicide or accidental fall, so everybody thought. Later, they learned that the order had been given from within to end his tenure as The Circle's leader, on a permanent basis, because others within the order deemed him too volatile and his domestic behaviour attracted unwanted attention. His position had been usurped by the island's good doctor, Stephen Walker, whose arrogance blinded him to the fact that he, too, could be usurped just as easily and for much the same reasons. Others had followed Walker and been brought to justice—like their former Detective Chief Superintendent, Arthur Gregson—while others had succumbed to the same grisly fate as their predecessors.

Nobody had questioned Andrew Taylor's death; the records were in place, and a headstone marked the spot where his body had been laid, in the little graveyard on the island. Anna chose not to visit, for very good reasons, and his memory had slipped into the distant past, along with his many misdeeds. But, if Ryan knew one thing, it was that a ghost couldn't leave DNA at a crime scene, nor inflict a series of killing blows upon a middle-aged author of second-rate mystery novels.

The more interesting question was not whether Andrew Taylor still lived, nor whether he'd killed Lin Oldman.

It was *why*.

If Anna's father had spent nearly twenty years as a dead man, what would motivate him to break his cover? What had Lin Oldman done that warranted such a risky and unusual step?

They were questions he meant to find out.

Ryan looked back at his wife, who was curled uncomfortably in the passenger seat, and pulled slowly into the driveway of their home so as not to wake her. A light burned in the porch to guide their way, and he saw a warm light in his mother's bedroom to let him know she was still awake, if they should need her. He smiled, and wondered if he and his mother would have become so close, had it not been for the gentle influence of the woman beside him.

"Anna?" he said, and placed a hand on her arm. "We're home, darling."

She didn't stir, so he unfolded himself from the car and crunched through the light sprinkling of snow covering the gravel at his feet, his pathway guided by bright, eerie white moonlight. He reached inside the car to unhook her seatbelt and then lifted his wife into his arms with infinite care. Her eyelids fluttered open for a second, she smiled at him, and then her head flopped back against his chest as physical and mental exhaustion took over.

"I've got you," he said, and brushed a kiss over her lips. "I won't let go."

With that, he knocked the passenger door shut with a flick of his hip, then carried his wife inside the house and up to bed. There, he undressed her with swift, gentle movements, and tucked her beneath the warm blankets.

"Ryan?" she mumbled into the darkness.

"Yes?"

"Thank you," she whispered.

He smiled, and kissed her again.

"Sleep now, darling. Sleep for as long as you need."

He waited a while longer, until he was sure she was in a deep sleep, and then made his way back downstairs to begin writing the e-mails he needed to draft to get things in motion for the next day's work.

Exhuming bodies was nothing if not a bureaucratic nightmare.

But first, *coffee*.

CHAPTER 20

The next morning

Frank Phillips yawned hugely, and tugged at his dark grey slacks, the bottoms of which were falling down to reveal more of his arse crack than was decent, even by his standards. They were several years old, and a bit roomier in the backside department now that he'd managed to lose a bit of weight during the intervening time.

"Remind me to buy you a belt, next Christmas."

Phillips turned to face Ryan, who stood beside him as they waited for a couple of takeaway coffees outside the Royal Victoria Infirmary, in the centre of Newcastle.

"I'll need it, since I'm skippin' so many breakfasts, these days," he said. "God only knows what time you knocked me out of bed this mornin'."

Ryan paid the vendor, handed Frank a large, milky latte and downed a couple of swigs of his own strong ristretto before answering.

"Sorry, Frank," he said, and they began walking towards the hospital entrance and, beyond it, the bright lights of the mortuary. "To be honest, I didn't manage to get much sleep last night, so I gave up in the end. I should try to remember that normal people like to get a solid eight hours, if they can."

Phillips licked the foam from his lips and nudged his friend with an elbow. "Howay, man, I don't mind, really," he said. "I'm more concerned about you losin' sleep. It's been a while since you had insomnia, lad. All this worry over Anna knockin' you out of whack? You never told me what happened at the station, yesterday. How did it go?"

Ryan knocked back the rest of his coffee while he thought of where to begin. "The DNA they found belonging to Anna could be explained easily enough," he said. "It was all over the manuscript she lost—the one Lin Oldman stole from the Lit & Phil."

He referred to the Literary and Philosophical Society of Newcastle, where Anna had attended the infamous creative writing session.

"We offered to hand over Anna's computer, so they can check the master file and the date stamp, to prove it was her work. They've already checked her account against the CCTV footage in the multi-storey car park and at the Laing Art Gallery, both of which confirm she was where she says she was, at the times she told them."

Phillips was relieved to hear it. "If they've accepted her explanation of how her DNA came to be on the manuscript, surely that's the end of it?"

"I'm afraid it's just the beginning."

"What d'you mean?"

"Remember, I told you they also found a partial sample matching her DNA profile? Well, that was a close familial match."

Phillips was a quick study. "She doesn't have any family left, does she? Apart from you and the kids, o' course," he added swiftly. "Biological family, I mean?"

Ryan shook his head. "Not that we know of," he replied. "The results have been checked, and checked again for any error, but the facts are there, in black and white. The partial sample belongs to a male member of Anna's immediate biological family."

"*Male?*" Phillips repeated, in confusion. "But Anna doesn't have any brothers or cousins, does she?"

"No," Ryan said, and cut to the chase. "Besides, the DNA profile was so close to hers, it could only be paternal. I think her father's still alive, Frank."

There was a short pause, while Phillips took a thoughtful sip of his own coffee, seeming entirely nonplussed by the bombshell that had just dropped.

"Reet," he declared, matter-of-factly. "I s'pose you'll be wantin' to exhume whichever poor soul is lyin' in Andy Taylor's grave?"

"Yes."

"And you'll be wantin' to know how the evil old bugger managed to fool everyone into thinkin' he was dead?"

"Mm hm," Ryan said, blowing on his hands as they rounded the corner into the main forecourt outside the hospital's entrance.

"Lastly, you'll be wantin' to find out why Andy Taylor likely killed Lin Oldman, and what the connection is between them?"

"If it isn't too much trouble."

"Don't ask for much, do you?"

Ryan gave him a sideways glance. "We're still working the Pearson case, as well," he said, with a bland smile. "Not forgetting any other serious crimes that happen to come in during the next few days."

"Oh, *well*, we'd better have it all done and dusted by dinnertime," Frank said, with an airy wave of his hand. "What could possibly go wrong?"

"Don't tempt Fate," Ryan warned. "Knowing our luck, absolutely everything could go wrong."

"Speakin' o' which, what d' you make of Charlie bein' caught up with that wrongun, Alexei Whatshisface?"

"Rachmaninov," Ryan said. "I think she must have been frightened for three solid years, which is heartbreaking."

Frank's paternal instincts reared up, with a vengeance. "He's a reet nasty piece of work," he growled. "And her bein' such a canny lass, n'all. Nobody deserves all that worry, but especially not when they're just a lovely, hardworkin' body like Charlie."

"What people do or don't deserve never plays into these things," Ryan said quietly. "Life isn't fair, otherwise we'd be out of a job."

Phillips inclined his head.

"Jack's suggested a meeting, out of hours, to discuss the best way forward," Ryan continued. "After work, at Charlie's place."

Phillips nodded. "Samantha's got some party or other with her ridin' friends, down at the Pony Club," he said, with the air of a man who considered the whole 'horsey' world an alien planet. "She's stayin' over at her mate's house, afterwards, so me and Denise will both be there for Charlie. Solidarity, and all that."

Ryan expected nothing less.

"What about your Anna? You don't need to come to the meetin' if she needs you with her, lad. We can update you, later."

Ryan thought of how his wife had looked when he'd left her, early that morning. He knew there were further conversations to be had, and investigating to do, but his overriding concern was to protect her from the past for as long as possible. On the other hand, there was work to be done, and nothing was ever solved by burying their heads in the sand.

"I'll speak to her and see how things are," he decided. "She isn't due back to work at the university until the first week of January, and she can always take some time off, if she needs it. As for this stuff with her father, there's a lot she hasn't told me about her earlier life, because it was too painful to repeat. I don't want to cause her any stress, if I can help it—especially, since we can't be absolutely sure whether he's alive or dead, at this stage."

Phillips thought back to when his own wife had been at her most vulnerable, during the long recovery that followed a traumatic time at the mercy of a man who'd kidnapped her and who might have killed her. Denise bore scars from those days, mental and physical, and she'd never be 'whole' in the same way again. That being said, he considered her an even stronger woman than she was before the attack, and all the more so for having been responsible for her own escape. Denise MacKenzie was not a woman who needed to be 'saved', and neither was Anna.

"It's just my penny-worth," he said, treading very carefully. "First of all, I'm not forgettin' that Anna's expectin' a bairn, or that she might be feelin' more sensitive than usual. Still, it strikes me that she's made of tough stuff, or, more to the point, she's *made* herself tough. I don't mean she's *hard*," he added quickly. "There's nobody that's gentler or more loving than Anna. What I mean is, she's walked through all kinds of fire and survived the ordeal. Aye, she's had a few burns, but she's tougher because of them. She doesn't suffer fools, gladly—apart from you, obviously."

"Har har," Ryan said. "Very droll."

"But true," Phillips said, and laughed his infectious laugh. "In all seriousness, there's a time for protectin' the people you love, and a time for empowerin' them. Just remember to respect the difference, when the time comes."

There were few people in Ryan's life whose advice he trusted, and even fewer whose advice he would actually follow, but Frank Phillips happened to be one of them. His wisdom was sound, because they'd come to learn that demons could only be slain by facing them, head on; otherwise, they had a nasty habit of lingering in the depths of the mind, living forever like a parasite, feeding on a person's soul. If Anna was ever truly to slay the memory of her father's cruelty, or mourn the man he once had the potential to be, she needed to face him if he was alive and deal with him in a way she was unable to do while he was supposedly dead. Likewise, to overcome the suspicion that remained like a dark cloud over their heads, she needed to find the person who had truly killed Lin Oldman, so her reputation would be free of any blemish. It didn't matter to Ryan, nor to Anna's friends, because they knew who she was, at heart; nonetheless, it mattered to her, because a good reputation was one thing that you simply couldn't afford to lose. Therefore, Frank was right: Anna needed to fight for her own vindication, as a matter of pride.

"I'll remember," he said, toasting his empty coffee cup. "Thanks, Frank."

"Don't mention it," came the cheery reply. "Have we got time for—"

"Nope."

"It'll only take a minute—"

"*Nein*."

"But—"

"*Non*. You're not stopping for a sausage and egg roll," Ryan said, having also spotted the sign beside the hospital canteen advertising breakfast baps. "Nyet. Nei. Nem."

"*Nem*?"

"It's 'no' in Hungarian," Ryan snapped. "Besides, you know it's never a good idea to eat before we go down to the mortuary."

"It's a risk," Frank agreed. "But one I'm willing to take."

"Well, I'm not," Ryan countered. "Look, we can stop for one on the way back. Okay?"

"Fine," Frank said, and tried to sound as though it wasn't the outcome he'd hoped for, all along. "I s'pose I can wait."

He gave an elaborate *tut*, and then immediately wondered if he'd overplayed his hand, because Ryan shot him a suspicious glare.

"Which body are we here to look at, anyhow—aside from Jeff Pinter's bony arse, that is?" Frank asked, changing the subject quickly.

"It's more accurate to say body *parts*," Ryan said, referring to what was left of the late Terry Pearson Jr. "I'd also like to have a word about his father, Terence, to find out whether anything flagged that might suggest foul play was involved in his demise. I also want to see who examined Andrew Taylor's body, back in the early noughties, and which coroner signed things off for burial."

Frank cast his mind back. "Pinter was workin' as a police pathologist, back then, but he wasn't Head of Pathology," he said. "If we're talking fifteen or more years ago, his boss would've been a bloke called Simon Winslet."

Ryan recalled seeing his name on a number of old pathology reports, but Winslet must have retired shortly before he joined Northumbria from the Metropolitan Police, because Jeffrey Pinter was the only Senior Pathologist he'd ever had dealings with.

"Let's see what Pinter can tell us," he said, and came to an abrupt stop outside the double metal doors leading into the mortuary. "Oh, not again."

"What, now?" Phillips asked, looking around the empty corridor for the source of annoyance. "Did you forget something?"

"The bloody code," Ryan muttered, and gestured to the keypad that required a four-digit code before allowing them to enter. "Pinter changes it every couple of months, and I'd only just memorised the last one."

The frequency with which the pathologist thought it necessary to change the security code begged the question of what a thief could possibly want to steal, and there had certainly been some *dire* cases of individuals taking other things from the dead…Ryan shuddered, decided against any further speculation of *that* nature, and dragged his mind back to code-breaking.

"Let's think about this, logically," Frank said, after a few seconds ticked by. "Did he give you the new code in an e-mail?"

"Nope," Ryan said, succinctly. "He refuses to write it down, in case the system is hacked."

"Who the *chuff* would want to hack any of his e-mails?" Frank blustered.

"Grave robbers? Anatomy nerds? Witches? Warlocks? Wannabe serial killers?"

"Crime writers, more like," Frank said, darkly.

"You've just jogged my memory!"

"Eh?"

"Crime writers, you said. Pinter changed his usual theme from the dates well-known musicians died, to the dates well-known authors died," Ryan explained. "Now, what's he been reading, lately?"

"The lonely-hearts column in *The Journal*?"

Ryan grinned. "In this case, I'm pretty sure he was poring over some old classic, but I can't remember whether it was from the eighteenth or nineteenth century."

"A real page-turner, then?"

Ryan pinched the bridge of his nose and then cried out, much as Isaac Newton might have done when the apple fell upon his head.

"Mary Shelley!"

"Frankenstein? Should've guessed," Frank said, folding his arms. "Trust Jeff to pick a book where some crackpot stitches body parts together to make a monster-man."

"The question is, in which year did Mary Shelley die," Ryan said, and gave up trying to guess at a number he simply didn't know.

"1851," Frank said, casually.

"Thanks, I wasn't—" Ryan stopped mid-sentence and turned to his friend in shock. "How in the name of Caesar's Ghost do you know the year Mary Shelley died, when you can barely remember what happened last week?"

"I happen to have a first-rate memory for names and dates," Frank said. "I also happened to text Jeff to ask the pin code while you were havin' an existential crisis, and he just texted me back."

Ryan gave him a solid punch on the arm, which was met with another peal of Frank's trademark laughter.

"You know what that was, lad?"

"What?"

"Thinkin' outside the box," Frank said, and tapped the side of his temple.

"You'll need to think your way out of a cold storage box, if you keep this up," Ryan said, and cattle-prodded his friend through the door.

CHAPTER 21

Detective Sergeant Lauren Bell scrubbed the sleep from her eyes and thought wistfully of mince pies and *Downton Abbey* Christmas Specials. She was sure there was a time when she'd enjoyed such things, but the business of murder, especially *celebrity* murder, didn't conform to annual calendar events. If anything, crime statistics tended to show that people grew even more rowdy and aggressive than usual during the festive season, probably because there was a surplus of alcohol to be had. Then again, it might be due to a surplus of period dramas, which, she supposed, weren't everybody's cup of tea.

As for the Jane Austen festival she attended every year, in full Regency costume?

That, she would take to her grave.

"Boss?"

Lauren's heart gave a solid thump against her chest because, for a moment, she thought she'd spoken the words aloud.

"What is it, Vale?"

Her detective constable pulled up one of the cheap plastic desk chairs and plonked himself down with slightly more force than he'd intended, which caused it to roll a few feet away, on wobbly castors. Swearing, he dug the heels of his shoes into the ragged carpet tile floor and used them to drag himself back towards her.

"Sometimes, I think you're just too smooth for the likes of us," Lauren said, with a half-smile.

"Respectfully, Guv…Mr Bean would be too smooth for the likes of you," he said, and gave her a cheeky wink which, after seven years of working together, she decided to allow.

"Considering the number of frogs I've dated, recently, I'd take Mr Bean at this point," she muttered.

"Have you tried Tinder?"

"How desperate do you think I am?" she demanded. "And yes, of course I have. It's a cesspit of catfishing grandads."

Kieron laughed with genuine mirth.

"Anyway, enough about my non-existent love life," Lauren said. "What have you got for me?"

"Right y' are," he said, all business now. "As you know, Oldman lived in a flat in a converted Victorian villa here in Durham, just off South Street. Nice area, but the place itself was pretty run down."

"I remember," she said, thinking back to their walk-through of the crime scene. "What about it?"

"There's a block of modern flats next door, with some off-street parking outside," he reminded her. "There isn't any working CCTV outside, but one of the tenants who leases a ground floor flat set up a little camera in his window, facing where he usually parks his scooter on the street outside. As it turns out, the parking spot covers the shared entrance to Oldman's place in the camera field."

"Handy," Lauren remarked.

"Exactly," Kieron said. "Anyhow, the tenant's a university lecturer, so he goes by the book—no pun intended."

"Every kind of pun was intended."

He grinned. "The bloke was happy to help any way he could, and he's already sent over the footage from the relevant period. Fast forward to shortly after five o'clock, which is when we believe Oldman was killed, and you can see a man in his sixties, or maybe early seventies, exiting the building at 17:13."

He handed her a still taken from the footage, which he'd asked their digital forensics team to enhance as far as possible.

"Not bad work," she said. "But his face is in profile, which doesn't help much. His clothing is dark and ordinary, the bottom of his face covered in a scarf and the rest of him is covered in a long winter coat, which might've concealed all sorts underneath. Height..."

She cocked her head to the side and made an educated guess.

"Must be somewhere between five-eleven and six-two, would you say?"

"Definitely taller than average," he agreed.

"That's useful," she said. "But you could be completely wrong about the age."

"When I watched the full video footage, there was something about his gait that gave an impression of the guy being a bit older."

"His gait?"

"Yeah, you know, he kinda hunched a bit," Kieron said, with the airiness of a young man who believed himself immortal. "Either that, or he had a limp."

"Was his name Quasimodo?"

Kieron looked at her uncomprehendingly, and Lauren felt every one of her forty-three years.

"Never mind. Okay, well that gives us something to work with," she said, and felt her spirits rise at the prospect of at least one other suspect who *wasn't* the wife of a fellow murder detective, even if he might turn out to be her family member. They'd cross that bridge if and when they came to it.

"Did the footage capture his entry time, as well?" she wondered.

"Unfortunately, the camera runs on a WiFi connection, and the signal went down for about twenty minutes while the electrics were turned off during some building maintenance works. Bad luck for us, because that's probably when our perp arrived."

"At first glance, Oldman's building and the neighbouring ones don't appear to have any camera coverage at all," Lauren observed. "If this man is who we think he is, then we know he was confident enough to exit using the front door. That kind of confidence is hard to come by, usually, after killing someone in cold blood. He may have believed nobody would clock him coming or going because he'd already cased the joint and come to the inaccurate conclusion there were no cameras in the vicinity. The idea of tiny home cameras sitting in windows might not have occurred to him."

"Which further supports my theory that we're looking for someone eld—"

"Careful," Lauren said, mildly. "*Careful.*"

"—someone who, ah...isn't as young as they used to be. That's what I mean. You know, someone who might not know about the kind of CCTV technology you can buy nowadays, for a fraction of what it once cost, back in the 1930s, or whatever."

"You're suggesting the man in this image is in his nineties?"

"No, but...I dunno. He's old, isn't he?"

Lauren treated Vale to a fulminating glare.

"Tell me again how you passed your detective's exam?"

"I shagged the examiner," Kieron replied, which teased another laugh from her lips, before she realised he could be telling the truth, for all she knew.

Studying his face for any clues, and finding none, she decided to pretend she hadn't heard that.

"Back to our perp, our next task is to trace his movements after leaving Oldman's house," she said.

"Already made a start on that," Kieron said, and pulled out a notebook full of his scrawled handwriting.

"Christ, that looks like a book of hieroglyphics," she said. "How do you decipher your own writing?"

"What's wrong with it?"

"Are you kidding? It looks like a spider landed in some ink and then crawled across the page."

"Blame technology again," he said. "I hardly need to write anything by hand, these days."

She grunted. "Okay, tell me what you've got, if you can still read, that is."

He made a show of holding the notepad up to his nose, then away again.

"It seems the perp left Oldman's house and turned left, making his way to the junction of Crossgate," Kieron said. "CCTV outside a Thai restaurant on the corner caught him turning right towards North Road. At that point, he could have crossed the Silver Street bridge into the centre of town, but we got lucky with another bit of footage caught on a camera outside Greggs' bakery, which is in the opposite direction. Several retailers and cafes captured his progress as he headed north-west along North Road, but that's as far as we've managed to get."

"Pretty good progress," she said, and brought up a map of the city on her phone. "Looking at his options, there's at least one multi-storey car park along Millburngate, so he might have parked there and returned to collect his car."

"I've requested the footage from Riverwalk Car Park," Kieron told her. "I'll let you know when it comes through."

"Good. Now, if he didn't turn along Millburngate, he might have continued along North Road in the direction of the train station."

"My thinking, too," he said. "I've also requested footage from the station, on the off chance."

"Great. Let's see what comes back."

Lauren paused, gnawing on her cheek.

"You thinkin' what I'm thinkin'?" he asked.

"That depends. Are you thinking about a bubble bath followed by the *Strictly* Christmas special, on catch-up?"

"Er, not quite." Kieron laughed. "I was thinking, we should assume the perp *was* heading for the train station."

Lauren smiled because, of course, she'd been thinking the same thing.

"What makes you say that, bonny lad?"

"If I'm right about us looking for an older perp—not *infirm* because he's clearly capable of wielding a murder weapon—but, given the way he walks, somebody who isn't as light on their feet as they used to be? Well, maybe he wouldn't be much of a driver."

"I agree," she said. "We can't rule out any possibility, but, until we're faced with evidence to the contrary, let's assume our perp caught a train. Where was the last sighting of him?"

"Outside a chicken shop on North Road," he said. "The image is poor quality, but it fits the same profile as the man captured on the camera outside Oldman's place."

"Good enough, for now," she said. "Focus on trains due to leave Durham station around that timescale, in either direction."

"Will do," he said, and scrawled another illegible note. "Anything else?"

"Yeah," she said, rising to her feet and stretching her arms above her head. "Don't pretend you didn't watch the *Strictly* Christmas Special."

Kieron grinned and folded his hands behind his head, enjoying the banter that flowed easily between them. Suddenly, a thought came to him out of the blue.

Lauren Bell was a good-looking woman.

She was intelligent, too, and made him laugh.

Yes, she was his boss; and yes, she busted his chops every now and then, but…still.

She was *hot*.

"You've seen right through me," he said, and there was a note to his voice that hadn't been there before. "Hey, d'you think—"

"Nope."

"Wh—you don't know what I'm going to ask, yet."

Lauren surveyed her constable with a knowing eye. Kieron was only six years younger than herself but, to a woman with old-fashioned ideals, it might have been a lifetime. He was younger, full of cocksure arrogance which she didn't mind, so long as he kept it within reasonable boundaries and did the job well. He'd been sensible enough to keep any philandering out of the workplace, so far as she knew, and that was precisely how she intended to keep it.

"I know exactly what you were going to ask," she said, with a slight shake of her head. "I'm a trained reader of people, remember? Now, stop fantasising about things above your pay grade, and get back to work."

"Yes, ma'am," he said, smiling slowly.

To her eternal shame, Lauren felt herself respond to that look, that *tone*, and the promise in his eyes.

Obviously, it was time to give the catfish on Tinder another chance.

CHAPTER 22

When Ryan and Phillips entered the city's mortuary, in the bowels of the Royal Victoria Infirmary, the first thing that assailed them was not the overpowering stench of chemicals, nor the sight of a naked cadaver being cut open by one of the technicians.

It was Ricky Martin.

His voice blared out around all four walls of the clinical space, regaling them about his love being into superstition, which led him to have a premonition. Ryan was about to pass comment about the pathologist's ever-declining taste in music, but, catching sight of Phillips' hips jiggling beneath a visitor's lab coat, decided he could be in the minority. When Jeff Pinter appeared from around the edge of an immersion tank and proceeded to dance his way over to them, Ryan decided he was surrounded.

"Morning!" Pinter sang out. "Great to see the pair of you! All rested after the Christmas break, I hope?"

Ryan and Phillips looked at one another, then back at Pinter, because there was something very, very wrong with the picture they were seeing. To begin with, his usual 'pastier than pasteurised milk' skin no longer rivalled the whitewashed walls, being a few shades darker, with a sprinkling of freckles to boot. Admittedly, it only elevated his pallor from a deathly grey to a creamy, off-white, but it was a noticeable improvement. Furthermore, he appeared to be wearing trendy fashion trainers on his feet, in a colourful medley of white, blue and red. To their dismay, his usual long chinos had been replaced by a pair of acid wash jeans, rolled up at the ankles, and his grey hair had been re-styled into some form of quiff. Upon closer inspection, he may have had a bit of Botox in his forehead, too, because he was looking noticeably *fresher* than usual.

"You look…different," Ryan said, suspiciously. "Been on holiday?"

"How did you guess?"

"You look like you've actually been in the sun, and we've not had too much of that around here, lately," Phillips said. "Where did you jet off to, then? Must've been a flyin' visit!"

The pathologist had been as busy as they had, dealing with the bodies coming in and out of his mortuary in a constant stream. Making time for any kind of holiday was an achievement.

"I managed to whizz off to Sharm el Sheik for four nights," he said. "Did me the power of good, too."

Phillips waggled a finger. "Ah, now, don't hold out on us, Jeff. You had yourself a little holiday romance, didn't you?"

"Now you mention it, I suppose I did."

His face became even more smug than before, if that was possible.

Ryan consulted the time and decided they could spend another two minutes quizzing the good doctor, before they got down to the real business of the day.

"Come on then," he declared, sticking his hands in the pockets of his jeans. "Spill the beans."

"All right," Pinter said, as though his arm had been twisted. "Her stage name's Amrita, and she was the belly dancer at the hotel."

Phillips' eyebrows shot into his hairline. "The *belly dancer?*" he repeated.

"Exactly! There was a competition, one night, and we all had to shake our hips a bit," he said. "Rita—that's what her friends and family call her, because she's actually from Leeds—well, she pulled me up to take part in a demonstration. I've never felt so *liberated*."

"Aye, it's like that, the first time you take to the stage," Frank said, with the sage wisdom of one who had often helped himself to the mic down at Paddy McGee's Irish Bar, whether it happened to be Open Mic Night or not.

"I lost myself in the music, and, the next thing I knew, Rita and I were having dinner together. The day after that, we went snorkelling and…you know, one thing led to another."

"You old hound dawg," Frank said, and gave him a slap on the shoulder which held enough force to knock the pathologist out of his trainers.

"The thing is chaps…*I'm married*!"

They stared at his left hand, which now sported a shiny gold wedding ring.

"Wha—" Frank began.

"Uh—" Ryan said.

"I know it's all a bit sudden," Pinter said. "But, when you know, you just *know*."

He grinned like a madman, the grooved lines of his face softening from something ordinary to something joyful and, dared they say it, something *young*.

"Well," Ryan said, recovering himself. "We're very happy for you. Aren't we, Frank? *Frank*!"

He nudged his sergeant, who continued to stare at the other man as though he'd grown two heads.

"Eh? Oh, aye. Aye! O' course, happy for you, lad," he said. "Are you goin' to introduce us to your new wife, then?"

"Love to, but she's still in Egypt," he said. "She's handed in her notice at the hotel, but she has to finish the Christmas season, so she'll be moving over in the New Year."

He grinned like a lunatic.

"If you think this gets you out of a proper stag do, you've got another thing comin'," Phillips warned him.

If possible, Pinter looked even more delighted. "I'll take what's coming to me," he said.

"To be honest, Jeff, and no offence intended, but I still don't know how you managed to pull a belly-dancer," Frank said.

"That can wait," Ryan said, cutting off another lengthy discussion. "Tell us whether Terence Pearson Senior was murdered."

"I'm not the one to make that determination," Pinter reminded him, unnecessarily. "But I can give you the facts, and you can use your good judgment. Come on through to my office and I'll show you the file."

They followed him through another security door and down a short corridor. It led to a series of private examination rooms, as well as a couple of small offices belonging to the senior pathologist and his second in command.

"Excuse the mess," he said, as they entered an office that was entirely free of clutter. "Have a seat, while I call up the file."

They settled themselves and, soon enough, Pinter swung around from his computer screen.

"Here we are," he said. "Terence Pearson, deceased…yes, end of October. He was in hospital for four days prior to death…" He paused to remind himself of the circumstances, and made a sucking noise with his teeth which grated on their frayed nerves. "Yep, yep…yep. Okay, so we've got a classic case of chronic liver disease, leading to a bad case of pneumonia which, in turn, was a major contributing factor to his death owing to widespread inflammation and fluid on the lungs. Essentially, respiratory failure combined with septic shock, but, to the layperson, you might as well say he drank himself to death and the rest followed as a foregone conclusion."

"What about the autopsy," Ryan said. "Did you find anything untoward?"

Pinter shook his head. "In short…no. I wasn't the one to complete this gentleman's autopsy, but one of my senior technicians, Donna, wrote up the report and her findings are cut and dried. Organ depletion and disease consistent with long-term alcohol abuse, compounded by short-term pneumonia. Excess fluid on the lungs, as I've said. Poor diet, in general, but decent muscle and bone mass, considering his age and the other relevant factors."

"What about toxicology?" Ryan prompted. "All clear?"

"In a manner of speaking," Pinter said, running his eye over the data, once again. "There's nothing sinister, at first glance. We're looking at a man who likely abused steroids, since there was a small quantity still swimming around in his bloodstream postmortem—"

"Don't they have some serious side effects?" Frank queried, having seen plenty of young men down at Buddles with the gleaming, top-heavy look of those accustomed to abusing that short-term fix.

"Of course," Pinter said. "Impotence, heightened aggression, long-term weakening of the heart, to name a few. However, when we looked at Terence Pearson's heart, we found it in a state entirely consistent with his lifestyle, and the impact of septic shock following pneumonia, which was recorded as the major contributing factor. To put it another way, steroids might kill someone slowly, in a long-term, cumulative fashion, but that would be their own daily choice. Now, if anybody wanted to see off Terence Pearson by way of premediated murder, there would be a hundred other more reliable and effective ways to do that."

Phillips tugged at his lower lip, thoughtfully. All the talk of steroids reminded him of the boxing gym which, in turn, reminded him that he'd meant to go back to Buddles to speak to his friend and informant, Harry. What with one thing and another, he hadn't found the time.

"There's nothing else that gives rise for concern in his toxicology report," Pinter carried on. "Terence was on a cocktail of hospital-prescribed drugs in the days before his death, all of which were properly recorded and within appropriate parameters. His blood tests are consistent with all of that. There's an elevated measure of alcohol, as you'd expect and, as for anything else that shouldn't be there…"

Pinter turned to them both with a shrug.

"Nothing whatsoever."

Ryan leaned back, looked at Frank, then nodded. "In which case, we work on the basis that Terence Pearson Senior died in accordance with the official record," he said.

"I would have offered to conduct a second postmortem, but I understand the body was cremated?"

"Mm," Ryan said, and found that highly convenient.

Then again, it was an occupational hazard to view with suspicion entirely normal decisions such as whether to have the body of a loved one cremated or buried; the fact that the Pearson family had chosen to have his ashes interred in a porcelain jar on Patricia's mantelpiece didn't necessarily mean anything beyond the fact she preferred to have him in the room with her, in some form or another.

"Let's strike his death off the 'suspicious' list, for now," Ryan said. "What about his son, Terry Junior?"

"Imagine callin' your bairn Terence, in this day an' age," Frank put in. "If I'd had a son, I'd never have inflicted the lad with 'Frank'. It's from another era."

"Your flat cap's from another era," Ryan said, looking pointedly at the soft hat stuffed inside Phillips' overcoat pocket, an olive green, tweed affair that might have come straight off the pages of *Tatler* or *Country Life*.

"Well, if anyone's to blame for this cap, it's *you*," Frank said.

"How d'you work that one out?"

"Simple. I'd never have got the notion to start wearin' one of these if I hadn't moved out to the blasted countryside, which you not only encouraged but facilitated," Frank said, triumphantly. "Everywhere I look, there's someone in a waxed jacket, or a pair o' ridin' boots. And, if I have to see another clapped out, old Defender driven by some batty old bird in a floppy hat—"

"What you're really saying is, you've found your people," Pinter said, in a rare move to join in their byplay. "Admit it, Frank. You've never been more at home."

Phillips thought of mornings looking out of his kitchen window at misty hillsides, or watching birds of prey swoop down in the twilight of dawn to nab an unsuspecting field mouse. He thought of friendly neighbours, of peaceful dark skies filled with stars, of sitting with Denise beside roaring fires and of Samantha riding her horse like the wind. It was a life he'd never believed possible, and he'd taken to it like a duck to water.

"Can I help it, if I wear herringbone blazers with the best o' them?" he said, affably. "As for me wearin' a flat cap, *you're* one to talk!"

Ryan pointed a finger at himself. "Me?"

"Aye, little Lord Fauntleroy—you! I bet you've got a dozen o' these back at your country pile, down in Devon."

That was very likely to be true, Ryan thought, with a grimace.

"Exactly," he parried. "They're hundreds of miles away."

"Much as I'm enjoying this," Pinter said, in the tone of a 1920s schoolmaster. "Can I drag us back to Terry Pearson's mutilated corpse?"

"I think I'd rather talk about flat caps," Frank muttered.

CHAPTER 23

Anna no longer drove a racing-green Mini, but she remembered a time when that little car had taken her everywhere, transporting her to sites all over the North East as she'd accumulated the knowledge to complete her doctorate, and then the many articles she'd published on early religious practices in her home region, mostly before the advent of Christianity. A decade ago, she'd considered herself an educated, self-sufficient woman, but, with the benefit of hindsight, she knew now that her world had been a small one. She'd kept a limited circle of friends and every element of her life had been planned, controlled, contained and, above all else, *predictable*, because that was how she liked it.

She'd been alive, but she hadn't really been *living*.

The possibility of a different kind of life had come the day she'd met Ryan, who broke down the metaphorical walls of protection she'd built, one crisp, sunny day in December, almost ten years ago to the day. She remembered the exact moment and the feeling, which she hadn't understood at the time, of coming face to face with her soulmate, if she believed in such a thing. He made her feel safe and secure, as though she was coming home whenever they were together. At the same time, he made her feel uncomfortable—in the very *best* ways. Everything changed, the day Ryan walked into The Jolly Fisherman, the pub where her late sister worked and which her father had once owned. By the time Ryan stepped into the bar area, her father was believed to be long dead, buried in the island's cemetery, and the cosy little pub had seen some investment from its new owner, Bill Tilson, a former friend of the family.

Anna would never forget the first time she'd seen Ryan, his tall frame silhouetted against the brilliance of the winter sun, lending his black hair a blueish sheen as he'd stepped into the quiet bar. His physicality had seemed ethereal, too perfect to belong to a living person, and she was glad that he'd disabused her of any unrealistic ideals she might have had on that score, as they'd come to know one another better. It would have been very hard to live with a paragon; someone too righteous ever to make mistakes. It was more than enough for her to know that the man she loved tried his *best*. He did what he considered to be right, and held himself accountable for the decisions he made, whether or not history proved them to have been the right ones. Above all else, she loved his integrity. Her only other male model had possessed very little of that priceless commodity, and the shortfall had been painfully apparent in every aspect of Andy Taylor's life. Though it upset her to think it, let alone to say it aloud, she'd felt relief when she'd been told of her father's passing, as though a great, heavy weight had been untethered, and her heart could beat freely and lightly without his spectre looming large over their lives.

Finding out that there was now a possibility of him being alive, somewhere out there in the world, was almost too much to imagine, so great was the sense of cognitive dissonance. Her mind had gone through several cycles of denial, in which she'd told herself the DNA results given to her by Durham CID were contaminated or inaccurate. If not, then perhaps some nefarious person had switched her father's DNA record with another person's, so they might avoid detection and pin the blame for Lin Oldman's murder on a dead man. Besides, even if her father *was* alive—and that was a big 'if'—what could he possibly have to do with Lin Oldman?

Andrew Taylor had been a prolific reader, but not of commercial fiction. He preferred classical texts or memoirs from great warriors and statesmen of the past, which took on new meaning in light of the other, secret life he'd been leading. Obviously, he'd had pretensions to the same echelon as Churchill, though the mark he made on society was not one they'd chronicle or teach children to revere in their history lessons at school. Her father had been a book snob, to tell the truth, and the irony of that hadn't been lost on her, either. He hadn't given much thought about raising his hands to the women in his life, nor about hurting many others, but he considered himself *much* too good to read anything so enjoyable as a mystery novel…

Her mind swirling with disturbing memories, Anna slowed the car as she reached the head of the causeway, which had opened to traffic around half an hour before. The tides had rolled back towards the sea, revealing a long, narrow road through the water and along the dunes. Visitors flocked daily to breathe in the spiritual peace of this place but, for her, the island carried too many memories ever to be called 'peaceful'. It was a place of secrets and lies, of good and evil, of light and shade, just like anywhere else.

It was still beautiful.

She pulled the car away from the road and found a parking space near the causeway, where she checked the time on her watch.

Two-thirty.

Not long, now.

She looked out across the Pilgrim's Way, a long walking route which had, for centuries, attracted those seeking to follow a journey through the fields and glades of Northumberland and across the water separating the island from the mainland. Barefoot, they walked over the sand, following a series of tall posts to guide their way to safety, until they reached the shoreline on the other side and, beyond that, the sanctuary of the Priory, now in ruins but no less commanding because of it.

Lost in thought, her mind far away in the mists of time, she barely noticed the car pulling up beside hers, nor the driver who stepped outside into the bracing wind and began making his way towards her.

Ryan rapped his knuckles gently against the window of Anna's car, and took an immediate, involuntary step backwards when she gave an ear-splitting shriek.

"*Whoa*! It's only me!"

Anna's heart was still beating wildly against her chest. "You scared the living daylights out of me," she said, and stepped out of her car to join him in the blustery afternoon sunshine.

"I could say the same," Ryan replied, enjoying the sight of his wife with her dark hair whipping around her face, lending a bloom to her cheeks. "Hello, Doctor Taylor-Ryan."

"Hello, Detective."

"How are you feeling?" he asked, and held her close, shielding her.

"I'm feeling about a dozen different emotions," she said. "I think...I think I feel *angry*, mostly. Betrayed. Disappointed. He was dead, and now there's a chance he's alive, after all these years. It makes me sick to think of it, and of *him*, getting away with murder. I feel so ashamed, because I came from him; he's a part of me, and I'm a part of him. For ten years, I tried to forget my past, where and *who* I've come from, but there's no escaping it, is there? There never is."

Ryan said nothing, because all that she'd said was true. There was never any escape from demons of the past; you could only face them, conquer them, and consign them to a distant corner of the mind.

Easier said than done.

"You don't have to come with me, you know," he told her, again. "I can do this alone."

"I know you can, and that it's your job," she said. "But we're both stepping over some boundaries, aren't we? By rights, you shouldn't be investigating the Oldman case at all. The jurisdiction lies with the team at Durham CID."

Ryan could only nod.

"As for me, if it takes finding the real killer to prove I'm not the person they're looking for, then that's what I'll do," she said. "I need your help, but you also need mine, because I know the man we're going to see today. No matter what Bill Tilson did, he was a friend to my family for years, and loved my sister, in his own way."

Anna thought of Megan, imagining a girl with dark hair like her own, building sandcastles on the beach beside her. Then, she remembered the discovery of her body years later, left outside to the elements, as though she'd meant nothing to anybody. Bill might not have killed her himself, but he did nothing to prevent it. She hated him for that, as much as for everything else he might have done.

"Tilson only got out of prison a couple of years ago," Ryan said, reading her mind. "He served eight years as an accessory to murder, but should have served a lot more. He was the one who drove you to the castle, where they planned to kill you."

"I haven't forgotten," she said, with a short, mirthless laugh. "Bill gave evidence against Steven Walker, and turned against them all, in the end."

"*Eventually*," Ryan said. "It took him more than two years to offer any information about Gregson, and that only happened once we had him in custody, bang to rights."

"Bill always was a coward," she said, and looked out across the sea to where the island rose up from the deep. "I want to be here, because I *have* to be here, Ryan. If I don't, I'll be as much of a coward as him, and all the rest."

Ryan pressed a kiss to her lips, tasting the sea on her skin.

"I'm here, beside you," he said, drawing away to look deeply into her eyes. "You never have to cross this causeway on your own again, my love."

He took her hand.

"Ready?" he asked.

Anna looked over at the causeway, memories nipping the edges of her mind, and then back into his eyes, which were steady pools of silvery grey.

"I'm ready."

"Shall I drive?"

She smiled, and shook her head. "Let me drive, this time."

CHAPTER 24

Ryan had often observed that a victim's recollection of their attacker varied wildly from what the reality turned out to be. In the midst of fear and panic, a victim might remember their attacker as being far taller and stronger than they actually were, their physicality having been exaggerated by the trauma of the ordeal. It had been much the same for Anna, when she thought of the island of Lindisfarne, and the part it played in the events of her life. To others, it was a pretty haven, a worldwide heritage site and centre of learning with a small, close-knit community who knew one another as well as any family might. For Anna, that community had been a blessing and a curse, in equal part, and the prospect of returning to a place where she'd experienced so much sadness was a daunting one, even if it happened to be fairytale-pretty beneath the golden rays of the afternoon sun.

"Are you okay?" he asked, softly.

Anna's hands were firm around the wheel of her car as she steered it over the causeway towards the village.

"I'll be fine," she told him, and was determined that would be true. "I'm surprised Bill came back here to the island, after his release."

"He didn't sell the pub, when he went inside," Ryan said. "It seems he put it into a trust, then bought it back from himself, if that makes any kind of sense."

She glanced across at him, then back at the road ahead.

"Bill was no fool, but I wouldn't have pegged him as someone who'd know how to arrange any of that."

"Gregson, or one of his cronies, probably helped," Ryan said, and the hardening of his jaw was the only outward sign that he was bothered by the mere mention of the man's name. In the early years, when he'd first moved from the Metropolitan Police to Northumbria, he'd been a fish out of water, in need of guidance and a professional mentor to help him walk the new terrain, in his city-boy shoes. For a while, Gregson had stepped into that fatherly role, building trust gradually. When the truth came crashing down, Ryan had been shattered to learn that his friend, the Detective Chief Superintendent in charge of their department, was nothing more than a stranger to him.

A stranger to all of them.

Then again, when Gregson's deception had ripped the blinkers from his eyes, it enabled him to see what had been there in front of him, all along—usually munching his way through a bacon stottie.

Frank.

It was Frank Phillips, not Arthur Gregson, who'd been the gentle, guiding hand throughout his time at Northumbria CID. It was Frank who'd picked him up after his sister died, and saved him from an action that could never be undone and for which he'd never have been able to forgive himself. It was Frank who'd taught him the true meaning of compassion, and the importance of listening first and speaking later. It was because of everything Frank had shown him and taught him, that he'd been able to see Gregson clearly, in the end.

"Do you think they're still in touch?" Anna wondered aloud, as they neared the village. "Arthur Gregson and Bill, I mean?"

Ryan considered this, and then nodded. "It's very likely," he said. "All incoming and outgoing mail is screened by the prison service, but their resources are already overstretched. It's easy for things to be missed, or for contraband phones to slip inside the prison walls. It's an endemic problem."

Anna had seen the impact of systemic failures within the criminal justice system over the years, and spoken with Ryan many times over a glass of wine at dinner as they tried to make sense of government cuts, or changes to procedures that actually worked in the communities they strived to improve. Their conclusion tended to be the same, every time: politics should have no place in criminal justice, to maintain a separation of powers. Politicians were always at the mercy of populism, and the pressure that came to bear from tabloid press and, nowadays, fast reporting—the kind Anna had recently fallen victim to online. It was that kind of viral information without filter, unchecked as to its veracity, that caused untold damage. Government decision-making should instead be based wholly on tried and tested data. In his work, Ryan had seen young men go into the system who might have been rehabilitated with some community investment, or a rehab programme. Instead, they met grown men like Arthur Gregson, and became their mules, their dogsbodies, coming out of the prison system far worse creatures than when they went in.

"Do you think Gregson would try to set up The Circle again?" she asked.

Ryan had wondered this many times, and had kept his ear firmly to the ground, checking in frequently with colleagues in other divisions and departments to ensure there could be no repeat of the past.

"He could try," he said. "But we have the advantage, now. Gregson is an old 'has-been', and Bill was nothing more than his muscle. I know where all of them are, and, as you know, I've made a point of giving an impact statement at each of their parole hearings. Usually, it's enough to keep them inside for the full duration of their sentence, but, in Tilson's case, he kept his nose clean and made himself the model inmate. I have to work within the system, even when those who come through it aren't rehabilitated or remorseful at the end."

"What if he *is* remorseful?" Anna found herself asking.

"What if pigs start to fly?"

She laughed, as he hoped she might. Presently, they entered the village, its squat, stone cottages just as sturdy as they'd always been and decorated with garlands of lights leftover from Christmas. They rounded a corner, and a charming pub came into view, the painted sign above its doorway reading, *The Jolly Fisherman, Prop'r William Tilson*. Its windows, which had fallen into disrepair over the years, had been repaired and re-painted, along with the stone walls, which had been re-pointed and looked freshly sandblasted so as to remove any graffiti or grime.

"The last time we were here, this place looked derelict," she said, bringing the car to a stop beside the kerb on the other side of the road. "It looks almost as it did ten years ago. Maybe even better."

Ryan looked at the shiny new windows and doors, and had one question uppermost in his mind.

Where had Bill Tilson found the money to reinvest in the pub?

He meant to find out.

The air inside The Jolly Fisherman was warm and smelled woodsy, thanks to a large, roaring fire crackling in a grate in the main lounge area. New leather sofas had been arranged either side of it, where some tourists were now seated, walking maps in hand as they pored over their next route while sipping pints of local ale. Trade seemed steady, Anna thought, with more than half of the tables occupied by small groups who'd bought drinks or were polishing off a late lunch. There was a buzz of conversation, and it looked for all the world as though nothing bad had ever befallen the old stone walls, or those who'd lived and worked within them. No sooner had the thought entered her mind, than she caught the flash of a young woman with a curvaceous figure and long, dark hair, similar to her own.

Megan?

Anna's chest contracted, the pain of her sister's loss a deep, physical ache in the pit of her belly. She opened her mouth, as if to call out to the woman, and then closed it again when she remembered.

The woman couldn't be Megan, because she was gone.

"Anna," Ryan said, gently. "It isn't her."

She looked up into his face, which was filled with understanding. "I saw her, and I thought..." She made a helpless gesture with her hand, and shook her head. "I knew it couldn't be her, but, just for a minute...silly of me, really."

Ryan curved an arm around her waist. "It's not silly. When I lost Natalie, there was a time I thought I saw her on every street corner," he said, swallowing the knot in his throat. "I know that feeling, that instant when you forget, and your mind allows you to pretend they're still alive. Your heart leaps, you feel elated, but on some deeper level you always know the truth."

Anna looked at the young woman again, now laden with a trayful of empty glasses, and saw clearly that it wasn't her sister. In fact, aside from having a similar shade of hair colour, the two women shared very little resemblance.

"Do you think this will turn out to be the case with my father?" she asked. "That there's been some error, and he's still dead?"

She hoped.

"It might be a mistake," she said again, when Ryan didn't answer immediately. "These things *do* happen."

"They do," Ryan agreed, hearing the desperation she was trying valiantly to hide. "But I don't think there's been a mistake, this time, Anna. If your father's still alive, then I wish he'd kept his miserable head below the parapet. That way, we could all have lived in ignorance, and been none the wiser."

Anna knew he was trying to sympathise, but he was a detective, through and through. Finding the bad guys was in his blood.

"A part of you is glad he's shown himself," she argued. "And I don't blame you for it, Ryan; I'm glad, too, in a way. He committed crimes deserving of society's punishment, and that's just what we already know about. We have no idea what else he may have done during the time he's been living his new life—although, there's a strong chance he was involved in Linette Oldman's death, for reasons that aren't clear to me. He needs to be stopped, as a protective measure, if nothing else."

It was humbling, he thought, to be understood so well by another human being.

"Of course, you're right," he admitted. "I want to know for sure, and that's partly why we're here, to speak to Tilson."

She frowned.

"Partly?"

Ryan sighed, not relishing the next piece of news he had to impart.

"I managed to push through an emergency exhumation order," he told her. "Morrison expedited it for me, this morning, so they're bringing up the body that's buried in your father's grave today. I need to be there to sign off the formalities, but you don't need to join me for any of that, Anna. We'll have a chat with Bill, then head back to the car. You could wait in there, while I see to things, if you like?"

"No," she said. "I want to come with you."

"It isn't pleasant," he warned. "We won't be opening the coffin, but the process of bringing up the dead can be disturbing. I only want to protect you and our baby from unnecessary upset."

"I know," she said, loving him all the more. "But, it's just as you said in the car: I need to face the demons of my past and do whatever I can to conquer them. I need to stop fearing my father for the man he used to be. The first step is establishing that he no longer has any power, whether dead or alive. He's human, and vulnerable to decay. Whether that decay happened in the ground, during the past eighteen years, or above ground while living a quiet life under an assumed name, doesn't actually make too much difference. He isn't the powerhouse he used to be, which is still only a fraction of the kind of man *he* thought he was."

Ryan smiled. "You're a hell of a woman, d'you know that?"

She began to smile back at him, but it fell away as she caught sight of another face she recognised, staring at them both across the bar. Not an echo of her sister, this time, nor any hallucination, but a man she'd once known well.

Bill Tilson.

Ryan followed her line of sight and saw a tall, broad-shouldered man he was fairly certain Frank would have described as being 'built like a brick shithouse'. It was an apt description, since Tilson's time in prison had done little to diminish his height or breadth; if anything, it seemed to have toughened his muscles, sculpting his physique into a solid wall of strength. His face was leaner, too, and hardened with time and experience into something like old leather. He was mostly bald on top, and he'd opted to shave off the remainder and grow an impressive beard, which added to the 'hard man' image.

"He doesn't look the same," Anna said, taking the words out of his mouth. "But I'd still have recognised him, anywhere."

"Some people, you don't forget."

Anna was sorely tempted to look away, to break the eye contact, but she held fast as a matter of pride. The last time she'd seen him, Bill Tilson had been complicit in drugging and then transporting her to Lindisfarne Castle, where others in his circle awaited her, ready to kill.

He was the first to look away.

CHAPTER 25

"Got it!"

Lauren almost choked on the scotch egg she'd been munching, and shot Kieron a filthy look as she coughed and spluttered, pieces of breadcrumbs and half-chewed egg narrowly avoiding her computer keyboard. He stammered an apology and rushed around to thump her on the back, which had the unfortunate effect of making matters worse.

"Will you…get…*off*!" she managed to say.

"Oh, sorry boss," he said, pulling another apologetic face. "Here, have some water."

He thrust a half-drunk, lukewarm bottle of formerly sparkling water beneath her nose. Ordinarily, she'd have told him to shove it where the sun didn't shine but, since she was desperate, she made a grab for it and forced some of the liquid down her throat.

"Better?" he asked, gingerly.

"Better," she said, once she'd caught her breath.

Then, she frowned at him again, more fiercely now that she could breathe.

"Vale, never, *ever*, frighten me like that again," she said. "I nearly shat my pants, thanks to you, and choking on a bit of sausage isn't the way I plan to leave this world."

Kieron's eyes gleamed.

"What, now?"

"It's just...you said..."

She stared at him, uncomprehending.

"Nothing, boss," he finished, but the smile spread across his face, all the same.

Lauren eyed him, still failing to understand the Big Joke, but decided to let it pass.

"Right, what information was almost worth killing me, over?" she demanded to know.

"Hm? Oh, right, right. I wanted to tell you we've traced the person of interest back to Berwick-upon-Tweed," he said. "Looks like he caught the 17:28 train from Durham, arriving at Berwick train station exactly one hour later."

"Exactly?"

"I know, I was as surprised as you that the trains were running on time, that day."

Lauren hid a smile. "Right, well, we need to know what happened to him, once he got off the train," she said.

"Today?"

She raised an eyebrow. "You've got better places to be?"

"Erm, well..." He thought of the blonde he'd met, down at *Klute* nightclub the previous weekend, and of the curry they'd planned to have together that evening. "Nah, I'm happy to stay late. I just need to make a quick call."

As he left the room, Kieron found himself wondering what he was doing, passing up an opportunity with a curvaceous blonde to spend a night in the office with his boss, who was more likely to shell out for a packet of crisps and a soggy petrol station sarnie than a nice bit of tandoori chicken.

He'd think about that, later.

Before he had time to call "Lisa Double-D from Crook", Kieron's phone began to rattle with an unknown caller.

"DC Vale."

"Vale, this is Frank, from the Northumbria office."

"Oh, y' alreet, Frank?"

"Aye, not bad, son, not bad. Listen, Ryan asked me to give you a bell about somethin'," he said.

"Oh? What's that?"

At the other end of the line, Phillips pulled a face at his own reflection in the computer's monitor. "Right, well the long and short of it is, Andy Taylor's body is bein' exhumed."

Kieron sucked in a deep breath, which whistled out again between gritted teeth. "Are you kiddin' me?"

"I'm not, lad," came the cheerful reply. "Ryan went o'er your head and got the order from the Chief Constable. He might've told her a couple of porky pies about your lot bein' on-board with it all, but I'd never swear to that."

"How am I supposed to break this to Lauren?"

Frank caught a whiff of gossip, and decided corpses could wait a minute. "Oh, aye, *Lauren* is it, now?"

Kieron felt his neck flush, right there in the middle of the corridor. "Lots of people call their boss by their first name," he hissed down the line. "You don't call Ryan 'Guv' or 'boss' anymore, do you?"

"Nah, but then, I rarely did," Phillips chuckled. "He'd know I was bein' sarcastic. I happen to recall you treatin' your senior officer with a certain decorum, until very recently. So, what's the craic? You hopin' for a bit o' Christmas nookie?"

"What? No..." The very thought of it made Kieron blush all the more which, for an experienced young-ish man about town, was an achievement in itself. "No. *No*, definitely not. *No*."

He closed his eyes, and shut his mouth.

"So, that's a 'yes', then?" Frank said, into the silence. "No need to be coy around me, y' nah. Remember, you're talkin' to the man who *married* his senior officer. Romance is rife, around here."

"Look, you've obviously got the wrong end of the stick," Kieron said, while his mind began to imagine Lauren dressed in evening clothes, sitting opposite him at a dimly lit table down at Shaheen's Tandoori. "Anyway, it's none of your business whether I hope for some Christmas nookie."

Kieron couldn't believe he'd said the word 'nookie' out loud, and turned a full three-hundred-and-sixty degrees to be sure nobody had heard.

"Well, good luck to you, lad, and remember, I'm here if you need any tips on how to woo a lady," Frank said.

Woo? Kieron thought, wildly. At best, he was thinkin' of a couple of drinks after work, followed by a drunken night—his place or hers—which they'd both agree to forget about in the New Year. But, even imagining that, he began to think of how nice it would be to have someone to come home to, and share the events of the day with. More often than not, he'd found himself dreading the silent walls of his flat, and it had been far easier than it should have been to think of cancelling the date he'd lined up.

Lauren had a great smile, he thought.

It gave him a real kick to make her laugh.

"Fine," he said. "Once this case is cleared, we'll have a pint, and you can give me some pointers and be the Love Guru. Until then, I want to know where and when the exhumation is due to take place, so we can take it over."

Frank heaved an apologetic sigh, which, even to his own ears, sounded disingenuous. "Sorry again, lad, but you'd be too late," he said. "It's happenin' in about ten minutes, up at the cemetery on Holy Island. If you leave now, you should get there in time to meet them at the mortuary in about an hour. Pinter's been told to expect you both."

Kieron swore, and then wondered whether he could make a reservation for two at a restaurant in Newcastle. Just two work colleagues sharing some dinner, chewing over the day.

"Fine," he said, the anger having been replaced by thoughts of his evening not having been wasted, after all.

"Kai Kai," Frank said.

"Eh?"

"It's one of the best Indian restaurants in Newcastle, and wor Lauren loves a curry," Frank explained. "Go on, fella. Push the boat out."

"Aye, thanks Frank."

"Don't mention it. Now, just one other thing—"

"*Bloody hell.*"

"Now, now," Frank chided him. "We're gonna need to know if you've traced a suspect matchin' Andy Taylor's description."

Kieron laughed. "I can't tell you that! It's a confidential investigation!"

"I suppose you're right," Phillips said, thoughtfully. "Just like the confidential information I happen to know about Lauren's likes and dislikes, not to mention her arse of an ex-husband. It's gold dust, that."

Kieron hated himself, but love conquered all. "It better be good," he said.

"Oh, don't you worry." Frank sensed victory was nigh.

"Fine. We've traced a man leaving Oldman's property in the relevant timeframe who's a potential match. He had a limp, though—did Anna's father limp, at all?"

"No idea," Frank replied, honestly. "I can ask."

"*We'll* ask!"

"Of course," Frank purred. "Of course, you will. Where did he go, after leavin' the property?"

"The train station. He got off at Berwick, but that's as far as we've traced him."

Frank made swift notes on a pad he kept in his pocket at all times. "Thanks," he said. "Now, a final bit of free advice—"

"*Free*?" Kieron cried. "I feel like you've taken my eyeballs, and then come back for the sockets!"

"As I was sayin'," Frank continued, blithely ignoring the outburst. "The key is to be a gentleman, lad. Hold open the doors. Pay for dinner. Walk on the road side of the pavement as you escort her back to—"

"Her place?"

"I like your optimism, lad, but you need to stop drinkin' the Kool-Aid," Frank said, drily. "The fact is, Lauren's well out of your league."

Kieron's face fell. "Wha—"

"Face facts," came the brutal reply. "You're smart, but she's smarter, and most likely always will be. That's fine, because you've got a couple of years on your side, which gives you a bit of well-placed energy, if you know how to use it. As for the rest, you've got a canny personality and you're not half bad to look at—"

"*Thanks*," Kieron said, testily.

"But, she's still better lookin', and that's just the way it is. Moreover, she loves her job, so she's not about to throw away a cushty situation on a one-night stand."

Kieron's face fell, again.

"That bein' said, she's had time to get to know you, and, if she's still talkin' to you with civility then it means she hasn't been completely put off."

"Stop, all these compliments will go to my head."

Frank chuckled. "The main thing that'll kick the dial in your direction is this: can you make her laugh?"

Kieron smiled broadly. "I can."

"Now, this next part is crucial," Frank said, conspiratorially. "Does she laugh *with* you, or *at* you? Because one'll get you a very different outcome over the other."

"I—I'm not sure."

"That's your homework, then. Oh—and start wearin' a tie! The lasses love something to grab, once in a while."

With that, Frank rang off, leaving Kieron standing in the corridor of Durham CID with the look of a man who'd just come through the eye of a storm.

CHAPTER 26

"It's been a while, Bill."

Anna moved to the bar with Ryan at her side, her eyes cataloguing the subtle and not-so-subtle changes on the face of a man she'd once known.

Tilson looked between them both, then around the bar to make sure they weren't drawing any attention.

"Look, I served my time," he said, unable to look Anna squarely in the eye. "If you're here to question me again about—about all that, then I'll tell you the same thing I've told ever other pissin' officer who's been around. *I don't know anythin' else.*"

"I wish I believed you," Ryan said. "But that isn't true, is it?"

At this, Tilson leaned across the bar, his bulk straining against the scarred wood. "Believe what you like," he snarled. "I have nothing else to tell you. That's all in the past, and I've moved on from it. The pub's back on its feet again, and I can't afford to have you stirrin' everythin' up."

"I'm glad you've moved on," Anna said, her soft voice commanding more attention than a hundred raised voices. "I haven't quite managed that, Bill, even after all these years. I remember you hauling me into your car, and driving me up to the castle, to my death. Do you remember?"

His eyes burned—whether in shame or sadness, they couldn't tell.

"I'm—I'm sorry for that," he admitted. "I was sorry about all of it."

"Oh, well, that's all right then," Ryan said, with false cheer. "Seems we've had a wasted journey, coming all this way to see whether you knew about Anna's father still being alive."

There it is, Ryan thought, catching the flicker of recognition that passed over Tilson's face.

"I don't know what you're on about," he lied, and began scrubbing the bar with a tea towel. "Now, if you've got owt else to say, you can say it to my solicitor. I've got rights."

"So did I," Anna reminded him, and then played her trump card. "So did *Megan*."

Tilson's hand stopped working, and he looked up then, grief still lodged in the space behind his eyes.

"I never wanted that," he said, in a low voice. "I would never have wanted to hurt her."

"You should be more careful, choosing your friends," Ryan snapped. "Now, do you want to continue this conversation here, where I can't promise my voice won't start to carry, or somewhere private?"

Bill bobbed his head towards the manager's office, behind the bar. "In here," he said.

"No, I think we'll avoid confined spaces," Ryan said. "Let's go into the beer garden, shall we? It's a nice day, and it's sheltered from the wind."

Bill said something to the bar maid, who took over serving drinks to patrons, and then joined them outside. They found an unoccupied bench in the far corner of the garden and sat down, Anna taking a number of deep breaths to remain calm in the face of a man she loathed with every fibre.

Bill scrubbed a hand over his beard, studying Ryan and Anna up close, and wondered what Megan might've looked like, had she been alive.

"Heard you got married," he said, and something of his old self rose up to remember the girl he'd loved, rather than the woman he'd forsaken. "Bet you made a beautiful bride."

"She did," Ryan agreed, and changed the subject. "Speaking of beautiful things, you've got the place looking nice, Bill. The last time we were here, it was looking a bit sorry for itself."

Bill nodded, warily. "It needed some work," he said. "I started the repairs as soon as I could."

"Really? When? Remember," Ryan said, "I can check with the residents, and the contractors."

Bill steepled his fingers. "What business is it of yours when I had the workmen in? I had all the proper permits, if that's what you're thinkin'. You'll not pin some trumped up charge on me."

"Wouldn't dream of it," Ryan said. "I prefer to pin entirely proper charges on those who earn them; like, that time when you tried to kill people, or were otherwise complicit in killing people, and I pinned an accessory to murder charge on your chest, which the jury agreed with. That sort of thing."

Bill glared at him. "What, then?"

"I'm simply curious to know how a man like you could afford to do it all, so soon," Ryan said. "By my calculations, and correct me if I'm wrong, you've been out of prison for almost two years, now. Is that right?"

It was a matter of record, so Bill nodded.

"That's what I thought. But you said you began repairs as soon as you could. I've been back on the island and there was no sign of any works happening until the past month or so. Should I check that, or do you want to confirm it for me and save time?"

Bill knew he would check, and simply nodded.

"So? Not everyone is born with a silver spoon in their gobs. I had to save up the money to reinvest."

"Now, that's interesting," Ryan said, conversationally. "Am I right in thinking, this is the only business you own?"

"You know, it is."

"I'll overlook the somewhat shady manner in which you managed to keep it, for now," Ryan said, with the ghost of a smile. "Since we've already established you aren't independently wealthy, and this pub was closed to patrons until very recently, I have to wonder…did you win the lottery? Did you secure a bank loan?"

"I—"

"Remember," Ryan cautioned him. "I can obtain a warrant to compel your bank records, if I have reasonable grounds, which I do. It isn't worth lying to me, Bill. I'll only keep coming back to darken your door and, next time, I'll be very loud about it."

Bill's eyes flicked between them, and they noticed the top of his balding head had begun to sweat, despite the chill.

"I don't have to answer these questions," he said, and pushed away from the picnic table so abruptly, he almost fell backwards. "If you want to bring me in, you'll have to do it by the book."

Ryan rose, drawing himself up to his full height.

"Gladly," he began.

"Bill?"

They turned, not having heard the arrival of the young bar maid, who looked nervously between them.

"What is it, Pippa?"

"There's a couple of police officers lookin' for a DCI Ryan," she said, her young eyes drinking in the sight of the tall man with the startling blue-grey eyes. "They say he's here."

She looked at Ryan, guessing correctly that he was the man they were looking for.

"Please tell them, I'll be there in a minute," he said.

She bobbed her head and then, with one last curious look at the three gathered around the table, dashed back inside.

Ryan turned back to the pub's landlord, intending to read the man his rights, when Anna cut across him.

"Bill," she said, quietly.

He focused on a spot above her head, still finding himself unable to look her in the eye.

"Bill, look at me," she said, more firmly.

He blinked, and chanced to look into Anna's eyes, which commanded attention and held him prisoner through sheer force of will.

"You know why we're here," she said. "You've known this day would come, and that we'd find out, eventually. We can guess where you found the money to do over this place, and why, but I need to know for sure. It isn't my father who's buried in the graveyard, is it?"

Her words were suspended on the air, time seeming to pause while the ramifications of what she'd said filtered through Bill's mind.

"I've already told you—"

"Don't lie to me," she said, and her voice slapped him like a whip. "I deserve better than that from you. Did you know I'm suspected of murder, Bill? Did you know that?"

As she spoke, Ryan studied Tilson's face and was interested to detect a look of surprise at Anna's mention of her being suspected of murder.

"I don't—" He cleared his throat. "I don't know anythin' about that."

"Did my father believe he hadn't left any trace?" she whispered. "Did he think they wouldn't match his blood against mine?"

"That's impossible," Bill said, a bit too quickly. "I mean, he's dead, isn't he?"

"Is he?" she said.

This time, the silence extended, broken only by the sound of the waves breaking against the harbour beyond, and the occasional hum of a car's engine as it passed through the village.

Without any further word, Bill moved quickly back inside the pub, leaving Anna and Ryan to contemplate all he had said, and not said.

"It was a wasted journey," she said, dejectedly.

"Oh, I wouldn't say that," Ryan replied, and offered her his hand. "Let's go and raise the dead, shall we?"

CHAPTER 27

DS Bell and DC Vale waited beneath a rain canopy outside one of the service entrances to the Royal Victoria Infirmary, the latter wishing fervently for divine inspiration. Ever since his conversation with Phillips, Kieron had found himself tongue-tied around Lauren, who must be thinking he was suffering some sort of personality shift.

"Er, they must be on their way by now," he said, before remembering he'd passed the same comment less than five minutes ago.

"Mm hm, thanks for stating the bleedin' obvious," she joked. "Are you all right, Vale? Had a bump on the head, lately?"

It sort of felt like it, he thought.

"Just a bit distracted," he replied, and that was the truth.

"Thinkin' about the hot date you might've had, this evening?" she said, and gave him a friendly nudge. "Maybe you can rearrange for another night."

"Ha..." he said, weakly.

Woo her, Frank's voice echoed, somewhere in his mind. *Wooo herrrrr.*

"Er, I might be a bit hungry," he said, in a rush. "I was thinkin'—"

"Kebab shop?" she suggested, with a snap of her fingers. "I don't mind stopping off there, on the way back to the cop shop, if you like?"

"Actually, I was just remembering this place someone suggested here in Newcastle, and, you know…since we're not often in this manor, I wonder if it's worth giving it a try?"

He kept his voice light. Easy-breezy. He even affected a yawn, to give the impression he didn't much care, either way.

"Let's see how we're fixed for time, once this is all over and done with," she said.

It wasn't a 'no', he thought, and almost punched the air.

"Here they are," she said, in the tone of a woman ready to commit murder. "If I end up throttling the pair of them, bail me out, will you?"

Kieron smiled, and she liked the way the last of the light caught the twinkle in his eyes. Embarrassed by the thought, Lauren frowned to herself, and then stormed off to confront Ryan and Phillips.

"Afternoon, Lauren."

She watched Ryan step out of his car, a smile already pinned on his handsome face.

He had a nerve.

"Where's your faithful sidekick?" she asked, in order to know whether she should save her breath and wait to let rip when the pair of them were in attendance.

"Taking care of other business," Ryan said. "So, if you want to let me have it, go right ahead."

Across the car park, Kieron leaned back against the wall and folded his arms, content to watch Lauren's arms gesticulating as the air turned blue above her head. He admired the curves of her body which she tried to hide beneath the boxy jeans and blazer she seemed to like wearing and which, despite not being something he might have described as his 'type', he found he rather liked. Her hair was swept up into a neat pony tail which swung around her back as she moved, and he had a strong urge to tug it while kissing her beneath the mistletoe which still hung above their break room back at CID and which, so far, had claimed no victims.

Kieron came to attention as they began making their way across the asphalt to meet him.

"Everybody friends again?" he asked.

"Shut it, Vale," Lauren said. "I still haven't decided whether to report him to the independent commission."

"While you're deciding, shall we go inside? I'm freezing my arse off, out here."

"Frank's rubbing off on you," Lauren noted, with a grudging smile. "Another decade or so, and you might be considered an honorary Northerner."

"I'll look forward to the commemorative plaque," Ryan said, and began to reach for the door, only to find Kieron there before him.

"After you," he mumbled, and stepped aside to allow Lauren to precede him.

"Oh," she said, shocked at the gesture. "Er, thanks."

As she passed them, Ryan gave Kieron the thumbs-up, signalling that, no matter how many cases they were juggling, there was always time for gossip.

"Bloody Frank," Kieron muttered, and followed them both into the hospital.

Ryan stood in one of the private examination rooms, flanked by Lauren and Kieron on either side, and all three stared at the soiled carcass of a coffin that had spent almost twenty years in the ground. Its lid had been removed by the mortuary technicians and, instead of the usual freshly-dead smell they were used to inhaling, all that remained within the rotten wood was a skeleton, so there was very little smell beyond the earthy aroma of fertile soil.

"Come on, it won't bite," Pinter said.

They edged forward as one, moving slowly, just in case something nasty was to crawl out of the woodwork. However, there were no ghosts, ghouls or vampires lying inside, only the grey-brown bones of what had once been an adult male.

"Fully matured, by the size of the femurs, and definitely male, looking at the torso and hips," Pinter told them, peering inside with the same excited expression Charlie had, upon stepping inside Mr Wonka's Chocolate Factory.

"Put us out of our misery," Lauren said. "Are we looking at Andy Taylor or not?"

Pinter was disappointed not to enjoy his usual theatrical revelations, however one look in the woman's eye told him she was in no mood for a performance.

"*Not*," he replied, succinctly. "Ladies and Gentlemen, say 'hello' to the bones of a man who's been masquerading as Andrew Taylor since 2007."

If he was hoping for a collective gasp of surprise, then he was disappointed.

"Ah," he said, holding onto the lapels of his lab coat. "I see this hasn't come as a shock, then?"

Ryan looked up from his inspection of the bones, which were still covered in the tatters of what had once been a man's suit and tie. It was uncomfortable to see, not least because it resembled the ghoulish effigies people often hung outside their homes on Hallowe'en. The only difference being, of course, that these were real bones that had once been covered in the flesh of a living person, and not something you'd pick up from the bargain shop.

"No, I think it's fair to say we had our suspicions, which is why I thought it was a good idea to have the body exhumed," he said. And then, turning to Lauren and Kieron, added, "I'm sorry to have gone over your heads on this, but I couldn't wait for the inevitable back and forth. We all needed answers, especially Anna. I want her name to be cleared, and I'll do whatever it takes to make sure that happens."

Lauren had been angry, but listening to the love he had for his wife, found it harder to remain so.

"Humph," she said, and then turned her mind back to business. "Right, well, I suppose you'll need some time to check the bloke's DNA against the database, to see if we get lucky with a match? Failing that, dental records? Vale and I could start trawling back through missing persons reported around the same time as this body was interred."

"Not necessary," Pinter said, trying and failing to hide his glee at having kept one last surprise up his sleeve. "There was a wallet inside the gentleman's jacket pocket, and its contents were remarkably well preserved, including—"

He paused, for dramatic effect.

"Jeff," Ryan said, in a warning tone.

"Sorry, sorry, I couldn't resist," he said, enjoying himself immensely. "There was a *warrant card* inside that wallet—alongside a couple of bank cards and some membership cards for the gym, and whatnot—belonging to a Detective Inspector Arnold Blythe, late of Northumbria CID."

It was before his time, so Ryan didn't recognise the name. He looked to his colleagues, who shook their heads.

"Don't look at me," Kieron said. "I was still watching cartoons around the time this bloke snuffed it."

As soon as the words left his mouth, he wished them back again. The last thing he wanted was for Lauren to be reminded of the small but significant age gap between them.

Idiot, he thought.

Reading him like a book, Ryan did his best to gloss over it. "The person to ask about this would be Frank, since he's the oldest member of our cohort, and it'll give me great pleasure and amusement to tell him that." "That's what friends are for," Lauren said, knowing she'd have done the same thing herself. "Anything else you can tell us at this stage, Jeff?"

"I'll have the lab check this fellow's DNA and dental records, anyway, to be sure he matches the identification cards," Pinter said. "I haven't had any time to perform a proper assessment, but, even without it, I can tell you one thing, straight off the bat."

They waited.

"This man died violently," he said, and produced a retractable pointer so he could indicate a deep crack to the side of the skull. "Heavy blunt force implement used, with a kind of chamfered edge to it, I'd say, given the force and impact to the bone."

"Could this injury have happened after a fall, or some other accidental death?" Lauren wondered aloud.

Pinter shook his head. "Different kinds of impact," he said, without providing any further embellishment, for it was a lengthy topic, and they had no time for lectures. "I'm fairly certain we'll find metallic remnants inside the head wound, which would be a strong indication of deliberate force."

He heaved a sigh, and strummed his fingers against the material of his coat.

"I'll run the tests and see what we can discover," he promised. "For now, I can tell you, this isn't Andrew Taylor. Even without the ID cards, the injuries this body sustained are inconsistent with a man who died after a fall. For one thing, the limbs don't appear to have been broken, which would have been a miracle for a man who'd fallen to his death from Lindisfarne Castle."

Ryan looked down at what was left of Arnold Blythe, and wondered what kind of man he had been. Had he left behind a family? Had he been one of Gregson's men, or one of the few who rallied against his corruption? How had he come to die—and, just as importantly, how had Andrew Taylor *survived*?

Every new revelation raised more questions, and they were no closer to finding the answers.

Twenty minutes later, the three detectives emerged from the dank interior of the city's largest mortuary, and breathed freely once more. It wasn't yet five o'clock, but the sun had disappeared beyond the horizon sometime while they picked over a dead man's bones.

"What do you make of it?" Lauren asked Ryan, throwing the last of any protocol and caution to the wind. "Oh, don't look at me like that. You've wheedled your way into this investigation, whether I like it or not, so you might as well tell me what you think of it all."

Ryan leaned against the side of his car and looked up at the sky above his head, wondering how their lives could be so complex, considering how insignificant they were, in the grand scheme of things.

"If the body does belong to DI Arnold Blythe, then I'm wondering why they left identifying documents inside the coffin," he said. "It's sloppy, if the idea was to have people believe the body belonged to Andrew Taylor. Far better to strip it of any identifying documents, and dress it in one of Andy's suits, I'd have thought."

"Maybe there wasn't time," Kieron remarked. "If the bloke was battered around the head, as Pinter says, then there'd have been blood spatter to deal with. You could see dried bloodstains on the material of the suit he was wearing. It feels like a last-minute murder, or one committed by someone who didn't think ahead."

"Or by someone arrogant enough to think their subterfuge would never be discovered," Lauren put in, and thought again of the person of interest they'd caught on camera leaving Oldman's building.

"There may be a bit of truth to all of that," Ryan said, and stuck his hands into the pockets of his windbreaker to stave off the cold. "Members of The Circle would have been at the height of their confidence, back then, safe in the knowledge they were protected by senior members of the police."

An image of Gregson popped into his mind again.

"You're saying they would've assumed nobody would allow the body to be exhumed, so there was no need to be especially careful about what they left inside the coffin?" Lauren surmised. "That would make sense, to a certain kind of mind."

"I did a quick search for information on Arnold Blythe," Kieron said, and turned his smartphone around so they could see what the man had looked like, when he'd been alive. "Detective Inspector in Narcotics, reported missing by his next door neighbour back in 2007."

"What actions were taken to find him?" Ryan asked. "Who was the last to see him alive?"

Kieron skim-read the summary note attached to the man's file on the missing persons database, feeling the ends of his fingers turning numb as the temperature continued to fall. Across the car park, a couple of doctors still dressed in their scrubs stumbled outside, so tired they appeared drunk to the casual observer.

"He was last seen at some gym in Newcastle... *Buddles.* Have you heard of it?"

Ryan nodded. "Anything else?"

"Ah, let's see. There was a token search, the usual door-to-doors—but, to be honest, it doesn't look as though the department made much of an effort."

Ryan nodded again, and asked a question to which, he suspected, he already knew the answer.

"Who was in charge of the investigation?"

"It was..." Kieron flipped through the file, searching for the all-important name of the Senior Investigating Officer. "Arthur Gregson."

"There we go," Ryan said, and exhaled the rage that threatened to suffocate him.

"So, it's safe to assume Gregson was involved in the cover-up, somehow," Lauren said. "The question is, why did they want Arnold Blythe dead?"

"He must have known something or uncovered something," Kieron guessed.

"Or he might have been a part of The Circle, and then made it known he wanted out," Ryan said. "Either one would've been reason enough for them to get rid of him."

"We can start digging up information on DI Blythe," Lauren said.

"Let my team help," Ryan said. "He belonged to our constabulary, and you know I'll only kick up a fuss about jurisdiction if you don't."

She gave him a disapproving look. "You're a pushy so-and-so," she grumbled.

"Not usually," he said. "There are extraordinary circumstances in this case."

"Anna," Lauren remembered. "How d'you think she'll take the news?"

"I think she's been preparing herself for this since the DNA results came back," he said. "That still doesn't remove the fact that her father isn't dead, after all, and she doesn't know how to feel about that. The overriding emotion she's been feeling is anger; at him, and at her relationship with him, which is something she's always felt ashamed of, given the kind of person he was...or is."

Ryan paused, wondering whether to say any more, and then took the chance.

"I know this won't make a difference to the investigation, but I have to tell you both again: Anna would never kill anyone in cold blood, the way Lin Oldman was murdered. It just isn't something she could ever do, no matter what the provocation."

Lauren happened to agree, but she had no intention of voicing that. "This new evidence is another major step away from her being considered our prime suspect," she did say. "You know how this goes, Ryan. We follow the steps, one at a time, and see where they lead us."

"The next step is to get something to eat," he said, catching Kieron's eye. "There's a very nice Indian restaurant, down by the Quayside. You should try it, while you're in town."

Kieron's face lit up, and he told himself to play it cool. "Yeah, I heard that, too. Kai Kai, or something?"

Ryan nodded. "That's the one. Let me know what you think of it."

"You aren't joining us?" Lauren said, missing the signals that had been flying freely above her head.

"I have one last meeting to go to, this evening," he said. "Bon appetit."

Kieron mouthed a 'thank you' and Ryan gave him a conspiratorial wink in return. Sometimes, you had to be a pushy so-and-so, or live with the regret of never having tried.

CHAPTER 28

Charlie plumped the scatter cushions on her living room sofa one last time and then perched on the edge, only to stand up and roam around again.

"You don't need to be nervous," Jack said, from his position in an armchair across the room. "They're your friends, and they want to help."

"Jack's right," her mother said, and rose to her feet in order to peck her daughter's cheek. "I'm going to make myself scarce, so you can talk shop, but I'll be in my bedroom if you need me."

She patted Charlie's cheek.

"I'm proud of you, love," she said. "It takes courage to face a man like Alexei Rachmaninov, and that's just what you're doing. You make me so proud, and Ben will be proud of you, too."

Charlie held her mother close, breathing in the scent of her. "Thank you," she whispered. "I love you, Mum."

The two women disappeared down the corridor and, Jack knew, Charlie would be protecting her mother's dignity by offering her any private, personal help she may need, now that her illness had taken more of a stronghold. Multiple sclerosis was a cruel disease, affecting sufferers at different rates of decline. So far, her mother's had plateaued, allowing them to fall into a false sense of security, but more recently the pace had quickened, like a train that was beginning to pick up speed. It was a worrying future, without any clear map of the journey ahead, except to know that the destination would be the same for all who followed it.

"Mum seems comfortable," Charlie said, when she returned to the living room a few minutes later. "It breaks my heart to see her struggle with things she used to do so easily."

"You're a good daughter," Jack said, rising to his feet to kiss her. "You help others all the time, so why not let us help you, for a change?"

Before Charlie could argue or dismiss the compliment, there came a quiet knock on the outer door. Ben was asleep in his nursery room, and she was grateful to whichever thoughtful soul had remembered.

It turned out to be Mel.

"Sorry, I'm a few minutes early," she said, toeing off her shoes so as not to drag slush through the hallway. "It's started to snow out there."

The curtains were closed, so neither Jack nor Charlie had realised.

"Oh! It's amazing how pretty everything looks in a blanket of white," Charlie said, and watched the flakes falling outside with a kind of wonder, before shutting the door again. "Thanks for coming, Mel. I can't tell you how much I appreciate this."

Unexpectedly, tears sprang to her eyes, taking them both by surprise.

"Hey," Mel said, and pulled her in for a quick, hard hug. "You don't need to thank me. We're gonna be mates, right? You don't have to thank your mates for being there, when you need them."

Charlie dabbed at her eyes with the cuff of her sleeve, and nodded.

"Mind you, I wouldn't say 'no' to a glass of something fruity," she said, waggling the bottle she'd brought along to share.

Jack overheard their exchange, and smiled to himself. He would always love Mel, for moments of generosity such as these. He was ready with glasses and a corkscrew by the time they came through to join him.

"Hydration," he said, and proceeded to uncork the bottle and slosh some of the wine into three glasses. "What should we toast to?"

"Friendship," Mel said. "And new beginnings."

"I'll drink to that," Charlie said.

"Me too," Jack added, and they clinked glasses.

The others arrived soon afterwards, and Charlie felt her home and heart swell with the force of their affection.

"It's bitter out there!" Frank declared, once he'd divested himself of several layers of woollen clothing.

"You might not be as cold, if you hadn't insisted on making a snowman with the comms team before we left the office," Denise said, drily.

"Aye, but it was a belter," he said.

"How about something to warm you up?" Charlie offered, and couldn't quite hide the awkwardness she still felt.

Phillips often made self-deprecating jokes about himself, but one thing he wouldn't joke about was his superlative ability to read people. In that moment, he read all that Charlie couldn't bring herself to say, and decided there was only one thing for it.

"Group hug!" he proclaimed, to the room at large.

Before she had time to protest, Charlie found herself enveloped in Frank's cuddly embrace, Old Spice swirling around her nostrils. The others didn't need to be told twice, and soon, other warm arms wrapped themselves around her.

"Looks like I missed the pile on," Ryan said, returning from the bathroom. "Room for one more?"

"Bring it in, big lad," Frank said, in a muffled voice.

Ryan's arms wrapped around the cluster, and Charlie couldn't help it...she began to laugh. A giggle at first, then full-blown laughter, at the ridiculousness of a group of murder detectives hugging one another like Care Bears.

"Okay, that's enough of the mushy stuff," she said, once her laughter dried up. "You can all let go, now."

They released her and, as they stepped apart, Charlie looked from one face to the next.

"Thank you," she said, whole-heartedly. "I've never had—"

Her voice caught on the last words.

"Just...thank you. All of you."

While the team discussed the best way to protect Charlie and her son from the man who had fathered him, Anna knelt beside her daughter's bed, watching Emma's sleeping face, loving the way her dark lashes fanned out against her smooth cheeks.

"Sleep well, beautiful girl," she whispered, and raised a gentle hand to touch her hair. "Happy dreams, angel."

Emma murmured something unintelligible and then, with a contented sigh, her body relaxed against the bedspread. Anna came to her feet and crept from the room, leaving the door ajar and a nightlight shining against the wall, projecting the moon and stars.

Her mother-in-law was waiting for her in the living room downstairs, a cup of camomile tea and a tray of biscuits ready and waiting to be eaten. The dog lay against her feet, snoring happily.

"All tucked up?" she asked, and set her book down.

"For now, at least," Anna said, and rubbed a hand against her womb. She'd been having some aches and pains low down in her stomach for the past couple of hours, but it might have been anything from a bad prawn in the sandwich she'd eaten, to the stress of the day.

Eve noticed, and frowned slightly. "Are you feeling okay, darling?"

"Just a bit achey," Anna said, and forced a smile. "It's been a long day, and I've probably done too much."

"On top of a stressful few days," Eve added. "When's Ryan due home?"

Anna moved to sit beside her on the sofa, wincing as the action brought a flash of discomfort. "Don't worry," she said. "He said he'd be home by eight, and it's only seven. He'll be on the road, soon enough."

Eve couldn't quite shake the niggle of worry that played on her mind. "Do you think it's worth calling for the doctor, just to check you over?"

Anna smiled. "They don't do house calls, any more," she said, and it was at times like these she remembered Eve had been used to a rarefied kind of world, back in Devon. "If I still feel a bit peaky in the morning, I'll make an appointment with the GP."

Eve took her hand. "Promise me?"

Anna nodded. "I promise."

They talked of other things, Eve listening while Anna brought her up to date on their trip to Holy Island, while an old Doris Day movie played quietly in the background. They fell into a comfortable silence, until Anna cried out suddenly, clutching her stomach as she doubled over.

"*Eve!*"

Her eyes were wild with grief, for she knew what was coming.

Pain. Loss. Heartbreak.

"Oh, no," Eve whispered. "Don't worry, Anna. Don't worry, sweetheart. I'm calling for an ambulance."

She rang 999 with a shaking hand, while her other one held onto Anna's tightly as she rode wave upon wave of pain.

"They'll be here as soon as they can," Eve said. "Here, lie down, that's right—"

Anna curled up into the foetal position, mimicking the tiny being that struggled for survival, deep inside her.

"I'm losing the baby," she whispered, and tears began to roll down her face and onto the cushion she clutched tightly against her head.

"We don't know that, yet," Eve said, stroking the hair back from her face, much as Anna had done with her own daughter not long before. "Hold on. Hold on to hope."

Where was the ambulance? she thought.

Ryan, she realised. *She needed to call Ryan.*

Anna cried out again, her body contorting with pain, and she began to crawl from the sofa, in search of a bathroom.

"I—I have to—"

Just then, the front door opened, and they heard Ryan's tread as he kicked off his shoes and hung his coat on a peg. Eve pushed to her feet and ran out into the corridor, where one look at the expression on her face galvanised him into action.

"Where?" he asked.

"In the lounge," his mother said, and he moved like lightning.

Ryan took in the scene like an old film reel, one shuttered image at a time.

His wife, in agony on the floor.

The television, playing some old film with Rock Hudson.

His mother's book, lying open on the table.

The blood.

The blood…

Eyes burning molten silver with unshed tears, Ryan surged forward, falling to his knees beside Anna to hold her, because it was all he could do.

"I'm sorry," she wept, clutching onto his arms for support. "I'm so sorry—I—I've lost our baby—"

"This isn't your fault," he said, kissing her face and finding it wet with tears. "None of it is your fault, Anna. It's beyond anybody's control."

She cried out again, a deep, guttural sound like an animal in torment, and Ryan couldn't prevent his own tears from falling, running in silent tracks down his face. He held Anna through it all, while Eve moved quietly around them, setting out warm towels, rubbing a hand over her daughter-in-law's back, preparing a warm water bottle for later and greeting the paramedics when they arrived a few minutes later. She watched her son lift his wife into his arms, a blanket wrapped around her, and hold her safely until they reached the ambulance outside. Eve followed and, once Anna was settled on the gurney, she handed Ryan a small bag of clothes and other useful things she'd gathered together.

"Ryan?"

He turned to his mother, eyes stark with grief.

"Talk to Anna of the *future*," she reminded him. "Of *hope*, and things you both have to look forward to."

He realised she spoke from experience, and wondered why he'd never considered the possibility of his mother having suffered a miscarriage at some time in her younger life. It was a common occurrence, but not something that was often spoken of, especially for women of her generation.

He leaned down to kiss her cheek.

"I'll try."

Unaware of the drama unfolding in their friends' lives, Frank and Denise wished Charlie and Jack 'goodnight', Mel having already made her farewells, and stepped out into the snowy night.

"You know, we have the house to ourselves," Denise said, and gave her husband a suggestive smile as they hurried to turn on the heating fans inside the car. "Unless you're too tired, of course."

"I'm never too tired when it comes to you," he said, and growled like a tiger to make her laugh. "But I have to make a quick pitstop on the way home. I promise, it won't take long. I just need to have a word with m' old mate at Buddles, then I'm all yours."

"You know, I don't blame Charlie for wanting to run," Denise said, once they were on the road and making their way towards the west end of town. "If I was in her shoes, I might be long gone, by now."

"If you were in Charlie's shoes, you'd have strung the bastard up by his bollocks, by now," Frank said, with a touch of pride. "Charlie talks a good game, and she's narf a good copper, that's for sure. But, when it comes to matters of the heart, she's a sensitive soul."

"It takes one to know one, so they say."

"Eh? I'm hard as nails, as you well know."

Denise snorted. "You're as soft as butter, you mean."

"I've got that *killer instinct*," Frank argued. "In fact, that's what they used to call me, back in the day: "Killer Phillips"."

Denise merely smiled. "You're a giant softie who stands up for the people he loves, and the things that matter," she said. "That's why we love you."

"When I'm not rampagin' around the city like a Geordie Rambo, y' mean?" he said, and wriggled his eyebrows.

"You daft bugger," she laughed, and swatted away one of his hands, which was roaming towards her leg. "Oi! Keep both hands on the wheel, and both eyes on the road!"

"Spoilsport," he said. "Which reminds me. Do you still stand by your edict about me not bein' able to give your arse a spank, every now and again? You said it was 'problematic' and sets a bad example to

Samantha, but it's hard to resist when you're bendin' over here, there and everywhere."

"It *is* problematic!" she cried out. "And the last thing I want is for her to think some lad can help himself to a swat, whenever he wants."

"Aye, that's true," Frank said, caught between a protective urge to coset his daughter, and a very *different* urge to grab his wife at every available opportunity.

It was a quandary, all right.

Then, the answer came to him, as a eureka moment.

"I've got it!" he said. "What if we make it equal opps, and you can spank my arse whenever you want?" he suggested, with the blind hope of a man who admired the fruits of his wife's Pilates classes.

"It's a generous offer," she said. "But I'll take a rain check, thanks all the same. Besides, if I wanted to spank your arse, Frank, I wouldn't bother to ask your permission, that's for sure."

Momentarily blindsided by the notion, his mind began to imagine the scenarios—

"I've been doin' all those gym squats, with those bloody heavy weights Ryan's always bangin' on about," he said, hoping to inveigle her. "He was on about bone density, longevity and all sorts of other stuff, but I told him he didn't need to worry about me bein' able to lift a weight or two."

"And, did you?"

"Hm? Did I what?"

She rolled her eyes. "Did you have any trouble lifting the weights? You know your heart hasn't been too good, lately."

Frank pulled a face at her, and indicated left. "I thought we agreed not to talk about my ticker until after 1st January?"

Denise sighed. "I know, but you can't blame me for worrying, Frank. You gave us all a fright, not so long ago."

"Aye, well, imagine the fright I had, when that bomb went off!

I'm surprised my heart didn't fly oot me chest and start leggin' it down the road!"

She had to smile. "Frank, I'll start legging it down this road if you don't give this car a bit more juice," she snapped. "We're crawling along at five miles per hour, and the roads have already been cleared and gritted!"

He risked another few points on the speedometer, and felt like Lewis Hamilton.

When they eventually made it to Buddles, they'd covered almost every conversational topic under the sun, bar one.

"I hope Anna's all right," Denise said, as Frank was about to exit the car.

He paused.

"Whatever made you think o' that?"

"I don't know," Denise said, with a troubled expression. "She just popped into my head, and I had a sense of…"

She shook herself.

"You know I don't believe in all that hocus-pocus nonsense."

"No, but you do have good instincts," he said. "Your knack of knowing when I've had a sneaky chocolate eclair is so uncanny, it might as well be witchcraft."

Denise wondered whether to bring up the fact that he often had chocolate on his upper lip, but decided not to ruin the illusion.

"Ignore me," she said. "Go on and see your friend, and I'll wait here."

She watched him make his way over to the entrance of the boxing gym, a cheap, brick and tin monstrosity tucked away at the end of one of the terraced streets in a part of Newcastle famed for its working class, industrial heritage. Frank's huddled figure disappeared inside and, soon after, her mind wandered north again, to Bamburgh, where she hoped her friend was safe and well.

CHAPTER 29

Ryan thought about calling Frank.

Sitting alone in the waiting room at the hospital, his finger hovered over the button on his smartphone, but he stopped himself, not knowing what to say or how to say it. The loss of a baby was a deeply personal thing, and he found he wasn't ready to say the words aloud.

"Mr Ryan?"

It was odd, he thought, when strangers called him that. Of course, they weren't wrong; Ryan was still his surname, although he'd taken it as his first name and that was how he'd been known for a long time, to everyone who mattered.

It was hardly relevant, now.

"Yes," he said, coming to his feet.

"The registrar has finished now, so, if you'd like to come back in, she'll speak to both of you at the same time," the nurse said, indicating the trauma room where Anna had been taken when the ambulance arrived at the Accident and Emergency Department.

"How is she?" Ryan couldn't wait to ask.

"She's doing as well as you'd expect," the nurse replied, and put a sympathetic hand on his arm. "Here we are."

The door opened and Ryan's eyes were drawn immediately to Anna's face, which was as pale as the pillow she lay upon. By contrast, her eyes were dark pools of misery, without any further tears left to shed. His mother's words came to him, then, and he set his own grief aside, drawing upon reserves he didn't know he had, to be strong when she could not.

"Anna," he said, and moved across the room to take her hand. "I'm here, my love."

Ryan leaned down to kiss her, a tender brushing of lips that was more about connection than anything else.

"I lost our baby," she said, so softly he struggled to hear. "I killed our baby."

"No," he said, snatching up her hand again. "*No*, Anna. You didn't. There isn't any rhyme or reason to why some babies survive, and others don't—"

Just then, the door opened again, and the registrar joined them, having cleaned herself up after performing some minor operative work to help Anna's recovery.

"Mr and Mrs Ryan," she said. "I'm Doctor Dalgleish, one of the registrars here. I've spoken to colleagues in Obstetrics, and we both think it's a good idea for you to spend a night or two under observation, just to be on the safe side."

Ryan assumed she was referring to Anna's recovery following the miscarriage, and was impressed they'd been able to find a bed for her.

"Thank you," he said, when Anna remained silent. "What happens now?"

"Well, it's important that your wife takes good care of herself, and I've elevated her risk rating to 'high' for the remainder of her pregnancy."

Both Ryan and Anna thought they had misheard.

"What—what do you mean?" Anna whispered, trying to sit up.

"Oh, please, *lie back*, Mrs Ryan," the registrar said, in the firm, schoolmarmish tone of one used to dealing with disobedient patients on a regular basis. "You should rest as much as possible."

"I'm sorry," Ryan began, wondering if he was suffering brain fog. "My wife suffered a miscarriage—didn't she?"

"Yes, I'm afraid so, and you both have our deepest sympathies."

Anna slumped back against the pillow again.

"I must have misheard you, when you said you'd elevated Anna to 'high risk' for the rest of her pregnancy," Ryan said, tiredly. "You must have been referring to any future pregnancies."

Now, it was the registrar's turn to look confused.

"No, I...Mr and Mrs Ryan, I was referring to the *other* baby."

Anna and Ryan looked at her with shocked faces, which, at another time, would have been highly comical.

"What other baby?" Anna said, finding her voice again. "*What other baby*?"

"Oh, dear," the registrar said. "I'm terribly sorry about this, I thought you knew you were expecting twins, Mrs Ryan."

Anna gripped Ryan's hand so hard, he yelped.

"Sorry," she muttered. "No, we didn't know I was carrying twins."

"Well, it's very possible the sonographer missed it, at your thirteen-week scan," the registrar said, and drew up a wheelie chair to rest her feet for a moment beside them. It also allowed her to speak more intimately to the couple who, by the look of them, were reeling from shock. "At this stage, the foetuses were tiny, and if the view was obstructed on the ultrasound, there's a chance he or she may not have picked up on the fact there was a second one."

She looked down at her clipboard, remembering there was no longer a second.

"Once again, I'm so sorry only one foetus has survived," she said. "These things happen far more regularly than you'd imagine, and, often the mother is entirely unaware a second egg had ever been fertilized. Even when multiple foetuses survive to full term, we often find there's a dominant one, who may have benefited from the lion's share of a mother's resources. This can happen at all stages of pregnancy."

Anna swiped away fresh tears, wondering how she had any liquid left in her body. "Was there anything I could have done, to—to—save the baby?"

The registrar smiled, sadly, having heard the same question so many times, from different lips.

"No," she said. "There was no physical trauma to precipitate this. As I say, sometimes Nature takes decisions that are best for the mother and foetus, but very hard to accept on an emotional level. In your case, there is a silver lining, Mrs Ryan, Mr Ryan."

The registrar came to her feet again, knowing that there were others in need of her attention.

"You still have a baby," she said. "Would you like to see?"

Ryan turned to Anna, his eyes shining. "Would you?" he asked, hoping she would say 'yes'.

"Of course," Anna said, caught between grief and elation. "I can hardly believe it."

The nurse rigged up an ultrasound machine, rubbing the gel between her hands to warm it before smearing some over Anna's stomach.

"Sorry!" She smiled. "It's always cold, this stuff. Now, let's see."

Ryan moved his head close to Anna's, and she rested her cheek against his as they waited for the image to appear on the screen that would confirm what the registrar had told them.

"There," the nurse said, pointing to what could only be described as a blob of shadowy cells. "Do you see it?"

They nodded, crying happy tears, now.

"I'll leave you alone for a minute," the nurse said, and slipped from the room.

Frank entered Buddles and felt immediately at home in its stale, sweaty interior. He'd been visiting the dusty old place since he was a nipper, when it had provided a healthy outlet for the anger he'd carried as one of many children from poverty-stricken homes, born to parents who'd lost their livelihoods to something called Progress, and turned to drink to numb the sense of shame and loss of purpose. When others fell into careers pushing drugs, or working as muscle for one of the city's gangs, Frank had walked the line between their two worlds. He'd palmed a wallet, or two, in his younger days, and used the proceeds to pay for food, when his father's dole money hadn't quite stretched to a session at the pub as well as a trip to the supermarket. He was a scrapper, back then, a stocky kid who knew how to handle himself but preferred not to, if he could help it. He made his pocket money fighting bigger lads in the back streets, making his training work for him, in the real world, but he'd known it was a mug's game. One day, there'd be a bloke he couldn't beat, as there always was, and he'd have the sense knocked out of him along with most of his teeth.

Frank had taken a different path to many he grew up with, and their worlds were very different now, but that didn't mean he'd lost touch with their daily struggles nor the choices they made. Some, he could sympathise with, others, he couldn't. He would always remember one of the few, truly useful pieces of advice his father had given him, in the days before the drink became his master. It was that a man was only 'poor' if he behaved poorly. Money didn't come in to it.

Funny, he thought, the things you remembered.

"Frank! You're in a bit later than usual, the neet," Mick, one of the regulars, said, before greeting him with a manly, one-armed hug.

"Aye, I was lookin' for Harry. Is he about?"

"In his office, the last time I saw him. Think he's got company, mind."

Frank nodded. "Ta, Mick. See you about."

The other man wandered off towards the showers, such as they were, and Frank decided to watch the two men currently going at it in the ring. They were young but disciplined, he was pleased to note, their actions controlled rather than aggressive for aggression's sake. He chatted to a few people he knew, moving around the room from one crowd to the next, while keeping half an eye on the manager's office, whose internal window was blacked out by an old blind, so he was unable to see inside.

When several more minutes passed, and there was still no movement, Frank wandered over to the office and listened for any sound on the other side of the wall. Rather than hearing voices in conversation, he heard nothing.

He knocked on the door.

No answer.

He knocked again and, this time, tried the handle.

When he opened the door, he found his old friend slumped back in his chair, his face covered in a spidery web of broken blood vessels which had burst as he'd fought to breathe, while a garotte had crushed his windpipe. Frank saw the angry red line against Harry's neck, the blood only just congealed, which told him he wasn't long dead and, if he'd only been a little quicker, if he'd only come to see him when he meant to, this might never have happened.

Too late now.

Much too late for Harry now.

Frank remained standing where he was, innate training preventing him from rushing forward to contaminate the scene, when it was very clear there was no life to be saved. There was an external door connecting the office to an alleyway outside, where Harry often smoked or made exchanges. That door was shut, but it would have been the perfect way for anybody to enter or exit without being seen by those in the main gym area. There was no CCTV there, either, because it simply wasn't that kind of place.

Harry's murder had been a cakewalk.

Frank said a prayer, one he remembered from the days when he and Harry had gone to Sunday School and worn starched white shirts, and then reached for his phone.

"Frank?" Denise answered, after one ring. "You'd better not be calling me to say you're having a pint, now."

He wished that was the case.

"No, lass. I'm afraid we'll have to cancel our plans for the evenin', though. There's been a murder, here."

There was a momentary silence, while Denise switched from being his wife, to being his senior investigating officer.

"Secure the scene," she said. "I'll call in the troops." She heard his soft sigh, and added, "I'm sorry, love. I know he was from the old days."

"Aye," Frank said. "He was one of the last links to the past, and now he's gone."

"We'll find whoever did it," she said.

Frank thought of all the characters Harry had known, all the years he'd operated in the shadows of the law, and wondered how they would even begin to narrow down a list of suspects.

Sometimes, justice was an elusive thing.

CHAPTER 30

The next morning

Detective Sergeant Lauren Bell opened one sleepy eye, then the other, feeling remarkably well rested for the first time in months. Her body ached a bit, but in the same satisfying way it might have done if she'd spent an hour or two at the gym, or so she imagined, since it was a place she never visited unless she was under duress.

Yawning, she made a grab for her glasses, which were usually kept on her bedside table, only to find a *different* bedside table staring back at her, with some sort of Japanese-style lantern lamp. She quite liked it, actually, but that wasn't the point. She sat up, then realised she was completely naked beneath the bedclothes, which she snatched up in panic.

Looking around, she saw a nice, if plainly decorated bedroom in shades of beige and cream, with the occasional bit of Japanese artwork on the walls, and an overly large television fixed to the wall.

It was a man's bedroom, she thought. Even if that hadn't already been a suspicion, given her state of undress, the television would've given it away.

Then, she remembered.

Kieron.

The man himself entered the room, bearing a cup of coffee in a mug with a worn image of Penshaw Monument on the side.

"Thought you might like some coffee," he said, and gave her a blinding smile.

Lauren told herself to stop staring at his bare torso, which didn't quite boast a six-pack, but wasn't too far off. She experienced a sudden flashback of how it had felt against her skin, as he'd pressed her back against the cushions, and—

"Are you okay?" he asked, coming to perch beside her. "I know, this is a bit of an unexpected turn of events."

Lauren dragged her eyes from his chest to look him in the eye, then wished she hadn't. Gone was the happy-go-lucky constable whom she bantered with daily, while apparently ignoring his considerable physical attributes until this very moment. Now, she faced a grown man with kind eyes, who was looking at her with genuine admiration. That was something she hadn't experienced very often, and, if her ex-husband was to be believed, it was something she didn't deserve.

"I—um—I should be going."

"Is that how you want to handle this?" he asked, mildly. "We're both grown, consenting adults, you know."

"You're barely an adult," she shot back.

"I'm in my thirties, Lauren."

"*Exactly*," she said, and then her nose caught the scent of coffee. "Are you going to hand over that mug or not?"

He took a long, slow sip from the mug, his eyes watching her over the rim, and then handed the rest to her.

"You've done that before," she said, but it wasn't an accusation.

"Have I shared a cup of coffee with an attractive woman before? Yes, I have."

"You know what I mean," she said, irritably. "That...that thing you just did with your eyes."

"What thing?"

"The *thing*! You watched me while you were drinking, and it made me feel..." She stopped, suddenly, and, saying nothing, he took the cup out of her hands and put it on the bedside table.

Then, he moved closer, bracing one hand either side of her.

"What did it make you feel?"

She opened her mouth to say something trite, but he caught her lips, capturing the words before they were spoken, taking her breath away.

"You've definitely done that before," she said, once they came up for air.

"I have."

"Good," she said, and made a grab for him, the bedclothes falling away. "Do it again."

"Is that an order?" he teased.

"It's a direct order."

Emma was polishing off the last of her Weetabix when Ryan arrived home from the hospital, shortly after eight o'clock that morning. He'd spent the night at Anna's bedside, until the nurse had given him a ticking off and told him that his wife would need some personal care, so he might as well go home and come back later.

"Ryan? Is that you?"

His mother appeared from the kitchen doorway, her face showing the signs of a night spent worrying and grieving. She moved forward to take him in her arms, remembering when he'd been a small boy and not the tall, handsome man he had become.

"I'm so sorry," she said, drawing back to look at him. "How's Anna doing? Emma's been asking for her, and I wasn't sure what to say. I thought you'd like to tell her what had happened, in your own way."

Ryan realised his mother hadn't heard the news of there being another baby—in the whirlwind, he'd only told her that he wouldn't be home until the morning, and that Anna was doing well.

"What?" she asked, noticing the subtle shift in his expression. "What is it?"

"They're keeping Anna in for observation," he said. "There was another baby, you see."

Eve blinked. "*Another* baby?" she repeated. "You mean…there were twins?"

Ryan nodded. "The sonographer missed it, at the first scan," he said.

"That's…that's wonderful news, isn't it?"

Eve wanted to dance for joy, at their unexpected good fortune, but she was never more aware that the blessing had come with a cost, too.

"It *is* wonderful," Ryan agreed. "But we're coming to terms with feeling two sets of emotions, all at once. We're incredibly sad for the loss of one little life that might have been, but also ecstatic to learn that there's another still there, fighting to survive."

Eve nodded, and opened her mouth to tell him something she'd never confided before.

Then, shut it again.

It wasn't the time.

"Emma, look who's home!"

"Daddy!"

She scrambled off her chair to give her father a hug but, this time, he was wise to her Weetabixy ways, and managed to hold her away from him at arm's length, like Simba.

"Oh, no, you don't!" Ryan laughed. "Let's clean your face up, before you smear it all over me again."

Emma giggled, and it became a game to see if she could splat him with her sticky fingers, while he evaded them with a series of ducks and dives, tickles and twists to make her laugh.

Once they'd finished larking about, and Emma was happily occupied colouring in pictures of Disney characters, Ryan turned back to his mother.

"I know you were planning to return to Devon, after the New Year," he said. "I wondered if you would mind staying a bit longer, until Anna's back on her feet again?"

Eve reached across to take his hand. "Just try keeping me away," she said, with a smile. "I've already told the staff that I won't be back for a couple of weeks."

Ryan thanked her, and, with an eye for the time, polished off his tea.

"I have to get moving," he said. "Before I do, I wanted to ask how you're finding it, managing the estate on your own, without Dad there?"

Eve thought of Charles, as she often did. In fact, she was reminded of him every time she looked across the table at her son, who was the image of his father, at the same age.

"At first, it was an empty place without him," she admitted. "Every room carries his memory, but I certainly don't want to become some old Miss Haversham character, living in the past. It's helped, so much, spending time with you all here in Bamburgh, but I know I'm not ready to leave Summersley, yet. I want to throw open its doors to the community, much more than we have in the past, because we travelled so much and were never there. I want to run art therapy classes for people. My fingers may not be as nimble with a drawing pencil or a paintbrush as they once were, but I can still teach and encourage creative expression in others. I want to be *useful*, not a remnant of a world that no longer exists."

Ryan smiled, happy to see a light shining in her eyes again.

"You can still paint beautiful pictures." He nodded towards the watercolour painting she'd completed the week before, capturing Emma sitting on a rug in front of the Christmas tree, with Rascal at her side.

"They're easy studies," she said, and then remembered something else. "Oh, Ryan? Just a minute."

"Yes?" he said, with a hand on the door.

"Someone pushed a letter through the letterbox for you, late last night," she said. "I only noticed it, this morning."

She reached for a plain white envelope lying beside the kettle. "Here."

Ryan turned it over in his hand. "Did you see who dropped it off?"

Eve shook her head.

He could check their household entry system, which came with a little camera above the porch, to see for himself. In the meantime, Ryan slid open the envelope to find a single sheet of paper containing a scrawled message:

MEET AT CHATHILL RAILWAY CROSSING, 9AM TOMORROW.
WE NEED TO TALK.
B.T.

Bill Tilson, Ryan thought, and his first thought was to wonder how the man found out where they lived. Then again, it was a small world, especially in the North East. Their window cleaner was a talkative man, for one thing, often sharing all sorts of information about his other customers which they neither wanted nor needed to know. It would be all too easy to imagine him chatting to others about, "the Ryan family, up at the big house in Bamburgh", following which he'd probably give them chapter and verse on the various renovation disasters they'd experienced with the old Georgian manor house. Bill could overhear a conversation like that from anyone in the neighbourhood.

He checked the time and, realising he was cutting it fine to make it to Chathill in time to meet Bill, he kissed his mother and daughter goodbye, made a grab for his coat, and hurried out the door.

CHAPTER 31

Frank and Denise had spent a long night spent interviewing every possible witness to Harry's murder, which came to more than fifty young men, women, girls and boys who'd been at Buddles Boxing Gym between six and eight-thirty the previous evening, which was the pathologist's best estimate of when Harry died. It was an unusually accurate window, because his body had still been warm when it was discovered by Frank, shortly before eight-thirty. Instead of the waxy, unnatural grey tone it would soon become once the blood fell to the underside of his body, his skin had retained a pinkish hue, which added further weight to the idea that he'd been murdered not long before Frank's arrival.

It had been a hard task for him to work the case objectively, and Denise soon established that Frank would be consigned to his desk thereafter, to avoid any bias that would naturally seep into the investigation, following a decades-long friendship with the victim. To that end, she'd called in Mel, who'd been glad of the opportunity for busy-work, and together they'd taken much of the load from Frank's shoulders as he strived to come to terms with the loss of a childhood friend.

"I still haven't been able to get hold of Ryan," Denise said, as they made their way into the office. "I've left a few messages, but he hasn't come back to me yet, which isn't like him. I wonder if everything's okay."

"Probably just run off his feet," Frank said, in a subdued tone that didn't suit him at all.

Even more worrying was that, for the first time in years, he didn't suggest they stop at The Pie Van as they passed its welcoming neon sign.

"Frank," she said. "Are you sure you shouldn't take the day off? There's the packing to do, for our trip to Ireland, and Samantha's still away with the Pony Club lot, so you wouldn't need to entertain her. Why not take a bit of time to yourself?"

Frank thought about it, then dismissed the idea.

"I'd only be climbin' the walls," he said. "Besides, we've got plenty of work to be dealin' with here, and we need all hands on deck."

There was no further opportunity to argue with him, because, at that moment, her phone began to ring.

"It's Anna," she told him, and then answered the call. "Hi, Anna! Is everything okay?"

At the other end of the line, Anna hesitated. "Yes, it'll be okay," she said, answering her own doubts as well as any Denise may have had. "Is this a good time to talk, briefly?"

Denise thought of all the work piling up, the calls and e-mails to make before it was time to collect Samantha, and shoved all of it to one side for the woman who'd been there for her more times than she could count.

"You can talk to me anytime."

Despite the grief that distracted him, Frank found himself tuning in to the second-hand conversation, concern for his friends trumping all else.

"I just wanted to let you know, I'm in hospital—"

"*What?*" Denise interjected, and turned around as if to head back to her car and drive to wherever Anna was being treated. Frank skipped after her like a puppy, following blindly until he was given further instructions. "What happened? Was there an attack?"

Anna loved her for the instant loyalty, the unquestioning support, even before she knew what the matter was.

"It isn't anything like that," she said, trying to keep her voice level enough to speak the news aloud. "We lost a baby."

Denise stopped dead in the middle of the car park, the noise of passing traffic fading away.

"Oh, love. I'm so sorry. Tell me where you are, and we'll come to see you. Or, can we help with Emma? Is Ryan there? What about—"

The questions flew from her lips, and Denise knew she was talking too much but couldn't seem to stop herself. She was one of life's fixers and menders, always the one to bring home a bird with a broken wing and nurse it back to health—just look at the job she'd done with Frank, who was now presentable in most polite company, and even had learned to pass wind only in dedicated toilet areas, most of the time.

"There's more," Anna said. "We found out there was another baby. I was expecting twins, and we lost one of them."

Denise didn't know whether to congratulate her, but took a chance and followed her instinct.

"That's marvellous news," she said. "I'm so sad that you lost one of them, Anna, but what a gift to still have one—especially one you didn't expect. But how do you feel about it?"

"The same," Anna said. "I also feel guilty for feeling happy."

"That's something you should never feel guilty about," Denise said, with absolute certainty. "Happiness is in short enough supply, so we should grab it whenever we can."

"Thank you," Anna said, and wiped away a tear that had somehow escaped. "I was also calling to ask if you'd heard from Ryan? He told me he'd be back at the hospital by ten, but it's coming up to that now and there's no sign of him. I spoke to his mother and she says he didn't even stop to shower and change, but went straight back out again and it seemed as though he was in a hurry. I wondered if something might have cropped up, at work?"

Denise looked to Frank, who checked his phone and then shook his head.

Still no word.

Conscious that additional stress was the last thing Anna needed, Denise made sure her voice held no trace of worry when she answered.

"I bet his mobile's run out of battery," she said, in a long-suffering tone. "It happens all the time, when we're trying to get hold of him at work."

That was a lie, but Denise told herself it was well-intentioned.

"I bet he'll turn up in the next few minutes, full of apologies. But, just in case he's been held up, why don't I head over to see you, and keep you company for a little while?"

Anna was tempted, but there was something to be said for having a period of quiet solitude in which to process what her body had been through.

"Thanks Denise, but I know how busy you are," she said. "Let me know if you hear from Ryan."

MacKenzie spoke to her for a few more minutes, making sure she really didn't need the company, before ending the call.

"Do you think Ryan's gone AWOL?"

"Never in a million years," Frank said. "If he's gone quiet, it's either because he's dealing with a problem, he's been kidnapped, or he's dead."

"Well, that's a cheerful thought."

"Just tellin' it how it is," Frank said. "And, as far as I'm concerned, if it's anythin' other than Option C, there's no excuse for him not droppin' us a line."

"Even if he's been kidnapped?"

"He could still send a message via carrier pigeon. I've shown him enough episodes of *Geordie Racer* for him to understand how to do it."

A pigeon landed on the bonnet of Ryan's car, and he thought seriously of taping a message to its leg, considering his smartphone flatly refused to pick up a signal at Chathill railway crossing, not far from Bamburgh. He realised that must have been a deciding factor in Bill's choice of location, though why he needed to concern himself with any of that was a mystery—after all, if he was to be believed, his criminal past was behind him, and he'd served his debt to society.

Ryan checked the time on the dashboard and swore.

Nine-fifty.

Bill was late.

He began to wonder if he'd wandered blindly into some sort of set-up, the events of the past few years having heightened his adrenal system to a state of constant fight or flight. Imagining different scenarios, he looked around the quiet, country road with its high hedgerows and distant views of the sea.

Five more minutes, he told himself. He'd give it five more minutes before leaving.

Just then, he spotted a car.

It was a brand-new Range Rover in a bespoke shade of rust-red, which Ryan associated with suburban families at school drop-off, along with an inordinate amount of what people called *loungewear*, which, as far as he could tell, was a fancy name for jogging bottoms and sports bras, baggy t-shirts and oversized sweaters—the kind he occasionally wore when he was a student, in the late nineties.

However, the driver of the Range Rover was not a parent with a back seat full of kids on their way to the nearest soft play, but a heavy-set man wearing a pair of aviator sunglasses.

"Finally," Ryan muttered, and flashed his lights.

There came a flash in return, and both men turned off their engines, having parked side by side in a lay-by more often used by tractors turning.

"I thought you'd changed your mind," Ryan said, as they walked towards one another. "What happened?"

"Got caught on the causeway," Bill said. "There was a bigger queue of traffic than I expected, so it took a bit longer to get off the island."

Ryan leaned back against his car, and folded his arms. "I got your note, and here I am," he said. "Before we get into it, I want to say something."

Bill waited.

"You never come to my home again," Ryan said. "You don't come within five hundred feet of it, or my wife and child, without my knowledge."

"How else was I supposed to get a message to you?"

"You have the number of the incident room," Ryan said. "You have the number for my office. Why not call either one of those, like a normal member of society?"

"I can't do that."

"Why not?" Ryan said. "You're a rehabilitated member of society now, aren't you?"

Bill swallowed. "Look, I wanted to get this off my chest. Not for you," he said. "For her."

"Anna?"

Bill nodded. "I owe her."

More than he could ever repay, Ryan thought, but he held himself back and focused on extracting information.

"Why isn't she here?" Bill asked.

"That's none of your business," Ryan replied. "I'm getting bored, Tilson. Say what you want to say, or stop wasting my time."

Bill looked around, half expecting to see the barrel of a gun poking through the hedgerow.

"I'll make this quick," he said. "But this conversation never happened. I don't want my name to appear on any paperwork and, if you try to drag me into it, I'll deny everything. Do you understand? I'd rather go back to prison and take my chances there."

Ryan was about to say something flippant, before realising something very important.

Bill was afraid.

No, more than that. He was *terrified*.

"You're not in a position to make demands," he said.

"Neither are you," Bill said, and knew he was right. "You need to know, and I'm the one who can tell you."

Ryan considered his options, thought of Anna, and gave a nod. "All right. You have my word."

Bill might have hated most of the screws and pigs he'd come to know, over the years, and he couldn't say he was any fan of Ryan's, either. But, if there was one thing he'd credit Ryan with, it was being able to keep to his word. "Done," he said. "Andy's alive."

Ryan's face didn't move. "Tell me something I don't know," he said.

"You didn't know for sure," Bill said, pointing an accusing finger.

"We would've found out," Ryan said. "They've already confirmed the body in Taylor's grave doesn't belong to him. You know who it belongs to, don't you?"

At this, Bill shook his head. "No, I swear, I don't know anythin' about that," he said. "I left that to—to other people to arrange. I only know that Andy survived, because I was the one who found him."

Ryan remained silent, knowing it was one of the best ways of encouraging people to talk.

"Look, Mark Bowers shoved Andy off a ledge at the castle," he said, referring to the fortress on Lindisfarne. "He was always jealous of Andy, and he saw his chance to get rid of him. There was no way he should've survived that fall."

Bill scrubbed a hand over his mouth, and checked over his shoulder again.

"Bowers thought Andy would be dead, so he sent me up there to make sure everything looked accidental," he carried on. "I went up straight away, while it was still dark, and found him. He was still alive. He'd broken his leg and maybe his hip…I can't remember. But he was *alive*."

"What did you do?"

Bill thought back to that night, and the risk he'd taken. "We made a deal," he said. "Andy had a pile of cash he'd built up, over the years. He offered to split it with me and chuck in the pub as well, if I helped him get away."

Ryan imagined them, and their desperate pact arranged under cover of darkness.

"How did you do that?"

"He used my phone and rang a few people, to call in some favours," he said. "I don't even know who he called; he kept the phone and probably destroyed it, later. All he asked me to do was to get him off the island, and keep my mouth shut. I don't even know where he got medical treatment…he was in a bad way."

"Where did you take him, Bill?"

Tilson ran a tongue over chapped lips, then shook his head. "That's all you need to know," he said, and began walking back to his car. "I've already put myself in enough danger, as it is."

"Why?" Ryan said, following him as he paced away. "Is it because Andy paid you another instalment, recently, so long as you carried on keeping your mouth shut? You used that money to do over the pub, didn't you? You know something else, don't you, Bill?"

"I don't know anything else!" Bill shouted back over his shoulder.

"You know why Andy killed that woman, that author, *don't you*, Bill?"

Ryan caught up with him, as Bill's hand reached out to open the car door. He slammed a hand against it, holding it shut.

"Had Olman found out his true identity, somehow? Is that it?"

"I don't bloody know!"

Bill wrenched open the car door, and Ryan stumbled backwards.

A moment later, the engine roared into life and Bill performed a wide U-turn. Ryan stood, a lone figure in the surrounding landscape, and watched him drive away.

CHAPTER 32

"This was Arnold Blythe."

DS Bell and DC Vale had decided to conduct a briefing at Northumbria Headquarters, rather than on their own turf. It was a small concession, because the dead man was found in Andrew Taylor's grave, whose connections with their team were a matter of record—and in consideration of the fact Blythe had been one of their own. All of Ryan's team were in attendance, except the man himself.

"Where's Ryan?" Lauren asked.

"Gettin' a bollocking from his wife, I should think," Phillips said, cheerfully. "Anna's not well, so they kept her in hospital overnight. Ryan's bringin' her home later today, all bein' well."

Lauren was sorely tempted to ask what the matter was and, more importantly, why Anna might want to give her husband the aforementioned 'bollocking', but it was none of her concern. Besides, she had her own problems, one of which was standing right beside her, so close she could feel the heat of his body in the chilly conference room.

"Well," she said, taking a subtle step away from Kieron towards the whiteboard. "Let's get started, then. As I was saying, this is Arnold Blythe, formerly a detective inspector within Northumbria Constabulary's Drugs Squad, from 1989 to 2007, when he was reported missing. He was thirty-six, no wife or children, clean service record."

"Amazingly clean, considering when he was working in that department," Denise remarked. "It would've been smack bang in the middle of Gregson's reign, and his reach spread throughout the whole constabulary. Drugs and Vice would've been especially vulnerable to corruption."

"Just because he has a clean record on paper doesn't mean that was the full story," Charlie remarked, thinking of other men she might have mentioned.

"It wasn't the full story," Mel put in, having spent some time on the phone to her contact in the archives department.

Lauren was impressed, considering the pathologist hadn't even returned a preliminary report yet. "Talk to me," she said.

"He was embedded," Mel said. "A plant. He worked undercover for almost seven years as one of the Pearson gang, from 2001 until he went missing."

"How'd you find out about this?" Kieron asked.

"Archives," she said. "There was a sealed file under his name, so I got Morrison's permission to have a little looksie. Turns out, Blythe was a dark horse."

They looked at the official photograph of Blythe on the wall in front of them, which showed an average-looking man with neatly cut red hair, in a dark grey suit and tie which had been fashionable in that era. He looked as though he worked as a customer service manager, not as a police plant on the mean streets of gangland Newcastle, during the late nineties.

"The fact he was found in a grave marked for Andrew Taylor tells us there was a possible connection—" Lauren began to say.

The door opened, and all heads turned to greet Ryan, who entered the room with his usual aura of dynamic energy. Watching him, Denise and Frank marvelled at his ability to conceal the tumultuous emotions he must have been feeling.

"Sorry I'm late," he said, throwing his coat across an empty chair. "What have I missed?"

"Before we get to that, can I check your bollocks are still where they should be?" Lauren asked, sweetly.

Ryan looked across at Frank, who shrugged and searched his friend's face for signs of the strain he must have suffered the previous evening. Aside from the dark shadows beneath his eyes, there was little outward sign of it. However, that didn't mean the suffering wasn't there, lurking beneath the surface.

"*Yes*," Ryan said. "Thank you for your concern, everyone, but my balls have lived to dangle another day. Now, will one of the detectives in this room bring me up to speed?"

"Gladly," Lauren said. "We were just about to discuss the possibility of a connection between the deceased—Arnold Blythe, who we've recently learned was an undercover plant within the Pearson gang, at the time of his death—and Andrew Taylor, whose grave he occupied for the past eighteen years."

Ryan hitched himself up onto one of the tables, and crossed his ankles. "The Pearsons?" he said.

"Aye," Frank replied. "In fact, you might say it's a—"

"*Coincidence*?" several voices chimed in.

Ryan's lips twitched. "Well, you know how I feel about those."

"What am I missing?" Kieron said, since he and Lauren weren't part of the joke. "What do you feel about them?"

"There's no such thing," Jack supplied. "He's been drumming it into us for years."

"Because it's the truth," Ryan said. "It can't possibly be a coincidence that, around the same time we discover Taylor is still alive—"

"We don't know that for certain, do we?" Lauren said.

"As of this morning, I have it on excellent authority that he's been alive the whole time," Ryan said.

"Whose authority?"

"I can't divulge my source," he said.

"What do you mean? You're not some old hack on Fleet Street, Ryan. We need them to go on record and give a statement, if that's the truth."

"They won't," he said, flatly. "Besides, the information they've provided is more important, since it'll help us to get to the next stage in tracking Taylor's whereabouts."

They listened, as he relayed the information Bill had given him.

"So, your source, who we must assume to have been a former member of The Circle, says that he or she drove Andy Taylor off the island to a safe place, which they refuse to divulge. As to the arrangements for faking the man's death, and substituting a body, they claim not to know any details about that. Is that the gist of it?" Denise said.

"Exactly," Ryan said. "Although, at this stage, I'd query whether a substitute body was even necessary for a successful cover-up. Whoever helped falsify Taylor's death record must have also bribed the coroner and the pathologist who signed off the fake autopsy report—they could have buried an empty coffin just as easily as an occupied one."

"Maybe Blythe was already dead," Charlie said, thinking aloud. "I mean, it's another convenient coincidence, if they were able to kill Blythe and transport his body up there at short notice. It seems far more likely Blythe was dead already, and his body was being stored somewhere, which is why they could access it quickly and bury him in Taylor's place."

Another thought occurred to Ryan, which answered the remaining questions he had about who had orchestrated the cover-up on Taylor's behalf, and why they would go out of their way to do such a thing. Certainly, he was out of favour with his comrades in The Circle, so he had few friends to rely on for help.

"The question is, who owed Andy Taylor a favour?" he said. "Who'd go to all that trouble, unless there was something in it that would benefit them, too?"

"There's also the related question, who would benefit from Arnold Blythe's death?" Mel added. "Someone in the Pearson gang? Maybe they found out Blythe was an undercover cop, and murdered him as punishment."

"Possibly," Frank said, and thought of his friend, Harry. "But it's not gangland MO. If they wanted to send a message, it'd be more likely they'd kill Blythe execution style, and make sure the body was found, so the word got out. It's the same issue we had with Terry Pearson's murder; if the idea was to punish him and send a message, why cut up the body and weigh the parts down underwater, so they wouldn't be found for a while? It doesn't make sense."

Whereas, in Harry's case, he'd been executed in his place of business and left for the first person to find. It was a gruesome, bloody death, designed to ward off any others who might be thinking of informing. For that, Frank would never forgive Harry's killer; he'd also never forgive himself.

"Frank's right," Ryan said, pushing to his feet so he could think more clearly—though, why standing up should help matters, he had no idea. "Added to which, although the pathologist hasn't completed his report, he has made a few comments on the state of Blythe's body. His head was caved in using a heavy, metal implement, like the end of a shovel, which isn't the usual method in gangland killings. It speaks of anger in the heat of the moment, using the first thing to hand, not an execution-style killing using a knife, a gun, or—"

"A garotte," Frank muttered.

"Or a garotte," Ryan repeated, not understanding the reference, since he hadn't caught up with Denise's case summary following Harry's murder the previous evening.

"You're saying it's more likely Blythe was killed on the spur of the moment and his body was stored until such time it could be disposed of without attracting attention?" Kieron said, working through the likely suspects in his mind.

Ryan nodded. "That's exactly what I'm saying. We're looking for someone who stood to lose, if Blythe spoke out about information he'd found out during the course of his duties—or perhaps Blythe wanted a cut of a deal which this person wasn't prepared to give? There are a hundred possibilities, but the field narrows when we consider the mindset. The death was unplanned, the disposal not thought through. It suggests a desk-jockey, a suit, not someone on the ground working as the muscle in an organisation. They're executive level, not entry level, which is another reason why they stand to lose out, if Blythe went public with information that would cause reputational damage. On top of all this, that person *also* had an interest in helping Andrew Taylor. Who do we think ticks all the boxes?"

"What if Andy Taylor was the one to dispose of the body, initially?" Jack offered. "Maybe the killer lost his rag, whacked Blythe around the head with a garden shovel, and then rang Taylor, asking for help? They're both members of The Circle, maybe; they're both connected. Taylor wasn't 'Master' in that cult for very long; maybe he managed to get a promotion after helping this person, but it wasn't enough to save him from Bowers, in the long term."

"That's a good theory," Denise said, nodding. "It feels possible."

Ryan agreed.

"I've read the files, the report and all that," Lauren said. "But I never worked on the investigation of The Circle for our command area. Are you sure they had this kind of clout, back then?"

"Very sure," Ryan said. "In fact, I'm also pretty sure I know who's the missing link in all this."

"Bloody Nora," Frank said, and slapped a hand to his forehead. "Gregson. It had to be Gregson."

Ryan nodded.

"Who had a public reputation to protect from scandal? Arthur Gregson. Who was supposed to uphold the law and set an example? Gregson. Who was profiteering from all his gangland connections, creaming off the top of their deals in hush money? Gregson. If Blythe was initially a straight arrow, which people seem to think he was, and he learned of Gregson's involvement with the Pearsons, he might have threatened to report his superintendent, or go public with the information. He might have tried a bit of extortion, if he had the mettle for it."

"Gregson lashed out to stop him," Lauren said, thinking of a man she'd seen on the news, but seldom in real life. "If Taylor helped him out by storing Blythe's body somewhere—"

"In a freezer, would be my guess," Frank put in, and waggled his smartphone. "Pinter just sent through some more observations, and there's a funny little one in particular that might be of interest. The little finger of Blythe's left hand was missing, and several toes."

"Cut off, as a form of torture?" Kieron suggested.

"He thinks not, in this case," Frank replied. "The bone snapped off midway, not at the joint. It's liable to happen when the bones are entirely frozen. They become more brittle and prone to breakage."

"Which is consistent with the idea of Blythe's body being put into deep storage," Ryan said. "Taylor helps Gregson out, and saves his bacon—sorry, bad analogy—which means he can call in a favour when he needs to disappear. Gregson's perfectly placed to make that happen, and to make sure the world believes it. Taylor tells him where Blythe's body is being stored, probably as leverage for an occasion such as this, and he offers it to Gregson in exchange for a new identity. Gregson agrees, and arranges for Blythe's body to be buried in Taylor's grave."

The room fell silent, following the logical pathway, and there were murmurs of assent.

"We think Taylor may be living in Berwick," Lauren said, having decided it was no use pretending they weren't all playing for the same team. Luckily for Kieron, she had no idea that everyone in the room was already aware of that fact, thanks to Kieron's little side-hustle with Phillips which, he had to say, had paid off beautifully.

"You don't seem at all surprised to learn that," she remarked, and the gathered crowd made elaborate 'surprise' and 'shock' noises to compensate.

She turned to Kieron, who smiled winningly.

"We'll discuss information sharing, later," she said, beneath her breath.

"We can share other things, if you like," he whispered, and she became flustered beneath her buttoned-up shirt.

Skating on thin ice, she told herself. *Never get into bed with a workmate.*

"It's all good conjecture," Ryan said, slicing through the tension that had gathered in the air above their heads. "But there's something I still don't understand. We've got a good working theory about how Andy Taylor forged a new life, and who he called upon to help him. We have another good working theory about how Arnold Blythe fell afoul of The Circle, in the course of performing his undercover duties. What we don't know is why, after all these years, Taylor would come out of hiding and murder an author he'd never met before, that we know of, and with whom he had no prior relationship. Likewise, why kill Terry Pearson around the same time as all this? What was the catalyst?"

"We found more trace samples of Taylor's DNA, after a second sweep of Oldman's flat," Lauren said. "There was a concentration around her desk area, her chest of drawers, her cupboards and kitchen units. It's possible she had something in her possession that he needed to take back."

"But what?" Kieron asked.

"She wasn't a rich woman," Mel said. "There would've been easier, less conspicuous targets, if he was running short of cash and needed to pick up some items to hock down at the pawn shop."

"Exactly," Ryan said, staring at the image of Blythe, which stared right back at him. "It had to be the manuscript."

The others turned to him in surprise.

"Your wife's original manuscript wasn't stolen," Lauren reminded him. "There wasn't any of his DNA found on it, or around it."

"Because it was in a hidden compartment," Kieron reminded her. "Our forensic guys only found it while they were stripping the place apart."

Ryan sat back, running a tired hand over his face, realising where all of this would lead.

"I don't quite follow," Frank said. "What does the manuscript matter to him, if Oldman had thousands of copies of the book out across bookshops around the land?"

"It was a different manuscript," Ryan said. "Anna's original one, which was plagiarised and formed the basis of the book Oldman went on to publish. It was never held in digital form, only as a print copy which she hid away, so nobody would find it. If someone happened to read her book, they would see the similarities, as we did, and there may have been something in there to give cause for concern. Taylor needed to see Oldman's original paperwork, and perhaps to speak to the lady herself, to be sure she didn't know anything else."

"Why kill her, though?" Mel wondered aloud. "If he learned she wasn't the original author, why would he need to kill her?"

"She'd seen him," Ryan said, shortly. "She'd seen a dead man."

"What do you think Anna's manuscript contained that gave him such cause for alarm?" Denise asked.

"I don't know," he said, and picked up his coat. "I need to find out, because, if Andrew Taylor knows Oldman didn't write the original, he'll know Anna did."

On which note, he turned to leave, then spun back around to look at Blythe's picture.

"I don't know why, but he reminds me of someone. Frank? Do you see it?"

Phillips screwed up his face in concentration, then shook his head. "I know what you mean, he looks familiar, but I don't think I've seen him before, or remember him from the old days," he said. "I'll let you know, if anythin' comes back to me."

Ryan nodded, and was gone.

Then, before they could do anything further, he was back again.

"Make up yer mind!" Frank joked. "What now, lad?"

"You're with me," he told Frank. "Sorry, Denise, but I need to steal your husband away. Lauren, Kieron? Congratulations."

"On—on *what*?" she stammered.

Ryan gave her an innocent look. "On pulling together a great briefing," he said. "What did you think I meant?"

Lauren's eyes narrowed.

"Mel, Denise, I know you're handling the case we caught last night," he said, and offered Frank a sympathetic smile, in lieu of the conversation they would have once they were on the road, chicken nuggets on their laps and driving towards HMP Frankland. "But, Denise, I wonder if you'd mind handing the SIO hat over to Mel, temporarily? I'd be grateful if you and Sam could sit with Anna, and protect her until I get home? I need to interview Gregson and find out the part he played, once and for all. If anyone knows which rock Andy Taylor is hiding under, it's him. It would make me a lot happier to know there was someone there who can handle themselves."

"We can help, too," Kieron said, entirely unprompted.

BERWICK

Lauren felt a mixture of pride and admiration, neither of which she relished feeling for *any* man, but seemed to be feeling more and more towards one, in particular. "Yes, of course, we can help," she echoed. "Denise, I know Anna's your friend, but you have your daughter to look out for. If there's any suggestion of danger, until we understand what's really behind all of this, I think it's a good idea for Anna to be under protection."

Ryan nodded. "Thank you, both. I won't forget it."

He turned back to his team. "Jack, Charlie, see if you can squeeze anything else out of the Pearson family about their dearly departed and, especially in light of recent information, find out everything you can about their connection to Arnold Blythe. Most of all, we need to find out what *Terry's* connection is, to all of this. Find that out, and we'll find his killer."

"Yes, Guv."

He turned and left the room again, but Frank lingered on for a second or two, to see if Ryan changed his mind and doubled back again.

"*Frank*!" Ryan bellowed from the corridor outside.

Phillips tipped his flat cap to the group, blew his wife a kiss, and hurried after his friend.

CHAPTER 33

"Anna can't be put under any further stress at the moment."

Ryan said this as soon as he and Frank were inside his car and headed south of the River Tyne, towards His Majesty's Prison Frankland, on the outskirts of Durham. It was a place they knew well; indeed, they might have said *too* well, considering their long and chequered history with the place. It carried painful memories, not only as a holding pen for all the living reminders of the cases they'd closed and of the crimes they'd seen. More recently, the prison car park was the site where Gregson had ordered a hitman to kill Ryan using a car bomb, and managed to target Frank, instead. The latter suffered a heart attack and, though he seemed in good health, none of them could quite forget the moment when they thought he would be gone from their lives far too soon.

"I should've asked," Ryan said, and could have kicked himself. "You might not want to interview Gregson, after what happened. You say you haven't suffered PTSD, but that might be different when you see the place again. I can turn around and drive you home, then come back later with one of the others?"

Phillips put a reassuring hand on his friend's arm. "Oh, ye of little faith," he said, with a smile. "Thanks for the thought, lad, but it takes more than a little old car bomb to put me off a trip to Frankland. It's always a pleasure to rub our freedom in Gregson's face."

Ryan laughed. "It makes the trip all the more worthwhile," he agreed. "Let me know if you change your mind, but otherwise we'll just go in and out, as quickly as we can. He'll be expecting us, after all."

"You reckon?"

"Of course," Ryan said. "Taunting us is one of the few remaining pleasures in his life—unless he's made a 'special friend' in the shower room, naturally."

Frank roared with laughter. "With a face like his? He'd be lucky," he said.

The drove on for a while, each man lost in his own thoughts, until Ryan broached the subject of Harry.

"I heard about what happened to Harry," he said. "Sorry, Frank. I know the two of you went back a long way."

Phillips looked out of the window at the passing lights of the city, and remembered a time before half of the buildings were there. *Was it simpler?* he wondered. People were fond of saying that; of harkening back to the past, as though it represented a halcyon time in comparison with the present, but he wasn't so sure. Frank thought of the childhood he and Harry had shared, and of the obstacles they'd faced. There was poverty now, but there was plenty poverty then, too. Harry was one of the lads he'd knocked about with, shared his lunch with, defended against bullies from other schools and other streets. They'd been part of a tribe, like the Lost Boys, but without half so much magic.

Had he agreed with all of Harry's decisions, over the years?

No, far from it. Their political views had been wildly opposing, for a start. While Frank believed in progress, opportunity and kinship, Harry had been far more protective of his funds and his country.

He didn't see the world as one big, shared community, as Frank did. He saw the boundary lines, and liked to enforce them, whether or not he had a right to. They'd often come to verbal blows on the subject, but what set them apart was an ability to overcome their differences and remain friends, for they shared one thing in common, always, and that was a desire to protect vulnerable children.

In Harry's case, that meant providing a safe space for them to work out their frustrations; a mentorship programme to show angry, neglected young lads how real men behaved, and it wasn't by smacking their kids about, or hitting their wives. Other members of the gym belonged to various trades and professions, so Harry had organised monthly workshops where the kids could learn a thing or two about what it meant to be a plumber, an electrician, a carpenter, or even a musician. Often, Frank had walked into Buddles and heard the sound of an acoustic guitar playing, or the old piano Harry had picked up at a jumble sale. Some of the wives and mothers came in to watch the matches, and made friends with one another. They taught some of the boys and girls, men and women, how to cook. They held part-time jobs, cleaning or carrying, running errands or doing the admin tasks Harry could easily have done for himself, but wanted to provide as a career building opportunity for others.

"Aye," Frank said, after a long pause. "We went back a long, long way, me and Harry. I kissed his sister, one year, and he almost threw me off the Scotswood Bridge, but otherwise we were pals, him and me."

Ryan smiled.

"Mel's good at what she does," he said. "You know she'll manage the investigation, while you and Denise are away."

"I don't know if I can face going to Ireland until we find whoever did for him."

"You deserve the break, and your girls have been looking forward to it," Ryan said. "As your friend, and as your boss, I'm telling you to bugger off to Ireland and don't come back for a week."

Frank heaved a sigh. "Ask me again, tomorro'," he said, and Ryan left it at that.

HMP Frankland was illuminated by a series of powerful floodlights, which broke through the darkness with long shafts of white light. In the daylight, the prison had very little kerb appeal and, in the darkness, its ugliness was compounded and its facade rendered even more ominous.

Ryan turned into the car park, after talking to the disembodied voice of a security guard manning the outer gate, and made a point of parking as far away from the site where his last car had blown up, almost taking his best friend with it.

"You okay?" he checked again.

Frank felt a flutter of remembrance, a pinch of discomfort, but he took several deep, deliberate breaths while reminding himself that those events were in the past.

"I'm fine," he said. "Let's get this o'er with."

Ryan couldn't have agreed more with that sentiment, and the two men made their way across the car park to the prison entrance, beyond which were several stages of security they would need to pass through. It was a tedious process, but a necessary one. Unlike some of the visitors who came to ogle the prisoners like human specimens, Ryan and Phillips had seen the impact of the crimes those specimens had committed. They'd read the criminology textbooks, the articles, the reports and interviews about what truly influenced recidivism rates, or how socio-economic conditions often led to disordered minds and antisocial behaviour. Early life trauma was another common factor affecting the likelihood of a person going on to commit crimes of varying severity, their own capacity to feel empathy having been so badly broken as children that they no longer felt remorse when hurting others, once they grew to be adults. All of that might be true, but those people remained in the minority. They'd met many more who'd suffered unspeakable traumas and *never* gone on to perpetuate the cycle themselves. Indeed, they actively rejected it, and instead made the choice to be productive, caring members of society. One of the first lessons Ryan ever remembered learning on the job was that it never helped to tar everyone with the same brush.

Nonetheless, their job was to enforce society's laws, and protect the general public from those who flouted them in the most violent of ways. Others could worry about the reasons why men and women chose to attack their fellow beings, and pontificate about it to their heart's content. In the meantime, the officers and detectives of Major Crime divisions around the country would continue trying to prevent them from committing those attacks, murders, rapes and assaults, without reference to their childhood histories because, sometimes, as Ryan had also learned to his cost, people were just *bad*.

The man they'd come to see was someone he'd have placed into that category. He'd committed violent crimes, or arranged proxies to commit those crimes for him, wholly in the name of self-interest. Though he was now in his late sixties, as a young man starting out in the world, Arthur Gregson had been afforded the same choice as every other person from a decent, working-class background. He could work hard, and climb up the ladder the honest way—or he could cheat. Cheating would lead to more deception, which would eventually present further temptations and a need to protect the reputation and lifestyle he built upon those lies. It led to enormous short-term gains, but came with a terrible cost to the soul and, as Gregson had come to learn, an equally enormous cost to his life and liberty. The safer road would have meant a more modest living for Arthur, growing in increments proportionate to his work ethic, but he would've been able to sleep at night. Power would have been a distant, abstract thing he could become accustomed to as his professional responsibilities grew, rather than being something he snatched for himself like a greedy child, trampling upon anyone who tried to stop him.

"I'm sorry, Detective Inspector Ryan, Sergeant Phillips," the night manager told them, after speaking with the Governor. "We don't have any pre-approved visits scheduled between yourselves and Arthur Gregson."

"I'm aware of that," Ryan said, and told himself to remain calm. "As I explained on the telephone, there's an urgency to our investigation which precluded the possibility of us giving the usual notice. I can obtain verbal or written approval from the Chief Constable, if that would help?"

Please, Ryan thought. *Don't make me call Sandra Morrison.*

"Yes, that would be very helpful."

Ryan swallowed the expletive on the tip of his tongue, and gave an empty smile.

"No problem," he intoned, muttering something about computers saying 'no' beneath his breath. "I'll just be a minute."

Chief Constable Sandra Morrison was in the middle of her weekly 'everything' bath, in which she addressed the most pressing needs first. Usually, that meant dealing with the alarmingly long hairs beneath her arms, followed by her legs, and, finally, the more intimate areas in need of pruning, so as not to attract local wildlife or birds seeking somewhere to build a nest. In her younger days, she'd booked a regular waxing session, even going so far as to whip the whole lot off, but age had taught her wisdom, and that wisdom was that you'd have to be a bloody numpty to want to rip the hairs off your hoo-ha without any better reason than, 'He likes it better, that way'. In her experience, *real* men didn't mind, and, as she'd also learned in her private experience, real *women* didn't mind, either.

That being said, she wasn't quite ready to 'free the bush'.

These thoughts circled her mind as she scrubbed exfoliating salts over her skin, Alanis Morissette playing from an Alexa she'd perched on the bathroom vanity. A glass of iced white wine rested on a side table alongside a book she'd been looking forward to reading but hadn't yet had found the time. She hummed along to the music, and was beginning to forget about the trials and tribulations waiting for her back at the office, when her phone began to ring.

"They know it's my day off," she muttered, and scrubbed her skin a bit harder. "Should've turned the damn phone onto silent mode."

It rang out, and she was about to sink back into the warm water, when it started to ring again.

Balls and bugger, she thought.

One ring could be ignored, but two? Two was never good news.

Annoyed at the intrusion, but unable to look past her duty to the department, she sloshed out of the bathtub and wound a fluffy towel around herself, hair dripping onto the floor as she snatched up the phone.

"Ryan," she said, accusingly. "I might have *known* it would be you."

"I'm sorry to trouble you at home, ma'am," he said. "I'm afraid I need your sign-off on a last-minute interview with one of the prisoners at Frankland."

"Is that *all*?" she almost shouted. "Ryan, you could've put in a request and visited whoever it is tomorrow, like a normal person!"

"I've never been accused of being normal, and, in any case, it really can't wait, ma'am. We have a dead killer at large, and I strongly believe Gregson knows where he is."

BERWICK

"Andrew Taylor's alive, then?" she said. "Are you sure?"

"The body we exhumed from his grave has been positively identified as Arnold Blythe, formerly an undercover officer working out of Drugs Squad, back in the late nineties, ma'am. Additionally, colleagues at Durham CID have traced the movements of a man matching Taylor's description leaving Lin Oldman's property around the relevant time she was murdered. He's been traced by rail from Durham to Berwick, where we're now liaising with our colleagues in Berwick to acquire any and all video footage of the area around the station to determine where he went, after that."

"Why does all this require you to pay Gregson a visit this evening, and not tomorrow morning?"

"We have strong grounds to suspect Gregson enabled Taylor to flee Holy Island, fake his own death and establish a new identity back in 2007," Ryan said. "We believe he did this because Gregson murdered DI Blythe, and Taylor arranged for the removal of the body to a place of safe storage. He may have used Blythe's body, and his knowledge that Gregson murdered him, as leverage to enable him to call in a favour for himself, when he was later in need. However, right now, the main thing is, we're very concerned that the reason Taylor has shown himself, after all these years, and the reason Oldman was killed, has to do with the content of a manuscript Anna wrote and which Oldman stole and plagiarised. We believe Taylor read Oldman's book, without knowing his own daughter had written the original manuscript, and that he confronted Oldman in order to find out the extent of her knowledge about something within the pages of her novel."

"And you think Taylor could strike again, if he realises Oldman didn't write the original story?" Morrison finished for him. "Would he do that, to his own daughter?"

Ryan didn't even have to think about it.

"Yes, ma'am, I'm afraid he would. Andrew Taylor's desire for self-preservation is stronger than any paternal feeling he ever had towards either of his children."

Morrison felt it best not to pass comment, though there were plenty of pejorative adjectives she could have employed.

"I understand the risk factors, now," she said. "Would it help to move Anna to a safe house?"

Ryan wasn't sure how to answer without giving away more than he'd intended.

"Ryan? Are you still there?"

"Sorry, yes. Yes, ma'am. It's kind of you to offer, but I'm afraid Anna can't be moved, at the moment. She spent last night in hospital, and has been discharged home on the strict condition that she remains in bed for the rest of the week and only gets up when she has to."

Morrison let out soft sigh, in sympathy for all he had left unsaid. "Oh, Ryan. I'm so sorry—"

"So were we, and we still are," he said. "However, we found out the baby was a twin, and one is still viable."

Sitting on the edge of her bath, Morrison perked up, the news as much of a surprise to her, as it was to all of them.

"I'm so glad to hear it," she said. "How can I help?"

"Just get me into Frankland to speak to Gregson, and I'll take care of the rest," he said. "Some of the team is with Anna and my mother, as a protective measure until I return home."

"Good," Morrison said. "In that case, put whoever is in charge on the phone, so I can lay the proverbial smack down."

Ryan grinned, and thanked her. "By the way," he said, before he went in search of the manager.

"What *now*?"

"Is that Alanis Morissette you're listening to? That's ironic."

"Oh, shut up," she said. "Before I change my mind."

CHAPTER 34

"Just can't stay away, can you? Have you missed me?"

Gregson shuffled into one of the interview rooms in his prison-issue jogging bottoms and sweatshirt, which bore the marks of several old food stains and washed-out brown patches where he'd suffered bloody injuries during the time he'd spent in lockup. Nowadays, he was kept in solitary confinement for his own protection, until a place became available at another maximum-security prison in a different part of the country.

"Sit down, Arthur."

"Don't mind if I do," he said, and took the seat opposite Ryan and Phillips at the shiny, metal table which was bolted to the floor. The prison officer took Gregson's handcuffed wrists and began to attach them to an anchor point on the underside of the table, but Ryan held up a hand to stop him.

"What do you say, Arthur? If I ask this kind officer to release your shackles, will you behave yourself?"

Gregson remembered a time when *he* was the man giving the orders, and *he* was the man commanding respect along every corridor. Back then, nobody would have dared to shackle him, nor to ask if he'd *behave himself*.

He'd fallen a long, long way.

"Fine," he said.

The handcuffs were unlocked, and he rubbed the skin on his wrists.

"There we are," Ryan said, magnanimously. "Now, let me take a wild, stab in the dark, and guess that you know precisely why we're here. Am I right?"

Gregson grinned like a Cheshire cat, and leaned back in his chair. The years had been both kind and unkind to Arthur; he'd always been a tall, imposing man with a military bearing not dissimilar to Ryan's late father, though his face was now a patchwork of scars thanks to successive revenge attacks perpetrated by the many inmates serving long-term sentences thanks to him. On the other hand, he'd spent time sculpting his body in the prison gym, and boasted a leaner, meaner frame than before.

"Quite right," he said, with a smile.

"Let's cut to the chase," Ryan said. "You've always known Andrew Taylor was still alive, because you helped him make a new life under an assumed name, didn't you?"

"Even if what you're saying is true—hypothetically-speaking, you understand—why would you think I'd help Andy Taylor? He meant nothing to me."

"That's not quite true, is it?" Phillips said. "We happen to think he helped you out by disposin' of a body, or, he let you *think* it had been disposed of. Turns out, he'd kept it in storage, for a rainy day, you might say. That rainy day came one dark and stormy night, when your old mate Mark Bowers decided to shove Taylor off a cliff to his death. Only, he didn't die, did he? He lived, and you got a call you didn't expect. He was callin' in the favour, wasn't he?"

Gregson said nothing, but secretly applauded the legwork. "Go on," he said. "I love a good story."

"Well, this *is* a good one," Ryan said, and leaned forward, forearms resting on the table, in Gregson's space and deliberately so. "You see, once upon a time, there was a guy—let's call him Arthur—who was never going to set the world alight. He was tall, alright-looking—"

"In dim lighting," Frank put in.

"Good point," Ryan nodded. "In *dim* lighting, he was a five out of ten. Now, Arthur managed to scrape and claw his way out of an otherwise unremarkable career trajectory, because he fixed his sights on the equally unremarkable daughter of Teddy Smyth, who was a pillar of the community back in those days. He flattered her, told her he loved her, and managed to convince this poor woman she was the only one for him."

"Was she blind?" Frank wondered.

"Now, then, Frank," Ryan said, in a mock stern tone. "As we all know, love is *often* blind, and it certainly was in this case. Arthur never loved this woman, really, but he married her and, sure enough, her father started to dish out opportunities that would never have come his way otherwise."

"A cynical ploy, you might say?"

"I'd say that's an accurate description," Ryan nodded. "What about you, Arthur? Or are you going to surprise us all and claim that you loved the woman, despite trying to cover up her murder?"

Gregson said nothing, but his eyes burned with hatred for the pair of them.

"I don't have to listen to this," he said.

"Oh, but you do," Ryan said, and gone was the jovial raconteur. "You do, because you murdered a man by the name of Arnold Blythe, back in 2007. It might have been your first kill, or it might've been accidental, because you panicked. You learned how to be more careful, later on, but in the case of poor Arnie Blythe, you saw red. That's right, isn't it?"

Gregson remained silent, but shifted in his chair.

"Struggling to remember? Let me help you out," Ryan said, and brought out an image of Arnold, as he'd been in life. "He reported directly to you in CID, way back when you were an inspector, like the rest of us mere mortals, so we *know* that you knew one another, Arthur. It's a matter of record that he worked on cases you signed off, as the senior investigating officer. Then, he transferred over to Drugs Squad, but something happened you might not have expected. He went undercover, working with the Pearsons."

Gregson remembered the day he'd heard from a DCI in the Drugs Squad, one of the remaining few he hadn't turned, only to be told Blythe had accepted an assignment to embed himself in the Pearson crime family on a long-term basis. It had given him many a sleepless night but, as time wore on and nothing seemed to come to light, he'd been surprised when Arnold came to find him on the golf course, one Sunday afternoon, years after he'd begun the assignment, to confront him about the evidence he'd found. He'd done what was necessary to shut the man up, permanently, and called one of his closest allies in The Circle who could be relied upon to get rid of a body without trace.

He hadn't expected Taylor to have the wherewithal to keep Blythe in cold storage, but he'd obviously underestimated the man and his capacity for strategic thinking.

He said none of this to Ryan and Phillips, of course.

"They paid you plenty of hush money, didn't they, Arthur? They paid through the nose, to be the big crime family in the region, didn't they? I wondered why the Pearsons seemed to fall off the radar, all of a sudden, but then it struck me that their decline began around the same time you were banged up. You weren't able to help them, anymore, and we were cleaning up the streets after the mess you left behind."

Gregson leaned forward, meeting Ryan almost nose to nose.

"Do you expect me to admit to any of this?" he snarled. "It'll be a cold day in hell before I help you out, Ryan. You want something on record? Then, listen up, because I'm only going to say this once:

no comment." Gregson followed this up with a series of expletives for good measure.

Ryan and Phillips turned to one another and tutted.

"His language has certainly gone downhill, since he was incarcerated," Ryan remarked.

"Worse than a sailor's skivvy," Phillips agreed. "Couldn't take him to any o' those fancy garden parties, now."

Gregson looked between the pair of them and wondered why they didn't seem too concerned by his refusal to cooperate. *They had an ace up their sleeves*, he realised.

"The thing is, Arthur, you might not want to say anything so unequivocal, until you've heard our proposal," Ryan told him.

"And what might that be? Because I've already got a radio, thanks."

"And plenty of illegal contraband, most likely," Frank said, with an affable smile. "But we're not here to strip away your simple pleasures, are we, Ryan?"

"No indeed," the other said. "If we strip away anything, it'll be something you really want."

The cogs in Gregson's mind began to turn, and then his face lost a shade or two of colour.

"You bloody ba—"

"No more bad language, if you please," Frank said, and pointed a stern finger.

"Now," Ryan said, linking his fingers. "We know you've been looking forward to a transfer to a nice Category B prison, with a few more amenities, maybe a big poster of Raquel Welch you can tunnel behind, that sort of thing. *Unfortunately...*" Ryan pulled an apologetic face. "We're just not going to be able to allow it."

"It isn't up to you!" Gregson argued, spittle forming at the corners of his mouth as he fought a rising tide of rage.

"Isn't it?" Ryan said, calmly. "On the contrary, Arthur. This is my world, now; not yours. Strange as it may seem to you, I never take shortcuts, but that doesn't mean I don't know where they are. I have contacts I could call, strings I could pull. Ordinarily, I wouldn't do such things, but, in your case, I'm thinking very seriously about making an exception."

He leaned forward again, quick as a flash, so they were eye to eye.

"Just think of it, Arthur," he whispered. "A *lifetime* spent in this place, where you can't take a piss without worrying it'll be your last. You've made yourself strong in here, because you've had to. You've built a rep, because you've had to. But you and I both know that you've been dreaming of a day, someday soon, when you could rest easily again. You could start to imagine a future, outside of the prison walls, no matter how deluded that prospect may be, where you could wander around where flowers grow and sun shines. Sounds good, doesn't it?"

Ryan sat back again, and shook his head.

"For you, that's all that'll ever be, Arthur. A *dream*. I can call those contacts, first thing tomorrow, and tell them to cancel the transfer you were looking forward to. You'll be off the list, and I'll see to it you're never put back on again."

"What do you want?" Gregson whispered.

"An address," Ryan said, without a pause. "Give me Andrew Taylor's address in Berwick, and I'll reconsider making those calls."

Gregson sat back, torn between his hatred for the man in front of him, and his hatred for the one who'd left him to rot. "I wouldn't know," he said slowly. "But I do know there's a very nice bed & breakfast up in Berwick. It's been open a few years, now. I seem to think that the owner moved abroad for a while, then came back over to live near the place he grew up. Or, so I heard."

Ryan came to his feet, and Phillips followed.

"Remember, you gave me your word," Gregson said, and grabbed his jacket sleeve as Ryan moved to walk past him.

"No, I didn't," Ryan said, flicking him off. "But I am a man of integrity, nonetheless. I won't impede your transfer application, but it isn't because of what you've told us this evening. It would always be a decision for others to make."

"So high and mighty, aren't you? Your conscience will be your downfall, one of these days."

"I'd rather *have* a conscience than none at all. Sleep well, Arthur."

"Lauren? Would you mind taking this tray upstairs for me?"

DS Bell looked up from where she'd been answering a seemingly never-ending list of e-mails, seated at Ryan and Anna's kitchen table. She and Ryan's mother had enjoyed a nice chat over tea and crumpets, during which time she'd heard all about Ryan's antics as a boy. She'd learned, much to her surprise, that he'd been christened Maxwell and had been known as 'Max' for almost thirty years, until life events led him to move north and reinvent himself. She sensed a certain unease from his mother about this, which was hardly surprising, since she'd chosen the name he'd discarded—the ungrateful wretch—but she'd offered the diplomatic opinion that both names had served him well, at different times in his life. Lauren could well imagine a younger Ryan, living his life in London and cutting his teeth at the Metropolitan Police, a dashing, twenty-something who would've been a vastly different person to the mature, family man now living in Northumberland. While they'd chatted about this and that, Kieron had stationed himself in the living room, which had a window overlooking the driveway. Ryan had given him access to the live CCTV camera footage covering the various entrances to his house, but Kieron claimed there was no substitute for manual surveillance, and she'd left him to it. Lauren supposed she could have joined him but she was avoiding him.

Why, she wasn't quite sure.

Yes, she was.

She was frightened.

Not of him, or, at least, not in the way that sounded. She was frightened of the depth of feeling she had for him, which had taken her utterly by surprise. Had she been repressing it, all this time, working alongside him? Perhaps she had.

Shaking herself, Lauren came to her feet and took the tray from Eve's hands.

"You should get some sleep," she said, thinking of her own mother. "It's been a long few days, for everyone, and you must be exhausted."

"Well," Eve said, wavering a bit. "I suppose a little nap wouldn't hurt. Emma will be up early tomorrow, as always, and I want to try to help Anna and Ryan as much as I can."

"I'm sure they're very grateful," Lauren said. "I'll take this up to Anna, now, and check to see if she's all right."

"Thank you," Eve said. "You're a lovely girl."

Lauren turned pink, partly at the shock at being called a 'girl' and partly at the pleasure in knowing that someone thought her lovely.

Kieron had told her the same thing.

She turned and fled upstairs, nudging Anna's bedroom door open with her bum.

"Only me!" she said, keeping her voice low.

Anna wasn't asleep, however. She was lying on top of the bedclothes in cosy fleece pyjamas, her long legs wrapped around a pregnancy pillow, for comfort. A tablet had been set up for her, and, by the sound of it, she was watching *Sense and Sensibility*—the superior film version, adapted by and starring Emma Thompson. Lauren would recognise it anywhere, since it was one of her all-time favourites.

"Come in," Anna said, and managed to dredge up a friendly smile. "Oh, you didn't have to bring that all the way up here. I'd have come downstairs."

"That's exactly why I was told to bring it upstairs," Lauren said, with a smile. "Eve's put together some iron-heavy dinner for you, which I'm under strict instructions to make sure you eat, or I'll be in the doghouse."

"She's so kind," Anna murmured. Not having had any appetite for the past twenty-four hours, it was a welcome relief to find that the delectable smell of Eve's beef bourguignon and buttery mashed potato managed to stir a rumble from her stomach. "Look, she's put another bowl on here for you. Why don't you join me, and we'll have a feast?"

"I don't want to disturb you," Lauren said, but her eyes strayed to the food like a starving lion who'd clocked a tasty-looking zebra.

"Pull up a seat," Anna suggested, pointing towards the chair tucked into her dressing table. "I was just watching an old period drama, but I know they're not for everyone."

"I love them," Lauren admitted. "But if you tell anyone, I'll have to deny it."

Anna laughed, and then gasped as the action brought fresh pain to her lower abdomen.

"Sorry!" Lauren said, and set the tray down for a moment. "Here, let me help."

She plumped the cushions behind Anna's head and lower back, then placed another one across her knees, as a base for the tray.

"There, how does that feel?"

"Great, thank you," Anna said, and waited until Lauren had made herself equally comfortable. "How's Kieron doing? I feel terrible, dragging you both all the way up here, at this time of night. There's a spare bedroom, you know, all made up for the pair of you. As soon as Ryan comes home, you should snuggle up and try to get some sleep."

Lauren froze, a forkful of beef stew halfway to her mouth.

"Um—Kieron and I work together," she said, as if that was the end of the matter.

"Yes, but you're also a couple, aren't you?" Anna said, without any artifice.

Lauren set her fork down, and told herself not to overreact. Just because her last relationship had been a monumental disaster, it didn't mean that every relationship was destined to have the same ending. Still, being referred to as a 'couple' made her feel…

Actually, it wasn't half so bad as she imagined.

In fact, it was a *nice* feeling.

Hell.

"We—er, no, we're not—I mean, we *have*, you know—but we're not—together. A couple. Yet. Well, maybe. Oh, *God.*"

"I think I followed that," Anna said, and scooped up another forkful of mashed potato. "Is it still early days, then?"

"Very early," Lauren said. "Unless you count the fact we've been working together for years."

"It's different," Anna said.

"Yeah, it is."

Anna continued to eat, saying nothing, until Lauren blurted it all out.

"I was married before," she said. "It didn't end well, and I share custody of our child. He's with his dad, this Christmas."

"Does Kieron know?"

Lauren nodded.

"That doesn't seem to put him off, which is weird."

"Is it? I think it's great," Anna said. "Some men are ridiculously old-fashioned about things like blended families and single mothers, aren't they?"

Lauren thought of all the timewasters she'd dated since her divorce, and how the experience had knocked her confidence. Usually, they were in it for a good time, not a long time, and that simply wasn't the kind of person she was. She wanted the fairy-tale, as stupid as that may seem to some.

"I've known Kieron a long time," she said, playing with her food. "He's never been shy with the ladies."

"So? He was a single man, wasn't he? It's not as if he should have been a monk, all those years. If he was, you wouldn't have enjoyed your sleepover with him half as much," Anna said, deadpan.

Lauren snorted, and was sure some beef came out of her nostrils.

"That's true," she said. "I guess I'm worried this is just a one-nighter for him, or a bit of a fling. I think I feel more for him than he may do for me."

"You can't be sure of that."

"The thing is, I don't have time to waste," Lauren said. "I like him a lot, but there's another obstacle."

Anna raised an eyebrow in question.

"He's younger," Lauren said.

"How much younger?"

"A few years."

"Well, if that's all!" Anna exclaimed. "For God's sake, I thought you were going to tell me he was a gamer, or into Warhammer, or that he'd fathered ten love children by ten different mothers, or something. Who cares about a few years?"

Lauren *had* cared, but, now she'd spoken to Anna about it, she realised she might have made a mountain out of a molehill.

"Maybe you're right."

"You know I am," Anna said, without false modesty. "Now, do you want to watch the end of *Sense and Sensibility* with me, or are you going to go and spend some time with the new man in your life?"

As much as she adored the film, Lauren found herself standing up to collect the dinner plates.

"I'll go and see him."

"Good choice," Anna said, before adding, "Remember Marianne Dashwood. She thought Willoughby was the one for her, because he had the looks and the charm, but it was Colonel Brandon who was the real winner. He played the long game."

"Are you saying Kieron Vale could be my Colonel Brandon?"

"Let's hope so," Anna said, with a smile. "He's one of the greatest romantic heroes of them all."

Lauren was curious. "Which one would you say Ryan is, for you?"

Anna thought about it. "He's a little bit of all of them," she said. "And the best part is, he doesn't even know it."

CHAPTER 35

The next morning

With New Year's Eve fast approaching, there was a heightened sense of urgency when Ryan's team reconvened at Police Headquarters. They were always hopeful of closing their open caseload before the first day of January, mostly because it represented a fresh start—for them and for the families of the victims. Only a few days ago, this had seemed a realistic prospect, with only Terry Pearson's death to contend with, discounting the cold cases and what they liked to call 'long term cases' which they knew would take months and months of investigative work before completion. However, their little workforce was now stretched, many of their usual administrative and research staff having taken annual leave, which meant fewer pairs of hands to make light of a caseload that was growing larger, by the day. The deaths of Arnold Blythe and Harry were both 'cases of interest', the details of their murders representing important intelligence in respect of other, linked crimes, not least Lin Oldman's murder, the assumed death of Andrew Taylor, and the question of whether Anna was now in danger from a man who was very much alive. Added to this was the need to protect Charlie and her son from his father. All told, it was safe to say they'd all be ready for a holiday, after the holidays.

With Anna feeling well enough to be left alone, Ryan weighed up the risks and decided the best thing he could do was try to find Taylor before anybody else was hurt, and eliminate the source of his wife's stress, which was the biggest danger to their surviving baby. Thus, he'd risen early, fighting sleep deprivation with two cups of strong coffee, before driving into Newcastle for a briefing he'd arranged for nine o'clock on the dot. The team had assembled without a grumble, and they'd been rewarded with an enormous tray of gooey chocolate brownies, baked by his mother to 'keep their chins up'.

"I'll have another chin to keep up, at this rate," Frank said, before taking a bite of his second brownie. "Ye Gods, that might be one of the best things I've ever eaten."

"Considering you'll eat almost anything, I'm not sure whether my mother will be flattered," Ryan said.

"Huff'n purgelspuhh," Frank replied, between chews, which they interpreted correctly to mean, 'Mind yourself, you cheeky git.'

"Okay, let's start with Terry Pearson," Ryan said, and walked around to the long whiteboard covering the entire back wall of the conference room, where a blown-up image of Terry Pearson Junior had been taped up beside a list of key dates and witnesses.

"Aren't we waiting for Lauren and Kieron to join us?" Jack asked, having forged a decent friendship with the latter, who happened to be a regular match-goer.

"They have their own caseload to deal with," Ryan reminded him. "But, don't worry, we'll arrange another play date, soon."

Jack flipped him the bird, and Ryan laughed.

"Where was I...right. Terence Pearson, the Younger. Pinter's full report came through, but it doesn't add much to the information he gave us verbally. He thinks Pearson's body parts were wrapped in heavy-duty black bin bags before being weighed down and dumped in the sea, although that didn't stop the fish doing their work."

If Frank had considered going in for a hat trick of brownies, that image alone was enough to give him second thoughts.

"Jack, Charlie, did you manage to get anything else out of the sister, Angela?"

Jack shook his head. "We took a drive up to Amble, yesterday, like you said, boss. Unfortunately, Angela was away in Edinburgh visiting friends," he said. "We had a chat with her husband, Kevin, and the son"—Jack consulted his notebook—"Jonah. We don't often get a 'Jonah', do we?"

"Not often, no," Denise chimed in. "It's quite a Biblical name, and—"

Ryan scrubbed a hand over his face. "Sorry to drag us back to the point, but I was hoping you might tell me what you learned from those conversations? If it isn't too much trouble," he added.

"Sorry," Jack mumbled. "Kevin basically stuck to his first statement, and Jonah—who was the most miserable, moody little teenager I ever did see, by the way—apparently knows nothing about anything, and hadn't seen his uncle for donkey's years."

"Which didn't ring true for us," Charlie said. "And, funnily enough, we've had some more footage come through from several outlets in the area."

After the initial trip to see Angela, Kevin and Jonah, Ryan had taken the decision to obtain CCTV footage from a number of places in the area that could have captured Terry Pearson driving in or out of the village of Amble, where his sister lived, within the month before he was reported missing. Patricia Pearson had seemed adamant Terry paid his sister a visit very recently, which was something Angela denied, so it was a matter of finding out who was telling the truth and who wasn't.

"Did you find anything?"

"We certainly did," Charlie replied, turning to the relevant page of her notes. "Terry Pearson was caught on camera entering the service station in Alnwick just after three o'clock on 12th July, but he wasn't there for any petrol. He parked up and waited until a dark blue Suzuki joined him, and the camera captures the two men talking for at least ten minutes. The car is registered to Kevin Riley, and the man in the footage matches his physical description."

"Well, well. Do we think that exchange slipped Mr Riley's mind, or was he hoping we wouldn't cast our net that wide?" Ryan wondered aloud. "I think you should try speaking to the Riley family again today, when Angela will be home. I want to know what Kevin and Terry talked about at the petrol station, and why Kevin lied to us about having seen him, especially right before Terry went missing."

"Will do," Jack said, but Charlie seemed distracted.

"What is it?" Ryan asked her.

Charlie was looking at an image of Arnold Blythe that was also taped to the wall. "Sorry, I was just thinking of what you said the other day, about Arnold reminding you of someone," she said. "It sounds mad, but…I think, he looks like Jonah Riley. Or, maybe I should say that Jonah looks a lot like *him*?"

Jack recalled an image of the surly teenager to his mind's eye, and made a startled noise. "You're right!" he said. "Bloody hell, I can't believe I didn't notice it before. It's the eyes, the hair, even the shape of the nose. Of course, it could be a co—"

"Don't say it," Ryan warned him, to a rumble of laughter around the room. "I haven't met Angela's son, in the flesh, but Frank and I saw a picture of him and I think you're absolutely right. Putting the timeline together, I seem to recall Angela leaving her family's restaurant business—and other business interests—for a new life with Kevin, shortly before Jonah was born. That means she would have been on the scene around the same time Blythe was working undercover in the Pearson crime family, which makes it conceivable that they were thrown together, socially."

"This narf throw a spanner in the works," Phillips said.

"If it's true," Ryan demurred. "I think it certainly provides another basis for questioning Angela, and it would have been more interesting if we thought Kevin Riley was responsible for murdering Arnold Blythe, but we're pretty certain that was Arthur Gregson's handiwork. Does the fact of Jonah's parentage have any impact on who we think murdered Terry, and why? How does it all connect?"

There was silence, as the others in the room tried to solve the mystery.

"Maybe Terry knew about Jonah not being Kevin's biological child, and threatened to make it public?"

"Yes, but…who would *care*?" Denise argued. "The Rileys live a quiet life, keeping well out of things, and they're not celebrities with a public platform. It doesn't make sense that they'd be especially bothered by anyone knowing about it, especially if Angela's family were already aware of it."

There was another thoughtful silence.

"On second thoughts, I want you to interview all three of the Rileys separately under caution," Ryan decided. "There isn't time to waste on the 'softly, softly' approach and they've had their chance to be honest. Clearly, Kevin chose not to be. Let's see whether his resolve wavers once he's sitting in an interview room, and let's see whether Angela and Jonah have anything they'd like to tell us, after all."

"Isn't Jonah just a kid?" Mel queried.

"He's nineteen," Ryan said, flatly. "He may look like a grungy teenager, but the law sees him as an adult, so that's how he'll be treated."

Mel nodded.

"This is an odd situation," Ryan said, turning to look at the board with its series of blown-up images and key timelines written beneath. "Initially, each death presents as a separate investigation. Terry Pearson started out as a body in parts, before we identified him and figured out the crime family connection. We still don't have any strong leads about who might've killed him, but we have a brother-in-law who lied about seeing him, recently, which corroborates Patricia Pearson's version of events—at least on that point. Separately, our colleagues are investigating the murder of Lin Oldman, or *Winterbottom*, if we want to use her proper name—"

Frank sniggered, because almost anything with 'bottom' in it was funny. He didn't make the rules of comedy; he merely abided by them.

"*Anyway*," Ryan continued, pointedly. "We find out Anna's father, Andrew Taylor, left some of his DNA at the scene and, from that, we've been able to find strong evidence to suggest he's still alive. In the process of which, we discovered poor old Arnold Blythe, who's been missing for years and buried in another man's grave the whole time. Arnold connects to Gregson; Arnold connects to the Pearsons. Taylor connects to Oldman, Gregson, and to Blythe, but not, as far as we know, to the Pearsons, and his connection to Arnold Blythe was limited to the disposal of his body, or rather, the storage of it. We don't know why Taylor connected to Oldman, except to suspect that he needed to obtain Anna's original manuscript, which puts her in danger, now."

Ryan paused to swallow the sudden fear lodged in his throat, and took a long gulp of cold coffee to try to clear his nerves.

"Not forgetting Harry Thomson," he continued. "Found dead by Frank, here, and I want to reiterate our condolences before going any further."

Phillips gave a sad smile in response to the murmurs of kindness from those seated around him.

"Thanks," he said, gruffly. "I appreciate the thoughts, but I'm keen to find the bastard who did it. That'll do me just fine."

"All right, then," Ryan said, briskly. "He was found strangled in his office at Buddles gym, which, on the face of it, seems a very public kill, done to make a point."

"Agreed," Phillips said. "It definitely sent a message."

"Even if it hadn't been you who had the misfortune to find him," Denise said. "There were more than fifty people in the main gym area over the course of that night, and whoever found him would have raised the alarm. The news would have spread like wildfire and served the purpose just as well."

She paused, considering the nature of the killing.

"Who did Harry upset enough to find himself on a hit list?" Denise wondered aloud. "There's another, very old connection, which is that Buddles is the last place where Arnold Blythe was seen alive, all those years ago."

"Who was the witness?" Frank asked, but he'd already guessed the answer.

"The witness statement was provided by Harry," Denise confirmed. "But, for a gym of that size, it's surprising none of the other statements taken would confirm the same thing. He would've been seen by others, wouldn't he?"

"It depends," Frank said. "If he was there to see Harry privately, he might've used the same side door Harry's killer likely used. Nobody would've seen him come in, that way. But, if he came in the main entrance, you'd expect plenty of others to have clocked him and given a statement."

"There weren't many statements given at all," Mel pointed out, having reviewed her notes whilst the others were talking. "That's unusual, anyway, wouldn't you say? Even if nobody saw Blythe at the gym, you'd expect a statement confirming that, at least."

"It is unusual," Ryan agreed. "Frank, do you remember Arnold Blythe being at the gym, back in those days?"

Phillips cast his mind back, looked at the picture on the wall, and then shook his head. "I can't say I do," he replied. "I don't recognise him at all, because he would've mostly been undercover rather than at the office, and I definitely don't remember seein' him from the gym. I'd have been a regular, back then. When Laura was dyin', I took a bit of time away, but that wasn't until later on."

MacKenzie gave his knee a squeeze, and he smiled, closing his hand over hers in silent acknowledgement. As the second wife, some might have found it hard to follow a dead woman who'd been greatly loved, but that had never been a problem for them—at least, once he'd found the courage to ask her out. Admittedly, Denise had forced the issue by planting a kiss on his unsuspecting lips, but that was neither here nor there.

"Do you think Harry had any dealings with the Pearsons?" Ryan asked him. "That could be a reason for Arnold Blythe to have been at the gym, if he was relaying a message to Harry in the guise of working with the Pearsons, with his undercover hat on."

Phillips sat back in his chair, and rubbed his chin while he thought. "It doesn't feel right, to me," he said. "Harry was many things, but he was always 'small time', if he was involved in anything dodgy. Back then, the Pearsons were big…really big. He wouldn't have had the stomach for dealin' with them, and that's the truth of it."

Ryan thought through the connections, and another thought struck him. "There's another possibility," he said. "Frank, who else from the office went to the same boxing gym, around that time?"

Phillips covered his eyes, thinking hard. "I'm goin' way back in my memory bank here," he muttered, and then looked up with dawning realisation. "There were a few lads from IT; the lad from the

Pie Van, because he was only a lad, back then; and, then, there was Gregson. He bloody went to Buddles for a couple o' years, before he gave it up."

"Would those years happen to be right before Blythe was reported missing?" Mel said.

"Yeah," Frank said, wearily. "I'd have to double check the dates, but…yes, I reckon' that's about right."

"So, what does this mean?" Charlie said, eager to learn from them. "Gregson knew Blythe?"

"Maybe," Ryan said. "But I think there's another possibility, which is that Gregson called in a favour from Harry, when he needed it, or applied pressure because he was in a position to. If Blythe was assumed missing, and Gregson needed someone to swear to the fact he'd been in another part of town when he was last seen—far from his own house, for example, where the murder might've taken place—then Harry could have been the fall guy for that."

Phillips sighed, again. "Aye," he said. "I could see that happenin'."

"There was no CCTV or other footage, from those days," Mel put in. "The Missing Persons file on Blythe was really thin, as we know, so there's no way to confirm our assumptions."

"Just a nose for the truth." Denise smiled, and then added, "That may offer an explanation about Blythe's supposed connection to Buddles, which may turn out to have been a false connection made by Gregson, as we've said. It still doesn't explain who'd kill Harry so horribly."

"Another gang member? What if Harry fell in with the…" Mel stammered to a halt, her eyes straying towards Charlie.

"The Rachmaninovs," Charlie finished for her. "Don't worry, you can say his name."

Mel nodded. "Okay, what if Harry fell in with the Rachmaninovs, and then got on their bad side?"

"There are so many possibilities but, the fact is, we need more information," Denise said. "We'll see what forensics can tell us, although Tom Faulkner's still away on holiday."

"Over *Christmas*?" Frank said, as if it was sacrilege.

"It's allowed," Denise replied, with a chuckle. "And, in any case, Christmas has passed. It's almost New Year."

"Aye, well, his timin' is narf inconsiderate," Frank said, and folded his arms. "We need him, and he's off gallivantin' somewhere." He paused, and wrinkled his nose. "Where's he gone to, anyhow? Sharm el Sheikh?"

"Skiing in the Dolomites, apparently."

"Well, I never."

They couldn't be sure if his response was intended to be a positive evaluation of their senior CSI's choice of holiday destination or not.

"I'm sure the team will do a good job," Mel said, in a soothing tone. "They've promised to get back to me within the week."

"Still too slow for my likin'," Frank said, and knew he was being unreasonable in saying it.

"Let's talk about Andrew Taylor," Ryan said, intercepting any further rant from his sergeant on the subject of absentee forensics staff. "He's alive, he's living in Berwick-upon-Tweed, and he runs a bed and breakfast, as of the past couple of years, prior to which he was living abroad. We don't know any further details beyond that. I want to know which B & B, what name he's using now, and anything else you can find out. I want him brought in, and made to pay for his crimes."

"I'll start looking into bed and breakfasts," Charlie offered. "There are quite a few in Berwick, but it's a good starting point."

Ryan nodded. "Thanks, Charlie."

Just then, there came a knock at the conference room door, and one of their administrative staff popped his head into the room. "Er, sorry to interrupt your meetin', only, I've got one of the DIs from Drugs Squad waitin' in the office…says he needs to have a word with you, urgently, sir."

It was an unusual occurrence for any of their fellow colleagues to interrupt a briefing, or to come down in person from their own division simply for a chat and a catch up. It signalled to Ryan that whoever was waiting for him had something important to impart, and hadn't wanted to say it over the phone or in an e-mail.

Ryan gathered up his things. "Meeting's adjourned."

CHAPTER 36

Detective Inspector Josef Kowalski was a man who seemed to have the weight of the world upon his shoulders. Indeed, when Ryan stepped back into the office, folder tucked beneath his arm, he spotted Kowalski easily amongst the sea of other coppers, chiefly because he was the only one holding his head in his hands.

"Kowalski?"

He looked up with a baleful expression on his unshaven face, and Ryan offered his best attempt at a smile. Apparently, one of the most effective ways to encourage a fellow detective to admit whatever cock-up he'd come to confess to, was by seeming approachable.

Or so Frank had told him.

"Oh, hi—er, hello," Josef said, his Polish accent barely detectable after almost thirty years as a British citizen. "Thanks for—"

"Shall we grab a coffee in the canteen?" Ryan suggested, cutting off any awkward, stammering small talk. "I could use something to eat."

Josef was instantly relieved, and the two men made their way downstairs, chatting about the weather and other inconsequential things until they were fortified with mugs of coffee and breakfast baps. Ryan selected a table in the far corner of the room and, after they'd swallowed a couple of bites, set his plate aside.

"Right," he said. "What do you need to tell me, Josef?"

Kowalski wiped his mouth with a napkin, then crumpled it in his hand. "It's about Terry Pearson," he said, before he could change his mind. "I need to tell you, he was going to be my informant. Off the books."

He took a file out of the rucksack he'd brought, and slid it across the table.

"It's partially redacted, but I can tell you what it says," Josef offered, when Ryan continued to say nothing, his sharp eyes scanning the pages of the cold case file until his eye fell upon a name he recognised.

Alexei Rachmaninov.

"Talk to me," he said. "Pearson was *going* to be your informant—or was he already an informant?"

Josef took a deep breath and launched into a stilted explanation of his dealings with the late Terry Pearson, who'd sought him out with an offer to provide information about his own family's business, along with everything he knew about the Rachmaninovs, who'd been muscling into the North East. Quietly, at first, and then more violently in the past twelve months."

"Why would Terry want to bring down his own family?"

Josef shrugged a shoulder. "He only had one condition for working with us," he said. "His sister, Angela, and her son, Jonah, would be given immunity and protection."

Not Kevin? Ryan thought immediately. *Not his own wife and daughter? His mother or father, who would have still been alive?*

"So, what information did he provide?"

"That's just it," Josef said. "The deal never went through. The next thing I heard was that Terry was missing. I assumed somebody had got to him, maybe after getting wind of what he planned to do."

Ryan took a gulp of coffee. "Why didn't you tell me this before now?"

Josef scratched the top of his head in a nervous gesture, and glanced around the room. "I felt responsible, okay? I know these people, and what they're capable of," he said, in a voice that shook. "The Pearsons might not be the force they once were, but that doesn't mean they don't have any clout. As for the Rachmaninovs…" Josef shook his head. "They have no honour," he said, swiping a line through the air with one hand, to be absolutely clear. "It makes them different because, at least with the rest, there's a code. Not with the Rachmaninovs."

Ryan thought of Charlie, and her son.

It was worse than he'd feared.

"All right, look," he said, thinking fast. "You know you should've come forward with this before now. I could report you, reprimand you, and I could speak to the Chief Constable. But I'm not going to do any of those things."

Josef had been staring at the tabletop, his head bent, but now he looked up again.

"No?"

"No," Ryan repeated. "You've done the right thing, now, and I have to credit you with having the integrity to do that much, when others wouldn't. But I want something in return, Josef. I want to know *everything* you have on the Rachmaninovs, especially Alexei."

The other man nodded, eager to make amends. "I'll get a file over to you by—"

"The end of the day," Ryan interjected.

Josef nodded again. "Thanks for—for understanding."

"I wouldn't go that far," Ryan said, and rose to his feet. "One last thing, Josef. What about Terry's daughter? His mother? Why didn't he want them to have the same immunity he wanted for his sister and her son?"

Josef wriggled in his chair, desperate for the loo now that he'd purged himself. "Terry was worried about his daughter, Mia," he said. "He said she was beyond his reach, now, whatever that meant."

Ryan nodded slowly.

"Bugger off to the gents, before you make a puddle," he muttered, and Josef scuttled off, his feet slapping against the linoleum floor.

As he made himself scarce, Ryan put a call through to his sergeant.

"Frank? I think we need to pay Patricia and Mia Pearson another visit….no, we're not stopping for brunch on the way."

While Mel and Denise occupied themselves investigating Derek's murder, and Ryan and Phillips made their way across town to Patricia Pearson's home in Woolsington, Jack and Charlie drove north to the village of Amble.

"How are you doing?" Jack asked, as they wound their way along the coastal route. "I know the last couple of days have been heavy going."

Charlie smiled at the understatement. "I've had better weeks," she said. "Then again, I've had a lot worse. The most important difference is, I don't feel like I'm navigating this alone. I have you, and I have a circle of friends I never imagined I'd find. For the first time, it feels as though I can take him on."

Jack glanced away from the road to smile at her. "That's because you *can*," he assured her. "We're going to do it together, and bring down a crime family in the process."

"And to think, I'd have been happy with flowers every once in a while."

"I think I can manage that, too," Jack said.

"If you're looking for a bit of post-Christmas nookie, you're going the right way about it."

He laughed, and then gave her a knowing look. "Have you been talking to Frank?"

"He was telling me all about the stress-relieving properties of regular—and I quote—'naked cuddling'," she said, and pulled a comedy face. "He *also* gave me a long list of unsolicited recommendations about background music while doing the aforementioned naked cuddling."

"Oh, God, don't tell me. I don't want to know."

Then, Jack reconsidered.

"Actually, I do. What was the first track on his bump 'n' grind playlist?"

"Half of them, I'd never even heard of," she admitted. "He kept talking about stuff from the seventies, and I didn't have the heart to remind him that was decades before I was born. That being said, I can get behind a bit of classic Motown."

"*Midnight Train to Georgia,* and all that?" Jack said, and, when she nodded, he made a mental note to download it for later.

Presently, they arrived at their destination. Amble was a lovely sight, with the late morning sun burning away whatever was left of the cold sea fret, and melting away any frost on the windows so the houses seemed to shimmer as they crawled through its narrow streets. There was a bustling energy to the place that hadn't been there before, and they could only credit the shift as being due to the change in the weather.

"Amazing, how different the world feels with a bit of snow and sunshine," Charlie said, as they made their way from the car park to Angela's café. "D'you think we're more likely to find her at home?"

"Let's start here, and see how we get on," he said. "It's a small place, so they can't hide from us, forever. One way or another, we're going to find out *why* Kevin Riley met with Terry and didn't think it was something we'd like to know."

"That, and we need to know if Kevin is really Jonah's father," Charlie added. "If he isn't, and his father was actually Arnold Blythe, we need to know if that makes a difference to anything, or if it's just a bit of interesting genealogical information."

Jack nodded, and held open the door to the café. "We're in luck," he said, after a quick scan of the dining room. "Looks like we've caught all three birds with one stone."

Charlie looked around and saw Angela stationed behind a till, while Jonah and Kevin were sitting at one of the tables, their half-eaten breakfasts growing cold while they scrolled their smartphones, not talking to one another.

"Divide and conquer," she suggested. "You take Kevin and Perry, I'll take Angela."

"You mean Kevin and Jonah?"

"Isn't that what I said?"

"Nope."

She gave a short laugh. "Slip of the tongue."

CHAPTER 37

When Ryan and Phillips arrived at the now familiar mock-Tudor mansion belonging to Patricia Pearson, it was to find her home alone, her granddaughter no longer guarding the entrance like a bouncer on a rowdy Friday night. They rang the preposterous 'Ring for Champagne' bell, waited for what felt like an eternity, and then the door opened. The first thing they thought was that Pat hadn't been expecting another visit from the police. She was decked out in a pair of black jeans, a matching cashmere jumper with some sort of glitter on the front, co-ordinating fashion trainers with leopard print and sequin details, and her hair and make-up were immaculate. Had they not been sure it was the same woman, who had previously given every appearance of being doddery and suffering from dementia, they might've thought a body swap had occurred sometime in the past few days.

"Oh, it's *you*...two," she tagged on, remembering that Ryan was not alone.

"Mrs Pearson, we're sorry to trouble you again, but we'd like to discuss some further matters that have come to our attention in the course of our investigation. May we come in?"

Pat stood aside for them to enter. "Mia isn't here, today," she said. "In case you needed to speak to her. I can give her a call, if you like—"

"That won't be necessary," Frank said, with disarming nonchalance. "How've you been?"

And thus began the charm offensive. In truth, Frank still hadn't recovered from their last visit, during which he'd been thoroughly overlooked in favour of His Nibs standing at six feet four inches tall, raven-haired and blue-eyed. He decided it was time to unleash the Frank Phillips Charm Offensive, not for his own sake, but for the sake of all shorter, stockier, slightly receding grey-haired men the world over.

It was a matter of pride.

"Well, it's been a worry, what with our Terry goin' missin', then his da' leavin' us like he did. It's been a lot to bear. Don't know what I'd have done without my Mia to look after things."

They had a moment to reflect that she didn't look like a grief-stricken widow, nor a feeble grandmother, for that matter.

"I bet you've been a tower of strength," Frank said, while hypnotizing her with his warm, brown-eyed gaze. "Must be hard, losin' your husband and your son, one after the other."

Pat said nothing to that, and looked away, her eye catching on a framed image of her grandchildren, before she took a seat on one of her silky embroidered sofas.

"Aye, it's times like these, you know who your friends are," she said, with a dramatic sigh. "As much as I'd love to chat to the pair of you *lovely* lads, I've got a WI meeting this afternoon, and I don't want to be late."

They dreaded to think how she had infiltrated the Women's Institute of the North East, unless they were already populated with the widows of mob bosses.

"Let me come straight to the point, then, Mrs Pearson," Ryan said, and proceeded to remind her of her rights, which she acknowledged. "Certain new evidence has come to light that suggests your son, Terry, was contemplating becoming a police informant. Did you know about this?"

Patricia's eyes widened, then narrowed again. "You're havin' me on," she said, and waggled a long, red-painted fingernail at the pair of them. "You know fine well he'd never have even dreamed about such a thing, let alone done it. He was no grass, my lad."

"I'm afraid it's perfectly true," Ryan said.

She folded her arms and gave them a very motherly, disappointed *look*. "I don't believe you," she said. "I'll never believe a word of it."

Ryan understood that, in the world she inhabited, the idea of a member of the family—literally, or figuratively—betraying them, was the highest form of insult. Evidence was the only way to settle the matter, and so he asked for her patience while he found a voice recording saved in the online version of the file DI Kowalski had given him. He pressed 'PLAY' and set the phone on the table. Immediately, Terry Pearson's voice echoed around Patricia's sitting room, speaking to Kowalski about his worries about his daughter and nephew, but also his sister, Angela. The two men discussed terms, meeting points and what both sides stood to gain.

All the while, Patricia listened, her face frozen like a waxwork mannequin.

"I think you get the picture," Ryan said, pausing the recording. "That was Terry's voice, wasn't it?"

She gave an almost imperceptible nod.

"Terry was speaking to one of our colleagues, who would have served as his main contact, had Terry lived."

Patricia stared at Ryan's phone, her eyes appearing ghoulish as the heavy make-up began to cake against the rolls of skin around them. She reached for a small, decorative box in mother of pearl on the table beside her, which turned out to be a cigarette case. She held it out to both of them and, when they shook their heads, she lit one up for herself and took a look, deep drag of nicotine.

"I s'pose this must come as a shock," Frank said.

Patricia inhaled some more tar into her lungs, and looked across at him through the swirl of smoke.

"Not really," she said. "I always knew he wasn't strong enough. My Terence left big footsteps for his son to fill, and Terry just didn't have what it takes to run a business like ours."

"Which is?" Ryan murmured.

"Import and export," she shot back, and gave him a glassy smile.

"No, I meant, what does it take?"

She laughed, then proceeded to have a coughing fit. Frank, ever solicitous, took himself off to her kitchen—which was equally ostentatious, in a late eighties sort of way—and procured a glass of water. "Thanks, pet," she wheezed.

They gave her a minute to dab away the mascara that had run down her face, and then she looked at Ryan again.

"Call it what you want," she said. "Guts, mettle, courage, loyalty, bein' a hard bastard…whatever. Terry just didn't have it and Terence always blamed me, for that."

She finished the cigarette and stubbed it out with a series of short, angry jabs.

"He said I was too soft on Terry, when he was growin' up, but he was just as bad. Used to spoil him rotten. Christmases, birthdays… No wonder he wasn't up to the job. We made life too easy for him."

Ryan thought of how coldly she spoke of her son, and couldn't help but compare it to his own parents. There might have been a degree of disappointment, especially on his father's side, when he'd told them of his plans to go into the police service rather than following in his father's footsteps; either, as a military man, with a glittering diplomatic career, or as master of Summersley. Despite this, he'd never felt any less loved, nor lacking in any sense. Then again, people quantified these things in different ways.

When it became clear Patricia had said all she wanted to say, the two men came to their feet.

"Thank you for your time, Mrs Pearson," Ryan said. "We're continuing to explore all avenues of enquiry in your son's death."

Patricia didn't acknowledge that, her eyes fixed on a framed picture of her granddaughter.

"You know," she mused, "Terry might not've had the stomach for hard work, but Mia does. She'll be anything she wants to be, one day, you just wait and see."

The words seemed prophetic, and Ryan found himself thinking again of what Terry had said to DI Kowalski, when they were discussing terms.

Mia's beyond my reach.

After ringing through the last order in a relentless queue of people needing a fry-up, Angela stretched out her back and looked up to find a young woman standing in front of her. She was quietly attractive, her hair pulled back into a neat ponytail, dressed in what she'd have described as practical winter clothing—offset by a forest green knitted jumper, which hinted that its owner was in possession of a cheery nature, when the occasion called for it.

"Good morning! Or is it afternoon?" She turned to check the time on an old maritime clock on the wall behind her. "Only just! It's table service, so if you'd like to find a seat, we'll come and take your order."

"Actually, I was hoping to have a word, Mrs Riley."

Charlie flashed her warrant card, and Angela let out a sigh she didn't make any effort to conceal.

Not an auspicious start.

"I understand you've already spoken with some of my colleagues—"

"Yes," Angela interrupted. "Which is why…and, I don't mean to be *rude*, but it's why I can't understand why your lot keep coming back. We've already told you everything we know."

"Not quite *everything*, Angela."

Charlie turned and looked pointedly at Jonah, who was idly picking at a spot while Jack introduced himself.

"Wait," Angela said. "You can't speak to Jonah, he's just a child."

"He's nineteen," Charlie corrected her. "He's a man, now. Remind me, what year was he born?"

Angela's lip quivered. "What does it matter? You can easily find out."

"Oh, it matters very much," Charlie said quietly, and paused while one of the other waitresses came over to deposit a new order.

"Mr Jamieson's in again, asking for his usual," the girl said, referring to one of their local elderly patrons. "Says the poached eggs were too gloopy yesterday. Oh, sorry! Did I interrupt your chat?"

She looked at Charlie with open curiosity.

"No, no, it's fine," Angela said. "This is, ah—"

"Actually, I *was* hoping to borrow Angela for a few minutes, if you think you can manage?"

"No problem! Take as long as you need."

Knowing it would look extremely odd if she backed out now, Angela gritted her teeth and signed out of the till.

"I'll be back in *five* minutes," she said, for Charlie's benefit.

"Jonah isn't Kevin's biological son, is he?"

Angela had been ready to let rip, and give Charlie a piece of her mind about being manoeuvred out of her own restaurant.

Instead, she found the wind knocked out of her.

"I—what do you mean?"

Charlie merely smiled, with a degree of sympathy.

"We found Arnold's body," she said, and left the words to hang on the air, before the sea wind carried them away.

Angela looked around, and perched herself on the harbour wall where she stared out at the choppy water and remembered a young man with messy red hair and a big, puppyish grin.

"How did you know?" she whispered. And then, "Do my family know? My mother?"

"I don't know," Charlie said, honestly.

"He and Terry were close," Angela continued, and found herself wishing for a drink for the first time in more than fifteen years. "Terry brought Arnold back to the house for dinner, one night, and that's when I met him."

Charlie took a seat beside her on the wall, and listened.

"I didn't want to fall for anyone in my father's business, you know," Angela continued. "I hated everything about what my father did for a living…and about him, to be honest. Terry wasn't so bad, he was just under pressure to follow in Dad's footsteps, whether he wanted to or not."

She rubbed the heel of her hands over her eyes, to stem any tears that threatened to fall.

"Anyway, for some reason, Arnold got under my skin. I know it sounds daft, but he seemed a bit different to the rest. As if he was trying to be as hard as they were, but it was just for show. It probably sounds ridiculous, to you."

"No, in fact—"

"So, how did he die?" Angela asked, before she lost the nerve. "Did a deal go south? Was it a revenge kill? All I know is that Arnold went missing, shortly after I told him I was expecting Jonah. Not exactly a confidence boost for a girl barely out of her teens."

Charlie realised the woman had no idea Arnold Blythe had been an undercover officer. She hadn't faced a situation like this before, and wished Ryan or Denise were on hand to offer some guidance, but she had to follow her gut.

"Angela, I have to tell you something that may come as a surprise. Arnold Blythe was a police officer," she said. "In fact, he was a detective inspector within the drugs unit at Northumbria CID."

Angela gave a little shake of her head. "You can't be serious."

"I'm *very* serious, and my next question's important, Angela, so I really need the truth from you."

Angela stared off into the distance, trying to wrap her head around the news, thinking back to the man she'd known. "He used me, then."

Their circumstances might've been reversed, but Charlie could understand the emotion. "We don't know that," she said, honestly. "Arnold could've found out plenty of intelligence from his position as your brother's friend without having to strike up a relationship with you. Especially if, as you say, you kept out of the day-to-day affairs."

Angela nodded. "That's true enough," she said, and then rubbed her hands over her arms, feeling colder than she ever had before. "In a way, I feel better, knowing I was right all along. He wasn't like the rest of them, was he?"

Charlie smiled, sadly. "No, he wasn't."

Angela sniffed, and took one of the paper tissues Charlie offered from a battered pack of Kleenex. "How did he die?"

"We're still investigating," Charlie said. "But we believe he was murdered."

"By one of my family?" Angela asked. "Do you think my father found out about him, and…and…"

"No," Charlie said, cutting off any speculation. "We have a suspect in mind, and they aren't a member of your family or the wider Pearson organisation."

Gregson could be counted on to have his fat, greedy fingers

in as many pies as possible, but, so far as they knew, he had only been a transient associate of the Pearsons at the time Arnold died. If anything, he didn't want them to find out that he'd been the one to murder Blythe, since they believed he was one of their own. It was a complicated web.

Angela didn't know why, but she was relieved. At least it was *one* person her father or her brother couldn't notch up on their tally sheet.

"You don't believe your family know about Jonah?"

"I haven't told them," she said, simply. "The only person I told was Kevin, before we got married. I wanted him to know what he was getting himself in for, rather than having to start our lives together lying every day. I know what you're thinking."

Charlie was surprised, for she hadn't been thinking anything specific. "What's that?"

"You're thinking, Kevin's not exactly the gangster type, and you'd be right. I told your colleagues how we met, and it was while I was still working at my family's restaurant in Newcastle. One of many they had, but this is the one Kev happened to walk into, with a bunch of his colleagues, for a work dinner. I thought he was kind, and steady. He'll never set the world alight, and he's not much of a conversationalist, but he's steady, like I say. He's been a decent father for Jonah to look up to."

Charlie didn't feel it was kind to mention that, in her observation, it didn't seem that Jonah had much respect for either of his parents.

"Kev's always known about Jonah, and he loves him. He loves me."

Again, Charlie didn't ask the burning question of whether Angela *also* loved her husband, because the answer was implicit in what she'd omitted to say. Some people were content to be companions, in life, and that served them well. In her case, Charlie could imagine nothing worse than a celibate marriage, but it was none of her business.

"Did he and Terry harbour any animosity towards one another?" Charlie asked.

Angela raised both hands in mute appeal. "Honestly, not a *thing*," she said, in frustration. "The last time he saw Terry was when I did; that time he turned up with Kerry-Jayne and Mia, here at the restaurant."

Charlie ran her tongue over her lip, considering the next thing she should say. "We have evidence to prove that Kevin met with Terry, at the petrol station in Alnwick, shortly before he died."

The colour drained from Angela's face. "You must've made a mistake," she insisted. "Kevin would've told me."

"Would he?"

Angela looked back through the window to see her husband and son, talking with a young male police officer.

"They—they must've run into one another, and Kevin forgot to mention it."

"No, Angela. The footage suggests it was very clearly a pre-arranged meeting. They spoke, and they argued. What do you think they might've argued about?"

Angela swallowed, and then looked away, drawing herself in.

"It's getting cold," she said. "And I don't have anything else to say."

She rose to her feet and, a moment later, she was gone.

CHAPTER 38

Kevin watched his wife leave with the female police officer but, before he could offer any support, he and Jonah were met with the arrival of her male counterpart, a young man in his early thirties with a mop of gelled hair and the whitest teeth they'd seen outside of *Love Island*, whom they recognised from a previous house call.

"Mr Riley? Jonah? You may remember me—I'm DC Jack Lowerson, from Northumbria CID."

He had his warrant card ready, but they barely looked at it.

"Can I join you?"

Without waiting for the affirmative, Jack took a seat at their table.

"Thanks," he said.

Kevin glanced at his son, who was paying only the most derisory attention to the fact a police officer was sitting at the breakfast table beside them. "Can we help you?" he asked.

"I hope so," Jack said, keeping up the cheerful act, for now. "I have a few questions to ask both of you, and I wonder if you might be more comfortable speaking to me privately, one at a time?"

"I don't have anything to hide," Kevin said, quickly.

Jonah shrugged, not seeming to care either way.

"Would you mind putting your phone down, for five minutes?" Kevin snapped at him, obviously as frustrated by the constant use of small screens in place of human interaction as the rest of the thinking world.

Jonah let his phone clatter to the table, face up. "Fine," he muttered.

On sparkling form, as always, Jack thought. "Thank you," he said, and kept a smile pinned on his face, hoping it didn't look too much like a grimace. "I wanted to ask you about your relationship with your cousin?"

The question took Jonah off guard, his entire demeanour closing in and closing down. "Why would I?" he countered.

"If you could just answer the question, that would be helpful," Jack said. "What's your relationship with your cousin, Mia Pearson?"

"You already said it," Jonah replied. "She's my cousin. That means she's my mum's brother's daughter, in case you didn't know."

He was pleased with his smart-Alecky response, but neither his father nor the murder detective shared that view. Additionally, and with superlative timing, the Universe chose that moment for Mia to send Jonah a semi-nude picture of herself, which flashed up onto the phone and was visible to all three men.

Jonah made a grab for it, but the damage was done.

"By the looks of things, I'd say you have a very *close* relationship with your cousin," Jack remarked. "In case of confusion, I'm talking about Mia, your uncle's daughter, the one who just sent you a picture of her naked boobs."

Jonah glowered, and Kevin swore softly, in frustration. "For God's sake, Jonah, what are you thinking of?" he said. "When did all this start? You barely know one another…"

Jonah sat back, arms folded. "Free country," he muttered.

"She's your cousin! How long have you been seeing each other, Jonah?" Kevin asked him, taking the words out of Jack's mouth.

Jonah kicked at the chair beside him, and then scrubbed his hands through his hair. "I dunno, a few months?"

Kevin swore again, and looked every one of his fifty-something years.

"I've told you a hundred times, Jonah. *Stay away* from that side of the family. They're no good."

Jonah became animated then, in defence of his beloved. "Shut up! You don't know anythin' about it or about Mia! You're just a borin' old man with a borin' life."

Kevin's eyes darkened, but he remained deadly calm. "You don't speak to me, like that."

"Why? You're not my father."

Kevin looked as though someone had taken a knife to his belly. "Wh—what?"

"You heard me," Jonah said, angrily. "I've known for ages you weren't my dad. It makes sense, anyway. Look at you!"

Kevin's hands were gripping the edge of the table and, sensing his control was nearing its limit, Jack stepped into the fray.

"Okay, Jonah, that's enough," he said. "You can sort this out, later, when there's less of an audience, eh?"

"You want to know why Mia and me get along so well?" he said, in response. "We both want to make something of ourselves. We want her father's death to mean something."

They sensed a breakthrough was near.

"Jonah—" Kevin began, but Jack held up a hand to silence him.

"To mean something?" he queried. "Like, what? Revenge? Do you know who killed Terry?"

Jonah looked between them, then his eyes went to the outer door, where his mother was stepping back inside the restaurant.

"It isn't about revenge," he said. "It's about succession."

"It must've been one of them," Jack said, on the journey home.

"Yeah, but which one?" Charlie said. "All three of them are equally weird."

"I know what you mean. I went in there, thinking it was Kevin, but now I'm thinking that son of his could've whacked his uncle and called it succession, on behalf of his girlfriend—also his cousin."

"I still can't believe that," Charlie said. "For all the obvious reasons, but also because Mia Pearson looks as though she could model for Armani on the weekends, while Jonah looks like something a fishing trawler dragged from Amble harbour."

"Harsh, but fair. He has all the personality of a wet fish, n'all."

"Maybe he has the...er, *attributes* of a seal?"

Jack laughed. "God knows, but the thought alone turns my stomach. What about Angela? She's a dark horse."

Charlie nodded, considering the woman she'd spoken to. "I think she had genuine feelings for Arnold Blythe," she said. "Not that it matters, really. She definitely thought nobody aside from Kevin knew about Jonah's parentage."

"Terry might've known," Jack said. "He seems to have had a soft spot for his sister, and a secret desire to get out of the organisation, considering his negotiations to become an informant. Added to which, he was friends with Arnold, or so Angela tells us."

Charlie looked across at him as they waited for a gap in traffic. "Angela had no idea about Arnold being a copper," she said. "That felt very authentic, to me. Do you think Terry knew about that?"

"If she didn't, there's no reason he would," Jack replied. "Arnold's cover wasn't blown; on the contrary, he'd found damning evidence about his superintendent, and that's the only reason he died. It wasn't a member of the Pearson family who ended him. They might've assumed he was dead, all these years, or that he was a deserter, but they wouldn't necessarily think he was part of the fuzz."

"We're still no closer to understanding why Terry and Kevin were fighting at the petrol station," Charlie said. "Angela wouldn't believe it, or seemed to put it down to the two men running into one another."

"That's total bollocks," Jack said. "The meeting was planned."

"Did Kevin say anything about it?"

"Clammed up," Jack said. "Said we'd have to bring him, or any one of his family in for formal questioning, and there'd be a lawyer present."

"Touched a nerve, then?"

"You betcha."

A breakthrough came an hour later, in the form of an e-mail from one of the intelligence analysts, back at Police Headquarters.

"Bingo!" Frank cried out, and trotted across to where Ryan was still removing his coat.

"Did you win the Postcode Lottery?"

"Even better," Frank declared. "I've just had an e-mail through with footage from one of the back lanes in Amble, on the night Terry Pearson went missing. It's Kevin Riley's car, again, and, what's more, he's followin' another car, registered to Terry Pearson."

Ryan's body tensed. "The same day?"

"Aye, the same." Frank nodded. "Only one car came back through Amble, and that was Kevin's. Here's the funny thing, though. He doesn't go the same route, back towards home. He goes the other way, towards the harbour."

"It would've been long past closing for the restaurant, wouldn't it?" Ryan said, as he watched the footage over Frank's shoulder.

Then, the answer hit him.

"What else would Angela keep at the restaurant, besides good soup, Frank?"

"Er…good fish 'n' chips?"

Ryan put a hand on his friend's shoulder and whispered the answer in his ear. "*Freezers,*" he said. "Lots of deep storage freezers, for all the fish, and perhaps other things. You remember, Arnold's body was frozen for a while, by Andy Taylor? That got me thinking. What if Terry's was frozen, too, and Kevin used his wife's restaurant as the storage depot?"

"Surely she would've known?" Frank whispered, in reply.

"Not necessarily, but that's something we need to find out. Call Jack and Charlie, and then get a search warrant. We're going in, tonight."

CHAPTER 39

Jack and Charlie parked their car in the station car park in Berwick-upon-Tweed, and consulted the list of bed and breakfasts she had compiled earlier.

"We won't get through all of them today," she said. "But let's give it a go."

As the northernmost town in England, less than three miles south of the Scottish border, the history of Berwick showed in its fine architecture—from its Elizabethan town walls to its impressive bridges, not least the Royal Border Bridge with its twenty-eight mighty stone arches rising a hundred and twenty feet above river level, first opened by Queen Victoria. There were also the castle ruins, the old barracks, the beaches and, above all else, the *people* to recommend it. However, they weren't there to go seal-watching, or to sit in the park overlooking the waterside. They were there to find a man who'd spent more than twenty years in hiding, and had chosen to return to the land of his birth, despite all good judgment. One of the first things he'd done was to kill a woman—an author he barely knew, by all accounts—and to frame his own daughter in the process, however unwittingly. Whatever Anna had written in her manuscript had been enough to serve as a death warrant for Lin

Oldman, so it was imperative they found him, and prevented any repeat performance.

"The next one is"—Charlie consulted her notebook—"the seventh on my list. It's pretty big, so I don't know whether it would be within Taylor's price range."

"I wouldn't rule anything out," Jack said. "Taylor probably had a contingency fund squirreled away in an offshore bank account. No way was the pub his only asset; he was violent, but nobody ever said he was stupid."

"That's a matter of opinion," she said, drily. "Here we are."

They'd made their way from the centre of town, eastward along Castle Terrace before dipping left along a narrow road leading down towards the riverside pathway. The road forked off towards various private residences, but they eventually took another left and noted a large, smartly-painted white and black sign hanging from one of the tall trees, which read, 'Bridge Villa B & B'.

"What do we know about this place?"

"It's the most secluded, as far as I can tell," Charlie said, as they stood at the top of the forest driveway. "Most of the others are based in the centre of town, in one of the larger terraces or old merchant's houses. It's probably better to describe this as a boutique hotel, because it's larger than the average. It's a Victorian villa, with colonnades at the front, a terrace where you can sit and look out at the river or watch the trains going over the bridge. It's a beautiful spot."

"Who's the owner?"

"That's the thing," Charlie said. "The proprietor is a gentleman by the name of Drew Lindis, who bought the place a little over two years ago and has been running it as a going concern for the past year."

"Drew Lindis?" Jack queried.

"That's what I thought."

"Any family?" he asked.

Charlie shook her head.

"That's a blessing," Jack said because, if there were, Anna would've acquired additional family members she might have wanted as much as a hole in her head. "Look, how are we going to play this?"

"Same as before," Charlie said. "We're a young couple looking for an affordable wedding venue, and we love the look of their place, with its views. We ask to speak to the owner, to try and cut a deal, and we see what he looks like."

"I don't know why, but..."

"You get a funny feeling about this one?" she finished, with a shiver. "Yeah, I know. I get the same feeling."

"Be careful," he murmured. "If he cottons on to the fact we're police, everything will be blown."

"You'd better act smitten, then."

"No challenge," he said, and pulled her in for a brief, thorough kiss to prove it.

"There's no answer from Charlie and Jack," Frank said. "Goes straight to voicemail, so maybe they're in a bit of a black hole."

"I don't remember Amble being that bad for mobile signal?" Ryan said, looking up from the search warrant that had just pinged into his inbox.

God bless Morrison.

"They're not in Amble, they've gone to Berwick to look into those bed and breakfasts, remember?"

Ryan sat back in his chair, feeling uneasy, though he couldn't have said why. He knew Jack and Charlie to be capable, professional members of his team, who didn't need babysitting.

But something still nagged at him.

"Frank, do me a favour and get on the phone to Kieron Vale and

Lauren Bell, will you? Tell them to get a team together and start heading up to Berwick."

"What reason can I give them? We've not found anythin' yet," Frank protested.

"We will," Ryan said, and set aside the search warrant. "Frank, you take over the management of things in Amble, and give Faulkner the 'go-ahead' to enter Angela Riley's restaurant and the Riley home in Amble. I want all three of them arrested and placed in holding until the search is complete."

Phillips puffed out his chest. "Y' nah you can count on me, lad. What'll you be doin'?"

"Driving to Berwick," Ryan said, shortly. "Pull Mel and Denise off whatever they're working on, and tell them to go directly to my house in Bamburgh. Where's Samantha?"

"Eh?" Phillips said, off-handedly, as he tried to keep up. "Oh, she'll probably be packin' the kitchen sink for the trip to Ireland."

"Okay, tell Denise not to worry, she and Samantha should stay away," Ryan said, re-thinking his strategy. "If Mel can handle it alone, I'll be back as soon as I know Taylor has been secured."

"He might not be where you think he is," Frank said.

"I know," Ryan said, shortly. "That's what I'm worried about."

Jack and Charlie followed the forest driveway down towards the main entrance of Bridge Villa, which was a beautiful, Italian-style creation built against the gentle hillside leading down towards the River Tweed. They supposed its architecture was incongruous, but it seemed to suit the landscape. It even boasted a little jetty, off which an attractive motorboat rocked gently on its mooring.

"Lovely place," Charlie remarked, taking in the creeping ivy, enormous lanterns and smart entrance portico, beneath which some guests hovered with their suitcases, having arrived in time for check-in at three o'clock.

"Let's see if the proprietor's in," Jack replied.

They smiled at the guests they passed, who were a couple in their sixties wearing the comfortable garb of seasoned travellers, and then entered the villa. They found themselves in a spacious, encaustic tiled entrance hall which carried the pleasant scent of pine cones. A captain's desk had been arranged in one corner, behind which was seated a young woman dressed in a navy suit that made her look slightly older, or so she must have thought.

"Hello!" she said, in an accent that was unique to the Borders, being the product of generations of warring Scottish and Northumbrian tribes. It was neither, yet it featured hints of both, and managed to be charming all the same. "Are you checking in with us, today?"

"*Actually*," Charlie said, grabbing Jack's arm, "We were in the area, and we were wondering if you host weddings, here?"

The girl's face lit up, and her eyes went immediately to Charlie's finger, only to find her hand stuffed inside her pocket. Disappointed not to see a ring, she focused on answering the question.

"I know the owner was considering it, a bit further down the line, but we only opened recently so we haven't held a wedding here, yet. We'd need to apply for a license, for one thing."

"Oh, we don't mind waiting," Jack gushed. "We want our day to be just perfect, don't we, darling?"

Charlie knew it was only play-acting, but it felt so natural, she was almost fooled into thinking they were venue-hunting for real.

"Um, yes, yes, we certainly do! I wonder, is the owner around? Maybe we can have a word with them, and talk it over?"

"I'm sure that will be fine but, unfortunately, Mr Lindis isn't here, at the moment. He should be back fairly soon, however."

"How soon?" Charlie asked, trying not to sound too interested.

"Oh!" the girl, exclaimed. "You're in luck. Mr Lindis! I have a couple here who are interested in having their wedding at Bridge Villa. They were wondering if they could talk it over with you?"

They turned to see the man known as Drew Lindis entering the front door, chatting with the other couple who'd arrived, wheeling the lady's bag inside for her. He was older, and walked with a slight limp, but it did little to detract from his stature. At over six feet in height, with hair now entirely grey and fashioned into a stylish beard, which served the additional benefit of hiding some of his face, he remained a handsome man with a powerful bearing. Despite his age and the facial hair to obscure him, they could see one thing very, very clearly. This man was not 'Drew Lindis'.

He was Andrew Taylor.

"You have a beautiful place, here, Mr Lindis."

Charlie gave Andrew Taylor a vacant smile, and mooned over the furnishings in the room he was calling a 'library'.

"Thank you," he said, with all the good grace of a well-heeled, middle-aged man. "So, tell me more about your plans. What made you think of us?"

"I see this place every time we cross the railway bridge," Charlie said. "I comment on how lovely it is, every time—don't I, love?"

Jack came to attention, and kissed the side of her head. "She's had her heart set on the place. It was unoccupied for a while, wasn't it? Imagine how happy we were to learn that it was now a guest house."

"Well, that's very flattering," Taylor said, and invited them to take a seat on one of the sofas dotted around the long room, which was lit by the warm, amber glow of the late afternoon sun shining in as it descended to the western horizon. "I'm sure we can come to some sort of arrangement. Unfortunately, we don't have a wedding license yet, but I was planning to apply for one, which shouldn't be too much trouble. What kind of wedding are you hoping for—summer? Winter?".

"Oh, I don't mind, really," Charlie said, smiling up at Jack, who draped his arm around her shoulders. "Late summer might be nice, though, and it would give all of our relatives plenty of time to mark it in their diaries."

"That would also give us plenty of time to arrange the necessary formalities," Taylor said, and, when he smiled, they were both struck by the resemblance to his daughter. That, and the deep, dark brown eyes; though, in Anna's case, they were more often warm and mellow, reflective pools of the kindness she carried within. In the case of her father, his eyes seemed almost black, and carried the glassy, onyx-like sheen of a predator. It might've been projection, given all they knew of his past misdeeds, but they didn't think so. There was a watchfulness to the man, a shrewdness that reminded them of a handsome bird of prey, its head darting this way and that before swooping down to capture some unsuspecting rodent.

"Do you run this place all by yourself?" Charlie asked, as artlessly as she could manage. "And what about the décor? Did you hire an interior designer?"

Taylor gave her a small smile. "I'm unmarried," he said, shortly. "Though, I wouldn't let that put you off. I lost my wife, years ago."

Charlie put a hand to her heart. "I'm terribly sorry," she said. "And, there I go, putting my foot in it."

"Not at all," he said, smoothly. "Perhaps, if she'd been around, she might've helped with this old place. As it happened, I hired a local firm to do the place over."

That would've taken some funds, Jack thought.

"Did I see a boat moored out there?" he said. "Are you a sailor yourself, Mr Lindis?"

Taylor crossed one leg over the other, and gave another one of his enigmatic smiles. "Yes, I used to be rather good on the water," he said, looking between them. "I could take you for a spin in the *Princess Sara*, if you like? The weather's picking up, but we probably have another hour before it becomes unpleasant."

"Oh, that's so kind of you, but we have to be getting home," Charlie said. "My mother's looking after the dog, today."

"What breed?" he shot back.

"Oh—a—a Labrador."

Taylor smiled again, and then came to his feet. "Oh, stay where you are," he said, when they made to join him. "I've asked Frances to bring through some tea and scones for you both. I'm going to go and print off some of our bedroom packages, as well as the menus we have here, so you can think it over. I'll be back shortly."

They thanked him, and, once he was out of earshot, slumped back against the sofa.

"I felt like he could see straight through us," Charlie muttered.

"Nah," Jack said, although he could still feel the sheen of sweat on his back, which had begun to flow as they'd faced him.

"This place has Wi-Fi, so I'll pop to the ladies and drop a line to the office, to update them," she whispered, before giving him a quick kiss.

"Anything happens—" he began to say.

"Not here," she said, looking around the busy little hotel. "He wouldn't dare attack either one of us here, even if he'd figured out who we were."

"Okay," Jack conceded. "But if you're not back in ten minutes, I'm calling the coastguard."

"I bloody hope so," she said.

When Charlie returned ten minutes later, she expected to find Andrew Taylor—or, rather, *Drew Lindis*—returned from his office, printed paperwork in hand. Instead, she found Jack exactly where she'd left him, eyeing up a tray of fluffy fruit scones.

"Might be poisoned," she said, and then laughed as his hand snapped back. "Isn't he back, yet?"

"Nope," Jack replied, leaning forward in his seat. "Didn't you see him in the hallway?"

"No," she said, and turned to look back along the passageway. "Let's go and see where he's gone. We can always say we need to head off, now."

They made the short journey back into the hallway, where they found a smiling Frances still seated behind the front desk.

"Did you have a good tour?" she asked them.

"Oh, lovely, thanks," Charlie replied. "Mr Lindis was printing off some information for us, but we really need to be heading off, now. Would you mind passing on our best wishes?"

Frances' ultra-smooth face furrowed, or, it *would* have done, if she hadn't gone a bit overboard with the filler at Bella's Beauty the previous week.

"Oh, dear," she said. "I wonder if he's forgotten…but, that isn't like Mr Lindis to forget something like that."

"Forgotten what?" Jack pressed her, while trying to remain patient in the face of a pervading feeling that their suspect had made a run for it, while they sat like the lemmings they were.

"To print off that information for you," Frances said. "I'm terribly sorry, but he's had to go out, again. He had an appointment in town, and he'd lost track of the time. Oh, he did leave a message for you."

She reached for her notepad, and handed it over so they could read it for themselves.

The note read: 'MY REGARDS TO ARTHUR'.

"Bugger," Jack said. "He knows Gregson led us here."

Frances' smile faded to concern. "Is everything all right?"

"How long ago did he leave?" Charlie demanded.

Confused by the sudden change of tone, Frances stammered a reply. "I—I don't know. Five minutes?"

"On foot, or did he take a car?"

"Foot," Frances said. "Mr Lindis doesn't drive, since his accident."

"That's something," Jack said to Charlie, before turning back to the receptionist. "Did he say where he was going?"

"Just that he had an appointment, in town," Frances replied, swallowing hard as she looked between their stony-eyed faces. "I'm sorry, that's all I know. But, please, don't worry, I'm sure he'll send you the wedding brochure…hey!"

They left at a run, Jack trying, but failing to put a call through to the Control Room.

"No bloody signal!" he called out to Charlie, as the pair of them raced back up the hill.

"He must be headed for the railway station," she said. "It's the only way he can go."

"What about…a…boat?" Jack panted, while cursing the number of vegetarian pigs in blankets he'd ingested over the Christmas period.

"Heavy rain's predicted, this evening—and his motorboat's still moored at the jetty," Charlie said, in a voice that seemed to betray no exertion whatsoever.

That clinched it, and they quickened their pace, knowing he had a good enough start on them to be halfway to the station already. There was still a chance, but it was growing slimmer by the second.

"We can't let him go under, again," Charlie called out, mostly to herself, as motivation to continue running up that hill. "If he does, we'll never find him again."

Jack knew it, and, thinking of Anna and all she'd done for him over the past decade, found the strength and the will to redouble his pace. "He isn't getting away this time," he ground out.

CHAPTER 40

"Well if it isn't the Wanderer, returned!"

Tom Faulkner turned at the sound of a booming voice he recognised instantly, his coveralls rustling as he did so. "Frank! How was your Christmas?"

"Never mind that," Phillips said, but pulled him in for a hug, anyway. "I don't know how we've managed, here on the front line, while you've been off God only knows where, livin' the life of Riley."

Faulkner only laughed, a broad smile wrinkling his freshly tanned face. "Riley's apt," he said, nodding towards the restaurant behind them. "The owner's Angela Riley, isn't she?"

Frank nodded, and gave him a potted summary.

"You sure you want us here, first, and not the family home?"

Phillips shook his head. "I'd focus your attention on this place, and on the freezer storage, in particular," he said, and pulled an expressive face. "That, and maybe any small saws or cutting implements."

"I take it this is where we think Terry Pearson ended up being chopped into parts?"

Phillips nodded, and tried not to think of the food he'd gobbled down, only days ago.

"We'll see what we can find," Faulkner said. "Since the kitchen is used every day for food preparation, it's safe to assume meat and fish will have been chopped up, leaving all kinds of blood traces, even in the most hygienic set-ups. If that's the case, we may have trouble isolating human blood amongst the layers, especially if this happened back in August."

"Do what you can, lad," Frank told him, and wandered off to one of the squad cars, where Angela was being held prior to being taken to the nearby station for questioning. Her husband was seated in another one, while her son was nowhere to be found, either at home or in the village.

"Any sign of young Jonah Riley?" he asked one of the bobbies.

"No, sir," she replied. "We're still searching, but there's no answer to his usual number. His mother says he only has the one phone."

"Aye, well, she had no idea about him crackin' on with his cousin, so I wouldn't rely too heavily on that," he said. "Let me have a word with her."

Frank ambled towards the squad car, tapping a knuckle on the window of the driver's side to let the constable know he was there.

"Open the door, kiddo," he said. "I'm goin' to have a little chat with Mrs Riley, if she'll let me."

The constable nodded, unlocked the doors, and Frank held it open for Angela. She stared at him, not moving from where she sat, looking utterly broken in the backseat.

"Howay," Frank said, and held out a hand. "Let's go for a stretch o' the legs, and talk it over, shall we?"

Angela saw kindness in the way he looked at her, and in the hand he held out to help her, and so she took it.

"Thank you," she mumbled.

"Are you warm enough?"

She'd been given the opportunity to wrap herself in her 'Big Coat', which was a long, quilted affair that covered her from neck to ankle, blocking out the worst of the winter gale.

"I'm fine."

They walked a little way away from the men and women in white suits, and away from the small crowd of rubberneckers already gathering outside the police cordon. When they came to the end of the harbour wall, Frank stuck his hands in his pockets.

"I'm telling you the *truth*," Angela said, after a few seconds passed. "I haven't killed my brother. I promise you, I haven't killed anyone. I know—I know my father was who he was—and—and—my brother wasn't much better. But, please. You have to believe me, I couldn't have killed Terry. We lived separate lives but there was a time when we were close. I still remember it."

Frank listened, and then cleared his throat.

"I had a friend called Harry," he said, glancing at her, then back towards the sea. "We came up in school together, got into all sorts of mischief…that sort of thing. Aye, we were proper scamps, the pair of us."

Angela smiled, finding it impossible not to like him, which was a malady shared by almost everyone who met Frank Phillips.

"Anyhow, you might say, our lives went in different directions. Harry took one road, and I took another, but, just like you and your brother, we stayed as close as we could."

"Sometimes distance is the best remedy," she murmured.

"Aye," he said. "It can be."

"What happened to your friend?" she asked.

"He died, recently," Frank said. "He was murdered, like your brother. I found him, as it happens."

"I'm sorry."

"The biggest thing for me is finding out who killed him," Frank continued, as if she hadn't spoken. "I know Harry would've done the same for me, y' see. If I'd been the one found with my neck strangled, he'd have moved Heaven and Earth to find out who was responsible and see them bang to rights. So, my question to you, is, don't you want to find out who killed Terry?"

"Well, of course, I do."

"And what if the answer isn't what you want to find?"

Angela closed her eyes, and felt the fight drain out of her. "You think it was Kevin, don't you?"

"Aye, love. I do."

"What reason would he have to kill Terry?"

"You tell me. I think you know the reason, don't you?"

She pursed her lips, still struggling, and Frank turned around to point at Faulkner's forensics van.

"You see that team over there?" he said. "I can guarantee they're going to find a load of trace evidence inside one of your freezers, and somewhere else in the restaurant, and that evidence will match Terry's blood and DNA. It'll be enough to corroborate our theory that, after he followed your brother's car, Kevin returned here with Terry in the boot of his own car. With a bit of digging, I bet we'll find Terry's car was burned out in some woods, nearby. I reckon you *had* seen Terry the day he died, because he'd been up here to see you, again. He told you about his plan, didn't he?"

Angela swallowed, thinking of her brother being cut into pieces.

"Yes," she managed. "He came up to see us…me and Kevin, that is. Jonah wasn't at home, that day."

"What did Terry say?"

"He…" Her voice hitched and fell, as she fought for control.

"Take your time," Frank said, and gave her a reassuring pat on the back.

"He told us he was planning to get out," Angela said. "He was going to become an informant, and bring down the organisation, along with some other crime family—"

"The Rachmaninovs?"

"Yes, that was it. He said he was going to help the police, in exchange for immunity for me and Jonah."

"Not Kevin?"

"He never liked Kevin, I'm afraid. Terry thought he wasn't good enough for me, and that I'd only married him for security, which is true."

She gave a short laugh.

"I can't say the current situation feels very secure," she tried to joke. "In any case, Terry seemed to think Jonah and Mia were spending time together, and that wasn't such a good thing. He thought Mia had inherited her grandfather's ruthless streak, and wanted to put the family back on top. Their goals were completely at odds."

"But Mia's only a lass, isn't she? How could she possibly have any sway?"

"You don't know Mia," Angela said. "She was the apple of my father's eye, and Terence invested every scrap of spare time in teaching her the rules of good business, as he saw it. She's beautiful, too, which doesn't help, and she looks a lot older than sixteen. Men don't see her coming."

Frank thought of the nude images she'd sent to Jonah, according to Jack's report from earlier that day, and wondered how to broach the subject.

"Well, we know Mia and Jonah found each other, despite the two sides of the family not spending much time together," he began.

"Yes, and that's just the problem," Angela said. "Despite not being his natural father, Kevin always loved Jonah. He's treated him like a son from the day he was born, and he cares about his welfare, as do I."

Angela rubbed a tired hand over her eyes.

"I know Jonah's nineteen, now, and he's really a man," she said. "I can't protect him anymore, and neither can Kevin. If he wants to be with Mia, and to go down that path despite the different life we've tried to give him, I can't do much to stop that."

"But Kevin tried, didn't he?"

Angela swallowed. "I still can't believe…" she murmured, shaking her head. "They had words, more than once. First, months ago, when Terry turned up here, on his own and broached the subject. He said it wasn't safe for him to stay long, so Kevin arranged to meet him at the petrol station in Alnwick, where they could talk a bit longer."

"Their conversation didn't seem too friendly, judging by the footage."

"It wasn't," she said. "Kevin came back and told me Terry was adamant about informing, and about putting a stop to his daughter's idea of making the family great again. He told Kevin he'd do his best for Jonah but, ultimately, he was of the opinion Jonah had made his bed, and he'd have to live with the consequences. Kevin thought he was putting Jonah at risk, and the best thing would be to try and separate him from Mia."

"Where are they now?" Frank asked.

"I don't know," Angela said, miserably. "I can't get hold of Jonah, and, when I spoke to Kerry-Jayne, she said she hadn't heard from Mia, either. Patricia took a fall, coming back from the Women's Institute and she's laid up in hospital."

Frank nodded, and wondered how much of a problem a nineteen-year-old lad, and a sixteen-year-old girl could *really* be—so long as they didn't have babies any time soon.

"Jonah's brilliant with computers," Angela said, seeming to answer his unspoken question. "He was expelled from one school for hacking into their systems and changing all the A-Level grades to 'A', amongst other things. It's terrifying, what he can do."

It was a sad thing for a mother to be afraid of her son, she knew, but there was no point in denying the truth any longer. Jonah was no longer the sweet-faced little boy she'd cradled in her arms.

"Terry was talking about a sting operation," she said. "That's what he was talking to us about, on the night he—the night he went missing. If Jonah and Mia were involved in family affairs, they'd have been caught up in it. Kevin didn't like it, but Terry said he needed to put a stop to things, once and for all, so the cycle would end with him. He already felt he'd lost his daughter."

"Kevin killed Terry, to stop him from orchestrating the sting, and putting Jonah in danger?"

Angela began to cry silently, as they stood there at the water's edge.

"Nearly there," Frank assured her. "Nearly there, now."

She nodded, and sniffed. "I don't know for sure," she said. "That's the truth. I really don't. But I do know, Kevin wasn't at home, the night Terry went missing. He left us here, and Terry left shortly afterwards, to go to the supermarket, he told me. But he came back with nothing, hours later. I knew something was wrong, but I didn't question it. God help me…maybe, maybe I was *grateful* he was trying to protect Jonah. I've always been so grateful to Kevin."

"Frank!"

They both turned to see Tom Faulkner waving his hand, and then giving the thumbs-up sign, to confirm he'd found some promising evidence.

"It'll take days to check the samples against DNA," Phillips said, quietly. "Kevin could save us a bit of time, and lighten his heart, if he wants to."

Angela thought of what her husband had likely done to her brother, and then of the hands he'd often held against her body, and felt as though she might vomit.

"I can ask him," she said, when she was sure her system was under control.

"That'd be the right thing to do."

CHAPTER 41

Ryan motored northbound towards Berwick like a man possessed.

Weaving in and out of traffic, every one of his advanced driving skills was put to the test and his progress delayed only briefly by the presence of a tractor on a stretch of single carriageway. Finding a gap in which to overtake, Ryan continued steaming ahead, every instinct in his body having been vindicated by Charlie's e-mail, which came through via his car's system to tell him that they'd found Andrew Taylor. He was, she said, most certainly alive and well, and didn't appear to be any the worse for being a dead man.

Good for him, the murdering so-and-so, Ryan thought.

Ryan had informed their colleagues from Durham CID, only to receive an update from Jack soon afterwards.

He's done a runner, Jack had told him, breathlessly. *We're in pursuit, on foot. Heading towards the railway station.* Even with a fair wind, there was no feasible way for Vale and Bell to arrive in Berwick within the next ten minutes, whereas, if he took a flexible approach to the traffic laws, Ryan could be at the railway station in under five.

At another time, he would have admired the surrounding landscape as he crossed the River Tweed, with the mighty Royal Border railway bridge rising in arched perfection to the west, and the Tweedmouth estuary spreading out to the east. The town rose up ahead of him, a perfect hotchpotch of stone buildings of varying heights, appearing like a mystical edifice in the dying of the light.

But there was no time to think of that, now.

Ryan swung his car into the station car park, narrowly avoiding a flock of pigeons which had congregated around one of the larger puddles on the tarmac. He came to a jerky stop in a disabled parking space, the drop-off area being already fully occupied. A train was imminent, he realised, and it was highly likely Andrew Taylor would be aware of the timetable.

He slammed out of the car and turned a full circle, scanning every face he saw.

There wasn't one he recognised.

Ryan took out his smartphone, and put a call through to Jack. "Where are you?" he asked, when the call connected.

Jack huffed and puffed, the motivation to keep running up that hill having evaporated once he realised Berwick had *several* hilly streets— long ones that seemed to stretch out like a journey in *The Never-ending Story.*

"Castle Terrace," he said, dragging in a couple of panting breaths, while Charlie continued to put him to shame with her easy running style and seemingly endless stamina.

Which, of course, he made no complaint about.

"How far away?" Ryan said, while continuing to prowl around the station perimeter, checking behind cars and outbuildings, in case Taylor was concealing himself.

"Two minutes, tops," Jack said, and could only hope that was the case.

"You're sure he came this way?"

"We can't be sure," Jack replied. "But it's our best guess."

"Good enough for me," Ryan said. "Secure the area when you get here. I'm going to check the platforms and the waiting areas."

There was no time for Jack to wish him luck, or to warn him to be careful.

Ryan had already gone.

Anna couldn't sit still.

While Samantha entertained Emma with a series of card tricks she'd learned years ago, during her days with the travelling circus, Mel and Denise kept Anna and Eve company at the house in Bamburgh.

"As if I'd just sit around at home, twiddlin' my thumbs, while you're all up here, waiting and worrying," Denise snorted. "Your man's either *had* a knock on the head, or he *needs* one."

Eve smiled, and decided she liked the sassy Irish woman with the fabulous mane of coppery gold hair.

"I've often said the same thing, myself," she said. "Ryan often thinks he's protecting people, but it's a fine line between being protective and being paternalistic."

Denise made a sound like *harrumph*, which she'd picked up from Frank. "He's too used to being in command, that one."

"Or, *thinking* he is," Eve said, and took a delicate sip of tea.

"Oh, don't I know it." Denise sniffed. "Don't get me started on Frank Phillips. I swear, that man'll have me committed, one of these days, and it'll be a relief."

They all laughed, even Anna.

"Why not come and sit down?" Mel suggested. "It'll do no good, being on your feet so much."

Since Anna was not a stubborn fool, she took her friend's good advice and settled herself on one of the comfortable chairs in the room they called the 'snug'.

"Maybe I should check on Emma," she said, only a minute later.

"I'll do that," Eve said, pushing her back into the armchair with a firm hand. "Although, by the sounds of it, they're having a lovely time."

It was true, for they could hear Emma's delighted peals of laughter while Samantha told jokes, did tricks, and otherwise played the generous older cousin she was, to all intents and purposes.

"You've got a lovely girl, there," Anna said to Denise. "Sam's a credit to the pair of you."

"To be honest," Denise said, "Samantha's been the making of us both. I never felt my life was lacking, before; but, since she came to us, we haven't been able to imagine our lives without her. It's as though she was meant for us."

The women spoke in easy pleasantries for a short while, then talk turned to more serious matters.

"I read back over my manuscript," Anna said. "I haven't touched it for a while, because thinking about it was too upsetting. I never thought I'd be able to publish it, because Lin Oldman had beaten me to it, and reading it over and over would rub salt in the wound. But, with everything that's been going on, I'm trying to understand what I wrote in it that upset my father, so much. What could be so bad he felt he had to kill someone?"

She reached for a folder containing a freshly printed copy of her book.

"This is the draft she stole from me. It isn't exactly the same as her version, because she made some token changes, to try to make it look less plagiarised, I suppose. I have a copy of her published version, here."

Anna retrieved a copy of *Island Peril* from inside her handbag, which Eve had purchased for her from the bookshop at Bamburgh Castle that very morning.

"I read through this today," she said, and it had been hard going, noticing all the little changes to words that had been hers. "I tried to put myself in my father's mindset, to understand what he saw in this book that concerned him so much. I don't know if it means anything, but I highlighted a few potentials, they're marked by the tabs on the side."

She held out the book to Denise, and Mel moved her chair around so that she could see the text.

"The story is about a woman who goes back to the island of her birth, only to find strange things start to happen, culminating in a series of murders that appear to have links to the occult. She has a bit of help with her amateur sleuthing in the form of a handsome police detective, who's licking some emotional wounds of his own while staying on the island for a while."

"I wonder where you found the inspiration?" Mel joked.

Anna chuckled. "It's not completely autobiographical, but there are definitely some strong threads," she said. "For instance, I've highlighted a couple of flashback sequences."

They were quiet for a moment, while they read through Anna's eloquent re-telling of some of her childhood memories, good and bad. There was a sharp intake of breath as they came to a passage in which she describes a woman called 'Tara' being thrown down a flight of stairs, while her two little girls stood helplessly at the bottom.

"Did—did this happen, Anna?"

She gave a brief nod. "Yes."

Eve moved to stand behind Anna, and rubbed gentle hands over her shoulders, while the others read the memories she'd chosen to share. Once they'd read through the passages Anna had highlighted, they fell quiet, trying to imagine what a man like Andy Taylor would see in it.

Then, the truth, simple and plain as it was, came to her.

"It isn't about any one incident, is it?" Anna said, softly. "I've been looking for something obvious; some memory dredged up from my deepest consciousness that hit a nerve, or somehow gave away one of his secrets, but that isn't the case at all. I've been giving him too much credit."

"What do you mean, love?"

Eve came to sit beside her, and reached across to hold her hand.

"It's about *image*," Anna said. "It always was, even when we were children. We weren't to speak to anyone about what happened behind closed doors, and he fed us the words we should use whenever we spoke about him. *My daddy's the best. My daddy's the strongest. He's like Superman,*" she parroted.

Then, shook her head.

"It was so far from the truth, and everyone knew what that truth really was, but didn't have the courage to intervene," she said. "He wanted the world to think of him as a 'big' man, a powerful man, who wielded the sword like an army general. He tried to create a sort of *myth* of Andy Taylor, at odds with reality. He wanted to be feared, revered, dangerous, powerful."

Anna lifted her chin.

"He was a *coward*," she said. "A coward who thought he commanded society's elite, but all they were was a motley group of mentally ill, violent criminals. He was always under the control of stronger, more powerful people. He was a pathetic creature, who ran from responsibility and left me with a legacy of shame; a weak, abusive man."

Denise leaned across to take Anna's other hand.

"You have nothing to be ashamed of," she whispered, her heart full of compassion. "I think you're right. If he's been surviving all these years by wilfully deceiving himself, adopting the alternate reality that he was 'all powerful' Andy, then reading Lin Oldman's book must have come as a huge shock to his psyche."

"The book turned him into an object of ridicule and pity, on the pages and in print forever," Mel agreed. "He probably recognised so much of himself, and wondered how Lin came to know it all."

"Naturally, she wouldn't tell him," Anna said. "She'd never admit to having stolen the story from me, so he'd have been furious. He probably killed her on the spur of the moment, which would suit his usual MO, because my father could never be accused of having any impulse control."

"Wrong place, wrong time for Lin, then?" Denise said.

Anna heaved a sigh. "I never liked the woman, but, knowing what my father is capable of, I wouldn't have wished that on her, or anyone. I don't think I have it in my heart to hate anyone as much as that."

Eve gave a small sob, and wrapped her arms around Anna. "You're safe now," she said. "We've got you."

CHAPTER 42

Ryan entered the railway station hall, with its pretty, Victorian painted balustrades and air of quaint yesteryear, to find it brimming with people. The loudspeaker announced the imminent arrival of a train bound for London, and there followed an exodus of bodies, all jostling luggage or small children, waving 'goodbye' as they shuffled towards the southbound platform. It seemed likely that Taylor would try to make his way to London, where there were far more opportunities for concealment and escape. However, just as Ryan thought this, there came a second announcement to say that the Aberdeen train would shortly be arriving on the northbound platform, and he found himself wondering whether Taylor would try to make his way to one of the eastern ports, where a ferry could take him overseas and into the ether, once more.

"Ryan!"

He spun around, eyes searching the sea of faces, and then caught sight of Jack and Charlie waving to him from the other side of the hall. It was impossible to talk, so he relied on a series of hand gestures to indicate they should fan out, covering as much of the station as possible.

They nodded, and, while Charlie made for the sides of the station, Jack hurried over the pedestrian bridge towards the opposite platform, pushing his way through a stream of irate people to make it across to the other side of the station before the trains arrived.

Ryan continued to move through the crowd on the southbound platform, searching bodies, faces, shadows and crevices. In the distance, there came the sound of a distant horn, heralding the arrival of a train passing over the high bridge. He saw it, in the distance, crawling slowly over the arches on the northbound line, making its way over the river that flowed far below. Turning back to the platform, he spotted Jack, moving swiftly through the bodies on the opposite platform, searching.

He did the same, continuing to move along the platform until he spotted the sign for the toilets. It was a classic ploy for anyone hoping to hide from a ticket inspector—or a murder detective—to lock themselves in a cubicle until the last moment. Torn between continuing the platform search and checking the stalls, Ryan made a split-second decision and shouldered into the gents, using the toe of his boot to kick open the cubicle doors, finding only one that was locked.

He dipped down to peer under the door, when it opened suddenly to reveal a young man dressed in a high-vis vest, wearing a look of extreme suspicion on his tattooed face.

"Oi! What d'you think you're doin'?" he said, squaring up to Ryan, ready to let one fly. "Pervert!"

"Police," Ryan corrected, but didn't hang around to argue about it.

The northbound train had arrived.

Running back onto the platform, he felt his phone vibrate and answered it immediately.

"Talk to me."

"I can't see him, anywhere," Jack said, still looking all around the now empty platform, as people boarded the train for Aberdeen. "I don't think he was on this side."

"Okay," Ryan said, thinking fast. "Tell the guard to delay the train for two minutes, and check the on-board toilets."

Jack acknowledged that, and ran off to speak to the stationmaster.

Meanwhile, Ryan turned his attention back to the southbound platform, and spotted Charlie behind him, having already checked the outdoor access points, without success. He made a circular motion with his finger, to indicate she should check over the ground he'd already covered, to be sure, and then returned to his own search, moving through the crowd with precision.

He had to be here.

There was nowhere else he could be.

The loudspeaker announced the arrival of the London train and, a minute later, Ryan heard the sound of a train's brakes squealing as the driver slowed to a stop. Passengers surged forward, obstructing Ryan's view along the remaining platform, and he swore, fighting to keep pace, to reach the end of the platform and finish the search. Time seemed to slip between his fingers, running like water as Ryan struggled on, tugging men around to see their faces, pushing others out of the way as gently as he could. The crowd had almost dispersed, the train readying itself to leave for London, when he saw it.

Just a flash, the motion of a tall, older man with an odd sort of gait, dashing from beneath a canopy at the farthest end of the platform, making for the closest carriage before the doors shut.

"*Taylor!*"

Fifty metres away, the man froze, turned to look directly at Ryan, and then back at the train carriage door, which had shut again. Ryan was already running towards him, long legs eating up the platform, with Charlie following hot on his heels.

Andy looked around—lost, alone, filled with panic.

Then, he did what he was best at.

He ran.

BERWICK

Despite his injury, Andy could still move ably enough, and, in any case, fear could give the most sedentary person wings. He shot along the remaining length of platform, flying past the 'NO ENTRY' sign that marked the end of the safe zone, and made his way down onto the tracks.

Bloody idiot, Ryan thought, viciously.

The northbound train moved off, and Jack saw a series of running figures through the windows of the London train, which remained on the southbound platform, ready to leave. Whistles blew, but Ryan shouted to the train staff, waving his arms to warn them a man was now on the tracks, picking his way over the rails in an attempt to evade an arrest that was more than twenty years overdue.

More whistles blew, and Charlie stopped to speak to the train staff, ordering them to hold the train while Ryan continued to give chase. Meanwhile, Jack spoke urgently on his mobile with Lauren and Kieron, who brought their small convoy of squad cars to an abrupt stop at the far side of the bridge, where they spilled out and made their way up a series of access ladders and stairwells to the top, where they could head Andrew Taylor off on the southern side of the river.

"There isn't anywhere for you to go!" Ryan called out, as he picked his way over the narrow walkway between the tracks, closing the distance.

Around their heads, the wind had picked up, battering their bodies. Glancing over the wall, he experienced a wave of vertigo, the river seeming to expand and contract as it moved beneath the bridge where he stood.

Gritting his teeth, he carried on, keeping his quarry in sight.

"Officers are already in position on the other side of the bridge!" he called out, spotting a line of men and women, dressed in uniform. "It's over, Andy! Come quietly, and we can talk!"

As they approached the middle of the bridge, Andy's feet slowed to a walk.

"That's right!" he shouted. "Stay where you are, and we'll walk back together!"

But there was no going back for Andrew Taylor. The time for that was long gone, if it had ever existed for him at all. He looked between Lauren's team, to his right, then Ryan, to his left, and finally straight ahead, towards the estuary and the sea beyond.

It was the end of the line.

"*No!*" Ryan bellowed. "*No,* Andy!"

Taylor scrambled up onto the wall, his hands and feet scrabbling for purchase, until he stood precariously on the edge of the old stone parapet, a king in his own mind.

Ryan would not have classified himself as an expert negotiator, but he'd been in plenty of high-stakes situations before, where every move and every word could make all the difference. The last time he'd walked over train tracks, their metal fizzing and humming with energy, it had been with the sole intention of bringing people off a train before it exploded. There'd been hundreds of lives to consider, hundreds of families who stood to lose loved ones.

And now?

Few, if any, would mourn the loss of Andrew Taylor. As far as Ryan could tell, his only distinguished act of service had been in fathering Anna, and that's where his contribution ended. Some would have questioned Ryan's commitment to saving the man's life, despite all he had done.

And yet, he didn't waver.

Justice and punishment would come later, but, for now, Ryan's sole responsibility was to ensure the man remained alive to face it. There would be no resolution for those he'd hurt, if Taylor ended it now.

"Don't be a fool, Andy! This isn't the way to go…not for a man like you!"

Flattery stuck in his craw, but Ryan said whatever was needed to ensure a safe removal from the bridge.

Andy seemed not to hear him, raising his face to the sky, feeling the wind and rain swirling around him, rocking his body on its axis, threatening to sweep him away. He felt the power of the elements around him, and was reminded of the old days, when he'd pretended to worship such things.

He started to laugh, and raised his arms aloft, in a crucifix formation.

"Andy!" Ryan called out again, closing the gap between them, one careful step after another. "You don't have to do this."

Andy looked down at the water, felt his stomach turn over, and then shuffled around so that he faced the man his daughter had married. They looked at one another—friends, perhaps, in another life. They might've shared a pint or two, and gone fishing, or climbed the fells. As it was, they represented two different sides to the world; one light, one dark, and each was aware of his place and purpose.

"Tell her, I wish her well," Andy said.

And then, he fell backwards. Down and down, into the watery abyss that awaited him, swallowing him alive.

CHAPTER 43

Andrew Taylor's body was not recovered.

The odds of him surviving a fall at that height were under fifty per cent, not counting the water temperature being almost freezing, nor factoring in his age and his various ailments. Ryan and his team remained on site for several hours to oversee the marine search, until Charlie made an astute observation, from their vantage point across the water.

"You can see Taylor's bed and breakfast from here," she said, and raised a finger to point across the river at a lovely villa, its colonnades lit up by a series of well-placed uplighters so that it resembled a sort of miniature Acropolis.

Ryan glanced at it, then grunted.

"Even if he did survive, there's no way he would've been able to swim back there, in his condition."

"His boat is gone," Charlie added.

Now, Ryan really did pay attention. "What d'you mean?"

"He had a motorboat, the *Princess Sara*," Jack explained. "It was moored on the little jetty outside the villa, but it looks as though it isn't there."

"That doesn't necessarily mean anything," Ryan said, but his gut told him otherwise. "Get onto the coastguard, Jack. Tell them to check their radar for any boats matching that description. Get a local team to trace the river inland, and see if any boats have been abandoned further upstream."

While Jack took off to see that it was done, Ryan thought of Anna.

"Are you okay, sir?"

He tucked his hands into his jacket pockets, no longer able to feel his fingertips. "Charlie, you know you can just call me Ryan."

"Sorry, I keep forgetting," she said.

"Thank you for asking, though," he added. "I feel as though I should be relieved, but I'm not. I want to see him dead, on a table at the mortuary. Until that happens, his ghost continues to walk the Earth, doesn't it?"

"In more ways than one," she said.

Ryan checked the time on his watch. "Your boy will be missing you," he said. "Thanks for everything today, Charlie. Have you had any trouble from Rachmaninov?"

She shook her head. "I don't think he's realised I'm here," she said. "As long as I continue to keep quiet, lay low and not do anything too ostentatious, it buys us some time."

Ryan nodded, and put a hand on her shoulder in support. "It'll come right."

She nodded, and scrubbed the hair from her face.

"Do you need me for anything, or could I head home?" Ryan smiled, and jerked a finger towards the car park. "Go on," he said. "Sling your hook."

Charlie passed on her love to Anna, and left to go in search of Jack.

At the waterside in Berwick-upon-Tweed, Kieron Vale and Lauren Bell stood side by side.

"What d'you think we should do?" she asked him.

Kieron blew out a breath, and thought about it. "Makes sense to do as Ryan suggests, and continue dragging the river," he said. "If Taylor doesn't turn up, he's likely to have been swept out to sea, in which case he'll turn up sometime in the next few days or not at all. Then again, maybe he made it back to his boat, and he's made a run for it, again. The man seems to have the fortitude of a cockroach, so it'd take a nuclear explosion to get rid of him."

"I know all that," Lauren said, and rolled her eyes. "I *meant*, what should we do about this thing between us?"

Kieron smiled to himself. "What thing would that be?"

"Don't you start," she warned him. "For one thing, we don't seem to be able to keep our paws off each other."

"It's an excellent development," he agreed.

"For another thing, I'm your boss, and I fear this will affect the respect you have for me in the office."

"Never," he said, and was telling the absolute truth. "If anything, I respect you more, knowing you better as I do. You're a sensitive, caring woman, not the foul-mouthed dragon I once thought you were—"

"Gee, stop with the compliments," she said, scowling heavily.

Kieron laughed. "I mean, you carry all this emotion beneath the surface, but manage to lock it away to be able to do the best job you can for the punters who come through our door. It's admirable."

Lauren blushed, for the third time that day, and was glad it was too dark for him to see.

"In answer to your question," he mused, "I say we carry on, just as we are. We're enjoying each other's company, having a lot of fun and pleasure. Does that help?"

She wished it did, but it fell short of what she was looking for in life. "It's been lovely," she said. "But—"

"Of course," he added, "if you really want to know, and so long as you won't be scared off, I should probably tell you that I have feelings for you. I don't know what to call them, yet, but it's more than just sex for me, Lauren. I want to be with you, all the time, just to be around you. I think about you, even when I'm with friends or doing something completely unrelated to work. You're in my blood, now."

She listened, heart and mind soaring like a bird. "I feel the same," she found herself admitting, and felt immediately vulnerable. "I mean—"

"You do? Oh, this is a happy coincidence," he said. "Do you fancy celebrating over a bowl of pasta and a nice glass of Montepulciano, on the way home?"

Now, she smiled to herself. "Look, Vale. Just because I fell into bed with you after dinner the other night, it doesn't mean that's going to happen every time."

He looked at her, and it was that *look* she loved so much.

"Of course," she amended. "It never hurts to eat before an energetic night."

"It's good sense," he agreed.

They waited a few beats, and then she asked, "Your place, or mine?"

"Don't care," he said. "So long as I'm with you."

"Vale," she said, narrowing her eyes at him. "Are you a closet romantic?"

He thought of the period dramas he loved to watch, and wondered if it would give her the 'ick' if he confessed as much to her.

Too soon, he decided. Much too soon.

Frank oversaw the arrest of Kevin Riley, for the murder of Terence Pearson Junior. After a heartfelt discussion with his wife, Kevin had eventually agreed to confess, having been reminded of the pain and suffering it would continue to cause her if he didn't. It was doubly heartbreaking for Kevin to learn that, despite acting from a desire to protect Jonah from the 'wrong' path, the young man had packed a bag and followed it, regardless. As Frank would later remark to Denise, from the comfort of an 'extra leg room' seat on their budget flight to Cork, a few days later, it was always the quiet ones you needed to watch.

And, she had replied, that put him well out of the running.

Samantha had rolled her eyes at the pair of them, and wondered whether Flynn, one of the grooms at the Pony Club, would ask her out for a bubble tea when she returned from Ireland.

It was a matter of priorities.

EPILOGUE

Anna stared at her inbox, and was sure she felt a flutter low down in her belly, either from excitement or from her unborn child's strong little foot.

"Ryan!"

"Mm?" he called back, from his position halfway up a ladder.

"Come and look at this!"

In his hands, he held a lamp shade and a bulb, which he looked at, then set aside with resignation. If there was one thing he'd learned from his wife's first pregnancy, it was never to 'test the hormones'.

Never *ever* test the hormones.

"Coming!" he called back.

"Did you manage to put up that lampshade?" she asked him, and Ryan opened his mouth to protest, before remembering his own mantra.

"Almost," he replied, with a smile. "What's up?"

"Is this a scam, do you think?"

She turned the computer around to face him, and Ryan leaned down to skim read a number of e-mails which had arrived in his wife's inbox since news of Lin Oldman's death had broken.

"Well," he said, pulling up a chair beside her. "It looks as though you've received several offers of representation from top literary agents in London."

"That's what I thought it said."

"It also seems you've received a direct offer of publication from three out of the Big Five publishing houses in the UK, who want to offer you wads of cash to publish your story properly, and hopefully turn it into a movie."

She nodded again. "Can this be right?"

Ryan laughed, and pulled her into his arms. "Of course," he said. "It's as it should be, Anna. You deserve to be recognised."

"I thought…after they pulped all the copies of Oldman's book, that would be the end of it."

"Apparently not. I see they want you to start working on a sequel."

"A sequel?" she squeaked. "I—I haven't thought about that—"

"Better start plotting," he said, with a wriggle of his eyebrows. "You'd better start taking over the literary world, so I can retire and become a man of leisure."

She laughed at that. "That'll be the day," she said. "Getting you to sit down for the duration of *The Lord of the Rings* is enough of a challenge."

Emma skipped in the room and, seeing them both, wandered over to burrow between them.

"Mummy," she said. "Have you been eating too many sweeties?"

Anna and Ryan grinned at one another.

"What makes you say that?"

"Well, your tummy's a bit bigger than it was," Emma said, and placed her hand against her mother's belly to pat it.

Instead, she felt something she hadn't expected.

A kick.

"Mummy! Daddy! There's something *inside*! It kicked my hand!" she cried, and then looked at them with wide eyes. "Is it an *alien*?"

Ryan roared with laughter, and picked her up into his arms. "It's no more an alien than *you*," he said. "We've been meaning to tell you, sweetheart. You're going to be a big sister."

Emma thought about it, her little face screwing up in concentration, then looked at the pair of them in horror.

"You've been having NAKED CUDDLES!" she said.

"I'm afraid, we have," Ryan admitted. "How do you feel about a baby brother or sister?"

In answer, Emma jumped off his knee and raced off to start building a baby cot using the materials from her craft box, after reminding them the new baby would need somewhere special to sleep, and they must be very careful with *her* new baby.

"I feel so lucky," Anna said, and blamed the tears that followed on the hormones, which were an unruly mistress.

"This is only the beginning," Ryan said, and kissed her deeply.

ABOUT THE AUTHOR

LJ ROSS is an international bestselling author known for her atmospheric mystery and thriller novels, including the DCI Ryan series which has sold over 12 million copies worldwide. Her debut novel *Holy Island* published in 2015 and reached number one in the Amazon UK and Australian digital charts. Louise has since released over thirty novels, most of which have been UK number one digital bestsellers. She is also the creator of the bestselling Dr Alexander Gregory series and the Summer Suspense series. Louise is a keen philanthropist and proud to support numerous non-profit programmes in addition to founding the Lindisfarne Prize for Crime Fiction, the Northern Photography Prize and the Northern Film Prize.

Born in Northumberland, England, she studied Law at King's College, University of London, then abroad in Florence and Paris, and worked as a lawyer before pursuing her dream to write. She lives with her family in Northumberland.

If you would like to get in touch with LJ Ross on social media, please scan the QR code below – she would love to hear from you!

LOVE READING?

JOIN THE CLUB...

Join the LJ Ross Book Club to connect with a thriving community of fellow book lovers! To receive a free monthly newsletter with exclusive author interviews and giveaways, sign up at www.ljrossauthor.com or follow the LJ Ross Book Club on social media:

@LJRossAuthor

@ljross_author